Kallum's Fury

Being the second part of
Lake of Dragons

E. Michael Mettille

TMR Books
PO Box 571978
Tarzana, CA 91357-1978
www.themikereynolds.com

All images provided provided by Adobe Stock

Cover Artwork – © 2016 L.J. Anderson of Mayhem Cover Creations

Published by TMR Books 05/31/2016

ISBN: 0-9975571-1-7
ISBN-13: 978-0-9975571-1-4

DEDICATION

For Shelia…again and always.

PROLOGUE
A GOOD DAY FOR HUNTING

It was far too late in the morning to begin a hunt. The sun already flirted with the very pinnacle of its ascent. Before Ymitoth reached the next clump of trees, the bright lord of the sky would be on its slow dive into the Great Sea to swim the dark waters until once again it was time to kiss Ouloos with the light of a new day. A late start didn't matter much to Ymitoth. The hunt wasn't really what drew him out of the throne room and into an unfamiliar saddle on an unfamiliar horse. It was the trail he yearned for—fresh air and freedom from the daily squabbles of those who called him king. The road forever beckoned, tugging his attention away from his duties and mundane questions of who did what to whom and why it wasn't fair. Sadly, the weight of his crown kept him firmly planted within the walls of his great city. Each day the freedom of the trail seemed to slip further and further away, a fond memory slowly fading into the murky obscurity of forgotten loves.

The horse shifted awkwardly, reminding Ymitoth of another lost love. Pride was a sturdy, black steed, built for miles on the trail and fast as the westerly wind ahead of a furious storm, but he was no Rumallah. More than merely an ample mode of transportation, Rumallah had been his only companion on many a journey. The king's heart ached even more for the old horse than it did for the open trail. In sixty summers he hadn't met a man he trusted more than that animal. If only he could have one more adventure racing over rolling meadows, stooping to drink from the cool waters of a forest brook, and battling fearsome, nightmare creatures from the darkest places where the feet of good folk don't tread. Alas, even if he could find a bit of freedom to do any of those things, his old friend would remain absent. Nothing could ever fill the empty spot Rumallah left in his heart when he departed this world.

"Ye think we'll be seeing anything for the wall, highness?" a voice from behind tugged him away from his melancholy, another stark reminder he could never be alone on the trail as long as the damned crown of Havenstahl called his head its home.

He turned the home for a crown enough to make eye contact with Egete as he replied, "Any life we be taking from the trail be filling our bellies not decorating our walls."

"Forgive me, highness," Egete's eyes dropped quickly away from the king's stern gaze.

Ymitoth ignored it. Egete was a solid soldier and a sturdy guard who still managed to wield a downright friendly personality. As far as guards go, he was probably the king's favorite. He certainly didn't earn Ymitoth's sour look. In fact, his statement hadn't really bothered the king at all. Any words leaving his mouth would have earned a negative response. His presence was what truly bothered the king of the greatest city of men. Not because of anything he had done, simply because the trail and Rumallah were the only company Ymitoth cared to keep just then. In Rumallah's absence, Pride would have to do. Egete and Scrih—the other guard accompanying Ymitoth on his hunt—were about as wanted as a three-inch thorn in the arch of a tired foot. The taste of sweet solitude on the trail was the one thing Ymitoth hungered for and the one thing he couldn't have as the king.

A brief flash of brown in a dark and familiar clump of trees caught the king's attention. "Whisht," something like a whistle without a tongue blasted sharp and quick from his lips as he raised his left arm and nodded toward the trees.

Egete and Scrih tugged the reins of their respective horses, halting them immediately behind the king. Ymitoth shot an intense, narrow-eyed scowl in their direction to stifle any words that may have been knocking against the backs of their teeth. The heavy look carried more meaning than anything the king had said since passing through the gates of Havenstahl. After a few moments of startling quiet, disturbed only by the sound of lightly rustling leaves blowing about in the random clumps of trees surrounding the three hunters and the slow rush of waters from the River Galgooth flowing behind them, Ymitoth pointed while nodding at the dark clump of trees.

Scrih sat just a notch lower than Egete in Ymitoth's eyes. They would stand equal if only Scrih had stronger control of his tongue. "I ain't be seeing nothing there, highness," he blurted.

"Shh," Ymitoth scolded before shaking his head and whispering, "These eyes have watched me friends toast me sixtieth summer and ye're telling me they be seeing more than the keen eyes of one so fresh to the trail?"

Scrih silently shrugged while Egete added, "I ain't be seeing nothing either."

"Fine hunting partners the two of ye have turned out to be," the king shook his head as he raised his bow and knocked an arrow.

As he drew his bowstring back and exhaled, Ymitoth's body relaxed. All the tension tightening up his muscles and hardening his face fled on a current of hot breath. His old eyes scanned the dark clump for the faint flicker that caught them in the first place. Finally, it came again, barely a shape and scarcely a color.

He remained frozen in odd, relaxed tension, all but forgetting about the two behind him. His intense focus sharpened and pierced deeper into the darkness beneath the mingling crowns of the trees. To Egete and Scrih he must have appeared stiff and rigid, more like a stone statue or a painting than a real, flesh and blood man. If only he could show them what he was feeling inside. That would be a lesson. They could marvel at the stillness of his form, the absence of even the slightest wobble or twitch as he held his bowstring back. The missing piece of the lesson, what he couldn't show them or even describe with words, was how completely at ease he felt. Adrenaline pumped no matter how many hunts a man boasted. Experience didn't stop the heart from racing. That was the thrill of the hunt, and it was always present. Controlling it was the trick. Learning to let your heart pound wild without allowing your body to fumble along behind it is what separates the hungry man from the fed man. He could have remained that way without flinching far into the darkness of night. However, the mighty hunter's composure crumbled when his target stepped out into the light. Ymitoth shrunk in his saddle like fat melting on a hot stone as three cloaked figures slowly approached from the shadows. Nearly eighteen summers had passed since he faced down the dead-eyed men in the cathedral at Havenstahl, yet his paralyzing fear was as fresh as the day that memory was painted on his brain.

"Run," he could barely hear his own voice as terror squeezed his lungs, only allowing him enough air for a hoarse whisper.

Egete and Scrih regarded their king with twisted, queer expressions.

After a few moments of struggling with his lips, Ymitoth finally found his voice and shouted, "Run!"

"From a mere three men?" Scrih's expression matched the incredulous tone of his voice.

"Damn it, that ain't no request. It be a command from your king," the volume of Ymitoth's voice filled the clearing. "Have ye ever known me to be fearing any man or anything?"

"Not in all me days, highness," Egete shook his head slowly.

"Not a chance, highness," Scrih's reply quickly followed.

"Well I tell ye true lads, fear be tearing at me spine as I be sitting here trembling before ye. Now run, damn it," Ymitoth's cheeks shook with the force of his words.

"Ye can be punishing me later, highness. But if there be a force in this land so awful as to be scaring the wits out of the bravest man I ever served, I'll be cutting that terror down," Scrih shouted as he drew his sword and slammed his heels into his horse's flanks, driving the animal toward the three cloaked men.

Egete fell in right behind Scrih shouting, "Make haste, highness," over his shoulder.

Ymitoth closed his eyes for the briefest moment, "Them boys damn hearts be far bigger than their damn brains."

Despite wrestling with the kind of mind-numbing fear that reduces most men to blubbering fools, duty prevailed. Ymitoth fired three quick arrows before charging after the stout, young soldiers who were so eager to prove their worth. Had they heeded his warning, all three of them would be on a hard gallop back to Havenstahl.

The arrows sliced the air one after another, splitting the space between Egete and Scrih. All of them bounced harmlessly away from the dirty, brown cloak they connected with. Confusion knotted up the expression on Scrih's face as he looked back over his left shoulder at his king. Then both he and Egete came to a halt. Ymitoth stopped directly behind his two soldiers before urging Pride in front of them.

"Highness," Egete complained.

"No, lad," Ymitoth kept his steely glare fixed on the dirty, brown cloak that led the group of three and stood a mere ten feet in front of him, "Ye ain't be having no idea what ye be dealing with here. I do, and it ain't nothing less than death."

A low, deep chuckle emanated from the cloak, as the shape beneath it raised both hands to draw the hood back. Ymitoth failed to suppress a gasp. Two black, dead eyes—lifeless orbs that had haunted his dreams ever since he faced the three in the cathedral at Havenstahl—glared at him. The last time he saw those eyes in the waking world had been shortly after celebrating Maelich's twelfth year. Even after all the years that had drifted by since the terrifying night so long ago, the horrors were as fresh as the breeze upon his neck. As his focus remained locked on those two empty globes, he was only faintly aware of something resembling a smile slithering beneath the orange mange under the twisted nose immediately below them.

Ymitoth drew a deep breath in through his nose. There was something foul about the aroma of the wet decay of leaves from the damp ground beneath the trees. Normally he found the scent rather appealing. Staring at the nightmares before him made the odor far less pleasant. Without averting his steely gaze, he growled through clenched teeth, "Race back to Havenstahl, lads. Tell them the king has fallen and a nightmare be coming to batter our gates. Find Maelich, and tell him dead-eyed men be walking about the woods of Havenstahl."

"No, highness," Scrih's voice carried a measure of authority.

"Aye," Egete agreed. "We ain't be going nowhere without ye, highness."

Ymitoth sighed and shook his head, "Lads—"

"Such fierce loyalty for their king," the dead-eyed man goaded. "I am impressed. And king, no less. That is equally impressive. When last we met, you were but a crude swordsman training an insolent brat to swing sharpened metal around. Look how far you have come."

"Aye," Ymitoth scowled, "a king I be. But I warn ye, this sword at me hip ain't for show. I swing this lady hanging at me side with vicious intent."

The dead-eyed man's stillness made the volume of his laugh seem impossible. The horrible sound filled the air around Ymitoth and his guards, startling the horses that stamped and whinnied in response.

Much like a cornered animal puffs up its chest in the hopes of frightening off a threatening predator, Ymitoth pressed on, "Ain't a jest left me lips, ye vile thing."

The horrible laughter ceased as quickly as it began, "Therein lies the brilliance of your humor. It is completely unintended." The foul creature paused. "I am still not convinced whether you believe your boasts, or if you are merely feigning bravery for the sake of your men. I assume the latter. Even a gruff swordsman parading as king must be wise enough to realize the folly in standing against a herald of the one true ruler of Ouloos, god of creation, and master of all things."

"I fear nothing," Ymitoth spat as he drew his sword and leapt off Pride's back with the grace of a warrior half his age.

Before the muddy bottoms of the king's boots kissed even the tip of a blade of grass, Egete and Scrih charged. Hooves tore into the wet trail, tossing muddy clumps of grass up into the air behind them. Ymitoth barely took a step toward the monster before the heavy air beneath the trees thickened once again with the deep horror of the dead-eyed man's laugh. Like a premonition, the next act danced out on the stage of a brief, waking dream flashing through his consciousness. Before he managed even a step toward the horror threatening his men, the nightmare manifested itself in two pairs of claws shooting out from beneath the sleeves of the other two dirty, brown robes. His feet froze as he helplessly watched his faithful guards dashed against the ground in heaps while their horses—life gushing from throats torn open by sharp talons—rose toward the treetops.

"No," a throaty shout grew from deep in Ymitoth's gut, filling the air and challenging the might of the dead-eyed man's laugh.

The dead-eyed men paid him no heed. Their leader offered Ymitoth that same silent, snaky smile as his two companions yanked back their hoods and leapt onto the broken piles Ymitoth considered the finest of his guard. The king remained frozen as half of a hand landed near his foot, and the air before him filled with pieces of Egete and Scrih. Mere moments later, lifeless eyes glared up at him from heads no longer connected to the bodies that had carried them around. Their dead stares seemed to accuse him. It was more than he could stand. The warrior charged.

CHAPTER 1
RETURN TO THE SOBBING FOREST

"Helias, the great Dragon, was a magnificent giant with menacing teeth, piercing eyes, leathery wings, and glowing skin like fire!" Maelich boomed.

The trees leaned in closer, almost oozing with anticipation. Nearly eighteen summers had passed since Maelich first walked among the cool, dampness of the Sobbing Forest. The same trees that had been so skeptical of his small group all those years ago, crowded closer, as if they wanted to hold him and keep him, absorb him into their oneness.

Maelich's tone became quieter, falling to barely a whisper before slowly mounting back to something just shy of a shout, "I trembled before her, terrified by the ferocity of her glare and the searing fire promised by her wicked smile. As I cowered before the beast, my fear quickly turned to rage. Glowing with the fire of that rage, my blade begged to be plunged into her blackest of hearts."

The trees gasped. Tension thick enough to be a real, tangible thing radiated from their trunks. He smirked as he paused, silently teasing them, holding back the climax, the slow, mounting crescendo ready to explode at any moment. Of course, there was no surprise. Since that day five summers ago, Maelich had failed to find a city—or a town, or even a settlement for that matter—where the story of the lad of the Lake facing down the last Dragon had not spread. Every man he encountered during his travels seemed bent on sharing their own version of the story with him. Even the birds chirped about it incessantly, sharing things they heard from here and there among the treetops. Still, the storyteller boomed with fierce intensity in his voice that promised a different, horrible ending.

Instead of continuing, erupting into a shocking climax that would shake the trees to their very roots, Maelich's tone became matter of fact, "I could not do it. I found her to be without flaw. With my blade aimed at that heart I knew to be blacker than the deepest pit of the deepest cave on Ouloos, I was prepared to destroy her. But she, the greatest power on Ouloos, breathed not so much as a spark to defend herself. Even with the bloody promise of my fiery blade poised, ready to punch a hole into her dark heart and end her existence, she refused to attack me. Without a shred of hatred or fear in her body, she completely lacked the ability to destroy. She was perfection. No, she is perfection."

A murmur fluttered through the forest. The tension quickly fled as the trees seemed to deflate, slowly drifting back down from the heights to which Maelich's words had taken them. Palpable joy oozed from them, surrounding him with feelings, meaning to all of their murmuring. The lad of the Lake had finally returned to them as he had promised so many summers prior, and with him he brought a firsthand account of the story that spawned a mountain of rumors. They slowly began to wave and shudder, fighting the desire to be close, to touch the boy who had grown into a legend of men. Trunks trembled and leaves shook, as the trees of the Sobbing Forest slowly inched closer and then stretched their limbs up and away from Maelich several times. Finally, the forest floor brightened, chasing away the darkness that normally suffocated it.

Filtered rays of sunshine warmed Maelich's face as a stoic expression crept onto it. He stroked his chin and continued his story, "Then came my battle with the father of lies, the father of hate, the father of evil, Kallum. He came to me as the mighty eagle, lord of the skies."

Again the trees murmured, passing whispers from twig to twig and leaf to leaf. None of them knew what an eagle was. Kallum had never visited them, much less in the form of an eagle. What did the forest know of eagles?

Maelich explained as he strolled among them, leaving the trail behind, "He came to battle as a giant bird, golden brown with a powerful, hooked beak and terrifyingly sharp talons. I rode Helias—the great Dragon, the last Dragon, the sweet soul who had once seemed the vilest of creatures to me—into battle. Kallum attacked us with the air, beating his mighty wings and sending whirlwinds to frustrate our flight. His command of the sky proved his boast of lord over it, and I was swept from Helias's back. Then—"

Maelich paused; a stiff breeze rustled the leaves above him and carelessly tossed his long, golden locks all about behind him. The air of the forest was normally still, almost stale. The uncommon wind weaving around tree trunks and shaking leaves all about the canopy wasn't what distracted Maelich from his story though. Since first he stepped foot into the forest that morning, the trees had—for the most part—spread their leaves wide to allow the sun and fresh air in, welcoming his long-awaited, heroic return.

Something else grabbed his attention, a new presence dancing among the currents, something foreign and out of place, something that did not belong.

Maelich's senses grew keener after his battle with Kallum, and each day since he became more connected to his surroundings. He could sense things he never dreamed possible, hear sounds no man could possibly hear, and smell odors no animal could hope to smell. Atmospheric changes were as noticeable as any sight, sound, taste, or smell. He was completely connected to everything on Ouloos, sensing changes in temperature, even sensing the coming rain hours before a drop fell from the sky. More immediately, he sensed the trees were completely taken by surprise. Normally each was aware of what every other one knew. This rendered anything known by one a surprise to none. Wrapped in the lad of the Lake's story, however, all of them missed the foreign presence until Maelich shared his awareness of it with them.

Maelich quickly glanced in several directions, slowly spinning a circle below a thick canopy of leaves rustling with anticipation. There was no need for strained eyes as he could see a great distance through the trees, even with the filtered sunshine. Silver light flickering in the distance— brilliant flashes lasting mere fractions of a second each—caught his attention. No person alive would have noticed, save Cialia, neither any animal for that matter. He drew in a deep breath through his nose. An out of place scent fraternized with the odors of rotting leaves, fresh dirt, and fragrant shrubs. It was something powerful, ancient, and primal. Focusing on the silvery flash and foreign smell, it only took moments for Maelich to be completely aware of the force that had entered the forest. It was the lion, Kaldumahn, the great, silver beast who stalks across the skies. A smile spread across Maelich's face. Though he never had an opportunity to speak to Kaldumahn, he felt a connection to the god. The same brotherhood he felt with all things on Ouloos.

"Kaldumahn," Maelich boomed as the massive, silver god approached, "the great lion who stalks the skies, I am honored to be in your presence."

Another murmur raced among the trees. They gushed with all the blessings this day had brought. The lad of the Lake—the one member of the race of men who could stifle their urge to squeeze and choke—had returned with tales of his adventures to share with them. As if that weren't enough, Kaldumahn had also come to stroll among them. The trees buzzed and swayed, humming the tune Maelich had honored them with so long ago.

The lion returned Maelich's smile as he raised his head high. The top of it sat easily twenty feet above the forest floor. His grand mane flowed behind his massive frame like a crown, the king of the gods. He spoke, his voice as deep and powerful as Maelich expected, "Maelich, savior of

Ouloos, it is I who am honored. Five summers have passed since you saved our world, and you have yet to rest. Have you finished the book?"

Maelich nodded, "Yes, yes I have. I did my best to present as much of the truth as I could to the people. I fear some of it may be too much for most to accept. Therefore, I have hidden some of it in metaphor. Only those minds great enough to unlock the secrets will have access to them. I believe a mind that desirous of truth will be able to accept it for what it is."

"Truth," Kaldumahn frowned. "Is that what you call your teachings? What have you written of Coeptus?"

"Only some of what they told me. Why do you ask?" his brows dipped toward his nose.

"Mind you, I seek no fault," Kaldumahn began, "but I must tell you now, I know everything you have written. You feel a connection to me and everything else on Ouloos. I feel the same connection to you, and I must confess something. I spied on you."

The corners of Maelich's mouth dipped slightly, "You spied on me? Why would you do such a thing? Why not seek me out to speak about my words? I would happily share my writings with you."

"Please, Maelich, do not mistake my intentions," the great lion replied. "I seek no fault in your words. I think what you have written is perfect. Your book will prove a wonderful guide for the people of Ouloos. It will give them hope and guidance." He paused, brought his gaze in line with Maelich's, and added, "My fear lies with your belief that what you wrote is, in fact, truth. It seems you believe things to be truths that are not truths."

Maelich shook his head slowly, "Everything I wrote was given to me by Coeptus themselves. How could they be anything less than truths? Coeptus are everything and everything is Coeptus. They are all and know all."

Kaldumahn softened his stance, "Maelich, your mind is as brilliant as the sun at midday. You are a god as great as any of us, probably greater. Yet, you are a man at the same time. You will always be hindered by your human qualities. You are so full of so many things you have been told and things you have seen. Still you do not realize you cannot always trust those things. Sometimes, you cannot even trust what your eyes show you. You truly believe Coeptus showed all of these truths to you. I know this. I know deep in your very soul you believe this. Unfortunately, I also know Coeptus are not anything that can be spoken to or seen. Like you said, they are everything, you, me, the trees, the ground we are standing on, and even the air you are breathing. But they are not tangible. Once you learn to quiet the man in you, you will be able to know this."

Maelich glanced down at his feet and thought for a moment. When he raised his face back to Kaldumahn, it wore a deep frown and a narrow gaze, "I must admit, great Kaldumahn, I am more than slightly offended. You doubt me. I spoke with them. My ears heard their words. I felt their presence." He raised his hands out to his sides and added, "Even Cialia saw and spoke with them. We discussed it endlessly after our encounter. Would you suggest we shared the same dream so completely real to have duped us both into believing in fancy?"

The great lion's gaze drifted toward the canopy, "I suppose, based on the connection you share with your twin, it would be completely within the realm of possibility. However, I do not believe it to be the case."

"What is it you believe, oh great and mighty Kaldumahn?" an edgy note of sarcasm loafed about in Maelich's tone.

"Of that I am unclear," the god frowned. "Whomever or whatever you encountered after your battle with Kallum must wield great power."

"Or perhaps I—being too much a man—am so easily tricked by a shimmering robe and wise words," he chuckled.

"Forgive me, Maelich. My intention was not to hurt your pride," Kaldumahn bowed slightly, "but I have. However, since it has been roused, I must counsel you to temper it lest it be your downfall."

Maelich humphed, "That sounds like something Kallum might say if not just a hair more polite. Please tell me the great Kaldumahn is more than merely another jealous god. I truly have been looking forward to speaking to you and sharing thoughts about Coeptus and Ouloos and the Lake. But you have not come to share these thoughts with me. Instead, you have come to find fault, to challenge truth." Maelich scratched his head and began to pace, "I presume Coeptus have never spoken to you."

Sadness spread across Kaldumahn's expression, "Of course they have not. They cannot. Coeptus are everything, not a man or being who can be conversed with. Surely if you search your heart, you will find you know this to be true."

"If it were not Coeptus speaking to me and not my imagination conjuring the encounter, oh great and wise Kaldumahn, then whom or what?" agitation crept into Maelich's tone.

"I do not know, Maelich. I believe you did speak to someone, or something, but I am certain it was not Coeptus."

Maelich stopped pacing and matched Kaldumahn's gaze, "I believe you are jealous that Coeptus spoke to me but have never spoken to you. I saw them with my own eyes. I felt their presence. I experienced them. This was not my imagination, not some fancy I concocted in my own mind." Again, he shook his head, "You have no faith in me."

Kaldumahn sighed, "Someday, Maelich, you will learn to see things through the eyes of a god. You will learn to disseminate fact from fancy. Until then, I suppose you will see me as this jealous thing you describe. Know this. We gods were first after the Dragons and we have seen Ouloos become what it is. It is unwise to dismiss any god as anything less than a powerful, wise creature who deserves to be revered with awe and worship. I do, however, understand where these ideas you harbor come from, and I do feel pity for you. I wish you only the best on your journey. You feel it is done, that you have conquered all and now need only to teach the men of Ouloos to follow your word. Hear me now, Maelich. Your journey has just begun and your path is not an easy one. You would do well to learn to control that pride. It is your biggest weakness. It makes you deaf to ideas not already haunting your mind. What is left to learn when everything is known?"

The lion was gone before Maelich could respond, leaving the lad of the Lake alone with a mouthful of angry words and a fire growing in his belly. Swallowing those words back down rather than spewing them into the face of that doubter made the blaze growing in his gut burn stronger. What a cowardly way to end a debate, throw a quick jab and then flee before a counterpunch can be thrown. He remained there; tense, staring impotently at the spot where Kaldumahn had stood showering accusations upon him. What else could he do, spar with a shadow? His adversary had fled leaving the moment unfinished, like a tender kiss stopped short by a sleepy-eyed child startled from slumber by a night terror.

Several moments passed before Maelich's rage dulled enough his mind could notice any signals from any of his senses. First his ears, the trees had stopped humming. Then his eyes, the forest had darkened. Trees that had at once stretched tall and spread their branches wide to allow the glory of the sun and the fresh relief of the north wind in to dance among the forest floor shrunk, huddled together, and cowered before him. They were afraid. It only took a few moments more for him to realize they had good reason to be. The warmth in his cheeks meant his eyes echoed the smoldering anger tumbling around his gut with the red glow of Dragon's fire. His body slowly relaxed as he sighed long and deep, gradually deflating. As the trees slowly gained back his full attention, their apprehension became more and more apparent. It stood tall like a thick, brick wall. The false sense of serenity he attempted to fill them with failed to penetrate. How could he fill anything or anyone with something he could barely secure for himself? With his power, he could burn the entire forest to the ground. He would never do that. At least, he believed he wouldn't. Apparently, the trees did not share his optimism. His return had been ruined. The story was finished. The redness in his cheeks shifted from rage to embarrassment that kept his apologetic thoughts to the trees short and awkward.

Damn Kaldumahn and his doubts, crushing a triumphant return to the forest with his needling remarks and his prodding questions. Still, the great lion's words were not without merit. A few simple queries managed to raise Maelich's hackles up far too easily. Is it wrong to question? No. It is never wrong to question. Had he never questioned, he would have killed Helias and all would be lost. Why did he react so poorly when his ideas were challenged? Perhaps it was pride that had him so flummoxed. Questions posed by one he held in such high regard cut deep. But should they?

The trees surrounding him trembled. With all of the doubt circling his mind, he couldn't calm them. Instead, he made a circle with the index finger and thumb of his right hand, pushed the tip of his tongue back with it, and gave a short, sharp whistle to alert Validus it was time to depart. The horse had been wandering the forest, probably looking for green things to chew on. Approaching hoof beats entered Maelich's awareness immediately after that whistle, but they did not match Validus's familiar gallop. The mystery solved itself within moments as the silhouette of Cialia astride Purity entered his field of vision. Intensity saturated the air surrounding the two. It was magnified by the urgency in Purity's hooves pounding the forest floor. Maelich gleaned enough from his sister's thoughts to know Havenstahl faced some form of danger. Sadly, the disjointed racing of her mind made its definition impossible to ascertain.

Cialia leapt from Purity's back before the white mare had stopped her gallop. Her words poured out as a frenzied shout, "Maelich! You must return to Havenstahl. Three cloaked men attacked your father. He escaped, but he is battered and slipping in and out of consciousness. Hagen tends to him, but he keeps babbling about dead-eyed men and the priests of Kallum. I thought they perished when we destroyed him."

Maelich thought for a moment. "Yes, they should have become rotting corpses when Kallum was scattered. How could they still be haunting our world? Unless—" his voice trailed off as he realized the implications.

At that moment, Validus charged up. Maelich leapt up onto his back and hollered, "We must make haste!" Once at a gallop, he continued shouting over the rumbling of horse's hooves, "Was there any sign of these cloaked men within the city walls?"

"No," Cialia responded, scarcely enough wind behind her words to be heard. "Ymitoth was barely clinging to his horse, but he was alone."

The trees made way for the two as they charged through the forest. The significance of Cialia's news was clear enough. Even as Maelich's attention shifted focus to Ymitoth's condition and the meaning behind the return of the dead-eyed men, he sensed the trees' fear of his fire slowly slipping away in favor of concern for one they held so dear. They resumed a soft hum of Maelich's song, the gift he had given them so many summers past.

CHAPTER 2
THEY LIVE

The sun burned bright in the sky as Maelich and Cialia burst forth from the forest. Even with the heavy weight of Cialia's news pushing him deep into Validus's saddle, Maelich couldn't help but feel slightly nostalgic racing out of the dark place. It reminded him of the first time he charged triumphantly out of the forest with Jom by his side. His eyes squinted as he gave in to a brief moment of reminiscing. Though his mind was elsewhere—traveling far ahead of him—he gave just enough thought to the trees to bid them farewell and promise to return again. He twisted back toward the trees and waved. They swayed back and forth as if to return the gesture. Their loyalty was humbling. He had frightened them to their roots, yet they still loudly sung his praises. He knew they would continue to sing them to all who stumbled within their midst. It felt more than he deserved. Hopefully another eighteen summers wouldn't pass before he could wander among them again.

Maelich pulled his attention back to the trail and the prairie spreading out before him, sloping on a slow, steady incline to the north. Too many thoughts and doubts swirled about his mind to focus his intent and urge the horses on faster. Kaldumahn doubted him, the trees of the Sobbing Forest had quaked in fear before him, and monsters bearing an uncanny resemblance to the priests of a dead god had attacked and battered his father. The immediacy of his need for haste was more than apparent, yet his mind continued to wander. Forcing and pushing, he tried to slip into the heads of Validus and Purity to urge them on and quicken their pace. Unfortunately, maintaining the concentration necessary to push the animals beyond their physical limits proved a summit too great to conquer. They charged ever faster toward Havenstahl, but they did it with little help from

Maelich. Even still, the sound of hooves pounding the earth echoed back off the trees like the hammering thunder of one hundred horses. Already wet from the trail, both of the sturdy mounts dug into the packed dirt, pushing harder and faster. If either were tiring, they didn't show it. They raced along as if sensing Maelich's urgency regardless of how incoherent his thoughts were.

Cialia detached herself from the moment long enough to enjoy the wind whipping at her face and blowing her golden hair back. The fresh, prairie wind filled her sinuses with the smell of wildflowers. They were so fragrant this time of the season. It filled her up, momentarily freeing her from the weight of life. Often times she felt a prisoner in her role as teacher of Coeptus's word. A young girl's dreams of adventure and battling against injustice that had once filled her head would probably never be realized. Her role was to teach and spread the word of Coeptus, giving hope to all those in need. Though the road endlessly beckoned, she had to ignore its cries in favor of a life of service. For a moment she was free from those shackles, flying far above the ground, riding the wind filling her sails.

Havenstahl came into view as they crested the hill. Maelich didn't let up. Their charge into the valley would be fast and short. As they approached its floor, the air around them became cool as the sun darkened in the sky. Maelich pulled up on Validus's reigns and Cialia followed suit. A swirling mist appeared before them. It seemed to have no origin, materializing from the air. Where there was nothing, something suddenly filled the space. Both Maelich and Cialia drew their swords. Spooked, Validus and Purity stomped about. They all watched as three cloaked men formed out of the receding mist.

Cialia's eyes widened until they were big and round like two moons, "It was no hallucination. Ymitoth spoke the truth."

Maelich's mind raced through explanation after explanation, but could find none other than Kallum still lived. Coeptus had said a god could not be killed, merely scattered. It appeared Kallum had managed to pull himself together. Maelich wasted no time. He let the fire come. Deep, blazing red filled his eyes as flames began swirling around his hands and forearms. At the same time, a perfect circle of flame surrounded the three cloaked men and licked up toward the sky. The most ambitious of those flames stretched up as high as their heads. Maelich had learned a thing or two about the art of controlling Dragon's fire since his last meeting with Kallum.

Maelich's voice remained completely calm as he addressed the three. "Show your faces and state your business or suffer the fury of my flame."

The leader of the three removed his hood, but the other two remained motionless. It was just as it had been when first Maelich faced them. A wild mop of orange hair crowned the leader's head. An even wilder, orange mange of a beard squatted across his face. His eyes were black and dead, and his sneer a thousand years of death. He showed no expression—save the wild sneer—as he reached his hand out into the encircling flame and allowed it to blacken and burn. It melted and then dripped from glistening muscles and tendons that also burned in the heat of Maelich's flame. Still, his expression remained unchanged. Even when the meat dripped off the bone, he didn't flinch. He slowly pulled his hand back and held it up for Maelich and Cialia to see. Glistening bone as white as Coeptus's robe reflected the smoke-filtered sunshine. Immediately, meat, tendons, and skin began to grow back. Within moments, there was no evidence of a burn of any sort. The monster's hand and arm appeared completely unscathed.

The smell of the dead-eyed man's flesh was still strong in the air as Maelich clenched his teeth and coaxed his flames to burn hotter, "State your business."

The leader spoke calmly and with great power, "You have become quite the master of your art, Maelich. You could burn all of Ouloos into oblivion, yet you could not kill me. Does that frighten you?"

"I fear nothing," Maelich's teeth remained tightly clenched, "especially a coward hiding behind soulless corpses. This world no longer belongs to you. I am the guardian of this place, and I will let nothing destroy it. Your reign ended when I bested you above the Lost Forest. You are nothing but a memory now, a bad dream this world once had."

The leader of the three continued to glare at Maelich with black, dead eyes, the kind of piercing stare that stabs right through the soul, "You belong to me Maelich. Your soul, your strength, and your power, they are all mine. Sadly, you are too wild for me to control at this point. You are a rebellious child, and you will pay for your insolence in time. For now, there is another child I want. Because you belong to me, he belongs to me."

"My child, you threaten the life of my unborn child?"

The flames grew brighter and hotter as the circle closed in on the dead-eyed men. Maelich's growing fury slowly took control of him. "Never," he hissed. "You will never lay your dead hands on my child's pure soul. I will destroy this entire universe, rip the sun from the sky, and crack the crust of Ouloos before I let that happen."

Maelich nearly lost control of his flame before feeling Cialia's presence in his mind. Though he sensed she was a victim of the same rage, she maintained control while his slipped away. The flames circling his forearms had spread the rest of the way up his arms and around his chest. Had Cialia not forced her way into his consciousness, he might have ended up standing above the ashes of his dead horse rather than seated upon it. Instead, with her assistance, his flame eased a bit.

The leader goaded Maelich, "Watch that temper son, lest those flames consume you. In five days, your bride will give birth to a son, my son. I will come for him then, Maelich. He will be more powerful than you could ever imagine. He will make your silly little tricks with fire seem just that, silly, little, fire tricks. He will rule this world by my side and be the son you should have been. You and your strong will. Pay heed, Maelich. It will be the end of you."

Maelich's reply had only made it to the back of his throat before the three vanished in the same mist that brought them. A few moments—and several deep breaths—later, his flame slowly diminished and eventually subsided. He placed his hand to his chest and sighed deeply. The thick smell of burning flesh still lingered. He shook his head. Could Kallum still live? He must. The scattered god's priests still haunted Ouloos.

Maelich's voice was just a hair more than a whisper as he reached out for Cialia's hand and said, "He said I am to have a son, his son."

Cialia shook her head, "He toys with you, Maelich. His words stab you where you are weakest. He exploits your emotion." She paused, "Do not let him have that control over you. Your emotions are your only disadvantage against him."

"Thank you for standing by me," Maelich whispered. "Thank you for helping me control the fire. My rage was getting the best of me." He paused and ran a hand through his golden hair, "How can he still live?"

Cialia shook her head, "I do not know. He certainly still lives though. You must teach me the art of Dragon's fire. The book is finished. You saw the way the priest toyed with your flame. You cannot do this alone."

Maelich stared far past Cialia, "I know. It is time. But first we must tend to Ymitoth and prepare ourselves for Kallum's return." His stare remained far off, "I must try to speak with Coeptus."

She placed her hand on his wrist, "Do not fear. We will not let him take your son. All of Havenstahl will fight by your side. You know this." Patting his hand, she added, "Come, let us prepare."

The sun had returned to its normal brilliance once the three had departed. Maelich squinted as the world grew brighter and brighter around him. Kallum's priests seemed more powerful than they had ever been. They darkened the sky. Doubt clouded his head as he and Cialia charged up the hill to Havenstahl, eager to swallow up the last bit of their journey.

The sun was still in the sky when they reached the gates of the city. Maelich's flesh pulled up into tight bumps. Entering the city gates invigorated him almost as much as exiting them would have eighteen summers prior. The few days he had been away felt more like years.

A crowd began to gather as Maelich and Cialia moved through the streets of the city. People seeking blessings and guidance from their savior crowded the path. Maelich tugged on Validus's reigns and brought the steed to rest among them. Then he raised his hands to them, palms out.

"Havenstahl," he began, "raise your eyes up from your troubles. Fix your gaze on the Lake, the great power that bore you into this world and ever beckons you home. Give your worries to the Dragon and heed her call as she guides you back to the warm embrace of the waters she protects."

He would have continued the blessing, but Cialia intervened, "My brother, how can you heal the souls of the masses when your soul is in such dire need of healing itself? Go to your father and leave the tending of the flock to me."

The weary and troubled prince smiled at his sister, "Thank you."

Cialia quickly hopped from Purity's back and worked her way into the crowd, touching and blessing people as she passed them. She drew them to her and guided them away from Maelich toward a fountain. Once satisfied she had their complete attention, she began to preach. The air lightened around the crowd as she gently lifted the weight of their worries off of their heads. In moments, she had them well in hand while Maelich escaped unnoticed.

CHAPTER 3
GOODBYE

Hagen waited impatiently for Maelich's arrival. His arms folded tightly across his chest as his foot nervously tapped the floor. Death was in the air. Ymitoth still lived but only barely. Hagen was losing his battle with death for the king's life, and the heir to the throne had duties far greater than ruling over a city of men. On top of that, his patient's attackers seemed to be no less than heralds of a dead god. Hagen still had yet to wrap his mind around that. Kallum's priests were merely corpses the god reanimated to do his bidding. Once he was scattered, those corpses should have collapsed and begun a natural process of decomposition. Somehow, Kallum must have survived his battle with Maelich. It was the only possible explanation.

Maelich hit the top of the stair fighting to catch his breath. He managed to choke a few words out between his labored breaths, "How…is he? Am I…too late?"

Hagen shook his head while his eyes rolled toward the ceiling, Maelich's condition momentarily interrupting his concern for Ymitoth's state. The lad of the Lake did much to frustrate the old healer, "Tsk, tsk. After all you have seen and done, you are still much of a man."

Maelich's breath still came in heavy, rapid gasps, but he was slowly gaining control of it. After drawing a deep breath in through his nose, holding it for a moment, and releasing it in a long sigh, he calmly continued, "Forgive me, Hagen. What is my father's condition?"

The healer ignored the question and continued his critique of Maelich's disheveled state, "At times it seems when you most need your power you forget what great power you wield. You could run from sea to sea as fast as a horse without exerting the least bit of energy. Yet, add a bit of concern to your mind and climbing a stairwell has you at the edge of consciousness.

Why is that? You are the master of your surroundings. Why in instances such as these do you pretend to be only a man?"

Maelich shrugged, "I do not know, and I do not care much right at this moment. All that concerns me is my father's condition. Please, if you have a mind to lecture, save it for later. Your lesson will be lost on me if you deliver it now."

"Yes, I suppose it will," Hagen sighed. "Well," he absently scratched the top of his head with his left hand as he grimaced and looked to the ground, perhaps hoping the right words might be carved in the stone there, "he still lives."

Maelich heaved a sigh of relief as he clutched his chest with his left hand and his chin with his right. Then he stroked his chin with his middle finger and thumb while nervously chewing at the side of his index finger for a moment, "Thank Coeptus for that. Is he awake?"

Hagen looked back to the floor, this time rubbing the back of his neck. His eyebrows rose as he continued his search for compassionate words, "Listen Maelich, I am not quite sure how to say this gently so I will just say it. I pray you can accept what I am about to tell you. Everything I can do has been done. I have toiled over him and filled him with my most powerful elixirs. The fight is his now. Yes he still lives, but only barely."

Maelich set his jaw tight as his entire face seemed to squint. He stared at Hagen with misty eyes, looking as if the old man had just slapped him across the face, "You sound as if you have given up. My father is strong, perhaps the strongest man I know. Surely he can survive a beating, even one as severe as Kallum's priests could deliver." Maelich's tone pleaded with Hagen as if he could lobby a change of the prognosis. He paused— quietly staring at the old healer for a moment—and then added, "With your help, I mean."

Hagen slumped, walked over to Maelich, draped his right arm across his shoulders, and pulled him close, "Maelich, Ymitoth was battered when they brought him to me. He was delirious, completely incoherent. His consciousness fled almost immediately. I cannot tell you how much blood he lost, but I can say it was more than enough to kill most men."

"No," Maelich shook his head and backed away from Hagen. "You are wrong."

"Maelich, his limbs and most of his ribs were shattered. His skull was cracked open. He bled from every hole in his head. Deep bruises cover his entire body. It is a miracle he still lives at all."

"Shut up," Maelich sobbed, absently wiping tears from his cheeks before pulling at his running nose. "Shut up. You are wrong," he repeated.

Hagen's eyes misted over as he watched Maelich break down. The words had to be said though. Not one to spread false hope, the old healer continued, "I do not want to tell you this anymore than you want to hear it, but the truth is the truth. You must be prepared for it. I do not believe Ymitoth is going to live. If he does, you will probably not recognize him, not his face or his mind."

"No!" Maelich shouted. His eyes flashed red as the fire grew inside of him, "Shut your old, stupid mouth! You know nothing! My father knows no equal in battle. He has cut down hordes of men and beasts. Surely you are mistaken. Perhaps your friendship with him has clouded your judgment."

"I wish it were so, my friend," Hagen slowly shook his head. "I wish it were so."

"I want to see him."

"I wanted you to, but now I do not believe it is a good idea. You are already very upset. Seeing him in his current condition will only serve to upset you further. Besides, he needs his rest."

Maelich had purpose in his steps as he pushed past Hagen to the door. The old healer grabbed at his sleeve and spun him around.

"Maelich, please," he pleaded. "You do not want to see him like this. All of those things you said about him are true. He was a great warrior, a hero among men. That is how you should remember him. The lump of dying flesh lying on the bed in there does not resemble the hero you just described. Believe me; you do not want that vision clouding your memories of him."

Hagen saw the fire burning in Maelich's eyes. There were no words, just a long, uncomfortable silence accompanied by squinted, burning eyes. The old healer trembled. That fiery stare could have burned a hole through stone. It was so full of anger and hate. Hagen stepped aside, slumped to the ground, dropped his head into his hands, and wept.

"I am sorry, Maelich," Hagen cried into his hands. "I have done all I can for him."

Maelich pushed the door to Ymitoth's room open and hurried inside. An acrid stench of stale blood saturated the air, mingling with the sharp sting of Hagen's medicines. The combination smelled like death. He gathered himself and walked over to the bed. Hagen's description had been mostly accurate, if not a shade tamer than reality. Ymitoth's skull had been crushed. It was wrapped in bandages, but the shape was all wrong. His face was the only part of his body completely exposed, and it was purple and swollen. The rest of him was a lump under the blankets that seemed far smaller than it should have been. Hagen had been correct. The poor, battered man occupying the bed bared little resemblance to Ymitoth.

An idea tore through Maelich's head like an arrow fired from a tightly strung bow. Hagen was wrong. This tiny, dying man was not Ymitoth at all. It was some other poor bloke who had gotten himself in the way of some creatures that were much too much for him to handle. Ymitoth must still be out on the trail. Thanks be to Coeptus. Maelich sighed. He had gotten himself all worked up over nothing. The idea that the battered lump of flesh lying in the bed was somebody other than Ymitoth had all but anchored itself in Maelich's head by the time Hagen quietly entered the room.

Words dribbled from Maelich's lips before he could stop them, "Is this really my father?"

"It is," Hagen responded somberly with tears still streaming from his eyes. "Go ahead and say something to him. Time is no friend of his now, and this may be your last chance."

Tears flooded down Maelich's face again as he asked, "Can he hear me?"

"I do not know. I think if you believe he can, then he can."

"What should I say?"

Hagen smiled slightly through his tears, "Whatever you want to say. Perhaps something he can hang on to until he makes his final journey home."

Maelich went to Ymitoth and kissed his cheek. Then he leaned in close and whispered, "I love you father. I am sorry." Heavy sobs took him. Burying his head into his father's chest, he continued, "I am sorry I was not there to fight those demons by your side. I am sorry I brought the wrath of those beasts down upon you. To them, you suffer so I might suffer. I am to blame for this." He sobbed silently for a bit. With his ear pressed against Ymitoth's chest, he could hear the faint, shallow breaths his father labored so hard to take. Maelich sat up, "You are still fighting. You are the bravest man I will ever know."

Suddenly, Hagen gasped. The startling sound prompted Maelich to raise his head off Ymitoth's chest. When he did, his father's eyes stared back at him. Maelich knew there was no way the king should have ever again seen consciousness. Yet there he lay with eyes wide open.

As Maelich gazed down on him, the battered king looked up and whispered, "Don't be blaming yourself, lad. Had I the chance to have another go at me life, I'd not be changing a thing. Sure I love ye, son. Don't ye be forgetting that on me."

Words escaped Maelich as he stared into his father's eyes and watched them slowly cloud over. Maelich's face contorted as his eyes began stinging once again. Shaking his head he shouted, "No!" Phlegm flew past his lips and he shouted again and again, "No! No! No!" He grabbed Ymitoth and pulled him close, hugging the lifeless body and wailing like a starving babe.

A lifetime of memories flashed through Maelich's head as he held his father's limp form. Throughout his childhood, Ymitoth had played the stern mentor. Everything was training and working and reading the book that had proven to be such a lie. The day his training had ended was the first time he saw the softer side of the man he called father. That day had been such a great celebration. Ymitoth was so proud, almost as proud as he was at Maelich's ceremony of the crest. Ymitoth had said many times that was the proudest moment of his life.

All of Maelich's attempts to blame something other than himself for Ymitoth's death completely failed. The closest he could get was also accepting the blame for his father's happiness. What would Ymitoth say? "Sure lad, ye have brought me a bit of pain and sorrow. What would I be without ye, though? I'd have never known the lifetime of joy ye brought me. I tell ye, lad, I'd not be trading me life for any other."

Hagen watched Maelich wailing over Ymitoth's corpse. The thought of intervening lived a short life. Instead, he let Maelich have his grief. Losing a father is a hard thing for any man. As the old healer left the room, he closed the door quietly behind him. Preparations were necessary. The final ceremony for the mightiest king Ouloos had ever known would have to be as great as the man it honored. There was much to do. Thankfully, there was much to do that would keep his mind off the loss of a friend so dear. His grieving could wait until all of his work was done. For the time being, Maelich would need him to be strong.

CHAPTER 4
REMINISCING

Maelich woke to the first rays of morning sun pouring into the room. His eyes squinted as he slowly blinked the sleep from them. The stench of death hit him, earning a groan from deep in his gut. He sat up, scratched his belly, and then absently rubbed at his eyes. Muscles loosened as he stretched his arms high above his head, arching his back and grumbling the entire way about the rank odor. Reality settled in as he slowly returned to consciousness. His father was dead. That was the smell. Quit grumbling.

Maelich looked down at Ymitoth's lifeless body. He stared at it so long his mind began playing tricks on him. A couple of times, he was certain his father's corpse moved. At any moment, Ymitoth's eyes might pop open again and they could laugh about how silly they had acted the night before. The idea was ridiculous, but he kept staring anyway, waiting. He sat like that until the sun was fully above the horizon. Then Hagen's harsh words from the night before swept into his head like rushing wind through a low valley. The old healer had scolded him for acting like a man. Maelich turned the idea around in his brain, flipped it over, and examined it from all angles. His mind began working much faster than it should, much faster than logic could possibly keep pace with.

After several minutes, Maelich knew what he was going to do. The plan was simple and clear. He was a god. Why behave like a mere man? Why sob and wail and wish when filled with such great power? The answer was beautifully simple. He wouldn't. In an instant as brief and powerful as the moment of clarity that hits a man just before the killing blow ends him, that moment when the world slows and all of one's memories crash down the walls of the dam that has held them back for a lifetime, the same moment that is at once instant and eternity, his decision was made. He wrapped

Ymitoth's body tight with blankets. The corpse was stiff and awkward to lift. He struggled with it for a few moments before telling himself again he was more than a mere man. 'Lift him like a god would,' he thought. Once his mind was flexing more than his muscles, he hefted Ymitoth up onto his shoulder and strolled out of the room with him.

Many an odd glance scrutinized him as he walked through the castle with the king's corpse draped over his shoulder. Even more met him as he walked to the stables and ordered Validus be prepared to ride. No one had anything to say. They all just watched as he walked about carrying a corpse wrapped tightly in blankets. That is until Talhomme—one of the stable hands—arrived with Validus saddled and loaded.

Talhomme was a round brute of a man. The skin on his face resembled wrinkled leather that had spent too much time drying in the sun. The top of his head was bare. The hair he did have was yellowish gray and hung in strings about his shoulders. As far as Maelich knew, the tightly squinting scowl Talhomme wore was the only expression his face was capable of making.

The pitch of Talhomme's voice was far higher than his gruff appearance would suggest, "Please forgive me prodding, your highness, but where ye be going with that body?"

"My actions are my own concern. Do not hinder me. I have much to do," Maelich snapped, uninterested in sharing his plans with anyone.

Talhomme bowed as he handed over Validus's reigns, "Forgive me, highness. Good day."

Maelich paid no further attention to the stable hand. He laid Ymitoth's body across Validus, tied it down, and hopped up onto the horse. In moments he was galloping out of the stable and onto the stone roads of Havenstahl. It was early, but they were already crowded with people heading to market for trade or off to work. Validus required only minimal guidance as they moved through the crowd. The horse had grown quite adept at keeping a swift pace without injuring any who desired to touch the savior. The crowds tried to move closer as Maelich rode by, but Validus's pace was much too quick. All they had time for were waves and well wishes. That was exactly what Maelich had hoped for.

The guards at the gate of the city came to attention as Maelich shot by them. There really was no need. He barely noticed them as thoughts of the task at hand dominated his mind. His eyelids gently closed as he pictured the old hut he and Ymitoth had shared through the first twelve summers of his life. The place was the setting for many of his fondest memories. It was also his destination. Though Havenstahl had become his home, his heart still ached for that simpler time of his life. A longing for those days filled with training and learning—like the longing of a starving man for the fat, glistening fruit dangling just out of his reach—consumed him. Life was so much easier before he was a hero, before people began to recognize him as a god.

Maelich's mind focused on the old hut, wrapping around the history he so desperately missed. As images danced about his awareness—trading blades with Ymitoth, running the trail around Yester's Pond, and even washing up bowls after the mid-day feast—he barely noticed the absence of Validus's hoof beats. Though they tore ever faster over the trail, the mighty thunder normally accompanying the horse's charge wasn't reverberating back off the huts they raced past. In fact, there was no sound at all, not even wind whistling past his face. The shapes before him quickly began melting into oozing colors, mingling with and bleeding into each other like a fresh scene on canvas battered by heavy rain. A moment before all the colors before him merged into one blurry mass, he caught sight of a young woman hanging shirts out on a line. Her lips mouthed something at the center of her shocked expression, and then she was gone. Everything was gone, black, still…for a moment.

Then hoof beats and horse sweat and the great, old oak crowning Keller's Hill; they were home. Maelich halted Validus at the base of the hill and gazed at the mighty tree upon it. From the tall grass around the fat trunk all the way up to the massive crown, the giant oak had remained constant, unmovable against the wind, the rain, and time, like an ancient warrior standing guard and patiently waiting for a challenge to his post.

Maelich dismounted, quickly surveying the rest of the area. Little had changed. The hut seemed mostly untouched. Aside from being a bit weathered, the planks hanging off the frame still appeared good and sturdy, and besides a few missing eaves, the roof looked structurally sound. Maelich allowed a smile to slip onto his face as he gently closed his eyes and drew in a deep breath. Then he threw Ymitoth back over his shoulder and hurried inside. The dead lump was stiff and difficult to bend. Before his mind had too much time to consider the condition of the corpse, he caught a whiff of it. He winced. It smelled like spoiled meat. Rot was setting in.

Then nostalgia hit. Inside the hut appeared nearly exactly as they had left it. A few minor details had changed. The hole in the roof had been repaired, as well as the shattered door. Other than those two things, it seemed like a time warp, like Maelich had just stepped back eighteen summers. Someone must have spent some time occupying the old space, but they hadn't changed much of anything. Judging from the thick coat of dust covering everything, even that had been quite a few summers past.

Maelich paused his reminiscing long enough to lay Ymitoth on the same cot the dead king had claimed back when he wore the title of mentor and Maelich, pupil. The corpse's stiff limbs bent in awkward angles and were stuck that way. It was too much for Maelich to look at, so he didn't for very long. Besides, a chill filled the small space. A nice fire would do it some good. He glanced over at the fireplace, empty save a small pile of cold ash spilling out onto the hearth. Despite its blackened brick, it appeared as frigid as the rest of the hut, as barren too. Moments later, the pile of spent ash was replaced by a healthy fire. There was no wood—or any other fuel, for that matter—in the fireplace, yet a cozy flame burned steadily within it. As the small blaze woke the musty odor of the old place, Maelich's smile finally returned. It was good to be home.

Maelich prepared some roast tubberslat and a sweet cake. The occasion seemed worthy of a feast. There were no tubber for miles. Nor was there the wheat necessary to make a sweet cake, but Maelich was in a different place. Free from the rules that shackle men, anything was possible. He moved as if in a trance. Two tall pints materialized and poured themselves out of nothing. Cooked meat and prepared vegetables appeared on the simple square table marking the center of the single-roomed hut. Everything was as it had been the last time they broke bread within those walls. Then the real work began.

The crackle of the fire was lost on Maelich as he focused his thoughts into Ymitoth. While his concentrated intent crawled around the dead brain squeezed inside of the crushed cranium, he unwrapped the blankets and bandages from the corpse. Not with his hands, but with his will. They dissolved into nothing. The wounds over Ymitoth's body began disappearing, fresh healthy skin replacing the broken parts. Bruises faded, busted bones mended, and the stiffness fled. Maelich fixated on his father's still chest. Suddenly, the heart within it beat strong. Blood filled the veins as the revived muscle pumped it through the body. Ymitoth's revitalized skin grew flusher with every moment until it was the healthy peach tone it had been before his final hunt.

Maelich spoke softly, "Rise father. Come to me."

Ymitoth's eyes snapped open and he sat straight up. He didn't look around or even seem to be awake. His head remained completely still, facing the direction his body faced. He spun his legs around to the side of the cot and stood with stiff, awkward movements. He walked like a normal man would—a man that hadn't been dead—straight to Maelich and then stopped.

Maelich threw his arms around Ymitoth and embraced him, but the former corpse remained motionless. "Hug me father," Maelich's voice dripped excitement. "I have pulled you from death's grip and brought you home. And look at this magnificent feast; surely you must be pleased with me."

Ymitoth remained motionless.

Maelich stepped back and beheld his father, mostly staring into his eyes. They were black and dead, two empty pits, void of color or life. They were just as the eyes of the dead-eyed men, blank and soulless. Maelich's own eyes misted and his voice cracked a bit, "Father, speak to me. Say something."

Ymitoth's reply was nothing more than a low, raspy moan.

Reality struck hard. The vessel carrying Ymitoth's essence around during his physical existence was nothing more than an empty shell. It was no more than Kallum's dead-eyed priests. He was just as Kallum was. No. No, this was different. He hadn't resurrected Ymitoth to carry out his bidding. It was a display of undying love and loyalty to his father. Surely there was a difference in that. Absently stroking his chin, he attempted to reckon the idea with himself.

Maelich stood for a good hour attempting to justify his own actions. When he finally looked back up from the floor, he realized Ymitoth still stared at him with those empty, dead eyes. Obviously, the corpse wasn't looking at anything. It had no will of its own. Maelich suddenly felt dirty and wrong, overcome with a sense of being watched, scrutinized, judged. Jittery nervousness toyed with his spine as he glanced around the empty hut. No one was watching, of course. It was just him judging himself.

Maelich had come too far to stop. He gazed at the standing corpse through squinted eyes and focused his thoughts into its head. He could see himself. He moved the dead head around, taking everything in through foreign eyes. He blinked those eyes several times and then turned the corners of his father's mouth up into a smile while raising the eyebrows up at the same time.

Maelich made another attempt at conversation, "Father, I have prepared a great feast for you, roast tubberslat and a sweet cake. I know they are your favorites. Would you care to join me for a meal?" Then he quickly added, "I even poured us a couple of pints. I thought we might reminisce."

Then he caused Ymitoth's corpse to respond in a way fitting of his father's personality, "Aye laddy, I been standing here wondering when ye might invite me to your table. That tubberslat smells fantastic. It be making me mouth water for a taste."

A broad, childish smile spread across Maelich's face. The fact Ymitoth's soul had made its journey home didn't matter one bit to him. His father was with him again, and that was enough. He made a welcoming gesture toward the table with his left hand and said, "Please, come. Enjoy."

Maelich controlled Ymitoth's every move down to the slightest gesture. It was queer and unsettling to experience senses through another's body. The scent of the fire was stronger from Ymitoth's nose than his own. Of course it would be as Ymitoth sat closer to the fireplace. He experienced the senses of both of them simultaneously, yet they were quite distinct from each other. He could feel the air on Ymitoth's skin as well as his own. He could hear himself talk through Ymitoth's ears, learning how his voice had been heard while the king still lived. It was all wonderful and strange.

Marveling at this new experience, he kept up the conversation he was having with himself.

"Ah Maelich, what a fine cook ye've become. The tubber be so tender. Ye must have been roasting it all day. And this Ale be the perfect complement for it," Ymitoth said as he chewed.

Maelich blushed slightly and smiled, "Oh it was nothing, really. I just threw it together."

"Well ye did a fine job of just throwing it together," Ymitoth raised his eyebrows and chuckled. Then he continued, "Hey, do ye remember the time I'd been showing ye sword techniques on horseback and me horse threw me?"

After a hearty laugh, Maelich replied, "I do. I laughed my fool head off and then you scolded and punished me for disrespecting you. You made me run the pastures a full three more times and then clean the hut from top to bottom. You sent me to bed with no food that night as well."

"Hm. Do ye suppose ye learned your lesson?"

"I sure did. Though I laughed plenty when your eyes were not upon me, I never laughed at you in your presence again," he finished with a chuckle.

Ymitoth laughed right back at him. "I tell ye, that lesson been no more than never be laughing at the master while he be mastering. Ye were just paying for me embarrassment. Ah, I'd been a proud man then."

Maelich's expression became somber, "I miss those days, father. More than you could know."

CHAPTER 5
THE MISSING KINGS

Hagen gently knocked at the door to the king's quarters. He'd given Maelich more time than he should have to say his good-byes. Ymitoth's body should have been well on its way to rotting. The corpse would need to be prepared for the customary hero's ceremony. One lost in battle received the most sacred and prestigious rite practiced in Havenstahl. For the great and mighty Ymitoth, there could be no less. He would forever be remembered in Havenstahl's history as one of her greatest champions.

Hagen knocked three more times at the door before gently pushing it open. His jaw dropped open as his left hand snapped up to cover it. The former king and the future king were gone. He groaned. Where could Maelich have taken his father's corpse? What would possess him to do such a thing? Hagen paced nervously back and forth. His eyes jumped from the bed to the window to the ceiling and to the door. How could Maelich have gotten the king's corpse out of the castle without being noticed? Someone had to have seen him. He rushed out to the hall.

"Guards!" he shouted. "Come quickly!"

Within moments, two men stood before him clad in the decorative armor of Havenstahl's Royal Guard, the elite. They wore red shirts with hoods covered by round, shiny helmets crafted of prang. Those buffed helmets sparkled brilliantly in the sun pouring through the windows. The better portion of both of the guards' faces was covered by nose and chin plates hammered out of the same piece of prang. Their chest and leg plates matched the helmets perfectly. Their boots were black leather as were their trousers. They all looked the same to Hagen; big, brutish men with more brawn then brains. That was fine with him. The less a man thinks, the more apt he is to follow orders without question. Doubt could kill a man in

30

battle.

The guard to Hagen's left was Artho. His tone was trained, "Aye sir. What be your bidding?"

"Have you seen Prince Maelich this morning?" Hagen kept control of his tone. He didn't want rumors to begin floating around the city about the king's heir stealing corpses.

"No sir. There ain't been none about on this morn. Though I been at me post but a few hours," Artho remained at attention as he spoke.

"Very good," Hagen folded his hands as he continued to work through his dilemma. "Begin a search. Question every soldier and castle worker that would have been about last evening or early this morning. I seek an audience with his highness."

"Aye sir," the guards replied in unison, bowed, about faced, and carried on down the steps.

Hagen followed behind them, "Report back to me as soon as you have information about the prince's whereabouts."

Hagen stopped at the next landing while the guards continued on. He walked down the hall, stopped in front of the door to Perrin's room, and lightly rapped it three times. His arms folded tightly across his chest as he stepped back and nervously tapped his foot. After a few moments—that may as well have been days—the door slowly opened. Perrin's innocent eyes peered up at him from her shining face while her great, round belly appeared ready to burst at any moment.

"Hagen!" she squealed and threw her arms around the old healer. "Have ye seen me love? I been hearing he be back from his travels."

Hagen paused a moment, "No, highness. I was hoping he had been in to visit you."

Her lips dipped into a shallow pout as she stepped back from him and complained, "At any moment I could be bringing his baby into this world and he ain't having cause to check on me well-being. What a fine gesture that be."

Hagen became somber as he regarded Perrin. Her crystal, blue eyes dampening with the emotions of a woman with child, her blond hair strong, healthy and full of life, her round belly looking full and ready to burst, she resembled a doll. Perfect and beautiful, she seemed more a portrait than a person as she pouted up at him.

"Alas, Your Highness, I am afraid I have some troubling news. The king has fallen in battle..."

Perrin interrupted, "What? Ymitoth...Ymitoth be..." her damp eyes widened as the sadness of her expression fled in the face of bewilderment, and her arms fell limply at her sides. Her eyes darted about the room behind their rapidly blinking lids. She remained silent for a moment, as she stepped backward into the room inviting Hagen in with a distracted wave.

Once inside, Hagen walked toward the window and continued, "Yes, I am afraid the king has perished. Maelich was with him last night. I left him alone with his father to say his good-byes in peace. Your husband was quite distraught, and I wanted to give him time to grieve the loss." He slowly shook his head as he added, "I am afraid that was a mistake."

Tears began to flow over Perrin's eyelids, "Where be me love now?"

Hagen sighed and rubbed at his jaw, "Well," he paused, "I do not know." He stopped short of telling her not only was Maelich missing, but Ymitoth's body was missing along with him.

Suddenly, the door pushed open and a woman wearing a blue robe hurried into the room carrying a basket. She considered Hagen briefly, raising one eyebrow in his direction. Then she addressed Perrin, "Your Highness, what ye be doing out of that bed? Have ye lost all of your senses? That baby be coming at any hour now. Lay yourself back down." Then she glanced in Hagen's direction, adding, "And what cause do ye have to be hanging about and bothering me pregnant misses?"

"Oh Chimarra," Perrin began, "Hagen be bringing us grave news." Then she slumped down onto her bed and stared out the window, probably at the same nothing Hagen had been staring at a few moments prior.

Hagen cleared his throat and turned to address Chimarra, "Forgive the intrusion, but His Majesty has expired and his son has gone missing."

Chimarra had been a midwife in the castle for thirty summers. Hagen—like most who called the castle at Havenstahl home—carried around a great deal of respect for her. She knew her task and took it more than seriously. Bringing royal blood into the world was nothing to be taken lightly. More than one dignitary had been ordered to move along to other business when they would get to making nuisances of themselves. Hagen knew he certainly wasn't above her strict rule over the pregnant princess's quarters. However, his news seemed to knock the edge right off her mood and left her with her jaw hanging slack. Meanwhile, her eyes asked the questions her mouth couldn't seem to get out.

Hagen answered the silent expression, "He fell in battle. Upon hearing the news, Maelich fled. I desperately need to find him."

Chimarra looked as if she'd been hit with a stick, "If I be seeing him, I be letting ye know."

"Thank you," Hagen left the room without additional comment, gently closing the door behind him. He had not even made the stairway before nearly bumping into Cialia as she charged around the corner.

Words flopped from her mouth as she stopped just short of toppling him, "Hagen, I have been looking all over the castle for you. Is it true? Is Ymitoth dead and his body missing with my brother?"

Hagen's tone was a sharp whisper, "Where did you hear that?"

"The guards are talking about it. They say Talhomme—one of the stablemen—said Maelich ordered him to ready Validus. He also said it looked as if my dear brother was carrying a body wrapped in blankets."

Hagen looked to the ground, shaking his head. It would be too late to control the rumors. Rumors born out of truth are the worst kind. The idea of the future king, a god even, stealing corpses would not sit well with most of the population of Havenstahl. He tapped his index finger nervously against his forehead.

Finally he spoke, "I will need to speak with this, Talhomme, immediately. I need to know exactly what he saw and what Maelich may have said to him." He sighed, turned his gaze toward a window sitting across the hall from them, and looked out at nothing in particular as he continued, "This is very serious. I fear for Maelich's mental condition and what his actions will mean for the people of Havenstahl who worship him."

Cialia's wide eyes and hanging jaw conveyed her shock far more effectively than her words as she quietly asked, "So it is true?" Then her face tightened as her head shook and she continued with more force, "I cannot believe this. Why would he steal Ymitoth's corpse? What will our mother say?"

"It appears it is quite true and quite worse than I hoped. My hope was he would still be somewhere here in the castle. Alas, with Talhomme's testimony, that cannot be true," his gaze remained fixed on nothing in particular. He thought for a moment before pulling his mind back to the present and continuing, "Come, we must not waste any more precious time talking about this. We shall go speak with Talhomme."

CHAPTER 6
THE STABLE HAND

Talhomme gently brushed Dixby's mane. The big oaf looked clumsy as a drunken dwarf on Maelich's Day most of the time. When grooming a horse however, he was an artist. He used long, slow, graceful strokes while humming softly in the horse's ear. His round belly, leathery skin, and stringy, yellow hair seemed a contradiction to the tender affection he showed the animals in his care. For all of his gruffness, he was gentle as morning rain with the horses.

Dixby was a wild one. Her coat was light-tan but glowed like shimmering prang in the sunlight. Her mane was a dark, luxurious brown. However, all the beauty oozing off the beast seemed a prank when one caught a glimpse of her eyes. Madness danced about their darkness like the frenzied insanity trapped in the desperate stare of a shackled prisoner yearning for sunlight and fresh air. None of the other stable hands could get within ten feet of her. She seemed to favor Talhomme though, nuzzling her head up into his chest as he hummed his songs softly in her ear.

Hagen considered the stable hand briefly before addressing him. Under different circumstances, the oddness of a brute such as Talhomme taking such tender care of anything might have earned a chuckle from the old healer. However, the cause for his quest kept even the slightest giggle buried deep in his gut. Instead, his tone was flat, carrying none of its usual flamboyance, "Talhomme, I seek an audience with you."

The rough brute absently turned and replied, "Aye?"

Hagen wasn't sure if he was impressed or irritated with the man's lack of interest. Commoners would typically fall all over themselves to bow in his presence. Talhomme just continued his careful brushing. Realizing he wouldn't get the usual salutary greeting he deserved, the old healer continued, "Yes, I understand his majesty had you prepare his horse for the trail earlier this morn. Would you tell me about that please, everything you know?"

Talhomme rolled his eyes as he turned and said, "Aye, he came to me looking for his horse. Had somebody with him too, all wrapped up in blankets. I don't be knowing who that might have been."

Under different circumstances, Hagen would have rightfully chastised Talhomme for his disrespect. However, the situation begged a more diplomatic course of action. Besides, the smell of horse waste filling his nostrils had him desperately battling back an urge to gag. Keeping the meager contents of his stomach down quickly occupied the lion's share of his attention.

"When was this?" he asked.

"Like ye' said, earlier this morn. What of it?" Talhomme shrugged.

Hagen forced a grin to his lips that did little to hide his impatience, "How early this morn?"

The frumpy stable hand grabbed his chin and looked up toward the sky, "I be guessing it must have been just after sun up."

"Did he give you any clue as to where he may be going?"

Talhomme shook his head, "No. He be in a mad hurry though."

Hagen sighed, "Is there anything else you can tell me? Did he say anything unusual, anything at all?"

Talhomme shook his head again and shrugged, "No."

"Very well, thank you for your time," Hagen turned to leave.

He made it as far as the stable gate before Cialia stopped him, "Well, did he say anything about where Maelich may have been going?"

Hagen shook his head, "Nothing we did not already know."

"Well now what? How will we find him?" Cialia pressed him.

"I do not know," he stared into nothing as his mind worked. "What about you? Do you not feel his presence? Why can you not track him?"

"He is not with me. I have been looking but…" she shrugged.

"He is hiding," Hagen decided as he hurried off to find the General.

CHAPTER 7

SWORD TRAINING

Despite the ale he and Ymitoth had drunk the night before, Maelich rose before the sun. After waking Ymitoth, he prepared a light snack of bread and fruit for them. A full belly wasn't helpful during the morning run. The two men ate in silence. Once they had finished, Maelich spoke, "Will we be taking the morning run, master?"

"Aye," Ymitoth replied, "always we be taking the morning run. It be keeping ye fit and keeping the fat off of your bones."

Maelich nodded as he cleared the table, carefully setting their dirty plates in the washtub. The water had grown cold overnight. He'd have to heat some more before the afternoon nap. Keeping clean dishes was one of his chores.

"Leave them, lad," Ymitoth said as he grabbed Maelich's shoulder. "Let's be getting to that trail before the sun does."

The two men ran east up Keller's hill and then turned south at the great oak crowning it. The path they followed was an old one, worn into the grass by the feet of many mentors and their pupils during years and years of training. Nothing grew there anymore. The old, familiar path would lead them along Yester's pond and then further south into the valley before turning back. A stiff breeze from the east gave the crisp, morning air a biting chill, perfect for the morning run. The sweat wouldn't come in earnest until well after they rounded the pond.

Maelich reached the hut a step behind Ymitoth. Neither he nor the wily veteran paused to catch their breath. Instead, both men grabbed their swords and moved through various techniques. The air gradually warmed and the breeze died down as Maelich swung his blade about at the air mimicking battle with the elegant movements marking a swordsman of

Havenstahl. His forehead quickly earned a glistening sheen of sweat. It was all but dripping into his eyes by the time Ymitoth turned to face him.

Ymitoth took a defensive stance and commanded, "Attack, lad."

Maelich lowered his sword and slashed at Ymitoth with a backhanded strike. His blade tasted nothing but air as the old swordsman leaned away from the attack. Maelich followed with a forehand. Again, his mentor dodged it effortlessly. Finally, Maelich finished the progression with a lunge. He didn't miss his mark. Unfortunately, his mark no longer matched his target, and he wound up in a heap at Ymitoth's feet.

"Enough!" Ymitoth shouted. "After all these years we been training, is that the best ye can do? Get on your feet and try again. This time don't be letting your body tell me where your blow be aiming to land."

Maelich quickly scrambled to his feet apologizing, "Sorry, master."

Ymitoth kicked him back to the ground, "Ye're sorry? Ye're sorry? This blade of mine will be taking the head clean off your shoulders if ye be spending your time on sorrow, lad. Get up and fight like ye're trying to keep the blood in your body!"

Maelich leapt back to his feet and attacked again. His blade devoured the air with urgent passion. He barely noticed a proud smile creeping onto Ymitoth's face. He couldn't let up. That proud smile would quickly gnarl up into an angry sneer if he lost focus for even a moment, so he didn't. Instead he remained aggressively on the offensive, attacking with a fury grossly excessive were his opponent any less than the greatest swordsman to ever live.

"Halt!" Ymitoth ordered. "Now, defend yourself."

Maelich retreated a full twenty feet before even considering standing his ground. He nearly lost himself marveling at the master's furious yet crisp and elegant technique. Each dazzling movement had purpose. Every step, every slash, every thrust, and every spin of the blade were strung together with the precision of an artist crafting a masterpiece. The attack seemed one long strike rather than several techniques executed in rapid succession. Maelich had all he could handle parrying, dodging, and countering in a desperate struggle to keep his master's blade from running him through.

A steady stream of commands poured from Ymitoth's lips, "Always be mindful of your opponent's eyes, lad. They be telling ye where next he'll strike. Stay loose behind your sword. Don't be stiffening up like that. Ye got to be bouncing on the balls of your feet. Always be looking to counter a blow. Attack when your opponent exposes weakness."

Maelich absorbed it all as he blocked and parried blow after blow, each moment searching for weakness, a rare opening in Ymitoth's assault. Finally, it came. Maelich slipped to the right as Ymitoth's sword slashed vertically down upon him. For a brief moment, the tip of it was trapped in the dirt. Maelich seized the opportunity and stepped on the old warrior's blade, pinning it down. Then he pounded a quick elbow into the master's chin while sweeping his feet in the same instant. With Ymitoth on his back a safe distance from his weapon, Maelich triumphantly placed his left foot on the master's chest and pressed the edge of his own blade against Ymitoth's neck.

"Submit," Maelich grinned.

Ymitoth growled.

A moment later, the horizon was vertical and Maelich could see Keller's hill between his feet. As he helplessly fell to the ground, he lost his grip on his sword. By the time his eyes came back into focus, he was lying on his back with Ymitoth's blade pressed up against his throat.

"Never be underestimating your opponent, lad, even when ye believe he be beaten," Ymitoth scolded.

Then the old warrior was gone. He was halfway to the hut before Maelich made it back to his feet. There would be no words of encouragement or further instruction. The lesson was finished and Maelich knew better than to expect any fatherly affection during training. An opponent cannot be counted on to show sympathy, compassion, or mercy. Therefore, none should be hoped for from the mentor. He hurried along behind Ymitoth who would rest in his chair while Maelich prepared the midday feast. It felt good to be back to training, normal.

CHAPTER 8
THE GREAT MOTHER

Cialia packed in silence with too many thoughts zipping around her head to focus on one idea. She paused from her toils and walked over to the window next to her bed. The valley stretched out like an empty void with the Sobbing Forest standing like an impenetrable wall at the other end. From Cialia's room, it didn't look like much more than a green smudge on the horizon. Her thoughts pressed deeper into that smudge, that barrier standing tall against her will, into the minute details of the trees. 'Are you there, my brother? If not, then where?' His voice had become such a common occupant of her mind its absence left her feeling incomplete, like she was less than herself without him. Even when their minds weren't speaking directly to each other, she could feel his presence. Since Ymitoth had passed, there was nothing. He simply wasn't there, completely lost to her. Where could he be?

She stared a long time out that window, searching. It was more an effort of her mind than her eyes. No matter how hard she focused her intent, there wasn't so much as a whisper from Maelich. A shiver crept down her spine as images of what must be going through her brother's head filled her consciousness. A man and his father share a special bond. Even though Maelich and Ymitoth shared no blood, Cialia knew that bond was exceptionally strong between them. The bruise had to be deep. If only she could slip into his head and fill him with soothing thoughts, massage his wounded psyche. How muddled and confused must his mind be? Ymitoth stood so tall in Maelich's eyes, as great as any of the gods, probably even as great as Helias or Coeptus. How could a force that mighty ever die? In her brother's eyes, he probably couldn't.

Where should she look? That was the question, the weight pressing down her brow. Maelich was always so busy catering to the people, spreading hope and preaching of Coeptus. She didn't really even know him anymore. He had become something else. It was as if his life didn't belong to him anymore and instead it belonged to the people who followed him. That same path had been calling her, but she didn't let herself fall in like Maelich had.

Suddenly, the door burst open with Leisha storming in behind it. The cadence of her words was frantic, "Where is he? Where has Maelich gone off to?" The normally smooth skin of her face twisted into tight knots, joining her tone to express her panic, "Can you not see him with your mind? Do you not speak to him always without words? Where is he? Where is my son?"

Cialia turned slowly from the window, stifling her own fears and worries to display a calm demeanor. Any appearance of tension would only add to her mother's fears, "I do not feel him, mother. I have been searching, but I cannot find him. Try not to worry though. His life has been quite tense of late. There is much that he has been tending, and then he suffered such a loss. You know how much Ymitoth meant to him. Perhaps he needed a break from the demands of his followers, some time to himself to work through the pain he is feeling. For five summers he has toiled day and night writing the words of Coeptus so the people might have peace. Perhaps he has worn himself thin and needs some time to forget the people and focus on himself."

Leisha waved her hand in the air and scoffed, "Indeed. That explanation might serve if not for the fact that many saw Maelich leave the city with Ymitoth's lifeless body." She shook her head quickly, "Yes, he is taking the loss of Ymitoth very hard. That part is true. However, the idea that his absence is nothing but a bit of frolic after some hard work is completely ridiculous."

Realizing her mother wouldn't be swayed, Cialia gave in, "I share your fears, mother. I too am worried for Maelich. I have focused my mind intently on him since his departure, but still I have found nothing. I do not know where he has gone or why."

Leisha's eyes darted around the room, widening as they settled on the packs on the bed, "Now you mean to leave as well? Where are you going?"

"I mean to enlist the help of Helias. I would call her with my mind, but I fear it is too muddled with concern for Maelich to effectively communicate my message. I feel I must go to her. Perhaps the great mother will have a solution to our problem. Perhaps Maelich has spoken to her or even gone to her. I believe she is our only hope."

"Ymitoth is dead, and Maelich has vanished. If you leave, who will protect the city? I have heard rumors about dead-eyed men. In fact, I hear dead-eyed men—the likes of which attacked Druindahl—are to blame for

Ymitoth's passing. Havenstahl is vulnerable. Who will be her champion if you leave?"

Cialia sighed, "Mother, Havenstahl still boasts the mightiest army on Ouloos, and father is the greatest general to ever live. Havenstahl is well protected even in my absence. We need to find Maelich. Nothing is more important at this moment."

Leisha conceded, "So be it. If you must go, then go. Be swift though, daughter. The people of this city need you as much as they need your brother."

"I will," she forced a smile. With that, Cialia grabbed her pack from the bed, kissed Leisha's cheek, and hurried from the room.

Purity was saddled and ready when Cialia arrived at the stable. She mounted and was off, urging the horse on with her will. By the time they reached the front gate, Purity was at a full gallop. They charged down into the valley, Cialia pushing the mare harder and harder. Images of the Lake filled her mind, visions as clear as if her eyes were seeing them. Dragons gracefully swam the air around the perfect circle of still water. They swooped and soared in all their glorious majesty. Cialia expanded and lightened as the elements bent to her every whim. It wasn't long before she and Purity were one with the wind, a streak of white light, a blur racing on the currents in the air.

CHAPTER 9
PERPLEXED

Moshat sat tense upon his throne, deep in a trance. His eyes darted about beneath his lids as if taken by dreams. Kaldumahn wasn't fooled by the illusion. He knew Moshat's conscious mind was hard at work. He considered his brother's mock slumber, 'Where are you off to now, brother?' Kaldumahn had recently risen from a similar state expecting a torrent of questions from Moshat. Sadly, their counsel would have to wait. The need was almost strong enough to disturb his brother's contemplation. Luckily the need vanished. As Kaldumahn scrutinized him, Moshat inhaled deeply through his nose and his eyes snapped open.

Kaldumahn's brows dipped toward his nose as he raised his head slightly and asked, "Have you learned much, Moshat?"

"I have," he replied and then added, "Sadly, much of what I learned is merely knowledge of what I cannot learn."

Kaldumahn humphed, "Riddles, Moshat? Why must you speak to me in riddles? What have you learned that you cannot learn?"

Moshat's eyes rolled as he turned toward Kaldumahn, "You fancy riddles, Kaldumahn, and you never tire of speaking them to me. You are impatient and nervous. That is why you accost me now. Furthermore, the words I spoke to you hardly make for a riddle. I learned nothing of what I sought to discover."

Kaldumahn sighed, "What did you seek to discover, dear brother?"

"Well, the whereabouts of fair Maelich of course," he replied. "You had the benefit of an audience with him in the Sobbing Forest. Sadly, I have not had the pleasure of speaking with him."

"You could have asked me about it."

"And you could have told me you intended to pay him a visit."

Kaldumahn shook his head, "You are correct, Moshat. I could have told you my plans. I did not. I am sorry. What have you learned of Maelich's whereabouts? He has proven elusive since I encountered him in the forest."

"Aha," Moshat exclaimed. "Therein lies the riddle. You see, his whereabouts are not. He simply is not. He is nowhere. It is as if he ceased to exist altogether."

Kaldumahn stroked his chin, "Well he has to be somewhere. Had he died, we would have felt it."

"I suppose so," Moshat agreed. "Yet, he is nowhere to be found."

"Interesting," Kaldumahn continued to stroke his chin.

"There is more," Moshat leaned toward Kaldumahn as he spoke. "Ymitoth, the great warrior who trained the lad of the Lake, has died."

"Yes," Kaldumahn agreed. "Yes he has. I felt great angst from Maelich when it happened. I decided not to pry. My thoughts were elsewhere. Perhaps I should have looked deeper."

"Perhaps," Moshat raised his eyes slightly.

"Did you?"

"I did."

"What did you find?"

"Immediately after Maelich's great outpouring of sorrow, he was gone," Moshat's eyes narrowed. "That is when he seemed to vanish."

Kaldumahn shrugged, "He discovered a means to block us. Your riddle is solved."

"Precisely," Moshat grinned. "Why, though? Now that is the real riddle."

"Yes," Kaldumahn sighed. "Yes, I suppose it is."

Moshat's grin widened as he continued, "We should have destroyed him when he was a child. I told you he would become far too difficult to control. He is still too much of a man."

Kaldumahn shook his head, "No. Maelich was the key to ending Kallum. He is the key to everything."

"He is," Moshat agreed. "He is the key to salvation or destruction. Which of those becomes the fate of Ouloos is completely up to him."

"Exactly," Kaldumahn sighed again. "That is why we must guide him to the correct destination."

Moshat's grin sank to something more somber, "How? How do we guide him when we cannot find him? He has gained enough mastery over his mind and this world to block us from discovering his comings and goings. Maelich is far beyond our control."

Kaldumahn shrugged, "The man in him has just suffered a devastating blow. He must digest it and move past it. We must give him time to do that. We must give him time to mourn. We must have faith in him."

"Bah," Moshat spat. "The luxury of time is something we currently lack.

The subject you have not touched is the return of the three. You know of Ymitoth's demise. I am certain you have felt their return."

"Yes," Kaldumahn agreed. "I have felt their return. That is another riddle we must solve."

"It would appear the lad was unsuccessful in destroying Kallum," Moshat replied.

"Perhaps," Kaldumahn spoke slowly as his mind worked, "or perhaps another wishes to disguise their own comings and goings and lay the blame at the feet of a scattered god. Any of us; you, me, Brerto, Ijilv, any of us could do the same thing."

"But would we?" Moshat asked. "Perhaps Brerto, but Ijilv was crucial in aiding Maelich against Kallum."

Kaldumahn rubbed his forehead with the index finger and thumb of his left hand, "We would not, no. Brerto would, but he is who I have been watching. I have been watching him closely. He is across the Great Sea raising an army of giants and trogmortem while his emissaries gather grongs together in the valley. His mind is clear. He means to march on the greatest city of men. He means to march on Havenstahl."

"What? Why do you wait to mention such things?"

"I have only just discovered them, and you desired to riddle me about Maelich."

"We must prepare them for battle."

"Yes," Kaldumahn agreed. "Yes we must."

CHAPTER 10
FISHING

Maelich woke to pokes, prods, and Ymitoth's voice, "Get off your lazy tail, lad. The fish be biting in the morn."

"What?" Maelich asked as he rolled over and rubbed is eyes. "It is so dark still. It cannot yet be time to rise."

"Aye it be," Ymitoth responded with a chuckle. "Ye been doing so well with your sword, I be thinking a day of rest might be in order. I strung up some poles. We be chasing chookers in Yester's Pond this morn."

"Fishing? I have not been fishing in ages! We shall catch ourselves a grand feast today," Maelich boomed as he leapt from his cot. Then he paused, cocked his head to the side, looked into his father's black, dead eyes, and added, "You rose before me."

"Aye laddy," Ymitoth agreed. "Aye, I did. With all of that snoring ye been doing, ye might of slept the whole day away."

Maelich smiled, "Yes, I suppose I would have."

Ymitoth shrugged, turned, and began packing two bags for the short trip to Yester's Pond. While Maelich watched him move, his mind puzzled over the idea of Ymitoth rising before him. Maelich had fallen deep into the fantasy of his father still existing among the living, not so far however, that he didn't realize the weight of this concept. He was in complete control of Ymitoth's every move and action. Obviously, since he had been sleeping, he had not consciously willed Ymitoth to rise and begin preparations for a day of fishing.

Ymitoth finished filling the packs with some bread, dried meat, and ale, then turned and said, "Have ye wiped all of the sleep out of your eyes, lad?"

Maelich started a bit and replied, "Yes, yes father. Yes I have."

"Well don't just be standing there watching while I be doing all of the work," he said as he shook his head and handed one of the sacks to Maelich. "Let's get to moving. That sun, she'll be on the rise before ye know it, and I want to have me pole in that pond long before she does."

"Right, sorry father," Maelich was still turning the strange idea over in his head, examining it from every angle.

Ymitoth grinned, grabbed the torch that was burning next to the fireplace off of the wall, and said, "Grab your pole, sleepyhead." Then he turned toward the door and pounded out of the hut.

Maelich grabbed the pole that remained and followed Ymitoth out. The chill morning air helped wake him up a bit more as a brisk easterly wind tossed his hair about. After a few moments and a brisk walk, both men were standing at the shore of Yester's pond fumbling around the torchlight and looking for the perfect spot to sit and catch fish. Finally, both of them found suitable spots for their rumps. Maelich sat perched upon a wide, flat stump while Ymitoth lounged on a large boulder that the elements had smoothed out and rounded off over the years.

Once he was comfortably situated, Maelich whispered, "Did you bring any bait?"

Ymitoth humphed quietly under his breath, "Did I bring any bait? Aye lad, I got lots of bait." Then he reached into his sack, pulled out two cans, and added, "This can here be full of corn." He raised the can in his left hand and nodded at it. Then he repeated the gesture with the can in his right hand and said, "And this can here be full of worms, long, thick, juicy ones, the kind the chooker be going crazy for."

"Perfect," Maelich smiled as he grabbed a worm, ripped a hunk off, and fashioned it onto his hook.

Chooker weren't the best fish for eating, a hair on the greasy side. They grew big in Yester's Pond though, and Ymitoth had a knack for preparing them. He would boil vegetables—usually corn, carrots, potatoes, and onions—until they were soft. While that was happening, he would rub the chooker with wild zaga leaves—the zaga leaves gave the fish a smoky flavor—and cook them directly over the flame. Once the fish were well roasted, he would stir them into the boiling vegetables. Then he would drain off the excess water, give the whole concoction a healthy dose of salt, and serve it with some bread and ale. It had been years since Maelich had a nice bowl of chooker stew.

As the two men sat with their lines in the water waiting for a bite, Maelich puzzled over what the morning's happenings could mean. He stole a glance over at the man he had grown to know as his father. That man wasn't in there anymore. He knew that. The fact managed to be forgotten sometimes, but when he gave it cognizant thought, he knew it. This though, Ymitoth rising and doing things seemingly of his own volition, this seemed outside the realm of possibility.

"Ye got a bite there, lad," Ymitoth whispered as he leaned toward Maelich and nudged his shoulder.

Maelich jumped, startled out of his trance, and felt a strong tugging on his line. "You're right, father. I do," he replied as he gave his line a good tug and grabbed hold of the handle of his spindle. "It feels like a big one too!"

"Don't be giving her too much line to work with, lad," Ymitoth coached. "Chooker be smart, as far as fish go. She'll drag your line down and wind it around the reeds, leave you with nothing but some broken wire to show for your trouble."

"I know. I know," Maelich grumbled back. "I have her," he added as he tugged again on his pole and started turning the spindle toward himself to reel the fish in.

"Oh well, aren't ye the great fisherman then," Ymitoth mocked. "I suppose ye'll be showing me a thing or two about landing a…" Ymitoth paused for a moment before adding with excitement in his voice, "I got one too, lad. She feels like a biggie!"

As the two men struggled with their respective fish, all thoughts of the queerness of the morning drifted from Maelich's mind. The fish, the fight, the pole in his hand, the pond, the sun just barely breaking the horizon, the smell of damp earth, and his father standing next to him pole in hand were all that mattered. The rest of the world could float away unnoticed. Everything that meant anything to Maelich at that moment was wrapped up in a boy and his father chasing chooker in Yester's Pond.

CHAPTER 11
NEW LIFE

"Now, now dear," Chimarra spoke in a soft tone that didn't match her rough exterior. The gray hair tossed haphazardly about her head and shoulders was streaked with sweat and continuously falling down in front of her eyes. She brushed it back again to reveal heavy wrinkles, deep set, dark eyes, a large hooked nose, and drooping jowls that hung almost even with her slight chin. "The future king be on his way dear," she added as she rubbed Perrin's back.

Perrin moaned, "Oh Chimarra, he be ripping me in two!" She sat upright in her bed, shaking, moaning, and occasionally screaming out as Chimarra sat beside her, helping her remain upright and continuing to rub her back. "Where be Maelich? Where be me love? I be bringing his heir into this world and he be nowhere to be found."

"Aye lass," Chimarra whispered. "He'll be found. Ye just focus on the task at hand. Ye be bringing a prince that will one day be king into this world. That be serious work, milady. Ye need to bring your head back in this room and let your love worry about where he be getting himself off to."

Perrin tensed up and moaned something that might have been a scream if it weren't so deep and throaty. The muscles all about her abdomen and back flexed uncontrollably. "Oh Chimarra," she groaned. "Get this child out of me."

Perrin's eyes followed Chimarra's finger as the midwife pointed to a plain girl with dark hair and bright eyes soaking cloths in a large marble basin by the window and said, "Meelah, bring a cloth and take me place here next to the princess."

"Yes, Chimarra," Meelah replied as she hurried over.

Once Meelah was in place, Chimarra moved to the bottom of the bed and tossed the wet cloth Meelah had handed her in favor of a dry one. Then she rested her right hand on Perrin's left knee and said, "Push with the pain now, dear. When ye feel your belly tightening up again, push with all your might. It be time. I be looking at the top of your son's wee head right now. He's got some hair this one."

It was a few moments before Perrin tightened up again. She squeezed Meelah's hand and said, "Here it comes again."

"Push with the pain, love," Chimarra responded. "Ye be doing a fine job. Push with all your might. Imagine holding your beautiful, wee lad in your arms. He be almost among us."

Perrin pushed as hard as she could for what felt like eternity. Finally, she had nothing left, "Oh I can't, I can't. I can't push anymore. It hurts."

"No, no lass," Chimarra encouraged her. "Don't be giving up on me now. His whole head almost be out. Give me one more good push."

"I can't," Perrin whined.

"Sure ye can, ye're the Queen of Havenstahl now," Chimarra assured her. "Ye be a powerful woman. There be nothing ye can't do. Come now, lass, one more push."

Perrin tensed up again, pushing against all of the pressure and pain. Her teeth clenched tight as her nails dug into Meelah's hand. All of her will focused on pushing her son into the world. Another groan left her lips among a good bit of spittle. Then there was relief. The pressure was gone. The tension slowly slipped away, and Meelah helped her lie back on her pillow. All that was left was a dull ache between her legs.

Perrin fought against the exhaustion and leaned up on her elbows trying to get a better look at Chimarra's efforts. No matter how far she stretched, all she could see past the mound of her belly was the top of Chimarra's head. Just as she was about to complain, Chimarra stood with a messy, peach lump in her arms. The midwife wiped at it a bit with the towel while her eyes moved all about the little bundle. Perrin was quickly losing her battle with impatience when Chimarra finally gave the new prince a quick swat on the butt to test his lungs and then swaddled him in the towel.

Perrin perked up when she heard her baby cry. "Oh thank Ouloos," she said as tears spilled over her eyelids. "That be the sweetest song I ever heard."

"Aye, lass," Chimarra agreed. "Would ye like to hold your son?"

"Aye, I may never be letting him go," Perrin whispered.

Perrin was planting soft kisses all over the new prince's forehead before Chimarra had even finished laying the child in her arms. "He be beautiful," she whispered, lifting her head to wonder at the new life she had just finished bringing into the world. "Look at all that hair he already be having. It be looking like a crown and the color of his father's." She paused and continued to look him over, "Aye, and his chin. Would ye look at his chin? If that not be his father's chin then I ain't be knowing what his father's chin looks like. Aye, he be looking just like his father. He be looking like a king."

"Aye, he be a beautiful lad, milady," Chimarra sniffled.

Perrin flushed as she glanced up at Chimarra and saw the wet streak on her cheek, "Be that a tear, Chimarra?"

"It just be the dust," Chimarra smiled as she patted Perrin on the leg. "Ye know I ain't the crying type." A look of admiration slipped onto her face as she looked down upon the new mother with her new son for a moment before adding, "Alright now, lass. Let's be finishing up this work. I be needing one more little push from ye to get the rest of this business out of ye.

Perrin didn't pay any further attention to the commotion happening in the room. She gave the last push that had been requested of her, but her attention remained completely focused on the glistening cherub in her arms. By the time she heard Chimarra say, "Now milady, ye will be needing to feed that lad," she already had the task well in hand. The child was latched firmly on her breast and didn't seem to be having any trouble feeding.

Perrin smiled up at Chimarra and shrugged, "He seemed to know what he be looking for."

"Aye," Chimarra agreed. "All be well. I'll be over in the sitting room if ye be needing me. Beckon once the young prince has had his fill. I'll be working the gas out of him and getting him in his crib."

Perrin barely registered Chimarra's words. Her attention had already moved back to the new love of her life. She marveled at his perfection as he fed. She played with his fingers and then toyed with his hair. She kissed his little forehead several times and then his pudgy cheeks. "He be perfect," she whispered as her eyes drooped and she drifted off.

CHAPTER 12
VISITORS

Daritus slumped in his chair, staring out the window of his room. Deep lines creased his forehead as he rested his chin on his right hand. Ymitoth had fallen at the hands of dead-eyed men that should themselves be long decayed and crumbled into dust, dead-eyed men that by all accounts seemed far more powerful than they had ever been. Maelich had stolen the king's corpse and vanished. Scouts had returned with word that foreign ships—big ships, possibly war ships—were anchoring on the western shore a mere three day's journey on horseback from the gates of Havenstahl. Rumors raced around his city faster than anyone could stomp them out or even hope to offer explanation, and fear gripped the people within his walls. All eyes looked to him as if to ask, 'What do we do next?' And he didn't know the answer. They say the king's crown is a heavy burden to bear. At that moment, Daritus thought the general's helmet might be just a bit heavier. Besides, the one who should be wearing the crown was damnably absent from its weight.

Daritus's strife was abruptly interrupted by the heavy door of his chamber slamming open with Leisha, in a panic, right behind it. Fear saturated her voice as she nearly shouted, "Is it true? Are foreign warships at our shore?"

Daritus sighed, slowly turned his head away from the window and toward his wife, and calmly replied, "It appears there may be. We do not know what their purpose is at this point. However, they do appear to be vessels built for battle, and their numbers are great."

Leisha wrung her hands as her eyes darted all about the room, "What are we to do? Do you have a plan? Ymitoth has fallen. Maelich has vanished and stolen his corpse. Cialia has left the city to pursue an audience with the

Great Mother. We are without a champion."

Daritus inhaled deeply and let the breath out slowly, "My love, you must calm yourself. Three of our champions have fallen or are absent. They are not the only champions that Havenstahl boasts though. I am a champion of this city, and I have many champions under my command that would take great offense at the idea that the great city of Havenstahl is vulnerable. This mighty city boasts the most powerful force on Ouloos, and that force will fight until all of the breath has left all of the bodies in it."

Leisha's demeanor calmed, if only slightly, as she continued, "Yes, my love. We have champions, all of which are men, mortal men. What do we know of our adversary?"

Daritus cleared his throat and rose from his chair, "Leisha, my dear," he began. Then he crossed the room and embraced her before continuing, "It is true, we do not know the nature of our adversary at this point. In fact, we do not even know if they are actually an adversary at all."

Leisha shook her head, "I think we do know. What other purpose would warships have at our shores?"

"That is a valid point," Daritus conceded. "I do not have a good answer. Truthfully, I am fairly certain whoever commands those ships means to wage war against us. I am even more certain panic will do nothing to aid our efforts in defending ourselves. In fact, I am completely certain it will hinder our efforts. What happened to the cool-headed queen commanding our fair city in the trees, the last defense of the race of dragons against countless attacks for so many years? Where has she gone?"

Leisha pulled away from his embrace, crossed over to the window, and stared down into the valley. "I do not know, but I fear she may be gone forever," she replied. After a brief pause she continued, "It was a simpler time. My children were not gods. Our adversaries were men or at least beasts that bled and died. It was before unstoppable, dead-eyed, soulless creatures came to batter men to death with their bare hands. It was before the gods showed themselves to us and waged battle right at the edge of our forest," she paused again and sighed. "Daritus, you know I have always felt the weight of this world on my shoulders."

"You have, my dear," he replied.

She turned to face him and said, "This world is so much heavier now. I cannot bear the weight. I need my children by my side. Maelich was lost to me for so long and now he is lost again, right when I need him most, right when Ouloos needs him most."

Daritus went to her again and gently held her shoulders, "The weight of this world has grown. I feel it too, but I take heart in knowing there are an army of men willing to give their souls to help us hold it up." He stared into her eyes in silence for a few moments hoping for evidence of even the slightest ease in her tension. Once he finally decided there was none to be had, he continued, "Not to mention, an entire kingdom of dwarves that—though small by the standards of men—fight as if they were three times their size stand ready to rush to our aid whenever the need may arise."

"Okay," she nodded. "What you say is true. Worrying over what might be will not help protect this world from darkness. What is your plan?"

Daritus quickly found himself pacing. His plan was not quite finished. That answer would never suffice, so he didn't say it. Instead, he said, "I have dispatched a small force to determine the nature of our new visitors; friend, foe, man, giant, or otherwise. Two emissaries from the force will attempt communication. If the effort is successful, the group will return with word of the nature of our visitors' expedition. If not," he paused.

Leisha prodded, "If not, what?"

Daritus stopped, "I have sent our army to build a camp about a half day's journey from the shore. There is a fort there from a battle that occurred many years ago when foreigners threatened Havenstahl after Maelich had Ahm's head in battle. The soldiers of Havenstahl proved mightier than their adversaries then, and the fort is solid. If our emissaries meet with anything less than hospitality, the rest of their small force will return with word of their demise, and we will go to war."

"War?"

"Yes war, my love," Daritus sighed. "We will take the battle to them, beat them back to their ships, and send them scurrying back across the Great Sea."

Leisha's form drooped as she replied, "I love you, Daritus. I have always loved you." She paused and straightened back up before continuing, "I have always known you better than you know yourself too. Your tone and your words are confident, but your eyes..." She trailed off.

Daritus turned to face her, "My eyes, what?"

"Your eyes are filled with doubt, my love."

Daritus shook his head, "Concern dear, not doubt, my eyes are filled with concern. It is my job to protect this city, and—as you have already pointed out—I am without the aid of my greatest champions. Doubt, however, is the furthest thing from my mind. I believe in our cause, and I believe in my men, my champions." His tone softened, "Most importantly, I believe in you. If our visitors are unfriendly to Havenstahl, if our forces fail and they breech our gates, I am depending on you to guide the people of this fair city to the safety of our beloved city in the trees."

Leisha began speaking before Daritus had even finished, "And I will. At the first sign of danger, I will gather them all and guide them to the safety of the Forgotten Forest."

Daritus nodded as he approached her, put his arm around her shoulders, pulled her close, and assured her, "I am counting on it. I know you as well as you know me, dear. You will have the full strength of the palace guard to protect you on your journey, and I will send word if the tide turns even slightly against us.”

Leisha nestled her head into Daritus’s chest and asked quietly, “Will you be on the front line with your men or here with the palace guard?”

“My place is with my men, dear. You know that.”

Her form drooped again, “I do know it, my love. When will you go?”

“At nightfall we ride,” he whispered.

She raised her head, grabbed his shoulders firmly, pulled him close, and whispered, “Lay with me awhile, love.”

“Of course,” he replied as he fell into her embrace.

CHAPTER 13
DRAGONS

Stretched across the wind, Cialia felt lighter both physically and mentally, almost unconscious, but aware on a different level. Her senses weren't triggering chemical reactions in her mind or sparking up memories of things she knew to be to feed her awareness, yet she was aware of everything. And not only aware, but she was a part of everything, like dancing between light and dark or physical and spiritual. Time, light, sound, space, depth, distance, nothing was beyond her control. Ideas grander than the entire universe or infinitesimally minute were as accessible to her mind as the feel of cool sand between her toes. Nothing seemed out of reach. That is, of course, except for her brother. She didn't feel the slightest tingle from him.

Cialia slowly grew heavier as her physicality returned, and she materialized out of the air at the edge of the Lake of Dragons. The perfect circle of glass-like water—known to all but for most merely myth—lay before her. A perfect ring of sand exactly fifteen feet wide surrounded the water creating a circle within a circle. Beyond the sand, trees—long and thin with wide, balmy leaves—grew haphazardly in small groups, bunches here and there like tiny forests. Flowers with petals of the most vibrant purples, yellows, and oranges grew in patches as random as the trees. Some with sharp looking petals stretched tall as if they were reaching for the tops of the trees, while others with softer, round petals drooped like they were sniffing the ground. Wrapped around all of it was lush green upon green; plants with long, wide floppy leaves resembling the trees mingled with plants bearing leaves so tall, thin, and frail they looked as if a stiff breeze might blow them down. Fruit bearing vines snaked around the plants, trees, and flowers as if sneaking between the giants to occupy all unclaimed space. Cialia inhaled deeply through her nose. Joy like no desire remained unfulfilled forced an uncontrollable smile to her lips. The earthy smell of the greens mixed with the sweet perfume of the flowers nearly wiped away all the heavy thoughts weighing her down and left her feeling so peaceful she nearly forgot her purpose. Movement in her periphery reminded her.

"Cialia, you have returned," the familiar voice was calm yet powerful.

"Delcinia," Cialia began as she turned to behold the mighty Dragon. "Your home is so beautiful. It always leaves me completely enchanted. I forget myself surrounded by the bright colors and the sweet air."

"Yes," the Dragon replied. "Yes, this place is quite peaceful and beautiful. If only the rest of Ouloos were so. You are one of few who can look upon it while still inhabiting your physical self. This beauty is mostly saved for those whose souls are called home. You and your brother returned it to us. We are forever in your debt."

Cialia shivered as a white mist slowly surrounded her and then moved on toward the Lake. It hovered like fog just above the ground but moved as if guided by intelligence. Within a few moments, it had traveled to the center of the Lake. Then it sunk slowly into the water until it breached the surface and in a flash of white light raced toward the heavens until it was out of site.

"Another soul called home," Delcinia noted.

"Indeed," Cialia agreed. "It was so cold."

"They are," Delcinia replied. "I honestly do not know why, but they are."

Cialia looked up to see hundreds of dragons flying long, lazy circles around the Lake. Thousands more must have been among the trees or beneath the water's surface. Cialia's broad smile grew as she looked back at Delcinia, "It is so good to have Dragons back where they belong, back at the Lake, the true origin of us all. I shudder to think of those dark days when misguided fears robbed Ouloos of your love and perfection."

"As do I," the Dragon agreed. "Kallum was pure evil. He opened the eyes of violent men allowing them to find this place. Then he poisoned their minds with lies and urged them to destroy. I cried for every soul he damned to that wicked forest, that prison holding us captive for so long. I even cried for him." She paused a moment and looked to the sky before continuing, "You did not come to reminisce or speak history with me though, fair princess. There is purpose to your journey. You wear it like a wound upon your brow."

"Alas my fair sister, you are correct," Cialia conceded. "I carry a burden quite heavy to bear."

"You worry for Maelich?" Delcinia asked. She paused only a moment before adding, "It is not just your brother you worry for. You carry concern for him, but your concern for what his absence means to the people of Ouloos is far greater. You seek the Great Mother, wisest of all our sisters."

"I do, Delcinia. I do," Cialia agreed. "I seek her wise counsel and her fair advice. I need guidance. I need help."

"She knows, fair sister," Delcinia assured her. "The Great Mother has been expecting you. She aches for Maelich as well."

Cialia allowed herself a faint glimmer of hope, "She sees him? She knows where he is off to?"

"Sadly, no," the Dragon replied softly. "You should go ask her about it yourself. She always does provide wise counsel."

"She does," Cialia frowned as she looked toward the rocky hill directly across the Lake from her. The greatest of all Dragons perched atop it. "Thank you, Delcinia. It is very reassuring to speak with you."

"Of course, my dear," the Dragon replied. "I missed you as well."

Cialia blushed as she smiled, turned toward the Lake, and dismounted Purity who tromped off into the foliage. With a wave toward Delcinia, she walked slowly toward the water until she reached the sand surrounding it. The Great Mother, Helias, perched upon the rocky hill on the opposite shore as if it were a throne. Helias, first daughter of the Lake—true beginning of all—was magnificent to behold. Her colossal body sat atop powerful, squat legs ending in mighty claws firmly gripping the peak beneath her. Thin, though muscular, arms ending in equally impressive claws folded across her belly. A head the size of a hut consisting mostly of jaws and horns sat atop a long neck that—though very thin—appeared incredibly strong. The Great Mother stretched and spread her wings. They must have spanned at least one hundred feet. Behind her stretched a mighty tail, long and thick, ending in a sharp point. As impossible as it seemed to her, Cialia felt her smile widen as she took in the perfect sight.

The Lake was a good two miles in diameter, but Cialia's eyes were far keener than any other, save her brother. The sight—as she and Maelich referred to their ability to see great distances without strain—was a gift from the Lake of Dragons. Through her eyes, she could see Helias's entire form as clearly as if she were standing beside her. Cialia gazed into the Great Mother's glowing, red eyes and felt the weight of her burden ease slightly. Helias was like a soft pillow to a sleepy head or a warm blanket to a cold traveler.

Cialia walked right up to the edge of the water and turned to her left. She could have willed herself to Helias's side, but she chose a slow stroll through the sand instead. It was an infrequent pleasure to be so close to the Lake, so close to Helias and the rest of her sisters. Why spoil it with haste? Ymitoth would still be dead, and Maelich would still be missing whether she hurried or not. And if Maelich were found in her absence, it would be all the better. Then there would be no reason to rush at all. She paused to remove her boots and walked with her toes in the sand.

The slow stroll lasted a little more than three hours. The warmth of the sun, the sweet scent in the air, the cool breeze lifting her hair off of her forehead, the glorious, blazing colors of the flowers all around her, the stillness of the Lake, and the perfect beauty of the Great Mother perched atop her throne all spun together lifting Cialia's cares away. For that regretfully short journey, nothing else mattered.

Finally, Cialia stood at the mouth of the cave at the base of the rocky hill Helias rode like a throne, the queen's throne. She looked up at the glorious mother of all Dragons and said, "Helias, my sister, my queen, Great Mother, I have missed you."

"I have missed you as well, my dear," Helias replied. Her delicate, almost vulnerable voice belied the power she possessed. "I fear you have brought a great burden with you."

"Alas, sweet sister, I have. Ymitoth has fallen at the hands of the dead-eyed men, those same men that should have perished with the scattered remains of their god. Yet it was them. There is no mistake. I saw them with my own eyes…" She trailed off and glanced down toward the sand.

Helias replied, "That is a puzzle. You know you have nothing to fear from them, my love. You have nothing to fear from any man, beast, or otherwise that haunts this world."

Cialia lifted her gaze back up, looked the Great Mother in the eyes, and said, "I fear no one."

The Great Mother smiled, "You are brave, my dear. Fear is a tricky adversary though. You have no fear for yourself. That fact is more than clear. You are able and there is not one in this world that could best you in battle. However, fear has little to do with might, fair Cialia. When you raise your sword in the defense of your city, it is fear that drives you. When you offer…"

Cialia interrupted, "Behind my sword is where I am most fearless. An equal to my blade does not exist."

The smile remained on Helias's face as she continued, "You are quite correct, my dear. You have no equal with a blade. Your skill even surpasses that of your fair brother. However, fear for yourself, for your own life, is not of what I speak. The fear troubling your slumber is fear for those who look to you for guidance and protection. Your fear lies with them. You carry many burdens, sweet child. Even in the tranquil peace of my home, I can see the weight pushing you low, bending your back, and forcing down your brow."

"You are correct, sweet sister," Cialia agreed. "I do feel fear. I feel it every day. In Maelich's absence, it has grown even stronger. Please tell me you have felt him. Tell me he has spoken to you, given you a glimpse. Your power is so great. Surely you have some happy news for me. Good news has been scarce of late."

"I felt great pain from Maelich," she replied. "The pain was so strong, so dark, and so deep it made me weep for him. I carry great sadness for his pain."

"Have you searched for him?"

"Why?"

Cialia sighed, raised both her arms out to her sides, and shook her head, "The people need him. I know you are the wisest soul on Ouloos, sweet sister. Surely you realize the significance of the presence of dead-eyed men. A dead god has no power. That can mean only one thing."

Helias's tone remained as sweet as spring rain, "A god cannot die, my sweet flower. Kallum was scattered, and he remains scattered. The presence of dead-eyed men simply reveals there is another sinister power as great as that which has been scattered to the wind, and that power wishes to trouble the lives of you and your brother."

Cialia's tone ran in stark contrast to Helias's, "How can you be certain? Please forgive the doubt, Great Mother. You are the greatest power this world has ever known, but you cannot even find my brother. Perhaps Kallum clouds your vision as Maelich does."

"Cialia, your mind is ever full of worry and so focused on what you do not want. How can you clearly imagine what it is you do want? Let go. Despite your belief in me, you and your brother are the greatest powers this world has ever known," Helias replied. "Once you forget your fears and learn to quiet the doubtful, timid, human part of your mind, you will know truth."

Cialia continued, calmer but unable to shake her agitation, "I do not feel powerful right now. The world spins out of control, and it is my duty to protect it." She paused as a thoughtful look crept onto her face, "Do you think we could find Maelich if we worked together?"

Helias's smile remained as she shook her head, "What makes you think Maelich needs finding? Why do you think he is lost? No one stole your brother. He left. He is experiencing great sadness. Yes, he is hiding. The fact in itself illustrates he wishes not to be found."

Cialia sighed deeply, "He stole a corpse, Helias. He stole Ymitoth's corpse. I am afraid for him. His mind must not be his own right now."

"His mind, your mind, they are very complex," Helias assured her. "He is in control of his mind. He has at least enough control to keep you from peering into his thoughts."

"And you?" Cialia asked.

"I have not the cause to search for him," Helias replied, "but yes, I am certain I would not find him if I tried."

"What should I do?"

"Sleep, dear," the Great Mother replied. "Your soul is far wearier than even your body. Rest on the sand for a while and let the sweet peace of this place soothe you. Then go back to your people, and do not fear for your brother."

Cialia contemplated arguing her point further, but Helias was correct. She was tired, and if Maelich didn't want to be found, he wouldn't be. The sand— lacking the course texture the sand of most beaches had—felt soft and warm beneath her as she lay herself down upon it. It was like lying on a thick, soft blanket. Mere moments passed before Cialia was far beyond the reach of Ouloos or any of her troubles.

CHAPTER 14
THE WHITE HORSE

Maelich stood alone in a small clearing surrounded by dense woods, completely unaware of how he arrived there or anything else immediately prior to being there. A thick, milky, white fog covered the clearing up to his waist. He waved his hand back and forth in it. The motion caused swirls and waves as if it were liquid. He walked a few paces toward the trees. The fog didn't hinder his movement or slow him at all. It just hung there surrounding him. Above him, the trees stretched toward each other forming a canopy allowing only the essence of light through, no rays, merely a faint glow. There was just enough light for Maelich to make out his surroundings which were rather unremarkable. Thick trees crowded so closely together he couldn't see past the fronts of them. The lake of fog he stood in and the very top of a pointed boulder jutting out of the fog to his left were all he could see.

He continued on to the edge of the trees and touched one. The bark was smooth and nondescript. It felt like a tree. He slid his hand to the left along the trunk until he reached the dark spot between it and the tree beside it. When his hand reached that place, it stopped. He pushed at it several times, but his hand wouldn't go any farther. It didn't feel like there was anything there to stop his movement, but he could not push past the darkness in between the two trunks. It took several attempts before he gave up the effort and stepped back to the center of the clearing to contemplate what to do next.

"Where am I?" he asked no one.

A deep—though clear—voice startled him, "You are standing in a dense fog near a large boulder in the center of a clearing in a very dense wood."

Maelich stroked his chin and looked around, "Thank you. That was extremely helpful. Although, I had deduced as much with a quick look around. What do they call the dense wood I occupy?"

"Who?" the voice asked.

"Who, what?" Maelich asked in return.

"You asked what *they* call this place," the voice replied. "Who are *they*?"

A bit of irritation found its way into Maelich's tone, "Anyone. What does *anyone* call this place?"

"Oh," the voice continued, "this place is not near famous enough to have a name. I guess the answer would be, anyone does not call it anything."

Maelich shook his head and began pacing, "Do you know where this is?"

"Do I know where what is?" The voice asked.

"Here," Maelich began. "Do you know where here is?"

"What is here?" The voice asked.

Maelich sighed, thought for a moment, and then continued, "Do you know where this dense fog near a large boulder in the center of a clearing in a very dense wood is?"

"Oh, why didn't you just ask me that in the first place? It is right where you are standing. As far as its relationship to other places, I do not know. I have never been anywhere but here," the voice replied.

"Well that is no help," Maelich sighed as he sat down upon the bit of boulder poking through the fog. Once he was seated, he continued, "And I did ask you that in the first place."

"It is some help. Now you know where you are," the voice paused almost long enough that Maelich thought it was finished, but then it continued. "You did not ask me that in first place. First you asked where you were, and I told you. Then you asked what they call this place. Once I determined what you meant by, 'they', I told you that too. Then you asked where this is and where here is and only after all of that did you ask me a question even remotely logical. Yet, even after asking all of those questions, you still haven't asked what you really want to know."

Maelich grinned. At this point he was too flabbergasted about the bodiless voice he was speaking with to be frustrated anymore. He stretched his arms wide apart above his head and in a mocking tone said, "Please, oh great disembodied voice of this dense fog near a large boulder in the center of a clearing in a very dense wood, enlighten me on what question I really want to ask."

"Ah, sarcasm," the voice replied. "I have so few occasions to speak with anyone I barely recognize it. Sarcasm is fun, isn't it? Still, laced within your sarcasm was a question far more important than you probably realize, and I will answer it for you. What you really want to ask me is, 'How do I get out of this dense fog near a large boulder in the center of a clearing in a very dense wood?' Although, after speaking with you for these past few moments, I know you would probably not ask me that at all. Instead, you would more than likely ask, 'How do I get out of here?' and leave me guessing what you really wanted to know."

Maelich laughed, "You are wise my friend, a tad too particular perhaps, but wise indeed. So then, how do I get out of this dense fog near a large boulder in the center of a clearing in a very dense wood?"

"Well that is very simple," the voice assured him. Then it added, "You just follow the path directly in front of you."

As soon as the last word reached Maelich's ear, the fog in front of him split to form a wide path. He followed it with his eyes to the edge of the trees and found an opening there. Then he said, "That was not there before."

"Of course it was. You simply did not know what you were looking for," the voice replied. "Safe travels, Maelich. Beware the black horse."

Maelich thought of inquiring about the black horse but decided against it. He probably wouldn't have asked the right question anyway. Instead, he stood up, walked over to the opening in the trees—that definitely wasn't there before despite what the voice of the clearing had said—and strolled into the dense forest surrounding him. As soon as he was beyond the edge of the trees, all but the faintest hint of light left him. There were no filtered rays like he had enjoyed in the clearing. The change was so dramatic he quickly turned around to see if the clearing had darkened at all. It was gone. He could faintly make out the trees where the opening to the clearing should be at the end of the trail he occupied. However, the opening itself had vanished, apparently closing up behind him once he passed through. He shook his head and turned back around. It didn't make any sense to try to go back anyway. That would just lead to another fruitless conversation with a voice obviously not in a hurry to get anywhere.

Maelich began to follow the trail. The whisper of light available was enough that he could almost make out the trees on either side the path for at least a couple of feet in front of him. It wasn't much, but it would have to do. He still didn't know where he was going. At least there was only one way to go. Wherever the trail led would be his destination.

"So where does this trail lead?" Maelich broke the silence.

This time there was no response.

"I guess you remained in the clearing," he continued to no one but the trees. "You were painfully irritating to talk to, but better than talking to myself."

Still nothing, the voice of the dense fog near a large boulder in the center of a clearing in a very dense wood had obviously remained there. That must be a horribly boring life, if it were life at all. The voice didn't have any form, at least none Maelich saw. Maybe it wasn't life at all. If it wasn't life, then what would it be? It did exhibit intelligence. Perhaps that in and of itself would denote some form of life. Of course, the meaning of life would then come into play and have to be reasoned into the equation. Does intelligence necessarily equate to life? A being doesn't have to exhibit intelligence to be alive, but does intelligence have to inhabit a physical form to be alive. If life is strictly dependent on a physical form presenting itself in the physical world, then intelligence wouldn't necessarily mean the voice represented life.

Suddenly, Maelich was surrounded by light. He had no idea how far he had walked or for how long. Neither time nor distance made any sense. The issue of whether or not the painfully particular voice in the clearing represented life—or what represented life at all—had proven to be a subject engrossing enough to suck his attention away from the details of his movement. In any event, he had left the dark forest and stumbled upon something else entirely. Thick grass grew wild up to his knees. It was a deep, intense green like no grass Maelich had ever seen, almost glowing rather than reflecting light. On top of that, it moved differently than grass should. Grass as long as the stuff he was standing in should sway and wave in the breeze. The breeze was there—strong enough to blow his hair straight behind him—yet the grass remained unmoved by its efforts. The stubborn, unmovable grass ended abruptly at a creek measuring about three and a half feet across. A steep hill covered in the same unmovable grass grew up from the edge of its opposite bank.

Maelich's eyes followed the odd grass up the hill to its peak. There, under a lone, tall oak, stood an impeccable, white horse. This was no ordinary white steed. The animal was without blemish. There was no grey or any kind of shading to its coat and, like the glowing grass, it appeared to emit rather than reflect light. As they made eye contact, Maelich felt something. It was something resembling nervousness or fear, but not quite either of those things. Anxious was perhaps a bit closer, but even that didn't quite describe the feeling. Something in his belly did not completely reconcile with his mind.

They stared into each other's eyes for a few excruciating moments before Maelich had to look away. Those eyes didn't make any sense. They weren't any particular color, but they had color. In fact, it appeared every color imaginable was present in them, swirling and twisting one moment, shifting and flashing the next. Simply maintaining contact with them for as long as he had left him feeling scrutinized and small. In an effort to avoid those beautiful yet terrible eyes, he looked to the sky. That offered little relief. It wasn't really sky at all, just a yellow glow. There was no blue, no clouds, and no sun. In fact, the glow didn't appear to originate from any one point. It was even and steady and it surrounded him from the grass on one side to the grass on the other. Maelich's mind grew tipsy as he scoured the non-sky with his eyes, examining it. His shifting equilibrium twisted his belly and brought bile up to the back of his throat. Even with all of that discomfort, the unsettling yellow glow posing as sky was far easier to behold than the white horse that filled him with such a queer and uncomfortable sensation.

"Maelich," the white horse addressed him, "I have been waiting a long while for you to finally arrive."

Maelich took a deep breath and exhaled deeply. Then he looked back to the white horse to find it still staring at him. He replied, "I did not know I was being sought."

The horse continued as if Maelich hadn't spoke, "A great journey lies before you, a journey that has been waiting for you since long before you were born. This journey has been waiting for you since the beginning of time."

Maelich thought for a moment. The simple act of searching for words shifted his focus from his peculiar surroundings, slightly easing his discomfort. Finding the perfect words was imperative. He didn't feel like entering into another tango like the one he encountered with the voice in the clearing. "Who are you?" was the best he could come up with.

"I am the white horse. I am your guide."

Maelich sighed, "I can see you are a white horse, but what is your name?"

The horse smiled and replied, "I know the fog had you befuddled in the clearing. It likes to play games and it is very particular about how people— or any other entities for that matter—choose their words. Essentially, it is lonely and bored. It very seldom gets any company at all. I am not lonely nor am I bored. I have no riddles. I also have no name other than the white horse. That is what I am. That is who I am. I am referred to as nothing else but that."

"Good," Maelich replied. "I am tired of riddles. What is this journey, and why should I accept it?"

"I cannot tell you what the journey is. I know the beginning. This is that. And I know the end. The journey itself is up to you. There are many paths you may follow, and there are many adventures you may encounter. Those are solely yours to decide. All I can tell you now is where you begin," the white horse answered in as matter of fact a tone as Maelich had ever heard.

Maelich's head dipped slightly to the right, "So if I understand you correctly, you want me to embark on a journey with no stated purpose to possibly encounter many adventures while I have no idea where my final destination lies based on the advice of a white horse with no name."

"Not exactly," the white horse replied. "My want has nothing to do with your journey. It is merely my role to guide you along your path. Like I said, the journey is yours."

"What if I do not accept this adventure?" Maelich asked.

"The journey has chosen you. There is nothing for you to accept," the white horse paused. "Before Ouloos existed, even before the slow cycle of time began, this journey was yours. Whether you leave now or postpone your departure, the journey will always be there until you make it."

Maelich shook his head, "So I do have a choice."

"Somewhat," the white horse agreed. "You can choose when you begin. However, at some point the journey will have to be made."

"What if I decide I will never make the journey?" Maelich asked.

"That is not possible. All journeys must be completed. We do not always choose our journeys, but they are all completed at some point. This journey has chosen you, and you will complete it. There is no other outcome."

Maelich shrugged, "Where does this journey begin? If I decide to make the journey, I need to know where to start."

"The journey begins where you are currently laying your head, in a hut with the man who once was your father."

"The man who *is* my father," Maelich corrected.

"Fine, the man who *is* your father," the white horse conceded. After a brief pause, he continued, "Your mind has become a puzzle that is not ready to be solved yet. In any event, the journey begins in that hut."

Maelich chuckled under his breath, "I'll tell you what a puzzle is to me right now. Where is my hut, and how do I get there from here?"

"You know the answer to that," the white horse replied. "Think about where you came from."

"I came from there…" Maelich began. He stopped short as he turned to point at the forest he had stepped out of and found it to be missing. There was nothing but more grass where the forest had been. As far as he could see in any direction—save directly behind him where a talking, white horse stood under a tall oak on a steep hill across a small creek—was the same waist-tall grass he was standing in. Slowly he turned back toward the white horse and was startled to find himself standing directly before him, both of them occupying the space under the tall oak at the top of the steep hill. Even more confused, Maelich began again, "I came out of a very dense forest. It was right there," he motioned over his shoulder. "It is gone now, but it was there a moment ago."

"Of course it was," the white horse agreed, "and now it is not. And you are standing with me under a tree on a hill. So what?"

Maelich scratched his head, "So, I thought you said you had no riddles. It most certainly feels like you are pulling some form of prank on me right now. How did you get me up on this hill without me realizing it?"

The white horse shook his head, "This is not a riddle, nor is there any form of prank afoot. The forest was there, and now it is not. You were there, and now you are here. I have no control of the forest or of you. You are the only one who has any control of anything here."

Maelich shook his head back at the white horse, "I certainly don't feel like I have any control of anything here. Everything is just happening."

The white horse shrugged and remained silent. Maelich puzzled at that for a moment. He had never seen a horse shrug before. He had never heard a horse speak before either. Compared to speaking, a shrug seemed far less impressive.

A few moments of silence passed before Maelich picked the conversation back up. "Where should I go from here?"

The white horse turned and said, "Walk with me." Then he proceeded to walk up into the yellow glow that was the sky.

Maelich sighed and followed a few steps behind. He strolled along in silence, steadily moving upward, surrounded by the yellow glow that served as the sky in this place. The tall, still grass expanded beneath him in all directions. After what seemed like a very short while, the white horse stopped. It didn't feel like they had journeyed more than a few hundred feet. However, when Maelich turned back toward the oak on the hill, he could no longer see it. He looked down and determined they had also climbed much farther than he felt they should have. The tall, still grass appeared very far away.

When Maelich turned back, the white horse stood before a large, wooden door set in a brick entryway and faced him. "But..." was all Maelich could muster before the white horse interrupted him.

"You should go through that door Maelich," the white horse said.

Maelich thought for a moment and then asked, "Why?"

The white horse sighed, "You have asked many questions about the journey. The first answer is on the other side of that door."

"But I haven't decided whether or not I want to make the journey yet."

"No you have not. How will you know what to decide if you do not have any idea what you are deciding upon? Besides, you cannot go back at this point. There is only one way to go, forward."

"I could go back the way I came," Maelich argued.

"No," the white horse countered. "The way you came no longer exists."

Maelich turned to see he was surrounded by sweaty, chipped rocks that had been carved into rude bricks. "Where is my choice now?" he asked.

"Your choice is to go through the door or not go through the door," the white horse replied. "You already chose to follow me here. Some choices cannot be undone."

"Fine," Maelich rolled his eyes. "I do not like this game, horse."

"There is no game," the white horse replied. Before he finished speaking, the bricks and the door vanished and were replaced with dusty, rocky ground. It was light brown—almost orange—and it was covered in giant boulders that looked like they had been there for centuries.

Maelich managed, "How?" before his voice trailed off. Then he spun a slow circle and took it all in. The yellow glow previously replacing the sky was gone. Above him looked like sky again, deep blue with fluffy clouds lazing about. The sun was nowhere to be found, but the vast expanse above him was quite bright nonetheless. Something just short of panic slipped into his mind as his gaze fell from the bright immensity stretching over him down past the end of the cliff he stood upon. His feet seemed far too close to the edge. The height of the peak was impossible to determine as clouds surrounded it, swirling a few hundred feet below him.

"There, Maelich," the white horse motioned with his snout toward the edge of the cliff. "Far to the south you will find the Sea of Sadness. Once you arrive there, I will visit you again."

Maelich turned toward the white horse now standing beside him and facing the same direction, "What is the Sea of Sadness?"

"For a god you know very little," the white horse replied.

Maelich turned to his right to ask more about the Sea of Sadness, but the white horse was gone. He looked back out over the clouds below him. They ended far in the distance, stretching almost to the horizon. Just beyond them he saw what could have been the shore of a great body of water. "That must be the Sea of Sadness," he said quietly.

Suddenly, he was pounded in the back. The force of the assault carried him toward the edge of the cliff. His arms flew out to his sides desperately seeking something to grab hold of as he spun back toward the rock wall that had been behind him. Nothing reached out to meet his hands as they flailed. At that moment, his balance was akin to an old man's youth, lost, yearned for, but out of reach. By the time Maelich had spun half way around, he saw the white horse smiling at him. He tried to lean forward, but was already too far off kilter from the shove. Leaning out over the edge of the cliff as his arms reached out in front of him, he hopelessly grabbed at nothing. "Why?" he cried out to the white horse as his momentum carried him over the edge.

Maelich raced toward a thick bank of clouds surrounding the peak he stood upon moments prior. It barely took a breath until he was in them. White upon white surrounded him as he began to roll end over end. Disoriented, he couldn't tell up from down. It no longer felt like he was falling, just spinning helplessly in a cocoon of white. There was no up or down, left or right, just one point where he rotated. Spatially, his body's movements made absolutely no sense to his brain. Then there was light. He plummeted through the bottom of the cloud bank and the sensation of falling returned. The rocky wall of the peak he fell from was gone. He was surrounded by a wide expanse of nothing as he charged headlong toward the tall, stiff, unbelievably green grass.

The ground grew closer and closer with every second. Maelich's heart pounded in his chest as all of his limbs flailed. The fingers on both of his hands still opened and closed on nothing, desperately seeking something, anything to grab a hold of and slow his descent. There was nothing to hold on to though. He was racing toward the ground and in moments he would shatter upon it. A scream ripped past his lips from somewhere deep in his belly, right as the ground was about to smash him into bloody pieces.

Maelich sat straight up in his cot and howled like he had been stabbed through the eye. Sweat poured down his face, his soggy hair dripping and sticking to it. His clothes were drenched. Hot breath poured out of him in rapid pants. He screamed again to make sure he were really still alive. Little by little his breathing became steady and he calmed. It was all a dream, a confusing and horrifying dream. Slowly, he turned his head toward the right. Ymitoth's black, dead eyes were inches from his own. The startling sight made him jump, and he howled again.

"Ye been havin' quite the dream, lad," Ymitoth remarked, undaunted by Maelich's scream.

"Why are you ogling me like that?" Maelich shouted. "Sitting with your face so close to me, you scared me nearly to death."

"Aye," Ymitoth replied as he sat back into the chair next to Maelich's cot, "either me or that dream. Ye were mumbling and tossing about, arguing it sounded like, talking in your sleep like someone be here in the room with us. Then ye screamed like ye were being torn apart by amatilazo. What could have scared ye so, lad?"

Maelich thought for a moment as he looked into Ymitoth's black, dead eyes, "How long have you been you been sitting here watching me?"

"Sleep, she be a frisky vixen sometimes," Ymitoth replied. "I chased her and wooed her for hours but she fled this way and that. I gave up the chase once ye started with all of that mumbling and tossing about."

"You couldn't sleep?" Maelich asked, looking deeper into Ymitoth's eyes and examining them as he continued, "What were you thinking about all that time? What thoughts kept you from slumber?"

"Ah, ye know, lad, the standard stuff that keeps a man from the warm bosom of sleep, hunting and fishing and fighting," Ymitoth replied as he stood and walked over to the table in the center of the hut, grabbed a mug that was sitting there, and took a long pull of ale. "We sure did have a time chasing the chookers the other day," he added after he swallowed.

Maelich swung his legs over the side of his cot, continuing to stare at the dead thing that used to be his father, "Did you just pour yourself that ale?"

"Sure, well, a few moments ago anyway," Ymitoth replied giving Maelich an odd look as he did. Then he asked, "What be that to ye anyway?"

"Why?" Maelich asked.

Ymitoth chuckled, "Because I'd been parched with the thirst. Why else? Ye been acting strange lately, son. What's that got ye acting so queer?"

Maelich shook his head, "Oh nothing, nothing's wrong at all. I've just been working through a little puzzle in my head."

"Aye? What kind of puzzle might that be, lad?" Ymitoth smiled.

"How an inanimate object can move around and do things on its own," he replied, never taking his eyes off of his father.

Ymitoth took another swig of his ale and nodded, "That be sounding like a doozy of a riddle lad. What kind of object we be talking about now, a tree, or a sword maybe?"

Maelich shook his head, "Never mind, it's silly to think about."

Ymitoth shrugged.

Maelich changed the subject, "How far off is the sun?" he asked.

Ymitoth looked up and to the left. Then his eyes scanned across the ceiling, down the wall, and eventually found their way to Maelich's, "Maybe an hour or just a bit more. Why, ye feel like chasing chookers?"

Maelich smiled, "I do, but that's not why I ask. Have you ever heard of the Sea of Sadness?"

Ymitoth nodded, "Aye, it be far to the south. Years ago tribes from across that sea marched all the way north to Havenstahl with thoughts of slaughter and plunder. I'd been a far younger man then," he paused and looked up at the ceiling. "'Twas me first real war, if ye could even call it war. It was more of a route really. The entire war weren't nothing but a handful of battles what weren't nothing more than slaughters themselves. We sent them treacherous bastards racing back across that sad sea."

Maelich reached back into his own memory. Had Ymitoth ever told him that story? He must have. How else would he remember anything from his living years? All his memories should be only what Maelich fed him.

"That be it then? Ye just be curious about that sea?" Ymitoth asked.

Maelich looked up to see his father's black, dead eyes staring at him, looking like two total lunar eclipses with a weird, negative glow. He shook his head and said, "No. Would you like to take a journey?"

"Aye, to the Sea of Sadness then?" Ymitoth smiled.

"Yes," Maelich replied, "to the Sea of Sadness."

"It be a long journey," Ymitoth continued to smile.

"Yes," Maelich agreed, "it is. We should leave now."

Ymitoth drained his mug and then replied, "Let's get to packing then, lad."

CHAPTER 15
THE TRAIL

Maelich and Ymitoth were packed and ready to bid farewell to their hut well before the sun peeked over the horizon. Clear skies to the east were just beginning to glow. The chill air surrounding the hut hung still, waiting to be warmed by the approaching sun. Maelich whistled for Validus. He paused a few moments, nothing. Glancing about the loose groupings of trees around the hut, he whistled again. No hoof beats, no rustling leaves, and no happy snorts found his ears.

"Well where do ye suppose that fool horse be off to?" Ymitoth asked.

Maelich frowned, "That is a mystery. Now that I think of it, I cannot remember the last time I saw him."

Ymitoth cocked his head to the right and looked up to the left, "I guess I could be saying the same."

"Validus," Maelich raised his voice and hollered toward the north.

A rustling in a small group of trees off toward Keller's Hill seemed a fitting response. Maelich charged up the hill. He didn't make it halfway up the incline before a fat squirrel crested the hill, noticed Maelich, and then raced up the giant oak crowning it. Maelich jumped a bit when he saw the critter. It gave him enough of a start to squeeze the slightest laugh out of him. The chuckle was short-lived. Where could Validus be?

"He must have run off," Ymitoth said somberly from the bottom of the hill.

Maelich turned as his eyes filled up, "He's been my horse for," he paused and thought, "since the end of my twelfth year. That would be..."

"Eighteen years today, lad," Ymitoth finished the sentence for him. "I be truly sorry. I forgot it was even your birthday."

Maelich looked at Ymitoth, thought for a moment, and replied, "I guess it is." Then he paused for a few moments and continued, "What a grand gift this is. My horse, my only companion on many a journey, is gone. I hope he still lives."

"Would ye like to look for him, son?" Ymitoth asked.

Maelich shook his head, "No. He could be anywhere. Besides, we have a journey to begin. He's always been a solid horse. He'll find his way."

Ymitoth's arm fell across Maelich's shoulders, "Thirty summers…old man, where did the time go, and when did ye get so old?"

Maelich chuckled, "If I'm old, what does that make you?"

"Ancient," Ymitoth snorted, and they both laughed.

The two men gathered their packs in silence. The sky to the east had brightened as the sun threatened to breach the horizon, splashing red, pink, and orange streaks across it. The brilliant, morning sun would rise at any moment. Maelich glanced toward the vibrant artwork, colors bleeding into each other and mingling like oils on canvas rather than rays of light refracted and split by the atmosphere. Thirty summers made for quite a few sunrises. Each one still filled him with awe.

Both men knew the trail they would take without speaking about it to each other. Without a map and only the loose beginnings of a plan, they would pick their paths based on the sun. Maelich truly had no idea where beyond the Sea of Sadness was their destination, and—according to Ymitoth—the Sea of Sadness was quite large. As long as they kept a southerly direction, they would reach its shore in three weeks.

The sun was fully in the sky as the two travelers rounded Yester's Pond and picked up a trail that headed straight east. They had hunted it regularly during Maelich's first twelve summers and both knew it well.

Maelich turned, took one last glance at the hut, and said a silent good-bye. Then he glanced at Ymitoth, smiled, and said, "We have never taken a journey this great together."

Ymitoth looked at him thoughtfully for a moment and then agreed, "Aye lad. This be an adventure indeed." Then he looked back toward hut and said, "Another good-bye, a fond farewell, I be thinking of ye always till the last chime of the bell."

Maelich smiled, "What was that?"

Ymitoth shrugged, "That be a short farewell poem we used to say to our folk when the road called us from home."

"I like it," Maelich decided.

The miles peeled off quickly as loose groupings of trees became less frequent and gave way to a wide prairie with far less dramatic hills. Maelich picked up the pace and jogged for a time. He glanced over at Ymitoth and could tell the old warrior was just as full of the pure excitement of boots pounding against the wide open trail as him. Of course, there was no need to rush, but the feeling of his heart beating wildly in his chest—surged on by every flex of his legs—was reason enough to race along that road. Nothing moves a traveler's spirit quite like the adventure of a journey. No matter how much joy his home and folk fill him with, his heart always longs for the trail.

As the sun reached its highest point in the sky, Ymitoth nudged Maelich and said, "Midday lad, let's be having a break and taking some nourishment. I be having a good share of salted tubber that will be just the thing to put a little fire back in our feet."

"That sounds perfect," Maelich smiled.

Maelich flopped down next to Ymitoth on a long, flat rock, slightly hidden by the tall grass. Ymitoth dipped into his sack and pulled out several strips of salted tubber. Maelich eagerly accepted half the booty and immediately began chomping on the biggest piece. The warm sun beat down on him as he absently chewed. Its warmth made the perfect complement to the cool air of the prairie.

"How be your legs, lad?" Ymitoth asked with a mouthful of tubber.

"Fine," Maelich stretched them out and leaned back on his left arm, "I'll be good until nightfall."

"Aye," Ymitoth agreed. Then he added, "We should be finding some horses though. We'd be making much better time if we be having a couple of steeds carrying us about."

"True," Maelich replied and then quickly added, "What's that over there?"

Ymitoth turned his face a hair south of straight east toward the large plume of smoke Maelich pointed at, "That be looking to be quite a fire. What of it?"

Maelich shrugged, "All that smoke, there could be an entire village burning over there. Maybe we ought to help them out if we can."

Ymitoth contorted his face like something awfully sour had gotten a hold of his tongue and replied, "That be like two days journey. If they ain't got that fire out by then, anybody that was alive will be long dead or long fled."

"Don't you think it would be heroic?" Maelich asked soberly.

"Aye, it be heroic, a heroic waste of time," Ymitoth replied. Then he picked up a blade of grass, spun it in his fingers a few times while he examined it, and added, "If we be having horses and riding into the night, maybe. On foot, it be taking us too long for there to be any heroic things left to do."

Maelich shrugged and nodded, "Probably. Rebuilding a village is heroic."

"Aye, that be a kind of hero what be helping build up a village what's been destroyed by fire or battle, but that ain't the kind of adventure ye be looking for on this quest," Ymitoth swiped at the air as if swatting the idea down.

Maelich shook his head, "No, no it isn't at all the kind of adventure I'm looking for."

Ymitoth smiled, "Straight south with the falling sun on our right side then. How be your water skin?"

Maelich shook the leather pouch at his side, "About half full."

"Good, we be crossing a small brook about halfway until nightfall. We'll be filling up there," Ymitoth nodded. "That brook she meanders a bit before growing into a small river, but she be emptying right into the Sea of Sadness. Maybe that be a good path to take."

Maelich nodded, "That sounds like a great plan. We may find a village or two on the way, maybe get some horses."

By the time both men had finished their dried tubber and taken good long pulls off of their water skins, the sun was just beginning its descent. They gathered themselves back up, stepped out onto the trail, and started along their afternoon of travel. Maelich glanced back over at the smoke toward the east, halfway between them and a small mountain range known as Branyon's Hills for the man that founded several villages and towns on and around it hundreds of years prior. The myths said he sold his soul to the Dragon for prosperity but was double-crossed and devoured instead. Maelich had learned that story and stories like it were completely false. He had never learned the real story and didn't care terribly much about it right at that moment. All he really wanted just then was to race into the fire causing all the smoke in the middle of the vast valley and save someone. He wanted to do something heroic. He wanted an adventure. Of course, Ymitoth had been completely correct in his assessment. By the time they could reach the fire, the need for heroes would be long gone. He silenced his mind and fell in step beside Ymitoth. Perhaps the river would provide adventure.

CHAPTER 16

GIRD YOUR LOINS

Daritus walked along a deep trench surrounding a wooden fort built on a small hill. As he looked up and beyond it, he could just make out Havenstahl crowning the peak of Mount Elzkahon in the distance. The fort was fairly small and simple but perfect for its intended purpose. Each wall was fifty feet in length and consisted of a series of fifteen-foot-tall, sharpened stakes fastened together on the backside with flat planks. At each corner flat, square platforms—ten feet long at each of their sides—stood an additional ten feet above the tops of the walls. They served as watchtowers. On the inside of the fort, narrow planks—just wide enough for a man to stand upon—ran the length of each wall, exactly four feet beneath the tops of them. The enclosure had no roof and one entrance at the back consisting of a ten-foot-tall, six-foot-wide door that doubled as a small drawbridge to span the trench dug around the other side of the fort. Sharpened sticks filled the trench, patiently waiting for victims to impale.

"You know all of the soldiers will not fit in that tiny fort, sir," Kantiim interrupted Daritus's examination of it.

Daritus turned toward his general, and replied, "Of course not. That was never the intention of this place. How much do you know about the history of Havenstahl, old friend?"

"I know much of it," Kantiim smiled, his dark eyes partially obscured by equally dark—though graying—waves falling just past his eyebrows. "Why?"

Daritus smiled back, considering the man he had grown up with, served with, and fought battles alongside. As he watched his old friend brush the wild waves back from his face to cavort with the rest of the dark—though graying—mop cascading off his head and hanging about his shoulders, he remembered how valuable Kantiim was as friend and counsel even when he missed some of the details. Unencumbered by all of that hair, the eyes of the man appeared far sharper, carrying the wisdom of all the years the lines on his face betrayed him of, the lines not covered by his massive, black beard. Finally he replied, "You must have missed the battle with Ahm's sons."

Kantiim's face reddened, "I suppose I did."

"Details, Kantiim," Daritus's smile widened.

Kantiim chuckled, "That, my friend, is why I have always admired you. You value knowledge. By the time you meet a foe on the battlefield, you know them better than they know themselves. That is why I would follow you into any battle against any army, damn the odds."

"I would follow you just the same, old friend. If you had a mind to lead, I would follow," Daritus smirked.

"Of course you would," Kantiim laughed, "but I have neither the mind nor the desire. No, the mind in that head of yours has no equal on the battlefield. Now, as much as I would love to stand here and discuss each other's greatness, I fear there are far more pressing matters to attend to. Go ahead; lecture me on the history of this damnably small fort and why it is perfect for our mission."

"You're an old dog, Kantiim," Daritus chuckled as the two men began walking along the trench again. "Fine then, let me educate you on this fort. Before Maelich could begin his journey to finish his training, he had to earn the crest of Havenstahl, the mark of a champion from our adopted city. In order to earn his crest he had to complete a trial. The man who wore the crown of Havenstahl at that time was a treacherous, double-crossing bastard named Yfregeof."

"I have heard stories about him," Kantiim interrupted. "He was the cousin of Ymitoth—may the Dragon rest his soul—who betrayed both of their fathers to a giant."

"Precisely," Daritus agreed. "The snake gave Maelich a trial he was certain the lad could not accomplish. He demanded the head of a giant. That giant was Ahm. Maelich proved his worth and won the giant's head in battle, earning the crest of Havenstahl and Alhouim's freedom with one clean slash of his blade. During his battle, Maelich learned of Yfregeof's treachery, and the foul king died a traitor's death."

Kantiim cocked his head to the side and squinted his eyes at Daritus, "That is a great story, old friend, but what on Ouloos does it have to do with this painfully small fort?"

"You know how much I like a good story, Kantiim," Daritus grinned. "I haven't gotten that far yet. Please allow me to finish." After a short pause, Daritus continued, "Everything seemed perfect for the two cities. The dwarves had earned their freedom and fair trade resumed. However, Ahm had sons who became quite distraught when they learned of their father's demise. Aht and Ahn, last in the line of Maomnosett, raised a small army and attacked. This fort," Daritus paused and corrected himself. "Well, not this exact fort. In fact, back then it really wasn't more than a trench and a bunch of stakes driven into the ground. No matter. It isn't important to the story. What is important is some semblance of a fort was erected on this very spot to defend against that attack. Now here is the key, this fort was never intended to be the stronghold of Havenstahl's army. It was merely meant to capture the enemy's focus, draw their attention. They did not even finish it until after the attack had been thwarted. Then it was built up, properly reinforced, and named Fort Maomnosett in honor of the family it defended our fair city against. You see, it has always been somewhat of a decoy."

"A decoy?" Kantiim asked. "Why are we working so hard to fortify a decoy?"

Daritus looked up at the sky, "Perhaps decoy is not quite the proper choice of words. It should be the focal point of the enemy's attack, and I believe it will be supremely useful in defending our position. Not to mention, it will give us a spectacular advantage to damage and weaken their forces. However, while your men are busy fortifying this position, Ycantle and Balgom have their men building and fortifying offensive positions to the north and south of this clearing." Daritus waved his arm toward the wide clearing sprawling out in front of Fort Maomnosett and then continued, "If Glord and Ygraml's forces fail to end the war before it leaves the shore of the Great Sea, this broad clearing is where the final battle will occur. And when our enemies reach this stronghold, they will be fighting a battle on at least three fronts. If it comes to it, this is where we make our final stand."

Kantiim smiled wide at his general, "You are always three steps ahead of your opponent. All the great feats I have watched you accomplish on a battlefield pale in comparison to the might of your mind."

"Please, Kantiim, do not congratulate me yet. Everything has to go exactly as I have planned for this to work. Hopefully Glord and Ygraml prove mighty enough to end this before my plan is tested," Daritus replied soberly.

"Ah, your humility is refreshing, my lord, but the compliment remains…" before Kantiim could finish, Daritus touched his arm and interrupted.

"It begins," he said softly as he watched a horse bearing the colors of Havenstahl charge out of the forest at the other end of the clearing with a man slumped over its head.

It took a few moments for the horse to make it across the clearing to the two men. Once the steed arrived, he stopped abruptly. The groaning man perched on top of the horse slid slowly off his saddle and landed in a heap on the ground in front of Daritus.

"You," Kantiim pointed at one of his men who was busy pounding stakes into the trench directly below him, "fetch Hagen and bring him as quickly as you can."

Meanwhile, Daritus knelt down by the man and examined his state. A large chunk of his right cheek and lower eyelid were missing. It appeared the flesh had been ripped off rather than cut. Daritus squinted as he watched too much of the young emissary's eye darting wildly around in its socket. The man's shirt was covered with far too many holes and tears to determine how many wounds his battered body carried.

"That is Kigan, my lord," Kantiim said quietly into Daritus's ear. "He was one of the emissaries we sent to speak with the visitors at the shore."

"My lord," Kigan choked, "they spared me to bring you a message."

"Shh," Daritus consoled the man, rubbing the one spot on his shoulder free from any noticeable wounds. "Hagen is on his way," he added quietly. Then he pointed to two men standing in the trench who had stopped pounding stakes to gawk at the scene, "You two get this man to my tent and fetch him some water."

Then he turned to Kantiim, but before he could speak his old friend said, "I will send two riders to get an update from Spang of the Dragon's Flame."

Daritus nodded. He had dispatched Spang and the rest of his flames just prior to sending the emissaries to greet the visiting ships. The elite of Havenstahl's army should be poised in the trees at the edge of the beach at Biggon's Bay prepared to strike as soon as commanded. Based on Kigan's condition, Daritus would be issuing that command before nightfall.

Daritus followed the two men carrying Kigan to his tent. Once inside, they laid the battered man down on Daritus's cot amid constant groaning and an occasional shout of pain from the poor emissary. After ensuring his instructions had been precisely followed, he slipped out to grab water and rags. By the time he returned from retrieving a bucket of water and a handful of rags, the bloody clothing had been cut off Kigan's mangled body. Daritus handed the water and rags to Shurm—the taller of the two soldiers—and said, "Here, clean his wounds as best you can. Careful though, try not to cause him too much more pain."

Then he turned to Nuuram—the stouter of the two—and said, "You go check on the whereabouts of Hagen. See if he is on his way."

"My lord," Kigan groaned. "My lord, I feel very weak. I think the Great Dragon, the Great Mother, she's calling me home."

"Nonsense," Daritus replied softly, "Hagen is on his way. I have seen him pull many a battered man back from the edge of death. Just relax. Save your strength."

Kigan's head shook so slightly it was nearly imperceptible, "I cannot, my lord. The house of Maomnosett yet lives. The brother of Ahm, Bok, leads this force. They killed the rest but left me alive to tell you he is coming." Kigan's body began to shake as his voice raised and his rate of speech increased, "He is coming to tear down the Fallon and tear down the Dragon and reclaim the city of dwarves that was stolen from his family. His force is mighty, my lord."

Daritus closed his eyes and rested his hand on Kigan's forehead, "His force may be mighty, but I command tens of thousands of men that will die before they see a giant comfortable in these lands."

Kigan continued, his agitation had not ebbed at all, "Bok's camp is immense, my lord. There are only twenty giants among them, but they are accompanied by thousands of trogmortem. I have always believed them to be myth, but I saw them with my own eyes. They are easily as big as the giants, but their arms are so long and powerful, and their hands immense. They have giant heads with pointy ears; big, swollen noses; and terrible, monstrous, green eyes, and not just any green, glowing green. But their mouths are the most horrifying, my lord. They are humungous and filled with sharp, jagged fangs. Always they hang open with slithery, black tongues that dart about constantly. All of these cuts and gashes my lord; all of them are from two slashes of one of those beasts. Except my face, that was a bite from a grong. I have never seen so many grongs in all of my days, thousands of thousands and more. I am afraid, my lord."

"Rest easy, son," Daritus reassured him. "You have done well. I am ready to face Bok. If he wishes to challenge the might of Havenstahl, he will find my blade, and he will learn two things from me, humility and fear."

Daritus looked down at Kigan and found the young man's eyes staring blankly back at him like two marbles. He hadn't even noticed that the boy had stopped shaking at the end of his rant. Daritus ran his hand down Kigan's face and closed what was left of his eyelids over the chilling gaze. "Your journey is done, my friend," he said quietly. "The Great Mother is calling you home."

Hagen raced into the tent, "Where is the brave, young man requiring my attention?"

Daritus turned to Hagen and shook his head, "He has been called to the Lake."

Hagen slumped, his chin dropping to his chest.

Daritus rose and patted him on the shoulder, "Steel your heart, my friend. War is upon us. Kigan is only the first of many we will mourn before the fighting is done."

"A little bit of me dies with every one we lose," Hagen sighed. "I think I am getting soft as I age, old friend. It ails me more and more each time."

"Then I fear you may not survive this war," Daritus replied as his gaze drifted far beyond the wall of his tent. "Our foe has no honor. He slaughtered our emissaries leaving brave Kigan here with just enough life in him to bring a threat to my ears."

Hagen sighed again, "What is the nature of our enemy?"

Daritus replied without breaking his stare, "Giants, trogmortem, and thousands upon thousands of grongs, according to Kigan."

"Trogmortem have come to our shores?" Hagen gasped. "I have studied the little bit of information available about them, but I have never seen one."

Daritus nodded, "As have I. Based on the description our poor friend brought me, I would say they are at least as terrible as described."

Hagen's hand fell to Daritus's shoulder, "I will not try to fool you, my friend. I dearly miss the presence of Ymitoth, Maelich, and Cialia. I have faith in you though, Daritus. You have proven yourself a great warrior and general. Havenstahl is in good hands. I trust you have accounted for far more potentialities than a lesser leader would."

Daritus finally pulled his eyes from the wall and looked at Hagen, "Thank you, my friend. Your faith gives me strength." Then he stood and added, "I only hope I prove worthy."

CHAPTER 17
THE RED DRAGON STRIKES

A heavy covering of clouds hung low in the sky blanketing Biggon's Bay in darkness far more pitch than an average evening when the bright moon would admire her reflection in the water. That was perfect as far as Spang was concerned. His troops would have no trouble avoiding the torches on the beach. Ninety-nine of the finest warriors ever to grace the face of Ouloos fanned out among the trees growing thick along the bluff overlooking the beach of Biggon's Bay. They needed no direction from him. When he moved, they would follow. Each knew exactly what their role was without words or instruction. Together with Spang they were one being, all in tune with one another.

The Red Dragon spared no worry for his flames. They were considered by most to be the finest force in all of Ouloos, at least of the known world. Even though the mission Spang laid before them would be their first in more summers than he could remember, his flames were equal to the task. Only the best soldiers who excelled beyond their peers in training and proved themselves in battle were considered for the trial. And the trial was no dance with a handful of grongs or a pack of amatilazo. It was—to any logical, thinking person—an impossible feat. Yet, all who had earned the honor of calling themselves flame had, in fact, conquered this challenge. A candidate would be stripped of clothing, supplies, and weapons. Then he would be deposited at the top of Mount Destiny—the highest peak of the White Mountains—far to the north where it always snows and the beasts grow large and terrifying. Warriors making it home to the temple atop Mount Zmajvatra—surviving the icy cold, the grizzly mongs, and the horrible halbakurs—became flames in waiting, serving the one-hundred who had already taken the oath. Only when a sworn flame died could their crest be passed along to the next warrior on the list. Lucky for those flickering in wait, the list was never very long. Under the cover of darkness, each of the one-hundred was worth a battalion of ordinary soldiers. Spang *was* worried, but not for them.

The hint of worry distracting Spang just then was spent on his old friend, Daritus. They had trained together and served together as riders of Druindahl. No man stood taller in Spang's eyes. In fact, had Daritus not turned down his invitation to the trial in favor of the love of a young queen, he would be squatting on a branch in the woods west of Biggon's Bay in Spang's place. That man never asked for help. It wasn't that he was too proud or unable to work among a team. He simply knew more about warfare than any man Spang had ever met. He always knew his opponent, and he always knew how to win. That fact troubled Spang more than anything else ever had. If Daritus felt he needed help, that meant he wasn't completely confident he could win.

Voices carrying from one of the ships on the water pulled Spang's attention back to the massive force gathered in the bay. Biggon's Bay was roughly five miles across at its widest point, and from the beach it was about a mile until a sailor would find the open sea. Thousands of ships carrying thousands upon thousands of nightmare creatures filled it. He would fight them all one by one if given the chance. That chance would never come though. It wasn't the mission. The directive given by Daritus was clear. Level the first blow and cause as much destruction as possible without losing any flames.

The Red Dragon pulled his gaze from the horror of massive warships to the equally horrifying tent city that had been erected on the beach. They were gigantic, capable of housing giants and the awful trogmortem. They would all burn. As Spang scanned the beach, it occurred to him that there wasn't enough movement down there. Only a handful of guards strolled about. They had to expect some kind of retaliation after slaughtering a peaceful group of emissaries in such a grossly dishonorable fashion. They were either stupid, arrogant, or he and his flames were walking into a trap. Hopefully it wasn't the latter.

The silent warrior slipped through the trees, moving to a place directly above the path leading back to Havenstahl. Two heavily armed grongs stood on either side of it. They appeared to represent the extent of the night watch. Within the space of two seconds, both grongs sported arrows through their necks, gurgling and gasping for breath as they fell where they stood. Immediately after those twitching, scaly bodies hit the ground, black shapes—barely discernable in the darkness—flooded down the bluff and onto the beach. Mere moments later, tents began burning. As the hungry flames grew, they stretched and expanded to other tents, engulfing and consuming everything in their path. Shapes began pouring out of the burning mess, disoriented grongs mostly. Panic ruled the beach settling into the mobs scattering from the heat. Many that managed to escape their tents fell with arrows poking out of their throats or chests.

Spang raced toward the opening of one of the tents. Fwip…fwip…two more grongs fell. One clutched an arrow jutting out of his chest while the other groaned, tugging helplessly at an arrow lodged in his eye socket. Just before reaching the door of the tent, Spang stowed his bow on his back and retrieved his sword. He was three steps from the door when another grong appeared and lost his head for the effort. The next to emerge earned an impaling through the heart. While still another lost a leg with one slash, an arm with another, and finally earned a boot to the chest that sent him careening into the wall of the tent he had just departed. Spang leapt high into the air flipping at the apex of his flight and landed softly on the sand behind the tent as it collapsed under the weight of the grong crashing into it. While the falling tent burned, several more grongs crawled, rolled, or stumbled out, desperate attempts to escape the flames. Spang paid them no further attention. Panic could have them.

Rolling to the right of the tent he had landed in front of, Spang shot a quick glance toward the shore. The twenty-five flames he had sent to antagonize the ships had begun their task. The hull of one of the largest exploded, brightening the dark sky and spreading flame all across the deck. A smile climbed onto Spang's face just before he ducked to avoid the club of a rather large grong. The Red Dragon spun low, slashing through both of the thing's sturdy legs before rising, spinning again, and slashing its throat. Confusion spread across the face on the front of the oblong head as it sailed skyward. Meanwhile, the grong's scaly body fell slowly to the sand on its stomach. Spang spit on one of the small, armor-like plates growing out of the thing's back as it twitched. Grong's were nasty creatures.

A black shape raced up to Spang's left. "Time to go," it said as it sped by him.

The voice belonged to Vaanx, one of the older flames. Spang quickly glanced around the encampment. Fires burned up and down the beach lighting up the sky above the bay and casting an orange glow all the way to the tress. Vaanx was correct. The first blow had been delivered, mission accomplished. It was time to pull back and wait for the next strike.

Just as Spang began to turn with a mind to race back into the woods at the edge of the beach, he heard a horrible, deep growl. It didn't sound like anything that should occur in the natural world, like the roar of a massive beast grinding boulders in its throat. His gaze drifted back toward the ships—the source of that horrible sound—and saw a gigantic shape leaping from one of the floating fires toward the shore. His eyes widened as he realized that—based on his trajectory—the giant would reach the beach with that one leap. The distance seemed impossible. It was at least three hundred feet, maybe more. Spang recognized Bok as soon as the massive giant's form pounded into the sand. Awe filled him as he sized the massive creature up. It was the closest he had ever been to a giant.

Bok stood nearly twenty feet tall, which is impressive even by giant standards. His features were that of a man—an extremely massive one but a man nonetheless. The head on top of his shoulders was easily the size of a large man's torso. Dagger-like teeth flashed behind an angry, wild sneer surrounded by a black bush of a beard. Long, black hair hung in dirty clumps all around his face. He raised his left hand toward Spang. It was curled around one of Spang's men, squeezing and crushing. The giant roared, "I will eat you all!" Then he bit the head off the body, spit it upon the sand, and flung the carcass into the trees.

The Red Dragon remained silent as he stowed his blade in favor of his bow and fired three quick arrows into Bok's chest. None of them stuck. They all glanced off the giant's immense torso. Spang stowed the bow as the furious animal charged toward him. He rolled between Bok's legs, and popped up behind him with his blade back in his hand. As the giant spun, Spang charged. He leapt toward Bok, planting his left foot on the giant's right knee. From there he sprung toward his left forearm, kicked himself off of it, and brought his foot across Bok's face. Then he pulled his knees in and fired them into the giant's chest before hitting the sand with his hands and rolling back to his feet. The entire beautifully executed move earned him barely a stumble from the massive beast who raised both fists high above his head and pounded them down into the sand. Luckily for Spang, he was spry enough to dive out of the way of those mountainous fists before being crushed by them.

"You're quick, wee man," Bok growled.

Spang remained silent. He leapt high up into the air causing Bok to stand straighter. The leap's trajectory was deceiving though, and he dove low between the giant's legs, slashing his right shin with a forehand before spinning and slashing his left shin with a backhand. Then he popped up behind Bok and stabbed him through his right knee. Bok howled and rolled forward. The giant's agility was surprising considering his size. Spang stayed right on top of him, slashing several times throughout the roll and earning shallow cuts with each blow. Suddenly, Bok stopped short, stood, and swung his hand toward the sand. Spang's momentum would have carried him between the giant's legs. However, Bok's timing was impeccable. Instead of rolling through and popping up behind the giant, Spang caught all four of the beast's knuckles across the entire left side of his body. The giant's hot breath blasted him as he careened back toward the trees. Spang fought to spin back toward the beast, but he was flailing out of control. He did manage to get his eyes around in time to see an arrow pound into Bok's left eye socket just before the monster got a hold of him. The world slowed for Spang as he watched the giant fall to his knees howling and damning all of the Dragon's Flame.

A moment later, Spang was snatched from the air by a black shape. Two more shapes joined and he was quickly shuffled back up the bluff into the trees. As he was carried away, he looked back at Bok. The giant scowled as he knelt, staring at Spang with his right eye. He flinched only slightly as he yanked the arrow out of his left and screamed at the trees, "I will crush you all and feast on your flesh!"

A few moments later, Spang and the black shapes carrying him were deep enough in the forest that the orange glow from the beach no longer reached them. Spang's feet made it back to the ground and all four of the flames scurried up into the trees. Once in the canopy, Spang whispered, "How many are we? Count the Dragon's Flame."

A moment later Vaanx answered quietly, "The Dragon's Flame is ninety-four. Count one hundred, we do no more."

CHAPTER 18
THIEVES

Perrin lay sleeping in her bed. Haleen sat in a chair next to the bed with her new grandchild lying on her lap and gazing up at her with bright, wide eyes that were still grey. Several months would pass before they found their color. She let her hair dangle about his face and shook it. His expression changed. "Oh look at there! Did ye see that? Might that be a smile from me young prince?" she asked, excited.

Kendal leaned in closer, shrugged, and replied, "Ah, probably a bit of gas. It be far too early for him to be smiling."

Haleen's voice jumped at least a full octave as she said, "Oh don't be listening to that grumpy, old papa of yours. I be knowing a smile from me handsome prince when I be seeing one." Then she shook her hair some more around the baby's face and asked, "Right? Right?" Finally deciding she was very correct, she answered for him, "Of course."

"When can I be getting a hold of that lad?" Kendal asked.

"Yeah, yeah," Haleen replied as she looked up at him, "it be hard to be letting him go, but I guess I be having to share."

Haleen handed the new prince up to Kendal who accepted him rather awkwardly, "Ye be minding his head now," she said.

"Ye be acting like I ain't never held a babe, love," Kendal replied as he worked his grandson into a comfortable position in the crook of his left arm, "it's been a time or so, that be all."

Kendal slowly rocked back and forth as he hummed softly at the child, "He be beautiful me dear."

"Aye, he be that indeed," Haleen replied.

Then Kendal looked up at her and asked, "When will she be giving him a name? I can't be calling him baby and young prince for all his days."

Haleen shrugged, "She be waiting for her love so they may be naming their child together."

Kendal humphed, "And where be the great prince?" Then he corrected himself, "I mean king. Where be the king to be minding his kingdom, not to mention his family? Our beautiful girl brung this precious blessing of love into this world, having no help from him I might be adding, and where be he to share the joy, or the burden?"

Haleen rubbed his arm and quietly replied, "I know, I know. Hush that talk now, Perrin won't be hearing that. She be in a fragile state what with his absence. Reminding her will only be serving to increase her sadness."

"Aye," he replied as he shook rather than nodded his head.

Suddenly, something in the periphery of Kendal's vision dragged his attention away. "Shh," he put is right finger up to Haleen.

"What be the matter with ye now?" she asked.

He shook his head, handed the baby to her, and whispered, "Gather Perrin and get her and the baby out of here."

"Why?" she asked again.

Before Kendal could answer, Chimarra screamed from the sitting room adjoining Perrin's bed chamber. Moments later, a shape flew past the archway between the rooms and crashed into the wall amid a shower of dark droplets. Kendal recognized the midwife immediately, but he couldn't see where all of the blood was coming from. Finally, he found his voice, turned, and yelled, "Go," at Haleen.

Haleen stood next to the bed, holding the baby. The commotion had roused Perrin who stumbled out of the bed and huddled in the corner next to her mother. Neither woman made any effort to move as they stared back at Kendal. His eyes bugged as he motioned toward the door with his head. Still they refused to move, the bed between them and the doorway.

Chimarra's screaming melted into gurgling and choking. As her last breath left her lips, the room grew completely silent. Kendal turned slowly toward the darkness, drawing his sword as his eyes scanned the sitting room through the archway. "Who be hiding there?" his voice was big and commanding. The sheer volume of it caused him to jump a bit. He sounded like a man twice his size even though he felt half of that and half again. Kendal was no warrior. He was a father and an inn keeper. Sword play was something he had only picked up from Ymitoth within the past five years as the two had become close friends. Blood was something his blade had never tasted.

The eerie quiet resumed after the boom of Kendal's voice faded. His temple dripped as his muscles tensed; one small bead of sweat slithering down his cheek. Kendal had nearly convinced himself he was brave enough to follow his sword into the darkness through the stone archway, when the silent horror in the darkness came calling for him.

Yellow lights glowing in a pale, blue apparition with smoke all around slowly floated into Kendal's line of sight. His mind groped for some kind of logical answer to the signals his eyes were sending. Perhaps it was a ghost, maybe Chimarra's spirit fighting the Dragon's call to return to the Lake. Maybe it was some form of energy or evil magic. Suddenly, the yellow lights blinked, and Kendall realized they weren't lights at all. They were eyes; long squinty eyes sparkling with a yellow glow when any bit of light hit them. Kendal felt only slightly better once he realized it was a face peeking around the corner at him. If it were a creature, he could probably kill it. If only he had even the slightest idea what type of creature owns a face so grotesque.

The face peeking around the corner at Kendal hovered roughly three feet above the floor. That's what had him so confused. The thing didn't look to be standing upright, but laying sideways on the wall and peering over it rather than around it. As Kendal's brain finally began slipping the pieces together, the yellow eyes blinked again. They seemed too wide and narrow. In fact, everything about the thing was too much. The bony forehead jutting above those eyes stretched too far compared to the rest of the features. The stringy, white hair dangling from the left side of it and falling over the top from the right was too long, too stringy, and too dirty. On the bottom half of the face, a wide, flat nose sat above a narrow mouth with tight, thin lips. The lips smiled as the body carrying that head around slipped out from behind the wall. The creature was about four feet tall with a very slight build. It wore odd, checkered trousers but no boots, and it had several decorations around its neck. The skin of its entire body was the same faint, bluish color of its face.

"What do ye want with us?" Kendal's booming voice was far more menacing than he felt facing off with the strange creature.

The thing continued to stare with those yellowish eyes as it slowly cocked its head left and widened its grin. Kendal took a step toward it. As soon as his foot touched the brick beneath it, a shape flew up from the pile on the floor that used to be Chimarra. Kendal had barely enough time to see that the thing flying at his face looked exactly like the little monster standing in the archway. There wasn't even time to swing his blade before the wee beast was wrapped around his face and biting into his forehead. A howl raced up the back of his throat and poured out of his mouth as teeth ripped up his skin and scraped against his cranium. Once the adrenaline racing through his veins finally reached his muscles, he grabbed hold of the little monster's hair and yanked back on it. At the same time, he brought his right hand up and forced his forearm in between the two of them. Pulling with his left hand and pushing with his right arm, it took every ounce of strength in his body to keep the vicious, blue thing's chomping jaws off of him.

The beast hissed and snapped at him as he turned toward Haleen and

Perrin and yelled, "Run, damn it! Run now!"

Finally, the two women found their feet and shuffled across the bed with Haleen still carrying the young prince. Kendal's eyes squinted as he willed them toward the exit. Perrin's hand had barely brushed the latch of the big, wooden door when Haleen screamed. Kendal watched helplessly as the other blue creature ripped at his wife's hair and violently snapped at her head. She held the baby out with both hands toward Perrin who grabbed him and fell back into the door. The creature stopped biting Haleen long enough to look at Perrin and hiss. Then it coiled itself up and lunged at Perrin at the same moment the new mother slid down the door with her new son. The creature missed its mark and crashed through the heavy, wooden thing leaving a jagged hole and sending hunks of wood and splinters flying all over Perrin and the baby.

Watching his wife stumble around with blood pouring from fresh bites on her forehead sent a surge of energy through Kendal. He re-doubled his efforts against the wee beast wrapped around his head; pushing with one hand and pulling with the other while the vile thing snapped and hissed again and again. He gave the thing's hair one final tug and managed to bring his blade near to its throat. The thing was too damn quick. It flipped away toward the wall before Kendal's sword could find its mark. He missed the throat he was aiming for but managed to earn a shallow cut in the thing's belly. The beast landed on the wall level with Kendal's head and then scurried up toward the ceiling. Kendal absently wiped at his eyes. It didn't help much. The room remained a blur beyond all of the gore pouring down his face. By the time he caught sight of the nasty, little, blue thing again, it was falling from the ceiling toward his face. He swung his left fist and sent it sailing into the carved, wooden head board of Perrin's bed. Then he charged, thrusting his blade as he came.

Slamming into the headboard slowed the beast down a bit, but not enough to give Kendal's sword time to hit its mark. Just before the point pierced its heart, it flipped up and over the blade and landed lightly on Kendal's back. It spun and sunk its teeth into the meat on Kendal's right shoulder as his blade pounded the headboard and he sprawled out on his belly in the bed. Kendal howled again as a chunk was torn from his shoulder. A wild swing behind him with his right hand sent them both flailing to the floor.

While Kendal struggled with the little nasty attacking him, Haleen jumped up and helped Perrin back away from the door with the fresh new hole in it. "He'll be coming again," her intended whisper was more of a shout in Perrin's ear.

"What be them awful things?" Perrin sobbed as she scrambled back onto the bed with her baby just before a long, thin arm ending in a hand with two claws in the front and one opposing in the rear swiped down from the hole in the door to the place where she had been.

Both women screamed as the thing poked its head back through the hole, smiled at them, and dragged a slimy, blood-stained tongue across its lips. Haleen shouted, "Run!" as she flung herself toward the door with both fists aimed at the nasty, little, blue monster.

Perrin slid off the bottom of the bed and bolted toward the sitting room. She gasped as she saw the bloody pile that used to be Chimarra. The sight of the midwife that helped bring her beautiful boy into the world bloodied and broken in a pile against the wall brought a bit of bile up to the back of her throat. She heaved slightly but managed to keep from vomiting. Turning her head away from the shredded, old woman, she crawled behind a heavy chair sitting in front of a large bookcase next to the fireplace. The baby whimpered a bit in her arms while she quietly did her best to console him. Screams and grunting from the other room kept her from peeking around the side of the chair.

In the other room, Haleen had missed the nasty, blue creature's face with both fists. Instead of pounding the little beast, she smacked into the door with her face at full speed. On the other side of the door, the blue thing grabbed her wrists and yanked them down, breaking both of her forearms. She screamed while desperately trying to pull her arms back through, but the thing held her fast and yanked her arms down again. Then suddenly, it sprang back through the hole and latched onto her throat with hundreds of thin, razor-sharp teeth. Haleen's eyes grew wide as she stumbled back to the bed with blood spraying from her throat, coating the walls of Perrin's bedroom along with the blue beast still gnawing at her. As the room darkened, she missed the blue shape fly across the room from the other side of the bed.

Kendal's head poked up over the mattress and came eye to eye with the blue beast that had stopped biting Haleen once her struggling ceased. The smile it wore dripped with satisfaction, as if it read the recognition of what had just happened on Kendal's face. His wife was dead. Tears filled his eyes as rage surged through his body. He dropped his sword and lunged at the monster that leapt up almost clearing the furious man's groping hands. Kendal expected the monster to respond that way and raised his hands high above his head to grab him. The momentum carried them both into the broken door and sent them smashing through it. By the time they pounded into the wall on the other side of the hallway outside Perrin's room, Kendal had a firm grip on the thing's throat. He squeezed with all of his might, causing the little, blue monster's yellow eyes to bulge and foamy red spittle to form at the corners of its mouth. He barely noticed the pain exploding in his destroyed shoulder.

Then the thing dug its claws into Kendal's forearms at the same time as it pounded both feet into his stomach. The combination of the deep, stabbing claws with the blow to his belly, loosened Kendal's grip enough for the beast to slip free of his grip. Once it had, it leapt up onto the window sill directly above them and quickly slashed Kendal's face three times, leaving a series of deep gashes to pour a fresh stream of carnage down his face and mingle with the blood already flowing from his chewed up forehead. Kendal swung wildly at the thing but missed. It leapt up and began flipping over his head, but an arrow stopped its flight before it could land behind him. Instead it landed in heap to his right side.

Kendal wiped his eyes again and looked over at the thing. It was still breathing, but they were shallow breaths. It didn't make a sound. It just lay there quivering and staring at him. Kendal considered the thing for the briefest moment before looking to his left to see the source of the arrow that ended the beast. Four of the palace guard raced toward him and began trying to help him to his feet.

He shook them off and shouted, "Not me, damn it! In there, me daughter and her newborn son be in there with another one of them monsters." Then he tried to get to his feet on his own but collapsed next to thing that nearly killed him.

All four guards charged into the room and through the archway in time to see the other blue creature sniffing around the chair Perrin hid behind. The guard in front—Braggon—pulled out his bow and fired an arrow at the thing. The beast was too quick and flipped backward through the air toward him, spinning and slashing as it reached proximity with his face. It left two shallow cuts in the small bit of cheek not covered by his helmet before spinning around him, hitting the floor, and leaping up toward the ceiling.

"He be a quick one," Braggon yelled as he spun and made ready to fire another arrow.

"Aye," Dirgal replied as he spun and fired an arrow.

Again the beast proved far too nimble and leapt from the ceiling toward Braggon's face. By that time, Braggon had readied his bow. Unfortunately, he released the arrow just a moment too late. The beast was on him, clawing, biting, and grunting. Lucky for Braggon, a fine, sturdy helmet cast of solid prang was standard issue for all members of the palace guard. All of the monster's fury amounted to nothing more than a vicious assault on a sturdy helmet.

Dirgal leveled his arrow at the small, furious creature's head, took a deep breath, and released both the air from his lungs and his arrow at the same moment. From four feet away, the beast never saw the arrow coming. It slipped into its temple with a quiet thwip. The thing turned its head as a look of surprise spread across its face. Then it went limp and would have fallen to the floor had Braggon not grabbed a firm hold of its head and launched it mercilessly at the wall.

Braggon's angry grimace slowly faded as he turned toward Dirgal and asked, "What in Dragon's Fire be that beast?"

Dirgal shrugged and shook his head, "I ain't never seen a beast such as this."

Ybrahm—one of the other two guards—piped up, "Them beasts be the palusculex. They linger in them swamps far to the south and east. They be wily, fast, and smart as any man, strong for their small size too."

Dirgal grinned, "Aye, Braggon will be attesting to that."

The fourth guard, Deegon, interjected, "Come now. Where be the princess?"

Before anyone could answer, Perrin slowly rose from her hiding place behind the chair in the corner. The blood splattered about her face was not her own, though she did own the tears that smeared it. She didn't speak, she merely stood there staring at them, clutching her son tightly, and trembling. Outwardly, she appeared terrified and small. She did feel those things, but they were mixed with rage. The entire assault sent her back to the hut she lived in as a child, that place where she watched a soulless beast maul her family while she hid, helpless, a bystander. This assault was the same. She did nothing but scream, cry, and hide while the people she loved most in the world fought to save her and her baby's lives.

A smoldering flame grew in Perrin's belly as she stared past the four guards. It burned the helplessness and fear away replacing them with something charred and hardened. This new rage wasn't for the blue monsters that attacked her. The fire in her belly blazed against her own weakness. As she stood damning herself, her mind drifted to another who deserved to feel the heat of her ire. There was another equally culpable in the carnage surrounding her, one who should have been there. His son entered the world, and he missed it. Blue beasts snuck into his castle to destroy his family, and he was absent. They had barely begun their life together after all of his adventures, and right after they did, he left again. A new tear formed on Perrin's eyelid. As it slowly rolled over the edge and worked its way down her face, she felt every tickle it made on her cheek. She logged each one in her memory. That—she promised herself—would be the last tear she would shed for fear. This would be the last moment she would be the damsel. From that moment on, she would be her own hero.

"Geillan," she said with strength in her voice.

"I be begging your pardon, princess," Braggon replied. "What be that ye say?"

She held her son out before her triumphantly and repeated the name, "Geillan, I be naming me son Geillan for me father and his father before him. The future king of Havenstahl be needing a name, and his father be absent from his duty. This boy, mine, will be Geillan."

The four guards bowed in unison, "Your Grace," they all muttered.

Suddenly, the outside wall of the sitting room exploded, sending bricks and debris flying about the place. All of the guards ducked, but Deegon took a brick to the back of his head. It carried enough force to send the big guard sprawling out on the ground. The three that remained standing spun, pulled their swords, and moved themselves between Perrin and Geillan and the new hole in the wall. However, Perrin wasn't waiting to be saved. She scurried over the chair with Geillan and raced toward her bed chamber.

A mist slipped into the room with three cloaked figures floating within it. Perrin had just made it to the edge of the archway by the time all three were fully in the room. She gave them the briefest glance as she sped around the corner, barely making it as far as the bed before hearing sloppy, ripping sounds, like muscles and tendons popping when bones are pulled away from other bones. Those horrible sounds were followed by screaming soaked in pain and fear. Perrin didn't slow at all. There was no need to pause and contemplate the ripping and popping sounds nor the screaming. She made the door, turned left out of her room, and raced as fast as she could down the hallway. By this time, Geillan had begun to cry.

Perrin made her voice as soft as she could amid the heavy breaths burning up the back of her throat, "Hush now, sweet child. Mama's here."

Geillan's crying didn't cease though. His screams increased until they hurt Perrin's ears. As the volume of his cries continued to grow, she slowed and looked down at him. The beautiful, bright eyes she had already fallen in love with were hidden behind tightly clamped lids as his heavy cheeks stretched around a wide-open mouth. The skin on those cheeks reddened as his screams continued to gain volume. Perrin held him close, rubbing and patting his back as the churning of her legs slowed. The wailing quickly grew so loud she couldn't focus on anything but the sound. Ideas blew away like dandelion seeds cast about on the heavy winds of the prairie, urged on by the fury of a scared baby's scream. It hurt to run. It hurt to walk. Everything hurt.

Suddenly, a flame shot up between Perrin and the howling child. Intense heat burned her immediately. Shocked by both the flash of light and the pain, she dropped the boy. Before the fact that she had just dropped her newborn child to the hard floor could register, she noticed her gown burning as well as her hair. She fell to the ground and rolled, beating at her clothes and her hair. After a few moments of panic, the fire was out. At least, the fire was out for her. When she glanced back over at Geillan, he was still screaming, but now he was burning too. His entire, tiny body was engulfed in flame. The harder he screamed the more intense it became.

The idea of trying to pick him back up skipped through her head, but a voice behind her pulled her attention away from the child before she could act on it. "My son," the voice boomed loudly enough to be heard over Geillan's wailing.

Perrin turned to see the three figures that rode in on the mist through the broken wall floating down the hallway toward her. All of them had their hoods down exposing wild, orange hair, mangy beards, and black, dead eyes. She immediately recognized the nightmares that had accosted her as a child in the Sobbing Forest. The fear she remembered from that horrible day so long ago had no time to settle in. It fled from the girl who had always played the damsel, hiding from danger and waiting for her brave prince to save her. A consuming rage filled her so quickly and completely she had no time to contemplate her actions or consider being afraid as she stood and faced the three. Placing herself between them and Geillan, she stalked toward them. "Ye can't have me son!" she shouted. "He all I be having now, and I ain't to be giving him up!"

"Poor Perrin," the one in front spoke, "always waiting for someone to save you, hiding behind this and that. Where is your prince now? Who will save you?"

Despite pain settling in on her forehead and down her right cheek where Geillan's flame had kissed her, she stood taller and continued to approach the dead-eyed men. Her volume grew with each step as she replied, "I ain't be having no more time for fear. Ye cowards challenge *me*, a new mother. What ye be having to fear from me? I'll tell ye what ye can be fearing from me. Ye just try and be taking me son from me, and ye'll be seeing what ye be getting from this timid girl. Ye'll be seeing a fury like none ye…"

The leader of the group ended Perrin's inspired rant with a backhand that sent her slamming into the bricks of the wall to her right before depositing her in a heap on the floor. Then he said, "You have grown bold, princess. Pity your brawn has not grown to match your bravado."

Kendal finally gained his feet. Though weakened from severe blood loss, he managed a charge at the back of the three dead-eyed men. After two steps toward them, a growl began in the back of his throat and filled his mouth before roaring out before him. He bore no weapons other than malice and wicked thoughts toward the bastards that would take what was left of his small family. The rearmost of the three turned to meet Kendal's fury and earned a barrage of fists about his face. Kendal moved as if in a trance, pummeling and smashing with all of his might. Despite all of his effort, no marks appeared on the man's face, no evidence of Kendal's brutality. The three began to laugh in one horrible voice.

"Die, ye soulless bastards!" Kendal shouted through clenched teeth as he punched and hammered the man with fists that grew bloodier and more bruised each time they struck.

The assault lasted moments. All the while, the laughter of the three grew. Finally, the dead-eyed man earning the brunt of Kendal's fury reached out with his right hand and grabbed a firm hold of Kendal's forehead. A slight squeeze caused a fresh stream of blood to pour from the wounds there. Exhausted, Kendal finally stopped swinging. The man tossed him against the wall rendering him just another unconscious heap in the hallway.

The leader stalked over to Geillan. The boy's wailing had diminished along with his flame. The dead-eyed man stooped, picked the cherub up, and smiled. "My son," he whispered in the child's ear, "you will be so much more than your father. You will be my champion. You will rule this world by my side. She called you Geillan. I like that. You will be Geillan. These pathetic worms will search for you. They will seek you out, but they will never find us. They will not see you again until you come to deliver them to the Lake in all your flaming glory."

With that, the three floated back to Perrin's chamber and out the hole in the wall they had entered through. Loud footsteps and shouts of guards filled the hallway behind them, but they were far out of reach. Not that the guards would have posed them any challenge, but they had the prize they came for. There was no further need for them to remain in Havenstahl. It was time to bring the king of Ouloos home.

CHAPTER 19
THE ROAD HOME

Cialia sat in the sand next to the Lake of Dragons musing at its stillness. Her perspective was so much different there. Several souls had found their way home as she lounged, yet she felt no sadness for them. Quite the contrary, each cold mist finding its way to the center of the Lake brought her spirits just a little bit higher. Sure they were losing their physical existence, perhaps in horrible fashion. But the freedom, peace, and the sheer joy the Lake represented erased even slightest speck of woe. They were returning home, back to the source, back to Coeptus.

Ouloos continued to spin on as Cialia rested on the beach completely detached, free from the weight of her duties and focused within. She felt so much lighter than she had for several years. No one sought any blessings. No one needed defending. There was only peace, quiet conversations with Helias and the other Dragons, and the perfect stillness of the Lake. She sighed and gazed up toward Helias.

"I am going to have to return home soon," she said.

"You are, fair sister," Helias smiled down at her. "Your people need you."

Cialia sighed again, "I know. Someone always needs something, a blessing to save their soul or a sword to save their hide." She pushed her hands as deep into the sand as she could get them, enjoying the coolness. Then she continued softly, "It is my duty to do all of that saving."

"Yours is a heavy burden, my dear," Helias smiled. "You are a very special soul who gives selflessly to all in need. This world owes you a debt, but you will never seek repayment. Serving others has always been your way."

Cialia frowned, "What if I stopped? What if I decided to stay here with my sisters and enjoy the comfort of this perfect place? Surrounded by my sisters until the end of time, I could be just like the rest of you."

"You could," Helias agreed, "but you would never do that. Even now, even when your mind is completely distracted by the perfection of the Lake, your thoughts are of what you are leaving undone. For a few moments you emptied your head, but even as we speak it all floods back in. Does it not? You are here, of course, but you are also elsewhere."

Cialia shrugged, "You are correct, as usual. My mind is elsewhere. Everything is cloudy though. Perhaps I have pulled within myself like Maelich has. Does that make me bad? Is it wrong to seek just a moment of peace?"

"Not at all, dear," Helias replied. "You have lived in the service of others your entire life. Focusing on you for a few days is not bad, or wrong. Obviously you know the things you are leaving undone now will be waiting for you when you return. You will get to them when you get to them."

"Wise advice," Cialia smiled, "wise indeed. I think I might visit Druindahl."

"Ah," Helias began, "the princess returns home. I think that is a splendid idea."

"Yes I think it is," Cialia nodded as she replied.

"Remember love, a restless spirit only becomes more restless the longer it rests," Helias warned.

Cialia paused for a moment, thought about what Helias had said, and then replied, "Do you think it folly to distract myself this way?"

"Not at all," Helias shook her head. "I think you have spent far too long in the service and spiritual healing of others, and your spirit could use some time of its own for healing. I know you far too well to believe you will give yourself that time. I believe you will ride to Druindahl, spend a few hours, maybe a night of rest, and you will slip back to Havenstahl in a flash, skipping across time like you and your brother are wont to do."

Cialia grinned, "You do know me well, sister. I promise I will try my best not to do that. You can rest assured I intend to take a slow ride to Druindahl. My plan is to enjoy the road for as long as I am on it."

Helias's eyes grew wide, "That could take a week or more if you ride slowly."

"That is my hope," she replied. Then she bowed low and said, "Farewell, good sister, Great Mother, love begotten by love. Thank you for the hospitality."

"Farewell my dear," the Dragon replied. "It has been refreshing to my spirit to have you so close again. You are always welcome here. This is your home as much as any of our sisters. May the road refresh you and bring you the peace you seek."

Cialia barely finished whistling before Purity charged up to the beach.

She mounted, turned toward Helias, pressed the fingers of her right hand to her lips, kissed them gently, and then held her hand out and blew. Helias dipped her head slightly and offered a glowing smile in return. Cialia gave Purity a gentle nudge as she waved to the rest of her sisters soaring about all around the Lake. Good-byes, miss-yous, and well wishes followed them as they trotted slowly away from the Lake of Dragons.

Approximately one hour had passed before Cialia spied the long strip that used to be the Lost Forest. She could see clear across it. The trees were different on the other side. Tall pines mingled with taller oaks. The distance was difficult to gauge, but she knew it to be roughly two miles across. The place had been a thick forest of sadness before Maelich had broken the spell and freed the souls. Of course, she had been there too. Coeptus had said Maelich could never have accomplished what he did had she not been with him. She never really believed that in her heart though. Riding along in someone else's body didn't make a soul feel very useful. Not to mention, after the battle everything was about Maelich. He wrote the book. He had control of the flame. He was the great protector. Fair Cialia babysat the sorry souls in need of saving while the mighty Maelich did all of the important work.

"Where are you now, brother," Cialia asked no one in particular.

She received exactly the response she expected as Purity stepped from the lush greenery covering the ground all the way back to the Lake and onto the dirt of the path Maelich had taken more than five years ago when the Lost Forest still stood, none. Cialia knew it was the same trail because it still looked like normal dirt, nothing special, just dirty, brown dirt like any other dirt anywhere. It bore a stark contrast to the deep red hue that stretched out in either direction from her. That burnt, red dirt marked precisely where the Lost Forest had been and it stretched all the way to the sea in the south. She wasn't so sure how far it stretched to the north. She had never been there, not even with her mind. According to the stories, there is a frozen sea far to the north where the snow flies almost all of the year, even for most of the summer. Those who believe the story say the forest grew all the way to that frozen sea and no snow ever landed upon it. They also say the red dirt remains just as free from snow. Perhaps someday she would challenge that story and investigate, but not today. On this day, she had no real desire to know.

Purity trotted along happily. She was as big a fan of the road as Cialia. Neither had seen it in far too long. The horse neighed as a little more spring entered her step. An uncontrollable laugh escaped Cialia as she rubbed the horse's neck. 'What a perfect day for the trail,' she thought, as she gazed up at the deep, clear, blue of the sky around her. The breeze tossed her hair about and she shook it even more in response. The freedom of the road had been sorely missed. Thoughts of Maelich fled along with thoughts of

Havenstahl. Cialia's mind was completely in the moment; trotting down a trail on a perfect, sunny day, riding her champion mare through a forest that was no longer there.

CHAPTER 20
THE BATTLE AT BIGGON'S BAY

Daritus leaned over a map of the battlefield and surrounding countryside he had spread out on a table in his tent. Kantiim stood across the table from him leaning in the same fashion. Two gold coins had been placed upon the map to describe the locations of the castle and the fort. Five small, wooden sculptures of fallon were placed at strategic points. Each depicted the location of one of Daritus's generals. To the west, the map ended at Biggon's Bay. It was filled with ten wooden ships representing the enemy fleet anchored there. Three of them were overturned. The report sent out by Spang suggested just over a quarter of that fleet had been sunk or at least burned to the point they would be useless for sailing. This fact brought little pleasure to Daritus being Havenstahl had no Navy. The bay was too far for any weapons fired from the ships to be effective on the fort or the castle. In the end, those broken ships would only serve to hinder any attempt at escape.

Along the beach, several simple, wooden tokens represented the various forces they battled against. Among the trees just east of the beach sat a wooden figure of a dragon. "The report from Spang was promising," Daritus said as he looked up at Kantiim. "However, I was quite surprised to learn they lost six during the mission."

Kantiim nodded, "I cannot remember the last time we lost a flame."

"How many await the call?" Daritus asked.

"Ten," Kantiim paused, looked at the ceiling of the tent, and then added, "maybe nine. I fear one may have passed along while waiting."

"It would not be the first time," Daritus looked back down at the map. He adjusted the wooden fallon to the north of the path, dragging it into the middle of the wide road leading from Biggon's Bay to Mount Elzkahon—

the peak crowned by the palace at Havenstahl. Then he added, "Glord has held at the beach, even pushed the vile beasts back toward their ships."

"Agreed," Kantiim nodded, "and Ygraml sits in waiting with twenty-five thousand horses. This war will be short my friend."

Daritus shook his head, "Glord has faced nothing but grongs thus far. The real nightmares have yet to join the fight. What is worse, we have not discussed the casualties he has taken."

"Where do his numbers lie?" Kantiim asked.

"According to the report I received this morning, approximately one full third of his force has fallen."

"After one battle?"

Daritus nodded absently as he continued to scan the map, "Chaag said these grongs fight with a passion and fury he has never seen from grongs before. He said they fight like they are possessed."

"Hmm," he began to pace, "possessed by what, I wonder."

Daritus reached under his cloak, pulled out a shiny circle of prang, and dropped it down onto the table. It landed in the center of the map on its edge and then rolled in a circle until finally coming to rest in the middle of the clearing Fort Maomnosett overlooked. Dread filled Kantiim as he recognized the symbol in the center of the emblem. It was an image of a tiger leaning back and slashing at the air with its claws.

"That is the crest of Brerto," he gasped.

Daritus nodded and frowned, "Indeed. It would appear our adversary is far more powerful than a handful of giants and an army of trogmortem and grongs."

"What will we do?"

Daritus rubbed his neck and replied, "We will fight until there is no fight left in us, and we will have faith our gods will give us strength to protect our lands."

###

While Kantiim and Daritus discussed the new insight they had into the nature of their opponent, the gods they prayed to strolled through the battlefield. Of course, they weren't physically present on the beach at Biggon's Bay or the forest surrounding it. Neither did their feet actually touch the dirt of the road to Elzkahon. They were present, however, and they did stroll among the men and grongs cutting each other down that day.

"Brerto is among us," Moshat said. "I can feel him like a shadow on my soul."

"You do not have a soul, brother. We are eternal," Kaldumahn replied as he surveyed the carnage surrounding them.

Moshat disagreed, "We have debated this before brother, and I do not share your opinion. Nevertheless, it was a figure of speech. The point is, Brerto is here somewhere, hiding."

"He is," Kaldumahn agreed but couldn't resist reviving their old argument. "If we have souls, why was Kallum not spirited off to the Lake when Maelich destroyed him?"

Moshat raised his right index finger next to his face and replied, "That is elementary, Kaldumahn. We were formed from the perfection of Coeptus which are all things. The same materials were used to create us, but we were created separate from all else and before all else, save Dragons. Ours is not to experience and feed the cycle, but to experience and remember so we may guide the cycle toward the path to true peace and enlightenment. That means we can never return to the source of our existence. It does not, however, mean we are not made of the same stuff. We have souls as everything else does. Our souls merely can never return home."

Kaldumahn shook his head, "I agree with all you say except that we have souls. The soul of man is what expresses itself in this physical place. It lives inside a sack of meat, an empty vessel that becomes the identity of a physical creature based on the experiences of that creature. It is limited by the laws of the physical, trapped as if by bonds holding it fast within that context. We exist beyond those laws. We express ourselves as we see fit when we see fit to do so. We can at one moment be a completely physical expression and the next be a completely spiritual expression. We can exist within or without all things. Souls do not share these characteristics with us."

"Then we are souls," Moshat sighed, "souls that are not bound by the rules of the physical prison they were born into because we were never *born* into this physical. We came before it. As usual, you have made my argument for me."

"I did no such thing," Kaldumahn disagreed. "We may be souls. You and I—as individual pieces of Coeptus that are everything—may, in fact, *be* souls. That is not what you said, however. You suggested that we *have* souls, that a soul is a piece of us, a building block. Obviously, that is not the case."

"You are arguing semantics, Kaldumahn. I swear you speak only to frustrate me," Moshat grumbled.

Suddenly Kaldumahn stopped and pointed to the northern point of Biggon's Bay. "There," he said.

Moshat followed the line from Kaldumahn's outstretched finger recognizing Brerto immediately. Long, straight, silver hair stretched back from the figure's face draping down behind his shoulders while his equally straight and perfect beard came to a point around the middle of his chest and bore the same brilliant, silver color. His white gown decorated with prang etchings carried a glow from within. The fact was unmistakable, three gods occupied the beach that day, and they represented opposing purposes.

Of course, none of the warriors battling on the beach could see them. They were there though, and they were all aware of each other.

"Kaldumahn and Moshat, my brothers," Brerto boomed. "How refreshing it is to see you both. It has been years since I bested you on the hill south of the Forgotten Forest. Welcome to the beginning of a new age for our world."

"I remember you fleeing after we beat you back over that hill," Moshat replied in just as mighty a tone.

"Ah Moshat, I would have destroyed Kaldumahn that day were it not for your interference," Brerto replied. "I owe you a debt for that, and it will be repaid in due time."

"Come then," Kaldumahn spat, "come test your might against me, you vile thing."

Brerto shook his head, "You are both simple fools. That is why you cannot hope to win. I will attack you, but I will not attack you yet. You will not know when I am coming, and you will fall."

"Why wait, coward?" Moshat asked.

"There is a plan far beyond the capacity of your simple minds," Brerto retorted. "I could battle you now, but that would not advance my purpose. What is more, I do not need to attack you yet. Though you are gods and bound by no rules whatsoever, you still impose them upon yourselves. I know as long as I sit and watch my work unfold, you are powerless to do anything but the same. Please enjoy what I have prepared for you."

Before the words had finished leaving his lips, thousands of trogmortem stormed the beach. They leapt down from the ships that hadn't burned and charged up from the water. In moments, bodies of men filled the air, tossed into the forest or back into Biggon's Bay. Some splattered against ships and others broke upon the trees. Horrible fangs and slashing claws ripped others to shreds. The surprise assault caught them off guard. Once the shock slipped away in favor of action, Glord called his men to return from the beach, and they formed back up on the path. A large number remained in the sand battling grongs and trogmortem, but those that hadn't made the beach, as well as those who escaped back to the path, fell in line. They numbered ten thousand, and they lined up ten across, shoulder to shoulder from tree to tree, one thousand deep. Shields and spears were all they showed their enemies.

One of the trogmortem charged the phalanx, smashing into it with two back hands, left and right. He earned a spear to the throat for his effort. Eight he killed with two swipes and one more he bit the head off of before breathing his last. More trogmortem came, three, then five, then ten, then twenty. The men at the front fell as the rows behind moved up to replace them. The trogmortem fell far too slowly, one here, two there. They tore through the ranks of Glord's army like a flesh eating disease, tossing men, clawing men, ripping them to shreds, or biting limbs and heads off their bodies. After only half of an hour, Glord's force numbered little more than five thousand men, five thousand men steadily losing ground. Glord blasted his horn. The sound peeled through the forest. Moments later, Ygraml's horn rang through the trees in response. A few more moments after that, the trail rumbled with the sound of twenty-five thousand horses.

Kaldumahn and Moshat watched as Brerto's monstrous force tore through Havenstahl's army. At this rate, they would reach the fair city inside of a week. Unless they rallied, the greatest city of men would fall. Moshat looked over at Brerto who remained at the northernmost point of Biggon's Bay smiling at the carnage unfolding before him. The waves in the bay ran red and frothy pink as they crashed on sand that was equally drenched with blood. Even the trees were spattered with it.

Moshat turned to Kaldumahn and said, "I am going to destroy him now."

Kaldumahn touched his arm and said, "Be still, brother. That is precisely what he wants. I am unclear of his ultimate plan, but I am certain if we attack him now we will help him achieve it. He has yet to assist his troops in their assault. As of yet, he is merely a bystander. We must be the same. Focus your energy into the hearts of the men of Havenstahl. Whip them up as Brerto has done for his monsters."

Then the horses came. Glord's men scattered into the trees and opened the path for Ygraml and his riders. Ygraml led a quarter of his ranks on the charge. His helmet—cast of fine prang and ornamented with a mighty fallon's rack cast of the same prang—shimmered in the sun. Six thousand men on horseback slammed into the trogmortem and grongs filling the road to Biggon's Bay, slashing beasts down and trampling them into the dirt. Arrows filled the air as some of the men fired bows from their mounts.

Once the first charge had passed, Glord's men charged back onto the path reinvigorated by Ygraml's success. At the same time, both Kaldumahn and Moshat focused their intention on the fighting men of Havenstahl, filling them with strength and reinforcing their resolve. Glord's men pushed the vile horde from across the Great Sea back toward Biggon's Bay. Men still fell, but they cut down trogmortem and grongs as they moved forward toward the bay.

When Ygraml's horses made the beach, they swept it and charged back up the trail. Few fell as they cut through the throng of beasts that became less and less cohesive as fear and confusion set upon their hearts. Great trogmortem fell with arrows jutting out of their bodies and grongs were trampled under the hooves of the mighty horses of Havenstahl.

Moshat smiled as the tide turned. He glanced back over at Brerto whose smile hadn't completely fled, though it was waning. "The men of Havenstahl stand tall against you, brother," he boomed across the bay.

"One battle, that is all this is," Brerto spat. "I did not think my army would take Havenstahl in one battle. Nor did I wish it so. I desire a long, punishing war that spreads fear across this land. I want the people of Havenstahl to suffer. Once I feel they have suffered enough, once I know Maelich and that wench Cialia have felt real pain and real fear, only then will I give them the peace of death. War is at your shores, my brother, and it will remain."

The battle raged on for most of the day. The push back to the beach was slow but constant. By the time the men at the front felt sand beneath their boots, the sun had begun painting the sky with pink and orange and red. Just before the sea swallowed it up, a horn blasted from the biggest of the ships in the bay that had not been kissed by the fires of the prior evening. At that signal, all of the beasts in Brerto's horde fled back to their camp. A few men broke rank and gave chase, but Glord blasted his horn. Those that would have continued the assault fell back in line, and then the entire force marched back up the trail to their tents scattered among the trees. Havenstahl had won the day.

Daritus stood at the opening of his tent, watching darkness choke out the last bits of color from the western sky. Twilight had settled into the vast clearing before him, but there was still enough light to see a rider charge into it off the road from Biggon's Bay. His form and standard were hard to make out, but he appeared to be one of Ygraml's men. In moments, he was across the clearing, dismounted, and bent to one knee before Daritus.

"I have news from the front, my lord," the rider's tone was even and emotionless.

"Rise," Daritus replied. "What do they call you?"

"I am Duvel, proud to ride under the standard of the Great Fallon, Ygraml, for the House of Havenstahl," the rider replied as he stood.

Daritus nodded his approval, "Hello Duvel. What news do you have from the front, hopefully pleasing?"

Duvel looked to the ground, "I bring good news and bad, my lord."

"Go on."

"Glord's army numbers only around five thousand men…"

"What?" Daritus interrupted. "That would mean that twenty thousand men died today." He looked up at the sky and continued, "I pray that is the bad news. Where do your numbers lie?"

Duvel nodded, "It is, my lord. Ygraml still boasts numbers over twenty thousand men and horses, somewhere closer to twenty three thousand. That is not even the good news though, my lord. Havenstahl has won the day at Biggon's Bay."

"How so?" Daritus shook his head.

"We pushed the army of grongs and trogmortem back to the beach and sent them fleeing to their ships," Duvel smiled proudly.

"So we have won the first battle," Daritus said quietly, "but at what cost?"

He looked back at Duvel, "Have any giants fallen?"

"None have entered the battle, my lord."

"What are your orders now?"

Duvel scratched his head, "I am to camp here for the night and return to my general by sunrise."

"I have one more mission for you," Daritus clasped Duvel's shoulder. "How well do you know this road?"

Duvel smiled, "Better than I know my own face."

"Good," Daritus patted his shoulder. "I need you to ride to Havenstahl and blow the great horn. I will send word to your general. I have a new plan." He paused, stroked his chin, and then continued, "Go now, blow the twin horn and call Alhouim to fight at our sides."

CHAPTER 21
PAIN

Perrin woke abruptly; feeling pain in every place her soft mattress touched her body. Her eyes darted around the room for a few moments before finally coming to rest on Leisha who sat beside her. The mother of the king sported hair that looked much grayer than Perrin remembered in its tangled and disheveled state. Beneath the tangled mess of gray, tears streamed steadily down a face that appeared to have aged several years in the few days that had passed since last Perrin saw her. The wet eyes dumping all of the tears on that aged face stared across the top of Perrin and out the window. As Perrin watched the tears pour, she realized she couldn't see anything out of her left eye, and the same side of her face throbbed.

The pain held Perrin's focus until the memories flooded back in. She had stood up to the dead-eyed men and apparently been knocked unconscious. Geillan had burned her face. They were there for him. "Where be me son?" she finally shouted.

Leisha jumped a bit, "Oh my dear, when did you wake up?"

"Just now I did," Perrin replied. "Where be me son?"

Leisha reached out and took Perrin's hand. "He was taken by the three."

"What?" Perrin screamed as she sat up. Pain exploded through her head as the dressing on her burns shifted while she rose. At that moment she wasn't sure which pain was worse, the fire burning in her head or the fist squeezing her heart. "Where they be taking me Geillan?"

"Geillan," Leisha began, "so you have given the prince a name? I thought you were going to wait for Maelich to return so he could share in that joy."

Perrin laughed, "Aye, wait for me love I should? Me son might be a brawny, young man before his father be returning from his adventures.

How long should I be waiting? How long do I be letting me son go without a name?"

Leisha squeezed her hand tighter, "I know, dear. I do. I miss my boy too. It pains me he is absent from you right now, and it enrages me that he left you, his son, and his city, unprotected." She paused, looked back out the window and continued, "I fear for him. I have no idea what is going on in his mind right now."

"I can't be caring about where he be off to or what nightmares be romping through his head," Perrin gazed up at the ceiling. "There be one thing on me mind at this moment and that be me son, me Geillan. While me husband be off tending to the road, me boy be needing someone to stand for him. Where did them evil things take me boy?"

Leisha sighed and shook her head, "I do not know. They killed four of our guards and floated off into the night. By the time I arrived, you were unconscious on the floor along with your father, and..."

"And what?" Perrin squeezed Leisha's hand.

Leisha closed her other hand over the top of Perrin's and leaned in closer to her. "My sweet girl, people died trying to protect you and your son, people you love very much."

Perrin's right eye filled, "Who died?"

"Besides the four guards that came to your aid, Chimarra, and..."

"And who?" Perrin's voice gained again in volume.

Leisha looked into Perrin's right eye—the one that wasn't covered by a white dressing—and said, "I am sorry, Perrin. I wish I did not have to tell you this, but your mother was struck down while trying to save you and your son."

Perrin had no more words. Sobs settled in and she submitted to them. Her body shook, her head ached, her face burned, and she wept.

Leisha pulled Perrin's head to her bosom and whispered, "I know dear. Those same three bastards took my son away from me when he was a babe just like they have done with Geillan. He was a man when he returned to me, but he did return. We will find Geillan, or he will find his way home."

"Highness, I need to check her condition, perhaps change her dressing," Meelah had been sitting quietly at the end of Perrin's bed. "That is probably enough for today. She has suffered severe burns, a fracture to her skull, and probably a concussion, not to mention all of the bruising."

Leisha's expression said more than her words as she shifted her eyes in Meelah's direction, "Give us a moment, Meelah. Her life has been turned upside down, and her heart needs just as much healing as her body does right now, perhaps more. You are without child Meelah, is that correct?"

Meelah blushed, "I am, highness. My training with Hagen has left me very little time to pursue any other interests." She paused, chewed on her lower lip, and added, "Please forgive the intrusion. This is very new to me.

Hagen has trained me for years, but this is the first time my training has been tested away from my mentor's watchful eye. He does everything and seems to be everywhere. The only reason I am being tested now is because he is needed at the front with our brave soldiers."

Leisha's expression softened, "I am sorry too. This must also be very frightening for you. Hagen does so much. I did not even realize he was training anyone. I suppose, he is not getting any younger. To be honest with you, I thought you were merely a hand maiden. I had no idea you were to carry on Hagen's practice at the palace."

Perrin lifted her head from Leisha's chest, "I ain't be having time for all of this. I need to be finding me son. Get me a horse prepared for the trail and a few stout soldiers to be accompanying me."

Leisha turned her attention back to Perrin as the corners of her mouth dipped into a frown, "And where will you look for him, sweet Perrin? The power behind the three is beyond you or me or any of the soldiers in our army. You can journey the trails for as long as you wish, but you will find nothing but sorrow and frustration."

"Then what would ye be having me do?" Perrin fired back with far more passion than her weakened state would suggest possible. "Would ye have me haunting the halls of this place like a ghost, an empty shell, weeping over me loss? The woman that would be doing that died when them bastards stole me son. This woman can't be sitting back and waiting for no heroes to come and save the day. I'll be saving it for me self."

Leisha sighed as she looked down at Perrin's face. "No, dear, I wouldn't have you roaming the halls of this place. I would have you leading your people out of it. You are the queen of the people of Havenstahl now, and as such it is your duty to lead and protect them. I am preparing a caravan out of our fair city for the safety of the Forgotten Forest and my former city, Druindahl. I think you should get out of that bed and lead that caravan."

"Why would I be leading me people away from their homes, to Druindahl or any other place?" Perrin shook her head.

"An enemy has landed upon our shores," Leisha replied soberly. "It is a large force; giants, trogmortem, and grongs, lots and lots of grongs. I refuse to take any chances with my people," she paused and then corrected herself, "I mean *your* people. In any event, I have the utmost faith in my husband and the great army of Havenstahl, but I have a bad feeling about this fight. The return of the three has me very afraid, Maelich's absence even more so."

"So we be fleeing then?" Perrin's gaze moved past Leisha. "Me first act as queen will be running away from danger while me soldiers fight and die."

"That is my recommendation," Leisha replied. "The men of Havenstahl often boast of the strength of our army, but they have never faced a force like this. There is a great and wicked power behind this assault. I can feel it. If I am wrong, we will return after the war is over; the only tragedy being untended fields. However, if I am correct and we do not leave, those fields will remain untended as no souls will remain to tend to them."

"Leisha?" Perrin's voice was almost a whisper as she rested her head back on Leisha's chest.

"Yes dear?" Leisha asked.

"How did ye get yourself to keep rising every day after they stole your baby from ye?" Perrin's voice remained soft.

Leisha stroked her hair. "It was not easy, and I remained in my bed for many days after they took Maelich from me. I even neglected my duties with Cialia for a time, counting on a midwife the men who came to fight for us provided. I wanted to die. To be honest with you, I almost did. I stumbled out into the forest and walked for days. I found a bluff. It was not terribly tall, but it would have suited my purpose just fine. I stood at the edge of it for hours, nearly convinced myself to dive off of it a few times. In the end, something made me stay my feet there at the edge of that cliff. Trackers found me standing there, swaying like wheat in the breeze, and brought me home."

"Right now I would be jumping right off of that cliff," Perrin sighed.

Leisha continued, "I thought I would too. Ultimately what kept me from dashing myself on the rocks below was an idea that everything happens for a reason. There are things about this world I do not understand. They are far bigger than me or you or Havenstahl or even— bless her name—the Great Mother. Your son has a purpose, like his father has a purpose, and like his mother has a purpose. If you survive this pain, Perrin, you will be a stronger person than you ever dreamt possible."

Perrin cuddled closer to Leisha, "I don't be feeling very strong right now. I be feeling small and weak and worthless."

"You are already stronger though, love," Leisha countered. "I can hear it in your voice, as soft and shaky as it is right now. What is more, you named your son without consulting your husband. I am unsure if you realize how bold a statement that is in your culture. That is why I questioned you about it, not because I found any fault in the action. Your people are very old fashioned, and women simply do not make decisions like that, no matter what the circumstances. Personally, I think it is wonderful, and your people have made much progress. However, even after Maelich and Cialia opened their eyes to the true nature of things, they still hold on to many of their old customs. The Perrin I knew even a week ago would make no decision, especially one as important as the name of the future king, without first consulting her husband. You are becoming a strong woman who can stand on her own. I am proud of you Perrin."

Perrin sat up and then laid her head back on her pillow, "I hope I be as strong as ye say and not just angry at me husband's absence. I tell ye, I don't be feeling it now."

Leisha patted Perrin's hand. Then she turned toward Meelah and said, "Please see to the queen, Meelah. I think it is time to tend to her physical pain now."

CHAPTER 22
THE OLD WILLOW

The Flagoon River ran from Lake Hirksham in the low hills just southwest of Havenstahl on a meandering route that eventually emptied into the Sea of Sadness. It wasn't much more than a brook as it skirted the edge of the Sobbing Forest and meandered through the prairie, but it became a proper river somewhere around the edge of Pikan's Wood. Maelich and Ymitoth were a good few days into their journey when they reached the forest, following the path of the river. The skies had been fair and the air favorable for keeping a good, solid pace. They certainly weren't rushing though.

Pikan's Wood was a forest basically marking the end of the prairie. Running all the way to the swamplands in the west and just shy of the Sea of Sorrow in the south, it was best known for the large population of willows growing there amongst the oaks. It was a dark, sparsely populated place that neither Maelich nor Ymitoth—nor anyone else in the civilized world—knew very much about. Maelich stopped before the first willow tree he saw. It was quite literally the first willow tree he had ever seen, and it stood apart from the rest of the forest like a sentinel. Maelich mused the massive tree was a wise old wizard far too busy thinking to be troubled with fussing over his hair.

"What an amazing tree," he remarked as he marveled at the long, dangling leaves reaching toward the grass beneath them. "We could live under there."

"Aye, the great willow, she's e'er been a mystery to me," Ymitoth replied.

"What is that?" Maelich asked.

"What?" Ymitoth asked in return.

"What you just said, it sounded kind of poetic."

Ymitoth shrugged, "That be no poem I been hearing of. I like them trees though, only seen them a time or two. This one ye're looking at though, don't she be looking like she be hiding some kind of secret?"

Maelich turned his head slightly to the side and replied, "I suppose so, but I was just thinking this tree reminded me of a wise, old wizard. Perhaps he is wise with secrets." He paused, thought for a moment, and then continued, "It is interesting to me you see this tree as being feminine, and I see this tree as being masculine."

"That be simple lad," Ymitoth smiled. "Ye see wisdom and strength as masculine qualities. When ye think of something wise, ye think of an old man with many years behind him. Ye were raised without a mother. Ye only had the benefit of one perspective on things, mine. Even though ye stood face to face with the wisest, most powerful being in this world, the Great Mother, ideas formed in your head when ye'd been a wee lad remain to shape your perceptions."

Maelich raised his left eyebrow as he shifted his eyes toward Ymitoth, "That doesn't sound like something the mighty Ymitoth would say."

"Aye," Ymitoth agreed. Then he smiled and added, "I had been training a warrior, a champion of Havenstahl. I had to be concerned with teaching ye about strength, courage, and survival. There weren't no room for sensitivity in your training."

Maelich looked back up at the tree, "So I see a wise, old wizard when I look at this tree because of my presuppositions about strength, wisdom, and masculinity. What do you see when you look at this tree?"

Ymitoth smiled and turned toward the tree, "I be seeing a strong woman, confident and proud, proud enough she be hiding her physical beauty behind a wild, shade of hair. She be wise enough to be knowing that if she lets that shallow, physical beauty shine, the dense will be using it to define her, and she be beyond definition. She don't be needing anyone to be flattering her or giving her assurances that she be acceptable. This be her world, and she be defining herself. And if ye be worthy, then, only then, will she be letting ye see her in all her glory. And when she does let ye in, she only be doing it because she be knowing that ye be knowing what she be showing ye ain't being what her true beauty be all about. She be knowing that ye be knowing her true beauty be what she be made of. That be on the inside and only the wisest can be seeing that."

Maelich puzzled over Ymitoth's words while he examined the tree and its long leaves waving in the breeze. "I can see that," he finally decided, "but I can't believe it came from your mouth."

"I be full of surprises," Ymitoth chuckled. Then he sniffed at the air, "Do ye smell that?"

Maelich sniffed, "It smells like roast tubberslat."

"Aye, it does," Ymitoth agreed.

"There must be a village, or at least a hut, nearby," Maelich added.

"Perhaps they be having a bit extra to share with a couple of weary travelers."

"Perhaps," Maelich agreed. "We should definitely investigate."

The two men followed the succulent scent away from the river. The trees became thicker as they walked a meandering path running between the oaks and mostly around sporadic willows. Each of those willows stood alone in clearings, as if the oaks were too shy or too afraid to get close to them. This added to Maelich's awe of this new discovery of his, these perfectly chaotic trees. A dopey grinned slipped onto his face as he looked up at an especially tall one that sat in a wide clearing with wildflowers and large rocks all around it. The branches dangling directly in front of him didn't reach as far down as the rest and gave him a glimpse of the tree's beauty unhindered by leaves.

Maelich left Ymitoth's side and strolled underneath the leaves. He stopped once he was safely in shadow and examined the specimen. Its trunk was a deep brown; similar to the oaks he was familiar with, but somehow richer. Thick branches started low and reached out in every direction, tangling around each other and overlapping as they stretched impossibly far from their source. Deep, green moss that almost seemed to shimmer—as if it were shining in defiance of the shade's darkness—grew in random patches over the trunk and branches. Maelich stood motionless before the beauty, the dopey grin upon his face growing ever wider. Leaves shot up from the branches and cascaded all around him like a fountain of green swaying rather than splashing.

"Why ye be lurking 'round me forest," a creaky, high-pitched, ancient voice asked.

Maelich started a bit and looked around, finally resting his eyes on Ymitoth who was standing behind him in the clearing. Ymitoth looked around and shrugged. Maelich turned his attention back to the tree. The voice certainly didn't fit his expectation of how a tree as beautiful as this one should sound. Moreover, he had never heard a tree form audible sounds. The Sobbing Forest moaned and hummed, but the only words it formed occurred to your mind rather than your ears.

"What is your name?" Maelich asked.

"If there be anybody to call me anything, they'd be calling me Goechal," the voice replied. "There ain't nobody 'round to call me nothing though. Ye can call me that if ye like."

"Okay, Goechal," Maelich replied. "They call me Maelich. My mentor, Ymitoth, and I are off to adventure, and our path led us through your magnificent forest. When I spied your beauty, I had to have a closer look. Please forgive my intrusion and the scrutiny."

Goechal made a sound like the scream of a fallon being taken by an ormacil and then said, "Ye must have something wrong with your eyes lad. This old hag ain't been a beauty in at least fifty summers. The wrinkles keep coming and me back keeps bending and me fingers and toes keep gnarling and twisting so as I be thinking they might end up in knots before I be leaving this world."

"I see the bent and twisted chaos you describe, and I assure you what I see is beautiful to me."

Suddenly an old face peeked out from behind the tree. Wild, ratty, gray hair stood off of the head wearing that face and stretched out in a wildly chaotic fashion before hanging down around it in a mess bearing an uncanny resemblance to the old willow's crown. "Did ye think ye'd been speaking to this tree?" Goechal asked.

Maelich blushed and chuckled, "I did."

Goechal gave Maelich a wide, toothless smile and asked, "Do ye still be thinking me the same beauty ye just described?" Then she hobbled out from behind the tree while leaning on a gnarled piece of wood to help her weak legs maintain her balance.

Maelich looked thoughtfully at her for a moment. A shapeless, black frock almost covered her round body entirely. The only parts of her exposed were the gnarled hands she described and tattered, old boots. Then Maelich noticed her eyes, deep set in the wrinkles carved about her face. They were a pale, creamy shade of green. Even with all of their cool creaminess and the dim light under the great willow, those eyes still sparkled like specs of silicone in sunbaked, desert sands. Wisdom of the years her bent form betrayed lounged about them, but it wasn't alone. It seemed impossible, given the weight of all that time, but youthfulness danced about with that wisdom, a spark refusing to be subdued.

"Your eyes," Maelich finally said, "the beauty I just described shines through in those eyes. They are mesmerizing."

Goechal cackled again, "Ah, ye be a sweet lad to fill up a tired old woman's sails with such compliments. I ain't seen me own eyes in quite a time, threw away all me mirrors years ago." Then she turned and motioned Maelich to follow, "Come ye two adventurers. I been cooking up some tubber for the midday. Ain't nobody else to share with, maybe ye be sharing a bite with me."

By this time, Ymitoth had stepped under the canopy of the willow and was standing beside Maelich. He nudged him and said, "What do ye think?"

Maelich turned to Ymitoth and said, "I think I am hungry."

"Aye," Ymitoth agreed, "I be ready for a feast too."

"Well come on then," Goechal beckoned. "Ye don't want your dinner to be getting cold before ye get to it. Me hut be just in the trees over yonder."

Maelich looked from the end of Goechal's cane to the edge of the clearing in the direction it was pointing and spotted a small, wooden hut; timbers laid upon timbers, a simple, wooden door at the front, only one window he could see, a flat roof, and a simple square chimney made of clay with a weak bit of smoke drifting up from it. He looked back at Ymitoth, shrugged, and the two men fell in step behind the old woman as she hobbled along on her makeshift cane.

The hut was cozy, a modest square room with a simple wooden table at its center, a wash basin against the back wall, and a fireplace on the wall to the right of the door. A small but strong fire burned in the fireplace, warming a large black kettle suspended above it on a hook. It also warmed a small cot covered with a pile of blankets sitting about a foot from the hearth.

"It ain't much," Goechal said as she scooped a bit of stew out of the kettle into two bowls and set them at opposite ends of the table, "but take a seat, warm yourselves from the trail, and fill up them bellies."

Maelich's stomach growled at the aroma of the stew filling the small hut. It was obviously tubber, but the scent was far more complex than the standard roast tubberslat he was accustomed to. "That smells wonderful," he remarked.

"Aye," Ymitoth agreed. "What ye be putting in there to have it smelling so good?"

"That be me secret," she winked. "It be nothing much really. I throw in some potatoes, some carrots, a few mushrooms, the standard stuff. That ain't the secret though. The secret be in the wild herbs what be growing in this forest. Oh they be smelling so wonderful, but just wait until ye taste them. Me Brakken loved me stew, said it be the reason he lived." Her smile drooped a bit and she added, "It's been ages since anyone else had a taste of me stew."

"Well if it be tasting a half as good as it be smelling, I think I'll be loving it too," Ymitoth smiled. "Who be Brakken?"

Goechal gazed over at the fire, "Ah, Brakken, he had been me life. I loved him with me whole heart. He married me when I still be nothing but a young girl, just the beginning of a woman really. He won me papa's heart and took me away. We had a grand life, for a time. Then Cardle, he being our eldest son, he reached that age when lads be aching for adventure. He heard about the myth of the witch of this forest, that vile wench what be calling men from their homes and be tricking them on the trail, Shellar."

Maelich's eyes sparked with recognition, "You mean the She Liar!"

"Aye, Shellar," Goechal agreed. "That vile creature stole me sweet boy and then she stole me husband too. Cardle heard the story from some boys in the village and got it in his head that killing that witch would be making a man of him. I ain't found that out until long after he'd gone, them same boys telling me a few days later. Well after I heard that I got into such a fret.

I begged me sweet Brakken to go find me boy, me heart, me eldest son. I never seen a one of them again."

A puzzled look found its way to Ymitoth's face, "Why ain't I heard of this myth?"

"Well she ain't a myth now, is she?" Goechal replied. "She got me husband and me favorite son."

"I learned about her when I was a lad," Maelich thought for a moment and then added, "I can't remember from where. It doesn't really matter anyway. The important thing is I know of this beast. The She Liar is a giant, formless blob. If you saw it with clear eyes, it would resemble an enormous, misshapen bubble filled with thick, swamp muck. It is wise though, one of the oldest creatures in this world, and it can introduce thoughts into a man's head," he explained.

"Yes, yes," Goechal agreed, "that be what them stories be saying about her."

"How does she be killing anybody?" Ymitoth asked.

Maelich continued his story, "She takes advantage of men when they are weary from travel and their minds are dulled from the trail, lifting herself up off of the ground and showing them a grand feast. As the story goes, men are enticed under her shade and imagine themselves in a grand ballroom filled with long tables overflowing with the most succulent dishes. When they fully give in to the illusion and begin to gorge themselves, she collapses around them holding only her middle up like a giant mushroom cap to trap them beneath her. Then she takes the vision away and exposes her true form. On her underside at her center sits her mouth, or at least the thing she eats with. It looks like a giant beak, as long and wide as a large man. Her tongue is twelve feet long and whips out the center of that beak-like mouth, wrapping around her victim's legs and pulling him in so that row after row of sharp, little teeth can grind his body to sauce. The She Liar feeds on men."

By the time Maelich finished his story, Goechal was weeping. Maelich draped his arm across her shoulders. Her frailty surprised him. "I am sorry for that description. I lost myself," he said.

"No," she shook her head, "I ain't thought of Brakken or me boys in quite some time. I been alone a long while and I ain't thought of nobody. It be good to remember those ones what left ye, even if it be hurting."

"Boys?" Ymitoth asked. "Ye be having other sons?"

"Aye, I did," Goechal replied, "Bingot and Drychal. They'd been wanting to chase after their papa and their brother, but I heard none of it. Them lads were good, twins they were. They stayed with me here until well beyond the time they should have been leaving for the trail that calls to all lads as they grow into men before they finally settle down with a nice lass." Goechal grew quiet, wiped her eyes, and looked at the floor.

"Where they be now?" Ymitoth asked.

Goechal sighed, "Amatilazo came one night, tearing up the village. A time ago this had been a village, small, but a village nonetheless. Well, me boys took up their swords and put a fighting to them evil things. The beasts bested Drychal with most of the rest of the village. In the end, it was Bingot what scared the last few away, or they be just fat enough from feeding on the rest that they ain't been having no energy or want of more blood to be having another go at him. They got him good before they ran off though, and me middle boy died in me arms. I buried many bodies that day."

"I am so sorry for all of your loss," Maelich pulled her closer. "How long ago was that?"

"Oh, years upon years I be guessing," Goechal replied as an aftershock of her sobbing caught her. She heaved a few times beneath Maelich's arm before her breathing became steady enough for her to continue, "Too many to be counting. Me hair had still been dark and beautiful then, just a wee bit of gray. It was a time ago to be sure."

Ymitoth slurped a bit of stew off of his spoon and then said, "Misses, we can't be bringing any of your boys back to ye. They must be long called home to the Lake. As sure as there be a mighty beard upon this grizzled, old face of mine though, we may be able to bring ye a bit of peace. Maelich here be looking for adventure. Might be a good cause to be ridding your beautiful forest of that thing what took your son and your husband away." After he finished speaking, he quickly stuffed another spoonful of stew into his mouth and chomped away at it.

Goechal's eyes glistened as she replied, "I ain't one for revenge mind you, but I'd be feeling a bit better knowing that wicked thing be dead and can't be bringing no harm to no other mother's sons."

Maelich gently rubbed her shoulders and said, "It is settled then. We will make camp out among the trees tonight and hunt down that nightmare in the morning."

Goechal wept again. "Oh ye be good men. I got nothing to offer ye but a hot meal and ye don't owe me nothing. I be resting easy if ye can really be doing this for me," her words came slow and choppy, laced among the heavy breaths accompanying her tears.

All three remained silent except for Goechal's sobbing and Ymitoth's slurping. The old woman cuddled closer into Maelich's chest, as he squeezed her just a little bit tighter. She would be his damsel, not quite a fair maiden but definitely in distress. Even though her peril wasn't imminent, Maelich knew she needed peace. He rested his head on Goechal's until her sobbing ceased.

Goechal's composure slowly returned as her crying lessened and then finally ceased. Once she had a firm grasp of her voice again, she said, "There be one more thing I be hating to even ask with all ye be doing for me already."

Ymitoth finished draining the last of his bowl and set it on the table, "Ye just be giving it a name."

She pointed to an artfully crafted wood carving mounted on the wall above the mantel of the fireplace, "That be a carving of me husband's crest. Maybe not as mighty as the great fallon the two of ye be wearing, but he hailed from a proud city just the same. His symbol be a great fish breaking the surf."

"Aye," Ymitoth nodded, "that be a fine emblem indeed. Your husband hailed from Belscythia, did he? That be a solid port town. Belscythians be sturdy folk."

Goechal looked up at the wooden emblem above the mantel and said, "If I could only be getting that crest returned to me, it'd surely be giving me a bit of peace."

"Of course it would," Maelich agreed. "As the summers have come and gone, you have been assuming your husband met his end succumbing to the wiles of that vile witch. Yet, you have never seen proof of this. Belief is all you have. I will do my best to help you justify the faith you have carried in your husband and your son. I will gut that beast and search her remains for that emblem. Did your son carry the same mark? Did Cardle bear the crest of Belscythia?"

Goechal shook her head slowly, "No, Brakken and me we talked of letting him travel to Belscythia to be taking them trials there, but we be simple, forest folk by then. We feared for what that big town might be doing to our good lad."

"That be quite wise misses," Ymitoth interjected. "Belscythia be a fine town, but she be having a dark side too. Some of them wharf folk don't be the type ye be wanting to encounter after the sun has bed down for the night."

Goechal turned her head toward Ymitoth and nodded, "Aye, that be just what me Brakken told to me." Then her eyes widened and the corners of her mouth drooped slightly as she turned her head toward Maelich and asked, "What if ye fail?"

"Fail?" Maelich smiled with left side of his mouth. "I had not thought about it."

"The lad typically don't," Ymitoth added as he helped himself to some of the stew Maelich hadn't given any attention to.

Maelich gave him a dismissive glance, "It is my duty as a warrior of Havenstahl to stand up for those who cannot stand up for themselves. You need me and that is enough to give me strength over any fear I may have." He paused, looked up at the crest of Belscythia, and then continued, "I assure you though, Goechal, I know all of the stories of the She Liar and I know all of her wily ways. My opponent will not be a mystery to me when I face her. I truly have no fear. If she bests me and I fall before her might, it is of no fault of yours. You are not sending me to face this wicked thing. I am making a conscious choice to free you from the pain of not knowing for certain what happened to your husband and son."

Goechal raised her bent, gnarly, right hand and gently patted the side of his face. "I believe in ye, Maelich. Moshat his self must have sent ye to me."

Goechal wiped her eyes one more time, then stood and hobbled over to the fire. By the time she returned to the table with the kettle, Maelich had managed to wrestle his bowl away from Ymitoth. The old woman refilled all three of the bowls, giving Ymitoth a wink as she filled his bowl high enough to give his stomach all it could handle. Ymitoth smiled up at her and shamelessly began stuffing his face again.

The three finished eating in silence. Goechal wouldn't allow her two heroes to sleep out under the trees, so they slid the table against the back wall of the hut and gathered their blankets upon the floor near Goechal's cot. The little fire kept the room surprisingly warm and sleep came easy. That was a blessing. The coming sun promised an adventure requiring the wits of men working off of a good night's sleep.

CHAPTER 23
REMEMBERING THE HERO

Purity trotted alongside the wide, red, dirt path that used to be the Lost Forest. Cialia sat astride her, loose and carefree. They had been following the border of the old, invisible forest for five days and had only just begun encountering loose groupings of pines marking the edge of the Forgotten Forest bordering it on the east. The green of the trees and the grass, the blue of the sky, even the red dirt that used to house a thick, terrifying prison for lost souls, filled Cialia with memories she longed to relive. Her world had changed so much since she faced the Eagle with Maelich and pushed Ouloos into a new age. Prior to that day, she had been a warrior and a soldier, the protector of Druindahl. She excelled beyond all of her contemporaries with a sword, bow, or knives. Her skills could best any young man in service of the Dragon. After that moment, when she and Maelich, fused together as one being, one presence, one intention, plunged that blade, imbued with the incomparable power of Dragon's fire into the heart of Kallum, she became something else. Now instead of being a warrior, she was a teacher, consoler, and spiritual guide. It was satisfying work, but it was like a prison for her free spirit that wished only to soar, free from the shackles of thought and worry.

She inhaled the fresh air and giggled as a stiff breeze blasted her. The scent of the pines and bush flowers of the forest launched her back to her childhood; a place where she could ride the trails bareback on the first mare she found ready in the stable, unencumbered by the weight of responsibility. If only she could go back there and live for a week as that free child again, or even as the warrior that child would grow into, just a week in the world she occupied before that great explosion of a god changed everything for her. She would race to there in an instant. Sadly, her world was what it was now. She had learned quite a bit about manipulating space and time, but she had yet to learn how to turn it back. Perhaps someday she would solve that riddle. For the time being, she would enjoy the shadow of days gone by and the break from the worries Havenstahl, the trail, and Druindahl could offer her.

A scream off in the distance where the forest began to grow thick around the trail snapped her attention away from her musings about the past. Urgency laced itself around the scream. Cialia focused her eyes toward the source of the sound and focused her intention toward that place. In an instant, she was hundreds of yards into the darkness of the Forgotten Forest. A young girl wearing a tattered and torn, white shirt, stained with dirt and maybe a bit of blood, sat against the trunk of a tree on the side of the path. Her bare feet pushed at the dirt in front of her as if she were trying to push herself into or through the great tree. Long, thin, dirty, light-brown hair hung carelessly all about the girl down to her chest. It mostly obscured her face, but Cialia could see enough of it to know the poor soul was terrified.

Cialia glanced up and located the source of all that fear. Four horsemen bearing the crest of the Dragon, the crest of her fair city, Druindahl, bore down on the girl. "What is the meaning of this?" Cialia demanded.

The man farthest left of the group, from Cialia's perspective, casually looked over at her, shook his long, brown hair so it fell behind his broad shoulders and replied, "Mind your business, wench. Move along or you can join this little trollop."

Cialia's eyes narrowed, "You are riders of Druindahl. What has this young girl done to deserve your wrath? Name yourselves to me!"

The man, who had first addressed her, pulled up on his horse's reigns and then gave the animal a couple of kicks to urge him toward Cialia. Once he was face to face with her, he leaned in a little closer and said, "They call me Antian." Then he motioned back toward his group and continued, "Those are my brothers, Bantios, Varmillian, and Limbriam, and yes we are riders of Druindahl. Considering you recognize our mark, you should also recognize how much danger you are in right now. You should recognize that the blades we carry at our sides are some of the most lethal weapons in all of Ouloos."

Cialia's face contorted uncontrollably at the foul odor of Antian's breath. She quickly composed herself and replied, "Now I know who you are. Perhaps I should enlighten you as to my identity to help inform the next words that leave your rancid smelling mouth. I am Cialia, princess and protector of Druindahl. I will assume you are new to the ranks of Druindahl's army as I do not recognize you and you, obviously, do not recognize me. Therefore, I am willing to forgive the transgression and disrespect you have shown me. However, I will not ride off without the satisfaction of an answer to my original query. What has this young girl done to deserve the wrath of Druindahl?"

Varmillian gasped and piped in, "Stand down, Antian. The king will take our crests and banish us if he hears we have treated the former princess of Druindahl so clumsily."

Antian ignored his brother and continued to stare stern-faced into Cialia's eyes. Through his scowl he said, "The man on the end over there, my brother, Limbriam, do you see his face?"

Cialia looked over at Limbriam. He had four fresh looking gouges on each of his cheeks. A bit of blood oozed from here and there among them. Though they still appeared fresh, a red tint and slight crustiness of his beard gave the impression the cuts had been oozing for a time. Cialia turned back to Antian and replied, "Your brother was scratched fairly well. What of it?"

"That lowly bar wench did that to him before she locked the four of us in a storage closet. She has some punishment coming her way," Antian spoke quietly through his scowl.

"Perhaps we should save it for another time," Varmillian interjected with a slight quiver in his voice.

"Get a hold of your balls man," Antian raised his voice. "This is the celebrated champion of Druindahl, a wee wench. I have been waiting for a chance to test my blade against this one." His expression softened into something that mocked a fun-loving smile as he laughed and added, "Imagine, the champion of a great city of warriors is a wee girl."

"I can see we are not going to be able to solve this matter with words," Cialia said calmly. "I can also deduce by your tone and foul demeanor that your brother earned the scars those cuts will become. It appears the rest of you have earned some scars as well. I am happy to bless your flesh with my blades if that is your desire."

As the final word left Cialia's mouth, she leapt up from her saddle so she was standing upon Purity's back a moment before she flipped backward off the horse and landed softly upon the forest floor with a sword in each hand. The moment Cialia's feet left Purity's back, the horse reared up and kicked its front legs at Antian, backing him off before trotting over to the tree and placing herself between the battered young girl and the other three riders.

Antian's horse took several steps back in response to Purity's action and almost spilled his rider out of his saddle. A moment later, the big horseman slipped off of the mount under his own accord, unsheathed his sword, and fetched his shield from the back of his saddle pack. The grime covering the shield and obscuring the shimmering prang it had been cast from bespoke Antian's time on the trail. Cialia could tell the massive man was an active rider who spent more time off on adventures than he did protecting the city he rode for. Aside from his shield, everything about his appearance from his trousers, to the random bits of fur decorating his jacket, and on down to his blade, betrayed him as a nomad.

Cialia examined the man as he raised his shield up with his left hand so the top edge of it sat just below his eyes and raised his sword up, bent-elbowed above his head with his right. He obviously had not learned his blade techniques from any of the master swordsmen of Druindahl. None employed an attack position or a defensive position resembling anything near what Antian displayed. The brute lacked the refinement of a well-trained soldier. Despite that, he carried himself with a confidence only gained through fighting and surviving. His huge frame and bulky build added to it. Standing a full two heads taller than Cialia and at least twice as wide, he was a giant by the standards of men.

"This is your last chance, wench," Antian growled, "get on your little mare and ride away, or die on the end of my blade."

Cialia wasted no additional words on the massive brute. Instead she lowered both of her blades to her sides, turned her wrists out, and charged him. After three long strides, she pounded both feet into the ground and leapt high above Antian's head, flipping and twisting at the apex of her flight. The big man spun beneath her, slashing with a backhand. Cialia crouched deep to avoid Antian's blade as she landed softly upon the dirt of the trail. Instantly, she spun to the left and fired her left leg out, sweeping Antian's thick legs out from under him. She rose and planted a foot in his chest a moment before his big body crashed to the ground.

"Bitch," Antian grunted as the trail knocked the wind out of him.

Cialia caught movement in the periphery of her left side. Bantios and Limbriam had dismounted, made ready for battle, and charged. She turned to face them just as Varmillian yanked on the reigns of his horse and fled back up the trail. A moment later, two blades were slashing at her in unison from different directions. She parried them both on her way into a dive and roll that left her behind her new opponents. Once back on her feet, she flipped toward them, turning her body so it was perpendicular to them, and smashing Limbriam with the handle of the blade in her right hand while her left heel hammered Bantios's jaw. She landed in a crouched position in front of the two who stumbled in either direction.

Cialia had only a moment to collect herself before Antian let out a wild howl and charged like a stampede of tubber from behind her. His feet pounding the trail betrayed his position to Cialia's keen ears. She waited motionless until he was all but on top of her before she slipped to the left leaving her right leg extended to trip the charging brute just as he was slashing his blade down with both hands. His momentum sent him crashing into his brothers who were themselves just regaining their balance from Cialia's attack. All three ended up on the ground in a pile of hairy, barbarous anger.

Cialia spun, struck a defensive stance, and chided the big men, "It looks as if this wee wench is too much for you big, strong men to handle. Now, get on your horses and report back to your general. I will be having words with your king concerning how roughly you have treated this young woman and how you have conducted yourselves in my presence."

Antian struggled to his feet and spit in Cialia's direction. "You won't be reporting anything to anyone," he roared. "You will have to do more than flip around and trip me wench. I am going to shatter your bones."

Cialia shook her head and replied, "So be it," as she sheathed both of her swords and brought her fists up to a guard position.

Limbriam chuckled, hit Bantios in the shoulder, and said, "Look at this arrogant, little runt now. She means to challenge us with her bare hands."

"Oh, let me flee in fear," Bantios replied in a mocking tone a couple octaves higher than his normal voice.

This sent both Bantios and Limbriam into fits of laughter. Antian didn't laugh though. He merely squeezed his sword tighter and continued to scowl at Cialia. "Boys," he began in a low, gravelly voice, "bring your minds back to the moment." He paused until their laughter subsided, "This wench is wily. She reminds me a great deal of Abrilan, Hebrom's son."

Limbriam smiled and said, "Ah yes, Abrilan, champion of the Angors. He was a wily one."

"Champion indeed," Bantios humphed. "The Angors are nothing more than a pack of savages. You elevate his memory to levels it doesn't merit, brother."

"Agreed," Antian's tone mellowed slightly, "the Angors are a savage people still. However, those savages pushed the mighty army of Balacyl to the brink. Remember how downtrodden King Prian was when he engaged us and the other swords for hire to assist him in the defense of his city? One name rolled about his lips like a bad taste. Over and over again he said it. What was that name?"

"Abrilan," Bantios replied quietly.

"Yes, Abrilan," Antian concurred. "King Prian was convinced that Abrilan was the champion those foul Angors rallied behind."

"He was quite correct too," Limbriam added. "Once Abrilan fell, the Angor assault ended quickly."

"Yes, Chief Hebrom fell into a deep melancholy at news of his son's death and his forces fell to chaos without any leadership." A wide smile spread across Antian's face, "Abrilan took us to the brink before I ran him through, and he fought much like this wee wench standing before us now. We'll do this one just as we did Abrilan."

Cialia had remained silent during the conversation. She lowered herself to her knees, folded her hands in her lap, closed her eyes, and focused on her breathing. A deep breath in carrying the sweet, earthy scents of the forest filled her lungs and reminded her of younger days. A long, slow breath out expelled anger, anxiousness, and hatred for the three foreign riders bearing the crest of her home. Vagabonds and marauders, they held no love for any land or cause, just coins in their purse and a place to victimize those weaker than them. They were takers. They would only remain as long as it suited their needs and then they would move on to the next patron of their services, like parasites seeking their next host. Cialia drew in another deep breath releasing more negativity out with it as she exhaled.

A few moments passed as Cialia knelt motionless on the forest floor, inhaling fresh, sweet memories and exhaling evil, violent thoughts. She was a protector, a champion of the people, all people, including the bad ones. Her motives could not be fueled by baser, human emotions. Duty was all that should drive her. As the breaths came in and the breaths went out, her mind grew quiet. Everything became quiet. The only perceptible sound to Cialia was the steady rhythm of her own breathing.

Cialia's steady breathing continued as she lay her head back on the forest floor barely avoiding Antian's blade. Her eyes snapped open and she rolled backward to avoid Limbriam's blade as it slashed down at her belly. She wound up on her feet between Antian and Bantios. Both slashed vertically at her. One step backward kept her safely out of the way of their hungry swords. A dive and roll forward carried her over the top of a horizontal slash at her midsection that Bantios followed his assault up with. From the roll, she leapt—flipping and spinning over Limbriam's head—and landed softly on her feet behind him. He spun, slashing with a backhand. This time, Cialia stepped into the assault, blocking Limbriam's forearm with her own and tripping him up by placing her leg between his as he spun. The befuddled warrior lost his sword as he toppled to the ground.

Limbriam had barely hit the forest floor when Antian leapt over the top of him, vertical to the ground with both of his feet aiming at Cialia's chest. She took one long stride to the left and launched herself through the air, pounding both of her feet into his stomach, crouching deep as if he were a flat surface, and then flipping backward off of him. Her feet hit the ground as softly as a butterfly landing upon a flower petal. The forest floor was far less forgiving to Antian who pounded into it like a falling tree.

Cialia had but a moment to collect herself while Limbriam and Antian struggled to regain their feet. That moment was cut even shorter by Bantios who charged at her, slashing his sword down as his heavy boots pounded the dirt. The momentum of his attack carried his right hand up to his left cheek. A backhanded slash brought his sword down again. This time the follow through carried his sword high above his head on the right side and he slashed down again with a forehand. As he came forward, he repeated these strikes with every stride, backhand, forehand, backhand. Cialia moved backward, matching his pace step for step and dodging left or right depending on which side the attack sprang from. Finally, after dodging right, she stepped in with her left foot and hammered his jaw with a left backhand that she followed immediately with a right hook. Bantios's eyes rolled as his knees went slack. He stumbled for three steps to his right before falling in a heap on the forest floor.

Without pause, Cialia continued to spin from the hook that helped Bantios to the ground, lifting her left knee up, just before firing her right heel across Limbriam's jaw, and dropping the big man where he stood. She landed softly upon the ground again and sized up the last man standing. Her face wore no expression as her eyes finally met his. No emotion troubled her thoughts. She merely had a job to do. A young girl had been misused and needed to be spoken for.

"You and your brothers have lost," Cialia informed Antian, her tone as expressionless as her face. "I would prefer not to inflict further injury on you. Please follow me to Druindahl and we will let the king sort this out, or gather your brothers, leave this forest, and never return."

There was nothing fun-loving or comical about Antian's laugh. It was dark, borderline maniacal, and saturated with bad intentions. After his laughter subsided he replied, "I am unimpressed with the former champion of Druindahl. How can you expect submission when you have offered no pain? For all of your acrobatics, I remain unscathed. Tossing and flipping your body around, you belong in an entertainment troupe. You are no warrior in my eyes."

Limbriam and Bantios managed to regain their feet while Antion mocked. Both gathered their swords and moved back into positions that effectively formed a triangle around Cialia with their brother. With quickness that didn't fit his large size, Antian reached under his jacket and fired something at Cialia. It glinted once, twice, three times as it approached her face. To Cialia, the movement was slow, as if it were floating down a lazy stream rather than cutting quickly through the air. It was a small throwing knife, its blade reflecting the sun every time it came around.

Cialia remained expressionless as she brought her right arm up across the front of her body in a circular motion. The knife glanced off her prang gauntlet a moment before it would have struck her eye. It careened to her right and continued its flight. Limbriam was not quite as fast as Cialia. A moment after the blade glanced off of her wrist, it buried itself in his throat. Her eyes remained locked on Antian as his expression melted from mocking hubris to shocked sadness, deepening as the gurgling sound coming from Limbriam increased.

Cialia inhaled deeply and slowly, held the breath in her lungs for a moment, and then released it just as slowly. Then she said, "Your brother Limbriam is on his way to the Great Mother. His journey to the Lake is about to begin. You have killed him with your own blade. Please submit so you do not have to follow him."

"Foul bitch," Bantios screamed as he lunged at her.

She spun to her right narrowly avoiding his blade and letting him charge by on her left side. As he passed, she brought the outside edge of her right hand down upon the back of his neck. His knees went slack as she connected, and he dropped like a stone. His limp body twitched twice and then lay still.

Antian had remained completely still, aside from severe trembling in his upper body caused by the intense grip both of his hands held on his sword. His eyes misted as his lips formed words with no voice to carry them forth. He stared at Limbriam lying on the forest floor and clutching at the dagger poking out of his throat. The vision of his brother bleeding out in the dirt was nearly as devastating to Antian as the horrible gurgling sounds spilling from the dying man's mouth as he tried to speak.

"That is your blade Antian," Cialia broke the silence. "Your anger has ended your brother's time among the living and sent him home to the Great Mother. I do not wish to cause you any further pain. Please stop this now."

Antian slowly moved his gaze from Limbriam's struggle to Cialia. His face tightened until it appeared as if the skin of it might rip right off of his skull as he said through clenched teeth, "This is the day you die, bitch. Your death will not be swift, and it will not be peaceful. I am going to punish you, break you, and cut you up before I let you follow my brother to the Lake. Then I am going to carry your lifeless corpse around as a trophy and do unspeakable things to it every time thoughts of my brother enter into my head."

"I am truly sorry you feel that way," Cialia replied quietly. "Come then, finish this."

Cialia unsheathed both of her blades and walked toward Antian who answered by bringing his blade up to an offensive position. The greatest hero Druindahl had ever known was three steps from Antian when he brought his sword high up over his head and slashed down at her. A quick step to the left kept the blade from tasting her flesh, and it hammered the ground instead. Immediately after hitting the dirt, Antian slashed again, horizontally, level with her waist. She leapt high over the blade and landed softly in the exact spot she had been standing prior to the attack.

"Fight me, bitch," Antian roared as he launched a furious assault.

Cialia remained silent as she danced around Antian's attacks. They were quick and random. The blade came faster and faster as she flipped, dodged, and contorted her body to keep it away from her flesh. She allowed the assault to continue for a few moments. Antian's rage seemed never ending. Finally, Cialia gave in. Death was all Antian understood. His soul would have no peace until he found it, so she gave it to him. The blade stabbed at her a final time. Parrying the thrust with the blade in her left hand, she stepped to the right and slashed Antian's throat open with the blade in her other hand.

Antian stumbled about a bit, his eyes blinking rapidly. A confused expression slipped onto his face as if his mind were troubled by some question he could not reason an answer for. The sword fell from his hand, chiming like a bell as it struck a stone on the ground. Two more stumbling steps proved to be the last he ever took, and he fell to his face amid a pool of his own blood.

Cialia knelt and bowed her head. Taking life was something she took no pleasure in. There had been a time in her life when she did. A warrior's death was honorable, and there was no greater gift she could give to an opponent than a glorious death. After battling Kallum, that all changed. More specifically, after Coeptus had opened her eyes—and the rest of her senses—to the truth of life, she gained a different view of Ouloos and all who inhabit it. That is when she decided it was not her duty to judge anyone. She was a guide to help souls find their way back to the Great Mother and back to the Lake. Sometimes it could be accomplished through words and teaching. Sadly, other times it could only be accomplished with a blade. Antian and his brothers were foul, villainous takers lacking the honor of real soldiers. They were mercenaries, swords for hire. Coin was the only cause they fought for. Someone taught them to be that way though, and the Lake would have them just the same.

Her thoughts were interrupted by arms around her neck and a head on her shoulder. Then a shaky voice whispered, "Thank you," quietly in her ear.

Cialia smiled, opened her eyes, set her swords down, wrapped her right arm around the young girl, and said, "It is my duty to protect those in peril or need. You look familiar to me. What do they call you, and what led to Antian and his brothers attacking you?"

The young girl cleared her throat and said, "My mother gave me the name my father picked for me, Keiryn. He died the day before I was born. I have been helping out at Glandon's Pub."

"I remember you now," Cialia interrupted. "You were the little girl always pinned to Tesha's hip while she served the drinks. I hardly recognize that little girl in the young woman before me. Five summers ago you were a hair more than a bright faced tot."

Keiryn blushed through the grime on her face and smiled, "I am not pinned to mother's hip any longer. I serve the drinks in her stead now. She has grown quite ill."

Cialia frowned, "I am sorry to hear that. I have fond memories of your mother. When I was a girl, she would keep me occupied if father was at the pub having a chat with the men. I would like to see her after I speak to your king. Now why were those men mishandling you?"

Keiryn shrugged, "They were at the pub drinking and having a merry time. At first they were fun and playful. They kept ordering drinks and telling jokes. Then that one," she pointed over to the heap that used to be Limbriam, "put his arm around my waist and pulled me to him. He told me I was beautiful and he would take me away. I pushed his arm off and he got back to laughing and talking with his brothers. They kept drinking though, and he began to get very grabby with me." She paused and stared off into the trees.

Cialia touched her hand and said, "Do not fear. You are safe now. Tell me what happened next."

A tear formed on Keiryn's right eyelid as she took a deep breath and continued, "I struggled and pushed him away, but he was persistent. Then he touched me somewhere I did not want him to touch so I slapped him. I regretted it as soon as my hand hit his cheek. He spat in my face, slapped me back, and threw me over his shoulder. Then he carried me into the supply room. His brothers followed him in. They slammed me on the ground and that one was climbing all over me, grabbing at my body and tearing at my clothes. He ripped my dress off of me. I was so scared. That is when I clawed his face and when he stood, kicked him in the groin."

A groan from Bantios startled Keiryn out of her story. She jumped, gasped, and buried her head in Cialia's chest, "Please do not let him hurt me."

Cialia rubbed her back and said, "That one will be awake soon enough, but for now he slumbers. Believe me, even when he does wake he will never lay a finger on you again. Go ahead and finish your story. Get it all out of you."

Keiryn took a deep breath, looked over at Bantios's unconscious body, and then turned to Cialia and said, "That is mostly all of it. He cursed me and fell into one of his brothers. During the commotion, I slipped between his legs and escaped the supply room. I managed to bar the door on my way out. I knew I would be in trouble for attacking a rider, so I fled."

"What?" Cialia was incredulous. "Why on Ouloos would you think you would be in trouble for defending yourself against the desires of a drunken brute like that?"

"Things have changed since you left Druindahl. King Blancus is fair and good, but he has hired mercenaries from far and wide to repopulate Druindahl's army. There were few riders left when you went away. The new riders rule the city now. Blancus never leaves his palace," Keiryn's reply was matter of fact.

A wave of anger rushed over Cialia. If Keiryn spoke the truth—and based on the four ruffians she had just dealt with, she did speak the truth—

it would mean it only took five short summers to destroy the glory of Druindahl. Leisha had pulled those people out of the dark ages of man and given them hope. Now all the people she once stood as champion for lived in fear of those who should be protecting them. She gave Keiryn a squeeze and said, "Come, I think it is time I speak with your king."

CHAPTER 24
THE CHAMPION RETURNS

The forest dimmed as Cialia and Keiryn made the slow journey into Druindahl. There were still a few hours of sunlight, but the dense canopy of the forest kept most of the sun's rays from reaching the forest floor. Unencumbered, Cialia could have made the rest of the jaunt in under an hour. Keiryn's condition slowed them down a bit. She sat behind Cialia atop Purity holding on tightly to her back. Injuries and weariness limited the young girl's strength and much of Cialia's attention was given to healing and keeping her passenger from falling off their mount.

The air changed slightly; a small current, ten men with mounts moved in the darkness of the forest, five each in the trees to either side of the trail. They were seasoned riders. Any ears on Ouloos, aside from Maelich's, would never have heard the faint rustling of hooves on the forest floor. The steeds of Druindahl were trained far too well to be heard when stealth was the goal. Cialia heard it though, and despite all of their techniques at masking their scent, she could smell them too. A hint of leather and oiled bicalchrin mixed with horse sweat wafted across the trail. She brought Purity to a halt a moment before torches blazed to life all around her, a clever trick she had come up with during her twelfth summer and taught all the riders of Druindahl.

"I am Boringas of the Dragon," a deep voice boomed from behind the torchlight on the trail about ten feet in front of Cialia. "You have entered lands that are guarded and protected. State your name and business."

Cialia smiled at the torchlight and replied, "It has been too long, old friend. You know very well who I am and my business is with your king."

Boringas approached and boomed, "I cannot believe it is really you! Varmillian brought word that he and his brothers were assaulted on the trail by the champion of Druindahl herself, but I had to see with my own eyes. I trust you gave them a sound thrashing." He chuckled and then added, "The mighty Cialia, princess of Druindahl, champion of the Dragon and her great city in the trees, you have never met your match with a blade."

"I sent them home to the Great Mother," Cialia replied soberly.

Boringas's laughter abruptly ceased, "What? You killed them? For what crime, challenging you? They were riders of Druindahl. I am sorry if they offended you, dear princess, but that is no reason to end their lives. They would have been punished."

"I offered them ample opportunity to relent, but they would have it no other way. The one they call Bantios still lives. He may even be awake by now. The other two have expired," she shrugged.

"You had no right," Boringas countered.

Cialia steadied Keiryn and leapt down from Purity's back. "I had every right. I lay my head under the crest of a different city, but I am still a daughter of Druindahl and a champion of all the men of Ouloos. Your men attacked and terrorized a young girl, Keiryn. You know her. She serves the drinks at Glandon's Pub. They would have killed her had I not intervened, and they would have done unspeakable things to her before extinguishing her flame. The caliber of men now bearing the crest of the Dragon saddens and disgusts me."

"We have laws, Cialia," Boringas replied. "I know Antian and his brothers are crude and rough, but we have laws to address this kind of behavior. It is no longer your place to enforce those laws."

Cialia took a deep breath and said, "You have the duty of your post, Boringas, and I have the duty of mine. This situation has placed us in opposing positions. I know the laws of Druindahl, and I respect them. I championed them. You know I do not kill without cause. My goal was to bring Antian, Bantios, and Limbriam before your king to answer for their actions. I tried. They would not allow it. As for Varmillian, I will see him stand before your king and face Keiryn, his accuser. She needs to know Druindahl will not stand for her riders mishandling those they are sworn to protect."

Boringas dismounted, walked over to Cialia, lowered his voice, and said, "Cialia, please forgive the stance I am taking. Things have changed drastically since you left. There are very few among us you could still count as friend."

"What about the riders accompanying you now?" Cialia asked.

"These men are my most trusted, but I must still guard my words. They all have developed relationships, and there are politics among the men," he paused and looked in her eyes. After a few moments of silence, he added, "My position is constantly challenged, not outwardly, but subtly, a comment here and a whisper there. Why do you ask?"

Cialia gave her old friend a sympathetic smile and replied, "Because two of them left. You cannot lead men who will not follow you, Boringas. I would take a force of twenty loyal soldiers over ten thousand I could not fully trust. You do not lead these men, old friend."

Boringas sighed and addressed his men, "Cialia will stand before the king. Keiryn's fate will be decided by him. We will lead the two into the city, and they shall remain unmolested."

A bit of grumbling from beyond the trees was the only response.

Cialia closed her eyes and slowly filled her lungs up, holding the breath a moment before releasing it as slowly as she had drawn it in. Then she grabbed Boringas's shoulder and said, "There are dark feelings in the hearts of your men, those among us as well as those in Druindahl. If you do not stand with me, old friend, you may not want to stand so close."

Boringas shook his head, "No one will attack you, but you must do as I say."

"Oh, sweet Boringas," Cialia smiled, "I am not afraid for me." With that she leapt back up onto Purity's back, checked Keiryn's condition, and added, "I will do as you say, but I fear we will not make the king's quarters uncontested."

The caravan moved at a slow trot. Boringas lead with Cialia directly behind him. Two riders Cialia was unfamiliar with brought up the rear. On either side of the trail four additional riders protected the flank. The trip was uneventful until they neared the hidden entrance to the city in the trees. Two men on horseback bearing the mark of Druindahl barred the path.

Boringas called out, "Halt," to his riders and then addressed the two men blocking the path. "Turin, Malto, what is this about?" he asked.

Turin put his arms out to his sides with his palms raised and lifted them toward the sky. The gesture set the forest around them ablaze with thousands of torches sparking to life at the same instant. A devious grin crept onto Turin's face as he looked left, then right, and then directly at Boringas. The grin turned into a wide smile as he said, "Your guests are unwelcome here."

Boringas sat up taller in his saddle, raised his voice, and boomed, "I am charged with the safety of Druindahl, and I lead the riders of our fair city. Cialia is a princess of Druindahl. She arrives as our guest and will be treated as such."

Turin shook his head slowly. "Your guests are not guests of Druindahl. Both of them assaulted the riders you claim to lead, and you expect to house them in this city unscathed? Where does your allegiance lie, brother?"

Boringas had barely spoken the word, "Treason," before Cialia interrupted him.

Keiryn had become uneasy on Purity's back. Cialia gently patted her leg and said, "I was born into this city and have stood as her champion since I was old enough to carry swords. I will have an audience with your king, and this young girl will have justice."

"You speak of history, princess," Turin replied, adding emphasis to the last word and drawing it out in a mocking tone. "You will not have an audience with our king, but you will have justice. Indeed, both of you will find justice on this day."

Boringas made contact with as many eyes as he could in the torchlight as he spat his words through clenched teeth. "If there were crimes, they will be answered for and punished appropriately. Murdering women—one an unarmed bar maid and the other a guest of our fair city—is not how Druindahl administers justice."

"The Druindahl you ride for is dead, Boringas," Turin replied. Then he stretched his hands out to his sides again and added, "We are Druindahl." His statement was followed by a short but loud cheer from the riders surrounding them.

Cialia's mind was terribly unfocused as she skimmed the minds of the men surrounding them. Thoughts like 'Kill the wenches,' and 'Vile whores,' were repeated in several of them. In others, even darker thoughts prevailed. Focused on the minds of savage men, she heard the fwip of the arrow and felt the air change too late. By the time she realized how close the danger was, Keiryn was gasping for breath as blood pumped steadily around the arrow jutting from her throat.

Boringas noticed it a moment later and shouted, "Damn you! Stand down! Are there none among you who remember the grandeur of our fair city and the true justice that made her great? Murdering a young girl for defending herself is not justice you foul brutes. It is loathsome and vile. What honor is there in cutting down an unarmed, defenseless creature?"

Cialia had no words. She reached back and pulled Keiryn close to her, cradling the young, dying girl in her arms. She bathed in the blood of innocence as the body went limp in her arms. A tear formed on her eyelid but quickly evaporated before it could fall to her cheek. Rage formed in her belly and sent a rush of heat through her body. Not the flushed heat of embarrassment or anger that reddens the skin, but real, tangible heat. Sweat poured out of her so quickly it soaked her clothes immediately. Her eyes darted around at the sneering faces glowing in the torchlight surrounding her. Keiryn's death—the death of an innocent—was far more than she could bear. A cry flew from her lips before she could contain it. More tears came but they evaporated as quickly as the first while the heat in and around her continued to rise. By the time she heard the whistling of another arrow splitting the still air of the forest, she—along with Keiryn and Purity—was surrounded by a swirling flame. The arrow turned to ash immediately. Then, in her rage, she lashed out at those who had so callously dragged her fair city down from the heights of enlightenment to the crude depths of savage brutality and stole innocent life for the sake of hubris and revenge.

Terror in Cialia's eyes burned red like hot embers in a roaring blaze as the riders surrounding her began erupting in brilliant flames and howling out in agony. The champion of Druindahl shook to the point of convulsion as her face twisted and contorted among expressions inhuman in the pain and fury they conveyed. All the while she squeezed the dead girl close to her body. The forest grew just a bit brighter with each exploding soldier who flopped to the ground and roasted in a ball of flame amid the chaos of hefty horses fleeing in fear of the heat the burning bodies produced.

Time slowed for Boringas as Cialia convulsed beside him. He watched those he called brother in name alone fall victim to her flame. Shock kept him from fearing his own demise as he witnessed her awesome power; the woman who as a girl had been the focus of his affection. Stronger even than his shock was a deep sadness, a wailing in his soul, as he watched one he loved so deeply fall so far from the honorable heights at which she once soared. The champion of Druindahl, the free spirit refusing to be bridled and encumbered by the affections of a man, the protector of the weak, the one individual he admired above all others, crumbled before his eyes, sinking to the very depths of injustice she had battled so furiously against. A single tear ran down his cheek as he watched his hero fall from her horse exhausted and still clinging to the image of innocence that had sparked her flames.

When the smoke cleared and all of the horses—now free from their riders—fled, Boringas looked upon his unconscious hero with eyes darkened by the sadness in his heart. The great mare, Purity shuffled herself between Cialia and Boringas, letting the warrior know he would have a fight on his hands if he attempted to molest her keeper. Shock maintained a hold on Boringas as unscathed riders began to emerge from the trees. By the time all that lived who could count themselves riders of Druindahl had emerged, they numbered only twenty, excluding Boringas. Surrounded by smoldering carcasses, they formed up behind him and looked on at the crumpled hero clinging to the young bar maid's corpse.

After a long silence, Alamond—one of the riders who remained— spoke, "Her rage was justified, Boringas."

Boringas looked back over his left shoulder, "Faithful Alamond, you have survived the fires of a god."

"Her rage was not directed at me or at the rest of us who did not taste her wrath. I could see fear and pain on the eyes of those around me before they burned in the flames. I felt nothing like what their eyes expressed," Alamond replied. After a short pause he added, "Queen Cialia the Dragon is just and fair."

"Queen?" Boringas's tone expressed his incredulity at the idea. "You would invite the rule of a tyrant into our home? Does this look like justice to you? Are these the actions of a fair ruler? These men were vile scrods, sure they were, but she killed indiscriminately. One man fired that arrow. For that, in her rage, she killed more than twice ten thousand."

Alamond's reply began before Boringas had even finished speaking, "The foulest of the foul, sir. The men she destroyed cared nothing for the standard they bore. They cared nothing for the vows they spoke. Her highness was right in her swift punishment. They were all vile, disgusting creatures bent on destruction and motivated only by personal gain. They were all shabby depictions of what a rider of Druindahl is, and we are better to be rid of them."

"You speak the truth, Alamond," Boringas sighed. Then he asked, "How far have we fallen?"

CHAPTER 25
SADNESS

Tears flowed freely from Helias's eyes as deep melancholy wrapped itself around her heart. A thick, white mist flowed toward the Lake before her, massive like heavy fog rolling across an open field. Many souls mingled in that mist. The great Dragon's tears fell not for those souls slowly creeping toward the Lake and their final journey home. The torrents pouring from the Great Mother's eyes flowed for the anguish of her sister. Cialia had found her flame at the precise moment she lost control of herself.

Delcinia spoke with her mind rather than her lips, "Oh sweet sister, mother to us all, what ails your heart and brings forth such strong currents from your precious eyes?"

"Alas sweet Delcinia, sister and true friend, one of us has fallen to rage and released her fire in a destructive fury. The volume of my tears pales when compared to the volume of sorrow in my heart," Helias replied also without the aid of her voice.

Delcinia soothed, "What has she done, fair sister, but brought vile men to an end they had been seeking for all of their days? Once a man lifts his sword against another man in violence, he invites violence against him, even yearns for the time when the fury of battle may take his life. Our sweet sister gave these creatures the gift they had been seeking for most of their physical lives."

Helias only wept harder and replied, "Is it our lot to judge what makes one man vile and one man just? Is it Cialia's place to pass judgment and execute, to interfere with the natural workings of this world, to relieve these spirits of their physical shell? We are guides, fair sister, nothing more. Our lot is to call the freed souls home to the Lake, to Coeptus, Mother and Father to us all."

Delcinia continued her delicate retort, "No sweet sister, it is not *our* lot to judge, and all of your thoughts bear truth well beyond their simple clarity, yet among them floats folly. Cialia is one with us, our sister; she is a Dragon that is true. However, she is more. The blood of men also flows through her veins. She is one with us but apart from us at the same time, and her role differs from ours. We are guides to the Lake while our sweet sister is a protector of those we guide."

Helias considered Delcinia's argument for a moment before replying, "As always sweet sister, you offer wise counsel. The unfortunate truth for me is my sadness is not lessened by it. Tears flow heartily forth from my eyes for the effect this event will have on our sweet sister. On one hand she may find regret and punish herself in response to the destruction she has authored. On the other hand, she may become drunk with the power she has learned to wield. I cannot decide or judge if her actions were just. I also cannot force my sadness to cease due to what it may mean for our beloved."

"Fear, Helias," Delcinia's reply was quick, almost curt. "You always counsel wisely against fear, yet here you are wallowing in fear of what may be. Sadness for our sister flows through all of us. Shed tears for sadness, but never shed tears for fear. What will be is meant to be. Fearing it will not change the outcome."

"You speak truth, my love," Helias conceded. "Thank you again, sweet sister, for your wise counsel. I will not fear, and things will be what they will be. I will let my sadness pour forth without shame or regret, and I will hope our sweet sister finds her way."

CHAPTER 26
CIRCLES

"We been at this a week now and ain't had sign of no beast or witch or whatever this Shellar be," Ymitoth grumbled as he stopped and lifted his right foot onto a ragged stump. Then he leaned down, resting his elbows on his bent knee, and added, "And this be the third time I leaned up against this very stump."

Maelich sighed as he surveyed their surroundings, "I am afraid you are correct, father. We have been going in circles. We camped at this very spot only two days ago."

"Based on where the sun be in the sky right now," Ymitoth chuckled, "I think we be camping here again on this night."

"I suppose you are correct," Maelich agreed. "This is a good spot to make camp, and we are quickly running out of light."

Pain suddenly tore through Maelich's head. It began at a point in the center of his forehead and exploded throughout the rest of his cranium with enough intensity to drop him to the ground in a heap. Both of his hands shot up to either side of his forehead and squeezed against the pressure. At the same instant, intense heat moved down his spine and filled up his chest, forcing a loud groan past his lips. He rolled onto his back and blinked several times at the bit of sky he could see through the trees. It wasn't blue and the leaves of the trees weren't green. Everything had a reddish-orange hue that was cloudy and murky. His chest felt as if it may collapse as the heat intensified. Then it spread through the rest of his body like a consuming flame.

Though the simple act of moving his lips increased the pain in his head exponentially, he cried out, "Am I burning?"

Ymitoth rushed over to him, knelt beside him, and replied, "No, there don't appear to be nothing wrong with ye, except for your skin being all clammy and pale."

"It feels like I am on fire," he moaned.

Ymitoth grabbed his water skin and splashed a bit on Maelich's face. Steam rose from him as soon the droplets hit his face. "Ye be burning up son!" the confused, old warrior shouted.

As quickly as the sensation had engulfed him, it left. He lay still for a moment as Ymitoth worried over him. Finally, he said, "It passed. I feel fine again."

By this point, Ymitoth had reached a state of frenzy. He quickly blurted out, "What in Dragon's fire be going on with ye, lad?"

"I am unsure," Maelich's words were quiet with barely a voice to carry them. "It felt like my body was burning. There was more than just heat though. There was pain, someone else's pain. It was like a deep fury caused by the most pitiable angst. I can hardly explain the mix of things I felt while wrapped in the strange heat, and a deep sadness remains like blackness on my soul. My heart aches but for what I do not know."

"Strange," Ymitoth decided. "Perhaps we be closer to Shellar than we be thinking. Perhaps…"

Ymitoth's voice trailed off as he reached into his cloak, pulled out his dagger, turned, and fired it into the trees. "That be a warning," he shouted in the direction his dagger had flown. Then he added, "Ye don't be creeping up on travelers in the forest."

Maelich quickly scrambled to his feet and drew his sword. "What is it?" he asked, as he scanned the trees surrounding them. Finally his eyes settled on a man struggling to free himself of Ymitoth's dagger that had him pinned to a tree by his cuff.

Maelich quickly fell into step behind Ymitoth who had begun stalking toward the man. 'That was quite a shot,' he marveled. The tree the man was pinned to stood at least twenty feet from where Ymitoth had been crouching over him. His mentor's ability with edged weapons had always awed Maelich, and the wily, old warrior was constantly doing things to maintain that awe. Maelich would have been far less impressed if he had killed or injured the man. At twenty feet, that would be a good shot but not awe inspiring. To trap a man and spare him until you can determine his intention was truly impressive. Few could make a shot like that in the heat of the moment when life may be on the line.

A loud growl followed by vicious barking tore Maelich's attention away from his thoughts about Ymitoth's great mastery with blades. A massive, shaggy, brown scrod—far larger than any Maelich had ever seen and at least twice the size Jom had been—lunged from the trees toward them. Both Ymitoth and Maelich stopped, raised their swords, and assumed defensive stances. Maelich had not desire to kill a scrod, but instincts often overrule cognizant thought.

"Please, no!" the man pinned to the tree shouted. "He's friendly! He won't bite."

The scrod stopped short in front of the hapless man pinned to the tree. The animal's shoulders hunched and his hackles shot up as a deep, menacing growl poured over his exposed fangs. The beast had eyes like blue ice, clear and shiny. Its thick, shaggy fur looked like it could be beautiful if not dirty and matted from too much time in the forest. "Mountain, heel!" the trapped man commanded the beast.

Maelich lowered his sword but Ymitoth maintained his stance and asked, "What business have ye sneaking around our camp?"

"I wasn't sneaking," the man replied as he continued to struggle with Ymitoth's dagger. "I'm hungry. My scrod is hungry. We haven't any food. I saw people and thought they might have a few scraps for a weary traveler."

"How well do you know these woods?" Maelich asked the man while he slowly approached the scrod with an outstretched hand. The scrod, in turn, approached just as slowly, the hair on his back smoothing out as he came.

"I should think I know them pretty well," the man replied. "I have lived among these trees for the better part of my life."

"The clothes ye wear be dirty but they seem far too fine for forest folk," Ymitoth interjected, "and ye got that funny talk like one of fine breeding."

"The clothes are stolen," the man replied. "As for my command of the common tongue, I was taught by a wise man to speak well. My family journeyed to this land en route to Havenstahl when I was a young lad. We were set upon by a small band of raiders. They killed all but me. Me they kept for a time; had me do odd jobs and taught me how to steal and survive in the forest. It went like that until I grew to a point I would call myself a man. Then I killed them all, slit their throats while they slept. Except Brandovan, I woke him a moment before I ran him through, gave him a chance to look around at his dead kinsmen before he expired. I have been on my own ever since."

"Ye killed Brandovan?" Ymitoth fell victim to a hearty fit of laughter. "That scoundrel be known far and wide, scourge of the great plains. Ha, to think, the mighty Brandovan, felled by a waif of a man such as ye."

The man frowned, "Please now, it is true my brain is far more reliable than my brawn, but I am no helpless babe. I am adequate with a sword and have faced down my fair share of nightmares in this dark wood."

"Ye failed to avoid me blade," Ymitoth's laughter had subsided to low chuckling.

"You are quite correct sir, I did. However, I would suggest my current circumstances are more a testament to your might than my meekness. Judging from the way you throw your dagger and the swagger with which you brandish that sword, I must assume you are a seasoned—probably great—warrior. Your keen ear—keen enough to judge my location with the ever so slight sounds I gave you to work with—assures me you are also a master huntsman. True, I would be no match for the likes of you. But then, who in this land would be?" The man had ceased his struggling.

"Ha!" Ymitoth laughed, "Ye do be having a silver tongue. What they be calling ye?"

"I am Braggon of the house Galzine, far to the south of the Great Sea. My father was Bragg, heir to the throne. My mother was Corintha of the house Panxelia. Both of them were killed by Brandovan along with Darcon and ten guards who served as our protection. Darcon was my uncle, the younger brother of my father," the man replied.

By this time, Maelich had made friends with Mountain and the two were wrestling and playing among the trees. Maelich looked up at Braggon and said, "You have a claim to that throne. Why not return and take your rightful place?"

"Aye," Ymitoth agreed, "Why not return and take what be yours?"

Braggon smiled and nodded his head, "Yes, yes indeed. That sounds so easy. Sadly, as you can see, I am a grown man. Honestly, I could not begin to guess my age, but I am far older than your companion, probably closer in age to you. That would mean I have been away from my home for near to forty summers. What could be happening there now? I have no idea. I was a young lad when I left that place, but not so young to be unaware of the intrigue. My grandfather's crown sat atop a worried brow. His throne was ever contested, even within his own house. His younger brother and his youngest son both had designs against him and that was just in his own house. I hail from a long line of treacherous bastards. If I were to return, I would need an army. That playful scrod is the only army I have. No, my desire to return simply does not exist. This forest is my home. Mountain and I do just fine here."

Ymitoth shrugged, "Much can be changing in forty summers. Ye probably be right to be staying away. I'd be storming the walls of the castle, alone if fate be making it so, but I'd be taking that throne back in the name of me father."

Braggon bowed his head, "You are obviously an honorable man. Far more honorable than me I am afraid, perhaps honorable enough to release me from this awkward prison you have placed me in."

Maelich piped in, "Forty summers is a long time. You say that you have lived among these trees the entire time?"

"I have," Braggon replied as Ymitoth yanked his dagger out of the tree and released him. "You will find no other who knows these trees as I do."

"Come," Maelich said, "eat with us. We had a very productive hunt the day before last, and we have plenty of meat to spare. You can share our bounty and perhaps tell us more about this forest."

The forest had grown quite dark and Mountain had long since found his way to sleep by the time the three men finished making camp. A stout fire along with the coziness of the camp the men had built made the effort seem worthwhile. Ymitoth turned a thick slab of tubber over the flame on a spit he had fashioned out of sticks. While the meat roasted above the flame, Braggon shared some berries from his pack.

Maelich smiled as he popped a berry in his mouth, "Are you always wandering Braggon, or do you have a place you call home in these woods?"

Braggon smiled back and replied, "There are many places among these trees I call home. There are small settlements all about these woods; too small to be called towns, but settlements nonetheless. Most of them sit empty for much of the time. The folk around these parts tend to be somewhat nomadic. One group will move in and occupy an area for one, maybe two summers, and then move on. Another group eventually takes their place. They leave much behind."

"Is that how you have survived all this time?" Maelich asked.

"Partly," he shrugged. "Most of what they leave is good for shelter and I have tended a garden or two when blessed with seed, but food is normally hard to come by. I've never been much for hunting. Aside from those throats I slit so many years ago, I haven't done much killing. Most of what I eat I have to steal. The trails are ripe with rich travelers for most of the year. I can keep both me and Mountain well fed without them ever knowing their good deed of providing us with sustenance."

"What about them darker things what be lurking in this wood?" Ymitoth interjected as he slowly turned the dripping hunk of meat on the spit. Then he raised his face toward the two men. The shadows playing across it made him look like some kind of demon or monster as they mingled with his features, especially those black, dead eyes.

Braggon chuckled, "I have yet to come across any amatilazo so bold as to challenge Mountain. I believe his scent alone keeps them far from us. This wood does carry a strong population of them, but they haven't bothered me in years. Prior to finding Mountain, I did quite a bit of running and a lot more hiding."

"What about grongs?" Maelich asked.

"Once in a great while a group of grongs will move through these woods. They mostly stick to the other side of the swamp though. They never stay in the same area very long, truly nomadic. Not to mention, if you don't have anything, they don't really bother with you. I was even accosted by a group of them once and they let me go. They checked me over, gave me a good pat down, found I had nothing of value, and sent me on my way."

Ymitoth piped in again, "We ain't looking for no amatilazo or grongs. We be looking for Shellar. What ye be knowing about that witch?"

"Ah, Shellar, the She Liar as she is called by men," Braggon said with a widening smile. "I should have known a couple of stout soldiers such as you would not venture into this forest without the promise of true glory. I know quite a bit about her. You are not the first adventurers to come looking for that prize."

"We will be the last," Maelich assured him.

"What is your cause?" Braggon clapped his hands loudly, rubbed them together, and then leaned forward. "Adventure, glory," he paused, "have you been promised a reward?"

Maelich shook his head, "I seek the monster to repay a debt owed to her by another."

"Ah revenge!" Braggon proclaimed loudly as he clapped his hands several times, leaned his head back, and laughed. "Revenge is the best of causes when dealing death to a vile beast. I pegged you for a hero right from the start; the strong build and flowing hair, you could be nothing less."

A frown slipped onto Maelich's face as his brow dipped, "You mock…"

Before Maelich could finish his statement, Ymitoth threw his opinion in. "I'd be counseling against mocking this one," he chuckled.

Braggon put his hands up to Maelich and said, "Please, I mean no disrespect. Sometimes my tongue gets away from me."

Maelich shook his head, "You have nothing to fear from me. I do not enjoy being made a mockery of. However, I have no desire to prove my worth against one untrained in battle. I would gain equal satisfaction from proving I could throw a stone."

"And I would be a fool to test your might," Braggon quickly added. "No more jest. I can lead you to the prize you seek. Of course she is not idle. She does not move quickly, but she does move about. Always she is in the swamp, very close to where we are right now."

"I knew we were close," Maelich said. "I learned all of the stories when I was a young lad. From where I do not recall, but I know what she is about. Her location is obviously still a mystery to me, or I would have slayed her by now. The bit we were able to glean from the owner of the debt we seek to repay was not much at all. It was enough to bring us this far."

Braggon's smile returned, "From this point, if you head straight east you shall find the prairie, veer at all to the south and you shall find the Sea of Sadness, head north and you shall find your way back to Havenstahl, but head west and you will find what you seek. Of course, she isn't straight west of here, more southwest really. You will find her in the swamp."

"We have been in and around that swamp for days and have found no sign of a monster fitting the description of the She Liar," Maelich complained.

Braggon shook his head and replied, "You have not explored the vastness of this swamp. I can tell by the condition of the clothes on your back. You are wearing your fair share of filth to be sure, but you cannot leave the swamp without bringing a good bit of it with you." Braggon popped a berry in his mouth and continued, "You may have tinkered around the edges of the swamp, but you have yet to penetrate its depth."

"Is that to say ye be knowing all the secrets of the swamp then?" Ymitoth asked.

Braggon chuckled, "Never. The swamp is a vast and ever changing mystery, as is Shellar. I feel quite comfortable boasting that there are few men living with a greater knowledge of the swamp than that which I possess though. I can lead you to Shellar if you truly believe she is what you seek."

"I made a promise long ago to stand for those who could not stand for themselves. At this moment, I stand for one in need of peace. I seek Shellar, the She Liar, bane of men," Maelich answered soberly.

"Very well," Braggon shook his head. "We shall rise with the sun, and I will deliver you to her by midday."

The conversation dwindled as Ymitoth pulled the roasted meat off of the spit and divvied it up among them. He even had a good sized hunk for Mountain who was also lucky enough to earn a large bone to gnaw on. The warriors would need a full belly and a good night's rest to face the challenge a new day would bring. They would find that deep, refreshing slumber beneath the trees.

CHAPTER 27
DOWN WITH THE FOREST

Bok sat upon his throne at the western edge of his tent. It had been erected on top of his ship and served as his war room. Fierce, amber eyes scanned the small group serving as his advisors. His father, Maomnosett Ott sat beside him along with Bok's younger brother Ohm. Based on the hierarchy of power in the giant community, Ott, by all rights, should have been at the helm of the great army. However, when Brerto, the great tiger, came to him in a dream and gave him his calling he demurred making way for his second son who still carried the fiercest fury at the loss of his brother Ahm. Hountmytall Dik and Laenkishot Kon were also present. Along with Ott, they represented the first generation of giants as well as the three most feared families of the proud race. They were seated in front of Bok along the southern wall of the tent on his right side facing north.

The trogmortem were represented in the war room by Chi-Ta, their king, and his three generals: Ka-Lita, Bim-Kalil, and Skivvi-Na. They sat across from the giants along the northern wall, facing south. Though the trogmortem were savage and terrifying in appearance, they were far from dumb animals. Their intellect did not match that of giants, but they had an advanced language, cunning, and the ability to strategize. Despite several historic clashes between the two groups, Chi-Ta was more than willing to accept an alliance with the race he admired more than hated. This was mostly because of a deep connection all trogmortem felt to giants. Sadly, the sentiment wasn't shared by the objects of their admiration. Bok's purpose for engaging the trogmortem had little to do with fostering unity or mending old scars. It was an engagement of necessity. The trogmortem had the one thing giants lacked, numbers.

According to trogmortem myth, Tal and Tol were the first giants. They are referred to as the houseless ones because they never adopted a name for their line to be recognized by as their children did. Tal grew tired of Tol when she refused to give him any more children. He left their cave and wandered the desert, searching for someone sturdy enough to bear his offspring. After years of exploration, he came across a mighty creature matching his size, the bintoosha. Bintoosha are beasts living in the land west of the Great Sea. They are massive, predatory animals who hunt the men of that land. Tal was inspired by the first one he found. She had lengthy limbs that looked strong and useful, with claws for tearing. Her face was long, mostly made up of jaws full of dagger-like teeth, and her body was covered in scales. Rather than being repulsed by her terrifying appearance, Tal found the strength in her form to be possibly the most beautiful thing he had ever seen. The beast was less fond of Tal though, and she attacked him. The giant was strong, agile, and adequate with his hands, proving a great match for her strength. They wrestled for days to a standstill until, finally exhausted, the bintoosha submitted to Tal. The eventual result of the union was Go-Rika, the first of the trogmortem. Tal would sire many more of the hybrid creatures with several bintoosha. Eventually, their numbers far surpassed those of giants and even rivaled those of men. This of course was the mythology of the trogmortem. Giants didn't believe any of it. The first generation was the first generation begotten by Coeptus as an image of physical perfection, an improvement on man.

Finally, the grongs were represented by Slurg, the choontah—loosely translated as chief in the common tongue—of the barbarous creatures. He was accompanied by his two most trusted generals; Glung and Banch. They sat together at the eastern edge of the tent, just inside the entryway. Grongs were ferocious, animal-like warriors who lived for battle and the hunt. Thinking and strategy were not among their strengths. Bok had only invited Slurg to the council to ensure the dedication of the grongs. They were easily distracted and fought for no real cause of their own. Keeping them engaged and focused on a goal was the biggest challenge in dealing with the brutes.

Bok made eye contact with Chi-Ta and asked, "Why are we still on this beach?" His voice carried an uneasy calm that seemed far too thin to hold back the madness swirling beneath it.

Chi-Ta shifted in his chair and replied, "Thousands of men have fallen, but they continue to be replaced. Their numbers seem inexhaustible."

"Perhaps the trogmortem are not as fierce as their boasts," Ohm interrupted.

"Be still, my brother," Bok said as he touched the giant's arm. "This meeting is not intended to disrespect our friends in this campaign." He paused and gave his attention back to Chi-Ta, "Forgive Ohm's disrespect, Chi-Ta, but there is validity to his point. You promised me the gates of Havenstahl in a week. A week of fighting has passed and all my forces remain camped on this beach."

Chi-Ta nodded, "I did make that promise. When I made it, I expected to see giants on the battlefield beside my kind. Instead, you all remain on your ships, idle, while we do all of the heavy lifting. Your numbers are small, but your might is great. Why do you hold back from the fight?"

Slurg had a weak grasp of the common tongue, but he did his best to voice his agreement with Chi-Ta. "Giants fight too," the words came slowly and his cadence was choppy.

Ohm scowled, but Bok smiled and said, "We have been building, my friend. The thick forests lying on either side of the road to Havenstahl have proven very helpful to the men defending it. At the dawn of each day, while you have gone off to fight the men of Havenstahl, we have been building great machines to tear that forest down."

"Fight," Slurg grunted, "no build."

"Well where are the fruits of your labor?" Chi-Ta asked. "Where are these mighty machines able to mow forests to the ground? Such a machine must be massive. I see no such thing on this beach. There are several catapults to be sure, but they are useless where they sit rotting in the salty air."

"They are on the beach south of the bay," Bok's tone remained cool, "four of them. "My sons and the sons of my kind have been camping there, building from before daybreak until well after nightfall. The full moon and clear skies have proved a blessing to their efforts, and they have finished ahead of schedule. As the sun rises on another day, they will wheel them up the coast and cut this forest down."

Slurg's chuckle sounded like loose stones being ground under the wheels of a heavy cart. He turned to Banch and said something in his own tongue, "Gaok hok hok mong."

To everyone in the room but the grongs and Bok it sounded like a series of grunts. Bok had spent time with a grong named Gorg. He had invited the beast to live with him for several months in order learn their customs in preparation for the war. Though he maintained his cool demeanor, his eyes narrowed, "I appreciate your assistance in this campaign, Slurg. However, I will not entertain disrespect in my war room. You can believe me now and see machines at day break."

Slurg's eyes fell to the floor before him, "Please forgive. No disrespect."

"You are forgiven," Bok smiled. "Remember that I know your tongue. It offers you no protection from my ears." His smile faded as he continued in Slurg's own language, "Bing ahk nok," which, loosely translated, threatened crushed bones.

An uncomfortable quiet settled over the room as Bok continued to stare through narrow slits at Slurg. After a few moments, Chi-Ta broke the silence. "What is the plan? How will we employ these machines?"

Bok's expression mellowed as he turned his attention toward Chi-Ta, "Each of the four machines carries two circular blades. Each blade has a diameter of thirty feet. The blades are mounted underneath a wooden platform leaving a ten foot arc exposed for each blade. At the back of the machine are two additional platforms—levers really—that will be pushed up and down by my giants. As they oppose each other up and down, a series of gears will spin the blades and move the massive wheels forward. We will cut the forest down."

"I am eager to see the mechanics of these machines," Skivvi-Na interjected. "You are facing old, mighty oaks."

"Small minds find big ideas challenging," Ohm answered the trogmortem general.

Bok added, "Our blades are sharp. I expect we will have cut a wide path to Havenstahl within another week. However, I do not expect their defenses to hold up that long. Without the benefit of the tight path to limit our numbers, they will be forced to retreat. Then we can march our catapults down the road to Havenstahl and pull their city down."

Then Ott, with a grim look upon his grizzled, old face quickly added, "And before you ask your next question, King Chi-Ta, yes there will be giants on the battlefield. My sons and the sons of my kind will lead you as we trample the men of Havenstahl under our feet."

Chi-Ta managed to keep his ego in check and replied, "Giants on the battlefield will be a glorious sight. I look forward to going to battle with you. You are the eldest and wisest among us. I count it a blessing to serve under the same banner."

Bok nodded and brought the meeting to a close, "By the time the sun rises, our machines will be in place. Laenkishot Kil's four sons will power the two machines to the north of the trail. Kik and Kol will manage one while Kal and Kan manage the other. Ohm's sons, Oyg and Oyn will power the first machine to the south of the trail while Hountmytall Mon's sons power the southernmost machine. Slurg, once the trees begin to fall, you will send a battalion to march up the trail and engage the warriors of Havenstahl. You will also send battalions to follow and defend the machines on either side of the trail."

"What of my forces, Bok?" Chi-Ta interrupted. "Where do the trogmortem fit in your plan?"

Bok turned his gaze to Chi-Ta, "Patience has never been a quality of the trogmortem. Chi-Ta, you will send two small groups, one hundred trogmortem to the north and one hundred trogmortem to the south to accompany me and the rest of the giants as we move through the trees to find and destroy Havenstahl's camps. The rest of your trogmortem should follow and support the grongs as they protect the machines and do battle with the forces of Havenstahl."

Chi-Ta smiled and nodded, "The plan is good. Lito-Bi, Stekka-Ha, and Ki-Falsa are my three finest warriors. They will be among the two hundred joining you in the forest, as will I."

"I will be glad to have you," he replied with a shallow nod. Then he turned his attention back to Slurg and said, "Once the sun has reached its highest point, pull back enough of your soldiers to move our camp. I expect to have a position to hold by nightfall."

Slurg nodded his agreement.

Bok quickly scanned the room with his eyes and said, "Now go. Prepare your warriors for battle. Tomorrow we turn the tide and begin the push toward Havenstahl."

CHAPTER 28
DIVIDED

Darkness had long settled into the clearing before Fort Maomnosett when Kantiim entered Daritus's tent to find him troubling over his map. He followed the general's gaze down toward it to see that some of the tokens had been moved about to different locations. The wooden, fallon token representing Glord's men had been moved far to the east of the prang coin depicting Havenstahl. A green, painted fallon figurine had taken its place. The dragon figure had been moved closer to the northern point of Biggon's Bay, and the simple wooden fallon that had been sitting on the coin representing the fort had been replaced with a figurine of a fallon painted blue. There were also four new figurines on the map. One of them sat beside the blue fallon, another sat beside the green fallon, and the other two sat at opposite sides of the clearing.

"You have been busy painting and planning I see," Kantiim noted.

Daritus glanced up and replied offhandedly, "Hmm, yes I have."

Kantiim continued as he made a swirling motion with his hand toward the map, "What is all of this? Your plan has obviously changed."

Daritus took a deep breath, rubbed his eyes, and looked up at Kantiim. "I received word from Alhouim. Just shy of a week ago I sent Duvel to blow the great horn. Thankfully, Alhouim answered. Her army is on the march and should arrive by mid-day tomorrow. Her generals are represented on the map by the four bears."

"I see," Kantiim nodded as he stroked his chin and moved closer to the map. "What of Glord's fallon? Why have you moved it so far from the fight?"

"For many reasons," Daritus sighed. "First, Leisha, my wife, is gathering as many of the people we fight for as will join her to flee Havenstahl for

Druindahl. The road to Druindahl is long and treacherous, and the palace guard numbers too few to adequately protect them. Glord has already been given orders to pull back from the front and escort our people along that dangerous path. I expect his force should arrive there in three days if they march with all the hours of sun. Aside from that need, there is also the fact that after one week of battle he only commands around two thousand swords; swords wielded by men who have faced down nightmares from sun up until sun down for seven full days. We need fresh men at the front."

"What of my fallon? Why have you have painted it blue?" Kantiim asked.

"You command fifty thousand swords, my friend. Half of them will remain here at the fort while the other half will move to the front and take up Glord's position," Daritus patted his shoulder as he finished.

"The finest soldiers on Ouloos," Kantiim's gaze moved to the back of the tent, but his mind continued far beyond that.

"Do you trust any of your lieutenants to carry your standard to the front and lead your men in your stead?"

Kantiim snapped to attention, "What? I do not *send* my men into battle. I lead them there. Some men can lead from behind. I cannot."

Daritus moved around the table until he was directly in front of Kantiim. Then he grasped both of his shoulders and said, "Old friend, none could ever doubt the duty you feel to your men and the city you ride for. I know my request is challenging. Do you think I do not ache standing idle in this tent, gazing at a map while my men die at the hands of monsters? A bit of me dies with every update I get from the front, but someone has to lead this effort. Your mind is far more valuable than your might in this struggle. I need you here to strategize with me. My plan has changed and it will continue to change. You must help me shape our effort."

Kantiim sighed, turned away from Daritus, and walked to the other side of the tent. The few moments he stood staring at the wall seemed far longer. Finally, he turned back to Daritus and said quietly, "I know what you say is true, my brother, and I will oblige. You are the true leader of all the men fighting and dying to protect Havenstahl, including me. I will stand by your side, old friend, but I will take no joy from my position." He paused and then added with a weak smile, "I fear you will not find me to be very good company knowing my men are at the front minus my sword."

"Of that I am sure," Daritus said as he crossed the room and patted his finest general on the back. "That being said, I am fairly certain you will not be without them for long."

"What do you mean?"

"Word from the Dragon's Flame is, though the giants have yet to enter the battle outright, they have not sat idle."

"Well, let us have it. What have they been about?"

"That is what I have been troubling over," Daritus stroked his chin. "The messenger described siege weapons, massive siege weapons, like nothing I have ever heard of."

Kantiim shrugged, "If they are so massive, how do they plan to get them within range to pose a threat?"

"That is a puzzle," Daritus gazed up at the ceiling. "Based on the description I received, these weapons would be far too large to transport down the trail. On top of that, they seem to lack any tools for battering walls and doors, or any mechanism for launching projectiles. They have giant, circular blades mounted to them so they could be used to literally cut our men down. It just does not make sense that they would be employed that way. They do have wheels for moving, but boasting such a massive size they would not be maneuverable. It would be far too easy to outflank and disable them. Giants are big and savage, but they are far from stupid."

Kantiim leaned his head back and shifted his stance. "No, they are not stupid at all," he replied. After a few moments of contemplation he added, "Perhaps they plan to remedy the very obstacle rendering those weapons so useless on our battlefield."

"That idea had crossed my mind," Daritus agreed. "They mean to mow down the forest."

"That should certainly change our strategy," Kantiim's expression turned grim. "Did the Dragon's Flame seek to frustrate their efforts at building these weapons?"

Daritus raised his hands, palms up, and replied, "Of course they did. Five more flames were extinguished in the effort. There were at least two giants guarding them at all times. Maelich is the only man, living or passed on, that I know to have slain a giant, and he is special."

"He is," Kantiim agreed. "He is also sorely missed on this battlefield. If he were among us, there would be no battle to fight."

"True," Daritus nodded. "Lamenting Maelich's absence will not help us achieve victory over our enemies though. How do we answer these machines if they serve the purpose we believe they serve?

Kantiim walked back over to the table and picked up the green painted fallon. Then he tapped it several times against the map as he scanned it. His eyes squinted, creasing up his forehead as his hair dangled about his face. He brushed it away several times before swirling it up and tying it off behind his head. His eyes closed as he bowed his head and began tapping the green fallon against the map again.

Daritus watched him for a few moments before asking, "Where is your mind taking you?"

Kantiim kept his head bowed but looked up toward his general and replied, "If those weapons are meant to cut down the forest, they will cut a wide path for Bok's army to outflank us on the trail. That is, if we continue to fight in the same fashion we have been. Yet, if we move into the trees, our men will be cut down along with them."

"Yes, neither of those options is appealing."

"Here," Kantiim stopped tapping and finally placed the green fallon figurine on the map at the northern point of Biggon's Bay. "I will send twenty-five thousand of my best to the north point of Biggon's Bay with Ymanchol. We will count on Ygraml's horses to hold the trail for as long as they can."

"The path to the northern point is narrow," Daritus interrupted. "It will take several days to get a force that size there."

"Yes it will," Kantiim agreed. "Meanwhile, Ygraml will give ground on the trail, more so if those weapons serve the purpose we believe they do. However, how quickly do you think even massive machines armed with gigantic blades can cut down those mighty, old oaks? Add to that the time it will take to clear the trees they cut down, and Bok's force will take far longer to make this clearing than my men will take to make Biggon's Bay. From there, it will be a short jaunt to take Bok's monsters from behind."

The essence of a smile slipped onto Daritus's face, and he began nodding before Kantiim had finished. "That is why you will remain here with me. I had completely forgotten about the northern pass to Biggon's Bay. We can outflank them and separate the strength of their force. Ygraml will give up ground on the trail slowly and the Dragon's Flame can frustrate the efforts of our enemies with their arrows."

"I will ready my men. They will march out before dawn," Kantiim bowed and left the tent.

Daritus watched him go. Then he looked up to the ceiling, scratched his head, and sighed. A new king and a dead king were missing. One of them could end this war with a whisper of his breath but remained damnably absent as his mother led the people in his stead. Packing them up and hurrying them off, yanking them from their lives, and fleeing like beasts seeking shelter from the coming storm. The proud fallon that had stood tall as the one beacon of hope in a world of violence and fear had been reduced to a quivering rodent, fleeing in the face of danger. Once Maelich had destroyed Kallum and opened people's eyes to the true nature of the nurturing mother, they were able to see the real terrors of this world, terrors that barely entered their planes of reality safe within the mighty walls of Havenstahl. The Dragon, the hated symbol that was at once a source of mind numbing fear and at the same time a source of the most violent anger and hatred, became a symbol for peace and love and hope. Sadly, for these people, hatred and anger had proven far more adequate in strengthening resolve than peace, hope, or love ever could.

The map spread out upon the table mocked him. The tokens he had placed on it jeered at him. He was fighting a war the people he led could not win. Most of them had only heard stories about the monsters they fought against; nightmares existing only in the imagination; stories used to frighten and impress your comrades around the fire. Those nightmares had been unleashed by an angry god provoked by an absent savior, and they had leapt from the realm of imagination onto the shores of the greatest city of men. The men Daritus led, men born of the house of Havenstahl as well as those who had followed the lad of the Lake from Druindahl, would stand tall before those nightmares, even with fear pumping coldly through their veins. They would ultimately fall though. No matter how Daritus worked it over in his mind, they could not hold at this fort and Havenstahl would be overrun.

The mighty fallon had held at the beach for seven full days, but so many had fallen. In seven more that number would double. Add seven more to that, and it would double again. That would continue until there were none left to defend the house of Havenstahl. Leisha would flee with the people. They would be safe in Druindahl, close to the Dragon, close to the source, the Great Mother. Great Brerto's nightmares would not dare venture that close to the Dragons again, lest they draw the fury of mighty Moshat and Kaldumahn. They would have Havenstahl though, and Daritus knew there was nothing he could do about it. He would lead his men with victory as the goal. Though he didn't really believe it could be achieved. The best they could hope for was to hold off the pummeling wave long enough to let the people escape to safety before the walls came crumbling down.

CHAPTER 29
FLIGHT

A line of wagons stretched from the front of the palace at Havenstahl nearly halfway down the hill into the great valley. Throngs of people hurried about packing up their belongings and fretting over what essentials they may have been forgetting. Only Coeptus knew when they may see their homes again. Even with the grand parade of village folk packing up their entire lives into rickety wagons, a larger number ignored the warning of the coming storm. The greatest army on Ouloos stood before the nightmares marching against Havenstahl. What beast could stomp so loud and roar so mightily as to cause a trembling in the great fallon? Surely none could make good on a boast so brazenly arrogant. Havenstahl had faced down terrible hordes of nightmares since her beginnings and brought peace and justice to the land. This threat would be no different than any other. The monsters would be turned away or skewered on the swords of mighty men. At least that was the sentiment of those who chose to ignore the warnings of Leisha and the soldiers sent from the front.

Outside the palace gates, Leisha readied her horse. Freedom was a wild mare with a blazing white coat speckled with black flecks. Three summers prior she had been brought into the stable wild from the prairie. No man could tame her, and not one of the stable hands could control her. After three weeks of trying to break her, the horse handlers were ready to give up and turn her over to the kitchen to be slaughtered for food. Had Leisha not laid eyes upon her and immediately fell in love with her free spirit, the wild mare would have perished. The great queen of Druindahl, mistress of the Lake, and mother of gods, approached the wild horse with her hands out at her sides singing a sweet song. The horse reared back kicking at the air and threatening to strike. However, when Leisha made eye contact with her, the fury fled. The horse bowed before the queen and submitted. Leisha named the beauty Freedom and after a few weeks was able to saddle and bridle the magnificent animal.

Perrin approached atop a brown stallion with a great white patch on his chest. His name was Trailfoot and he was custom fit to his rider by Talhomme. Perrin held her head high as she rode showing her face to the sun. One night of tears was all she gave to the burns on her face. That night after beholding what her son's fire had done to her she decided she would not try hiding her deformity. Those burns were all she had left of Geillan, and she would wear them proudly; a badge she earned defending the life of her child. She gave Leisha a smile and said, "I be ready for the trail."

Leisha eyes closed gently as she shook her head, "What on Ouloos are you doing on that horse? You have never been a rider."

Since she faced down the dead-eyed men, Perrin's voice had achieved an authority it had not carried prior to the event, "I ain't never been a fighter neither. Yet here I be sitting alive after facing down those dead-eyed men what killed four of our soldiers and both of me parents."

Leisha sighed, "You should be in a carriage with Meelah. You are still weak from the attack and your wounds still require care."

Perrin was undaunted, "Me wounds be me own concern. I won't be hiding out when others be dying for me no more. I ain't nobody's damsel no more."

Before Leisha could reply, Glord walked up and interjected, "Neither of ye ought be out riding along the caravan. Ye be finding a carriage and staying hid. That trail to Druindahl be a treacherous one."

"Ah, Glord," Leisha smiled at the old general, "you have been a faithful protector of Havenstahl since you could call yourself a man. Had you ridden under my banner, you would understand how wasteful your words are right at this moment."

"Please, me lady," Glord's tone was far softer than his battle-hardened face, "ye know we can't be protecting ye properly if ye be out galloping alongside them wagons instead of sitting comfortably in one."

Leisha smiled, "I appreciate your effort in softening your tone in my presence, and I also appreciate how furious you will be with me when I tell you again that I will not be hiding away in a carriage. The people in this caravan are fleeing from their homes in fear of the monsters beating at our door. I am the mother of the king of the people of Havenstahl, and the people that followed me from Druindahl still see me as their queen. I will not hide in fear. They need someone to lead them. In my son's absence, I will adopt the people of Havenstahl as my own. Perhaps I can be a small beacon of hope."

Glord bowed and shook his head, "And what if ye be killed along this trail, me lady? How much hope be they having then?"

Leisha patted the old general on the shoulder and said, "I have faith in you, Glord. I am unafraid."

"Wish I could be saying the same, me lady," Glord mumbled.

"And I be riding at your side, Leisha," Perrin finally interjected.

"Perrin, please…" Leisha began but the young queen cut her off.

"Ye be saying much about being a queen to your people and spreading hope and all else with all of your fancy words. Well I *be* the queen of these people. Me husband be their king, and I be their queen. And ye'd been right when ye said I'd be stronger for the pain, because there ain't none in this land that I be fearing. I won't be needing no men with swords and armor to be protecting me none either. I be keeping meself alive until I be finding me son." Perrin's lower lip slowly stopped trembling as she collected herself, turned her attention to Glord, and said, "All that be going be loaded up, general. Call the order to get this caravan moving."

"Highness, the scouts ain't returned yet," Glord complained calmly.

"And the sun be steady on the rise," Perrin countered. "I gave ye an order, general. Be making it so."

Glord bowed, scowled, shook his head, turned, and shouted, "Fallon, move out."

The command was echoed all up and down the ranks of soldiers lined up on either side of the caravan. Thousands of carriages churned to life as the horses pulling them were urged on by their drivers. Many men walked in and around the carts. They were armed with swords, spears, or rude farming equipment that would possibly never see the field again. There were few eyes that didn't look back upon the great city of the north as the sad caravan slowly crawled away from the mightiest stronghold of men.

Leisha gave Freedom a nudge to catch up with Perrin who had dug her heels into Trailfoot's sides and was already charging toward the front of the wagon train. The mare closed the distance with little effort and then kept pace. Men bowed at the two queens as they passed, but neither of the women noticed. Perrin's focus remained locked toward the front of the long trail of wagons and Leisha's eyes remained on Perrin. She had grown from a scared young lady into a fierce woman ready for battle seemingly overnight. The determined look on her burned face reminded Leisha of her own countenance when the same dead-eyed bastards that stole Geillan from Perrin had stolen Maelich from her. Perrin would lead her people. Leisha felt a great deal of pity for any with a mind to challenge her. Pure rage could only fuel someone for so long, but this was different. This rage came from the blackest pits of a person's soul, a place where only the most primal emotions live. A person living in that place could do things most men could never dream of.

By the time the two women had made it to the front of the line, four of the scouts that had gone off to secure a safe place to make camp were charging hard toward the caravan. Glord trotted off ahead to meet them. Perrin and Leisha followed close behind. When the three met the four, Glord motioned back the way the riders had come to lead them away from the rest of the group.

Glord looked them over as they slowly fell in line beside him. Then he asked, "Where be Harinot, and why ye all be looking so wild?"

"Me lord," Fielstag—the rider on Glord's left—began, "Harinot has fallen. We been set upon by a small band of grongs, thirty or forty. They had us by surprise. Harinot took five to the Lake with him, but his fire be burning no more. The road ain't safe."

Glord grunted something inaudible and then said, "Take a hundred men and be making it safe again." Then he snapped his fingers, whistled loudly and pointed forward along the trail.

With that, the four scouts charged back down the trail. A few moments later, one hundred additional men on horseback charged up the trail behind them. Glord looked at Leisha and Perrin. Both women wore expressions daring him to correct them or to attempt giving them any type of order.

"Me lady," he bowed toward Leisha. "Me lady," then he bowed toward Perrin. "Please be accompanying me back to the line. There be grongs about. I ain't asking ye to come down off of them horses, but please be keeping with the tight formation. Them grongs be vicious and they be looking for the stragglers."

The two queens demurred and fell back in line with Glord alongside the line of wagons slowly meandering into the trees like a fat snake slithering into tall grass. Neither had anything else to say as both had far too many distractions in their own minds to give further attention to much of anything else.

CHAPTER 30
LOSING GROUND

Daritus slumped in his chair with his eyes closed resting his head on his left thumb while three of the fingers on that hand rubbed slow circles on his forehead. The tokens representing the various factions of his forces lay strewn about the tent and scattered across the map. Everything was going exactly as he expected which meant Havenstahl was losing. Only three days had passed since the giants brought their great machines to the battlefield to cut down the forest, and they had already succeeded in mowing half of it down. His men stood their ground, brave in the face of the nightmares attacking them. Unfortunately, they were horribly outnumbered, and their opponents were far too strong. Once the protection of the trees began to be mowed down, any advantage they had enjoyed quickly melted away.

Doentaat poked his head into the tent. He stared at Daritus's slumped form for a few moments in silence. Once he realized the troubled chief was far too deep in thought to look up, he cleared his throat and said, "Daritus, me friend, have ye a few moments to talk about what be happening out on that battlefield."

Daritus raised his head slowly, his eyes cloudy with confusion as his mind tried to work its way back into his tent. He stared at Doentaat for a brief time in silence. Finally, he shook his head slightly and replied, "Yes, yes highness, please come in."

Doentaat chuckled as he entered the tent, "Ye can be keeping that highness crap. We both be knowing that if not for the great warriors of Havenstahl I'd be king of a mighty puddle of giant's piss. Ye not be a king Daritus, but ye be kingly. I've known many a proper king that can't be saying that about themselves."

The deep lines of Daritus's frown smoothed a bit as a smile just failed to make it to his lips, "It lifts my heart to know I have your support in this campaign, Doentaat. Our friendship has been brief, but it feels like I have called you friend my entire life. I am grateful to have the furious fighting spirit of the dwarves of Alhouim at my back. We will give these foreign invaders a fight they will never forget."

"Aye we will," Doentaat boomed. "Chase their sorry carcasses back across that Great Sea, we will." A broad smile spread across his face, lifting the bottom of his beard a full inch above his beltline. Then he added, "Them be the ones that ain't fallen to the mighty axes of Alhouim."

"Your vigor sends my spirit soaring, Doentaat," that smile finally succeeded in lifting the corner of Daritus's mouth, if only slightly. It lasted only moments before fleeing. Daritus looked earnestly in Doentaat's eyes for a long moment before adding, "Sadly, I am finding it very challenging to share your confidence in victory."

Doentaat's smile made way for a stern expression as the dwarf king puffed up his chest, "What kind of talk be that for the greatest leader of fighting men I ever been having the pleasure of fighting beside? The mighty Ymitoth could not even be counting himself your equal; with a sword maybe but never in the realm of strategy. In that ye be standing alone among any that I've met."

"It is a good plan," Daritus agreed, "but the trees are falling. With each tree that falls, our advantage decreases."

"Aye," Doentaat nodded, "so be letting them have the forest. The fort be where we be making our final stand. Them trees have let them bastards know they be fighting a furious force of men. They ain't been having no easy time of it. The Dragon's Flame been constantly frustrating them as they be knocking them trees down, and the mighty horses of Havenstahl been cutting them to pieces."

Daritus nodded, though the grim look had returned to his face, "Yes, our horses have proven useful and the Dragon's Flame has been more effective among the trees than we could have expected. However, our efforts to outflank the monsters have been frustrated. The giants must have learned of the northern pass to Biggon's Bay, and the force Kantiim sent to follow Ymanchol has met strong resistance. There is no way they will make Biggon's Bay in time to catch the bulk of Bok's force before they reach this clearing."

Doentaat scoffed, "Aye they met some resistance, but they be mowing them down. Kantiim's men be stout and strong and ever pushing them grongs back to that beach."

"But far too slowly," Daritus sighed and scratched his head.

Doentaat stomped his foot and planted his right hand on Daritus's chest, shoving the general deeper into his seat. Then he grasped both arms of the chair and shoved his nose to within an inch of his wavering friend's nose, "Now ye be listening to me and hearing me message well. These men that be dying in them trees and on that pass don't be needing a general that ain't believing in the fight he's got them fighting. They be needing a general that be confident and sure of the mission, even if he be knowing there ain't Dragon's spit of a chance that they be winning. Ye need to get off your arse and get on your horse and ride out to show them that ye be believing in them. Keep your arse off the front line, but ride among them and whip up their spirits. Quit your damn pouting and get out of this damn tent." The dwarf king was shaking and spitting by the time he finished his rant.

Daritus stared into Doentaat's eyes as they flashed a fury that had been absent from his own. The dwarf king seemed far bigger looming above him. Daritus opened his mouth to respond but was interrupted before he could begin.

"What in Dragon's fire is going on in here?" Kantiim asked as he stormed into the tent, grabbed Doentaat by the arm, and spun the dwarf king around. "How dare you?"

Doentaat grabbed the top of Kantiim's chest plate and pulled him down so they were eye to eye, "Ye could stand to hear me message just as much your friend. Ye got men out there dying for a cause ye ain't believing in. They be needing ye both to get out of this tent and give them somebody to follow." He gave the big man a stiff shove and turned back toward Daritus, "Ye have me support, Daritus. Be making sure ye got your own."

Daritus stroked his chin for a moment. Then he slammed both of his fists down on the arms of his chair, stood, and said, "Thank you my friend. That is wise counsel and I would do well to take your words to heart." He walked over to Doentaat, firmly grabbed his right shoulder, and continued, "I have been spending all of my time strategizing and worrying in this tent, paralyzed by the idea of what may come. No more I tell you. The plan has been laid and now we must execute it. I ride out with the sun in the morn."

Kantiim composed himself and said, "It heartens me to hear you say that, old friend. It would greatly raise the men's spirits to see you among them and perhaps receive some words of encouragement from their leader."

Daritus looked from Doentaat to Kantiim and back again, "Forgive me, friends. I have forgotten myself. I am not a man that sits idle in tents playing with maps and tokens while my men fight and die. My sword will taste the blood of grongs, trogmortem, and giants when the sun brings us a new day." He looked back at Kantiim, "Do you bring news from the front?"

Kantiim nodded, "Ymanchol has proven himself more than worthy of my confidence. They are severely outnumbered on the northern pass to Biggon's Bay; yet he has his men charging forward and cutting hordes of grongs down. Even the trogmortem are proving no match."

"What of the Dragon's Flame?" Daritus asked.

"There numbers have been replenished, and they hold strong," Kantiim replied soberly. "Every night since the giants have brought their great machines out to eat the trees, the Dragon's Flame has been running missions to frustrate their efforts. They managed to disable one of the contraptions for a day. It is running again, but they are slowing Bok's progress considerably."

"And Ygraml be stout in holding that trail," Doentaat spoke up. "Though it be shrinking as the forest be falling to them damn machines. The horsemen of Havenstahl be having ice in their veins."

Daritus finally allowed a genuine smile onto his face, "This is all very good news. If Ygraml can hold and Ymanchol can continue his march down the northern pass, Bok will be facing a battle on all fronts when he reaches this clearing."

"Exactly as you planned, old friend," Kantiim smiled. A sober expression replaced the smile as he added, "Sadly, I do have less heartening news."

"Of course ye do," Doentaat sighed, "grim bastard."

"What is it then?" Daritus asked.

"Many of Havenstahl refused to heed your precious wife's warning. They believe that nothing on Ouloos can challenge the strength of Havenstahl's mighty army, especially with the aid of the stout forces of Alhouim. At least half of the townsfolk remained with none to protect them," Kantiim replied, his voice far softer than it had been.

"Bah," Doentaat waved his hand, "ain't a dwarf left Alhouim. Them bastards ain't getting past this clearing."

Daritus stroked his chin again, "I appreciate your bravado, Doentaat, but this is something we would be wise to put some thought to. We may crush Bok's forces in this clearing and win the day, but can we be certain we will completely contain them here? Imagine the destruction a handful of giants or trogmortem could wreak on unarmed, untrained townsfolk. Even one giant could kill them all."

Doentaat chuckled gruffly, "The women of Alhouim will be giving any of them monsters that dare be trying the walls of Alhouim all they can be handling."

"I am certain they would, my friend," Daritus patted the dwarf's shoulder, "but I am not quite so bold as you. I am unwilling to take a chance like that."

"I have already sent one hundred men to mind all of the paths leading into the city and given strict instructions to send word to the front if they should fall under attack," Kantiim piped in. "One thousand more are briefed and ready should the need arise."

Daritus nodded, "Hopefully boredom will be the only enemy they encounter."

"Them bastards will be running the other way," Doentaat scoffed.

"That is the hope," Daritus agreed. "Let us rest now. In the morn we shall rise with the sun and light a fire under our troops."

CHAPTER 31
A NEW QUEEN

The room slowly came into focus as Cialia blinked several times and rubbed the sleep from her eyes. A dull throbbing in her right temple made her want to close them again. She sat up and brushed back the wet hair matted against her cheek. Something wasn't quite right. A slow scan of her surroundings assured her she was in her room in Druindahl, high atop the trees of the Forgotten Forest. Everything was where it belonged, but somehow she felt completely out of place. Her gaze fell upon the bureau across from the foot of her bed. Her music box was missing. Someone had been in her room.

Cialia leapt from the bed and almost fell as soon as her feet hit the floor; her legs quivering from lack of strength. Leaning back against the bed, she steadied herself with her right hand. Crouching slightly, she drew in a deep breath and collected herself. Weakened, from what she did not know, her entire body felt limp and exhausted. Why couldn't she remember the night before? She looked up toward the ceiling and thought for a moment. It wasn't merely the night before escaping her. She couldn't remember anything.

After a few slow, deep breaths, she tried her feet again. This time her legs responded a bit more agreeably. At least she didn't feel like she was going to fall to the floor any longer. Three slow, slightly unsteady steps had her at the door. The latch had never seemed so heavy. As the stout, wooden thing swung slowly open, the fresh forest air filled her lungs and fluttered through her hair. That was better. Her eyes closed as she pulled in a few more deep breaths. The throbbing in her head eased up a bit as her legs grew steadier. Food seemed a wonderful idea. Before she could take one step onto the open corridor outside of her bedroom, a guard blocked her way.

"I need to speak with you, Cialia," he said.

"I am hungry," Cialia replied. "Please do not hinder me."

The guard's eyes narrowed as he examined her and asked, "Do you feel no remorse for what you did last evening?"

Cialia sighed and ran her hand through her hair, "I do not remember last evening. In fact, I do not remember much at this moment. The only thing I am completely certain of is that I am starving. What is your name, soldier? Unless you are interested in challenging my blade, I suggest you let me pass and make my way to the kitchen."

"I am Boringas," he replied. "You know me."

"No," Cialia's head dipped slightly to the right. "You are a man. Boringas is a lad."

"Cialia," Boringas began, "do you truly remember nothing? You burned…no, you obliterated tens of thousands of men to ash. You killed them with fire that *you* created. It was like you pulled it from the air and they all exploded into bits of charred bone and crispy flesh. You wrought impossible destruction. If you truly cannot remember, it is a shame."

"That is horrible," Cialia replied. "If I honestly did such things as you said, how would it be a shame if I could not remember them?"

Boringas shook his head, "Because I cannot make you pay for your crimes. You are far too powerful. Someone should make you pay though, and if you are still the same lass I knew so long ago, you will administer your own punishment."

Recognition filled Cialia's eyes as her mouth slowly opened. There were no words. Her eyes merely widened as the truth of Boringas's words became clear in her mind. She had found her flame and lashed out at those barbaric, dishonorable riders in a furious rage. Her lips quivered slightly then moved as if to form words but no sound sprang forth from her lips.

"You do remember, princess," Boringas said quietly.

"I do," Cialia agreed as sternness crept onto her face and she set her jaw tight. "I also remember why those vile scrods earned my fury. Where is Keiryn's body?"

"She was washed and burned on a pyre as is customary," Boringas replied. "Then she was scattered on the wind high among the canopy, free to float until she finds a place to rest among the trees."

Cialia's expression remained cold as she said, "I would have liked to have been there to bid her flesh farewell."

"You were there to see her off to the Lake," Boringas shrugged. "The flesh is merely a vessel to carry our spirit around this place. You know that. In fact, I believe it is you who taught me that." He sighed and looked out into the trees, "That was so long ago. We were so innocent then. Everything seems so soiled now."

"Children grow old and innocence dies when we learn to pull truth from among the lies."

"You taught me that silly little poem as well, after the first time you killed."

Cialia lifted her chin and squared her shoulders, "It is the truth. Not the truth they tell you but the truth you must learn for yourself. This world is a vile, dirty place where foul men spread their filth until it infects everything, taking all they can while never caring who they break."

"What about the truth Coeptus gave you? You returned to us so righteous, ready to save Ouloos and bring peace to all her people." He looked earnestly into her eyes and asked, "Where did that beautiful soul go?"

A chuckle chased the stern look from her face, "She has been slowly dying over the past five years. The sickness you and your king allowed to settle into this place was the final strike, the dagger that pierced my heart. Coeptus gave me a truth, and I tried to share it. I faithfully spread their word to every ear I could find." She paused and rubbed her forehead, "There is another truth though, the truth that there will always be those who will exploit and terrorize those weaker than themselves."

"I suppose that is true," Boringas shrugged, "and I suppose you will make it your mission to punish those who would do so."

"To protect those too weak or frightened to have a voice," Cialia nodded, "yes. I will make it my mission to protect those who cannot protect themselves. There will be justice in this world."

Boringas remained silent as his eyes moved about her face.

Cialia let out a deep sigh, "Now, I am hungry. If you wish to continue this conversation, please let us do it on our way to the kitchen."

Boringas fell in step beside Cialia as she pushed past him. She could feel his eyes on her face. Was he scrutinizing or admiring? After a few steps she asked, "What is it you hope to find in the lines of my face?"

"I truly do not know?" he replied soberly. "Perhaps I am trying to decipher whether the scowl upon your hardened face is proof you truly feel no remorse for your actions or your effort to convince me of such. Maybe I am trying to determine if you have changed or if my adoration of you blinded me to the darkness in your heart."

"Darkness?" Cialia chuckled dryly.

"I am unable to think of a better word," Boringas's tone remained flat.

A light breeze danced among the tree tops urging the leaves into a gentle waltz. They rustled while they lightly kissed each other and sounded like gentle waves caressing the beach. Each strand of Cialia's matted hair was like one of those leaves and all of them together danced the same waltz in the peaceful, forest breeze.

Boringas broke the silence again, "Even with damp, matted hair waving all about around your head, I find you more beautiful than anything I have ever seen. How can a being so soft and delicate be so hard and lash out with such fury?"

Cialia didn't respond. Neither did she turn her gaze toward Boringas at all as they travelled along the open corridor so high among the trees. Down four steps and then curving around tree after tree, she walked with her chin raised and her eyes facing straight ahead. Even when they finally reached the kitchen and she found herself a slab of meat, some bread, and a little fresh, berry wine, it was as if she were alone. Boringas may as well not even have been there.

Cialia set upon her meal like a ravenous beast, devouring it in silence until Boringas broke the silence again. "I loved you once," he said quietly. "I think I still do. Though I am not sure how."

Cialia finally looked at him, "You did not love me, sweet Boringas. You wanted to own me, to shackle me, to stifle my free spirit."

"No," he smiled as he shook his head. "I loved you. I loved your free spirit. I loved that you refused to be shackled. I loved that you would stand your ground and fight for what you believed in no matter what the cost. I would never dare throw chains on something so perfect and free. That would be like trapping the mighty wind in a jar. Everything making it perfect and wonderful fleeing as it stales in its cell."

"You are such a romantic, Boringas," she finally smiled at him. "You may not believe this, but had I submitted to you, you would have shackled me. I wanted the wind and the trail, freedom. You are sweet, probably the sweetest man I have ever known, but I will never live under the rule of a man."

Boringas shifted in his chair as he laughed and shook his head, "Rule you? Would I ever dare to risk my skin in a game like that? I am far too fond of myself, dear Cialia. I know you. Like a precious gem I have admired you since we both were mere children. During this lifetime of admiration I have gleaned a few truths about the object of my desire. The most important of which is she will defend her freedom violently. I am a damn fine swordsman, but as a warrior you have no equal. It would be a foolish jest on my part to imagine imposing my will on the great Cialia."

Before Cialia could argue, Boringas raised his right finger at her, shook his head again, and said, "No, wait. I am not finished. The things I admire most about you are the things that would be stifled if I even had the power to hold you down and force you to submit to my will. What must you think of me if you see me as this thing so arrogant to believe I could rule over you? I would never conceive of the idea. I did not wish to rule over you but to accompany you, to bask in the sunshine of your presence. To me you are like a beautiful full moon, perfect as it rules the nighttime sky showering its radiant glow across the land." He paused, sighed, and scratched his head before looking around the room and adding, "Apparently you have never felt a similar affection toward me. If you had, you would know me better."

Cialia finished chewing and splashed a bit of wine down her throat. Once her palate was clean enough to speak without spewing moistened crumbs all about the table, she reached across it, took both of Boringas's hands in her own, and said, "Oh Boringas, my dear, sweet friend, my childhood companion, to say I never felt a similar affection for you is a lie. I have loved you for perhaps as long as you have loved me. Alas, that is not my life. My life is to serve; to protect those who cannot protect themselves. And look at the effect that has on you. I saw the fear, even loathing in your eyes as you chastised me. You say you love me; you admire me, but you are seeing me. I am not sorry for what I did to those men in the forest. You take exception to that. You would have me regret actions I cannot regret. I searched those men's souls and found nothing but evil. Then I sent them home where they can do no further harm to anyone."

"You are correct," he shrugged. "I do not agree with your idea of justice."

Cialia smiled as she continued to hold both of his hands, "And you would seek to change that, scolding me about how I am wrong. A weak, innocent girl was set upon by beasts and her sentence for defending herself was an arrow through her throat. That entire band of marauders—who you would call riders of Druindahl—was culpable in her death. Though only one of them drew the string firing the brand into her flesh, all of them wished it could have been them. They were all evil, wicked fiends hungry for blood."

"This is hard for me to say to you, but I think you should leave," Boringas pulled his hands away. "Please, fill your horse sacks, clean yourself up, and prepare for the trail. Whatever you need, we will provide. I do love you, but you are dangerous and I have to protect the people of this fair city. What you call justice does not resemble what we call it here."

She raised her eyebrows, "That must have been very difficult for you to say. I am not leaving though. After I have cleaned myself up, I will see your king and give him an opportunity to stand aside. You are correct. The people of this city, my city, need to be protected. However, you and your king have proven you are incapable of providing that protection."

"How dare you?" Boringas scoffed. "You vile usurper, you know none in this city can oppose you. Do you think that gives you the right to impose your will upon us?"

"Yes, I am imposing my will. I have searched the hearts and minds of the people you are sworn to protect and found nothing but fear. You cannot protect them. I will protect them. They are my people, and this is my city," her smile fled as she spoke.

He folded his hands and leaned back in his chair, "I did the best I could with the tools available to me. You and your brother took our general and most of our riders. What was I to do?"

Cialia shrugged, "I am not accusing you. I am stating the truth. You did the best you could, and it is not good enough. You peopled your army with filthy scum. I eradicated that scum, and I will rebuild Druindahl's army. I would ask you to remain as my general. Your heart is pure and you do mean well."

"The one who fears being ruled by me would ask me to submit to the same," he chuckled. "I will serve as your general, princess, but I will continue to counsel restraint. You have powers it seems you are only just learning to understand. I would hate to see you burned to ash by your own flame."

"I understand my powers," Cialia smiled. "The flames are new for me, but fire is only one element."

A red glow bled into Cialia's eyes as they narrowed. As her gaze looked far past Boringas, she barely noticed the terror twisting itself up in his expression. She couldn't blame him for being afraid. After all, he had witnessed firsthand how destructive her power could be the night before. Right at the moment she thought her old friend may give up on bravery and flee, the kitchen door suddenly popped open and thin vines pushed past it. They slithered in along the floor like snakes. In moments those snaky vines were slipping up Cialia's leg, onto her lap, over her shoulder, and then circling around her head. They wrapped around her skull several times before breaking off their tails and slipping quickly back out the door they had entered through.

Boringas's eyes remained wide as he said, "A crown for a queen."

"Indeed," she replied. "Let us go speak with your king. My people must know they will never live in fear of anything again."

"Of course," his head bowed slightly. "But first, I would ask you to accompany me on a short walk of the forest floor."

Cialia rolled her eyes. "To what end, Boringas?" she asked. "Do you mean to profess your love to me again, weaken me with the fresh fragrance of the forest air, and then take advantage of my weakened state to seduce me?"

Boringas's eyes narrowed as his tone betrayed his injured pride, "No, dear Cialia. You have made it abundantly clear any love you hold in your heart for me is insufficient to stifle your desire to exist as a free spirit unencumbered by the weight of a relationship. Even more, my eyes are finally seeing you clearly for what you truly are. I will always love you, sweet Cialia. However, after seeing your idea of justice, my fear of you has grown far greater than that love. It has grown so massive it eclipses any other feeling for you I have ever had." He smiled and shook his head as his tone gained a bit of strength, "I have no grand schemes of seducing you. I would merely like to show you the carnage you authored against those you deemed unfit for this world."

"And what purpose will that serve?" her tone remained stern but her expression softened slightly.

Boringas shrugged, "I merely want you to witness the result of your strength. The Cialia I remember would not be able to look upon the kind of destruction you caused without feeling something. You sit there so smug and satisfied in your actions with your talk of justice." A scowl crept onto his face as he continued, "But here in this room you are safe from the sight of it. I watched those men burn. I heard them scream in agony as your flames roasted them to nothing but charred bits. Your consciousness fled so quickly I am afraid you had not the time to properly experience it. I want to look in your eyes when they behold the terror of what you have done, and then I want to hear you justify your actions to me."

Cialia's eyes widened, "Who do you think you are speaking to me in such a way?"

The words had barely fallen from her lips when Boringas spat his response, "I am a man, just the same as the men you burned in the forest. Sometimes I make the wrong choice, and sometimes my thoughts are impure. Dare I say, sometimes my thoughts are downright evil? Does that mean I should be killed? Does that mean I should be damned to the fires of an angry god?" Boringas's voice had grown to a shout as he pounded both of his fists on the table, eyes wide with fury. He remained like that for a few moments before closing his eyes, taking a deep breath, and continuing in a far calmer tone, "Perhaps the sight will not move you at all. Still, I beg you. Please join me on the forest floor. I need to know if you are at all affected by what you have done. I need to know if there is any remorse in your heart at all."

Cialia's expression had lost all of its fierceness and her tone fell to just above a whisper, "What will that prove?"

Boringas chuckled and shook his head, "Whether or not I should hope for anything in this world. If you can look upon those charred bits of the men you so brutally punished for having hateful thoughts and remain unmoved, I will know there is no reason for me to ever put faith in any person again. You have no idea what heights you have soared in my eyes. Sure, I have confessed my feelings for you, but you will never know what it is like to look upon you with my eyes. You were flawless, perfect. This," he waved his hands toward her as he paused, searching for the perfect word. After a few moments of his lips soundlessly moving around several that were insufficient, he finally found the one he was looking for, "thing sitting across from me childishly defending her tantrum with nonsensical talk about justice is not you. And if it is, you have fallen, sweet Cialia. You have fallen from the very heights to someplace so low I dare not even look."

"Fine," sternness had crept back onto Cialia's face as she sat quietly listening to her accuser. "I will walk among the remains of those vile creatures you led; those vicious beasts so completely deserving of their fate. I warn you though. When I look at you with eyes completely free from remorse, eyes brimming with justification, then you can turn and walk away from me."

Boringas nodded, rose from his chair, and walked over to the door. Pushing it open, he motioned with his right hand, and said, "Come then, princess. Walk with me amongst the carnage."

The journey to the forest floor lasted roughly ten minutes. Boringas glanced over at Cialia only once during the walk. She didn't look back at him. The smug look on her face fueled the bitterness festering in his gut. His head shook slowly as he rifled through thoughts as quickly as a young lad tossing stones on the beach, looking for the smoothest, flattest one to skip. He wanted to jab at her again with another clever barb. That perfect stone—the one he could skip across the waves six times before pelting her in her smug face—simply wasn't there. He had nothing left. If she could truly look upon the charred remains of the thousands she sentenced to a painful, horrifying death, he would leave the city he loved as well as the woman he had loved for so long. If she could truly look upon that terror and not feel something, anything, the flame he carried for her would finally be extinguished.

As the two stepped off of the cart, Boringas gently touched Cialia's left elbow with his right hand, and said, "This way, princess. There is a clearing to the east. You may not remember it, but we used to play there together as children."

Cialia failed at suppressing a smile as she replied, "How could I forget? You always wanted to play king and queen, and I always wanted to play warriors and grongs."

"Yes," he replied. "And you always won."

The words that were set to leave Cialia's mouth stalled at her lips as her eyes followed a line from the end of Boringas's pointing index finger to the clearing they had played in as children. The twenty remaining riders—the sum of Druindahl's army—pushed carts full of what appeared to be charred wood. As she looked closer, very human looking shapes became clearer among crispy chunks. The clearest one was unmistakably an arm. It had broken off at the elbow. Two of the fingers had burned away or fallen off, and the skin—if it were skin—was charred so significantly it seemed impossible it held together. The three fingers left on the hand attached to that arm were gnarled up as if they were trying to grasp at some invisible thing.

A gasp slipped past Cialia's lips a moment before she found some words, "What are they doing?"

Boringas had expected to smile when he saw the reaction he was hoping for on Cialia's face. Somehow the shock painted across her bulging eyes and slack jaw didn't fill him with the satisfaction he believed it would. The weight of what was left of those thousands of corpses was far too great to feel any joy. "So the god hasn't completely destroyed the girl yet," he muttered through slightly downturned lips.

"I can't...I don't..." Cialia stammered as she fumbled over thoughts that wouldn't quite come together into something cognizant.

"There is no need," Boringas loosely draped his arm across her shoulders. "I just wanted you to see it and digest it." He pulled her closer and added, "I don't suppose I'll ever see you the way I used to see you. In fact, I don't think I'll ever see anything in this world the same way again. You have burned away any innocence my eyes held. However, your expression tells me the Cialia I remember hasn't been completely burned away. I will remain here for you as your general, or whatever else you need me to be."

Cialia's head slowly shook as her loose stammering devolved into nothing more than brief groupings of sounds. Eventually, she laid her head down on Boringas's shoulder and those sounds melted further into quiet whining. By the time they made it back to the cart that would return them to the heights of Druindahl, the whining had matured into full and hearty sobbing.

CHAPTER 32

SHELLAR

Maelich woke shortly before the sun to Mountain licking his face. The mammoth scrod had taken a fond liking to him. Maelich scratched Mountain's head on both sides as he scrambled up to his knees allowing for more effective scratching. His efforts were definitely not wasted. Mountain's rapidly wagging tail and profusely slobbering tongue were evidence of that. "That's a good boy," Maelich whispered, pulling the big animal close and hugging him tightly around the neck.

Maelich stood, patted his leg, and said, "Come on, boy," as he started down a path that led straight east from their camp into the rising sun.

Mountain charged out behind him, gaining, overtaking, and finally falling in place beside him. Both held their heads high as their feet—or paws depending on which species you consider—gobbled up the trail. A cool, breeze played among the trees, far stiffer than what normally blew around the stale air as deep in the woods as they were. The forest's perfume was damp earth and rotting leaves. Somehow it was far more fragrant than the description would suggest. The morning run had always filled Maelich with a sense of freedom nothing else could muster in him. On this particular run, that free feeling was joyously mixed with a bit of nostalgia, as Mountain's panting reminded him of days long past, attacking the trail with Jom by his side.

Back at camp, Braggon woke to find Ymitoth sitting on the other side of the fire he had rekindled and staring at him with those black, dead eyes. Those eyes were unsettling to the wanderer. He hadn't mentioned them the night before. The eerie way they stared at him above and sometimes through flames that danced higher and higher proved to be too much for him. He sat up, scratched his head and asked, "Who stole the color from your eyes, or have they always been as they are?"

Ymitoth's gaze didn't shift at all; those black, dead eyes piercing the orange glow of the fire and appearing to stare into Braggon's skull. "Ain't none stole nothing from me eyes," he said. "I don't be knowing a thing about what color they might be."

"Well I assure you they are quite unique," Braggon replied. "Here," he fished around under his cloak for a few moments and produced a small looking glass. As he handed it over the flames to Ymitoth he added, "Have a look for yourself."

Ymitoth took the thing and gazed into for a few moments. Then he shrugged, handed it back across the flames to Braggon, and said, "Aye, me eyes don't be looking a thing like yours. They maybe always been that way."

"You are a curious man, Ymitoth," Braggon decided as he leaned back against a log and laced his fingers together behind his head. "On the surface you seem straightforward enough, but I cannot help but believe there are many mysteries hiding behind those unique, colorless eyes of yours."

Ymitoth scoffed, "Ain't no mystery to me. I been a warrior all me life, a soldier, a general. There don't be no mystery to that. I be a master with this blade and that be that." He patted the hilt of his sword as he finished.

Braggon's eyes narrowed. "Perhaps you are more than think you are," he said, somewhat offhandedly. Then he slapped both of his thighs in unison, stood, and asked, "Have you anything I could prepare as a meal for us, or should I wander off and find what the forest has provided?"

"Nah," Ymitoth waved the idea off. "There be plenty of meat and bread to fill our bellies before we be off hunting Shellar."

By the time Maelich and Mountain returned from their morning run, juice was spitting and bubbling out of the big slab of meat roasting on a spit over the fire. Mountain curled up on the ground next to Braggon's legs as Maelich sat down upon a log. He removed his shirt and used it to mop the sweat off of himself. Then he grabbed his water skin and took a long pull off of it. Once his thirst was satisfied, he grabbed a small bowl from his pack, filled it with water, and set it in front of the panting scrod.

Ymitoth looked over at Maelich and said, "So I been replaced by a scrod then? Ye leave the master behind for the morning run?"

Maelich laughed, "You were sawing logs so hard I was afraid for the trees. Forgive me father. You looked so peaceful and the time to rise was still far enough off. I decided to let you enjoy the rest."

Bah," Ymitoth croaked, "I be resting when I be dead."

"That will never happen," Maelich replied.

Braggon looked over at Maelich, squinting with his left eye and asked, "What do you mean?"

Maelich glanced back at Braggon and smiled. "What?" he asked.

"What you just said," Braggon began. "You said Ymitoth would never die. What did that mean?"

Maelich shook his head, "I didn't say that."

"Not in so many words," Braggon shrugged, "but you alluded to it. When Ymitoth said he would rest when he was dead, you suggested it would never happen."

Maelich shifted and pulled his shirt back over his head. Then he cleared his throat and said, "Ymitoth of the house Havenstahl is the greatest warrior to ever grace the sweet face of Ouloos. His name is known and feared through all the land. It will remain on the people's lips long after the Dragon has called him home to the sweet solace of the Lake. He will live on in glory evermore."

Braggon nodded slightly, then shrugged and said, "I suppose that might be so."

The three men ate in relative silence. There was a bit of small talk here and there, but the meat they eagerly shoved into their faces kept most of their attention. At one point, Mountain rose, walked over to Maelich, rested his head on the warriors lap, and sighed repeatedly until he began scratching him behind the ear. They remained that way until all had finished eating. Then they broke camp and made ready for the swamp.

"Have ye any weapons in that pack there," Ymitoth asked as he eyed up Braggon's gear.

"I do," Braggon nodded. "I count a small hatchet and quite an impressive dagger among my arms. I had a good broadsword for a time. Unfortunately, it proved quite a bit quicker at hacking up the brambles than my hatchet did."

"Unfortunately?" Maelich asked.

"Yes, unfortunately," Braggon replied. "You see, it also proved far less durable to the task. After a few, short hours I had managed to work quite an impressive bend into the blade. At that point it was no longer worth its weight."

Ymitoth chuckled and said, "Aye, always be knowing your tools."

"Indeed," Braggon smiled. Then he pointed just a hair to the south of due west and said, "We shall find your prize there near midday. How long before or after depends on our pace."

"I am feeling mighty this morning," Maelich said. "I could run the trail if the two of you are able." Then he patted Mountain's head and added, "I believe I speak for him as well. We are ready."

"You have yet to see the trail," Braggon's smile widened as he stepped into a thick bramble on the west end of their camp. "It is this way."

Their path could not be called a trail by any stretch of the imagination. They had left the proper trail that held them lost and walking in circles for so many days far behind. Through thick banks of wild bushes, over—and sometimes under—fallen trees, and through an increasingly large number of mucky puddles that seemed to grow deeper as they progressed; the small company scrambled and trudged. Thorns poked them while stiff branches scratched all the exposed parts of their skin. All the while burs grabbed hold of their clothes and matted up their hair. After what seemed a solid week of traveling, Braggon stopped.

"That was the first mile. Are you completely sure the prize you seek is worth the journey?" Braggon asked.

Ymitoth replied, "I'd be fine finding an easier way out of this swamp, but the lad here won't be turned back. I can tell ye that."

"I have given my word," Maelich replied.

"As you wish," Braggon's grin was painfully forced. "The trees and brambles thin a bit from here, but the footing becomes far more treacherous. The swamp grows deeper as well. There are more than a few points that will swallow you up completely if you miss a step."

They continued on, and true to Braggon's word, the brambles and trees thinned a bit. Though the foliage wasn't as thick as it had been, the dense canopy still kept the travelers in something like twilight. It was near midday yet thick tree trunks, draping vines, and gnarled, twisted roots—that had become the only sure place to set a foot—appeared dim and gray. Browns and greens were lost in the slim breath of light filtering down to the swamp. Even wild berries that should have boasted vibrant, reds, blues, and purples were all but indistinguishable from the drab, colorless murk of the swamp.

"Shh," Ymitoth stopped and raised his right hand. His eyes narrowed as he cocked his head to the right.

Maelich's head snapped up and he whispered, "I just heard it too, a scream, close and to the northwest."

Mountain's hair stood from the base of his head to the base of his tail as he maintained a low growl. The massive scrod bent on his haunches and then leapt in the direction of the sound. Far nimbler on the slick roots than his large form would suggest, Mountain was out of sight in three long strides announcing his approach with vicious, furious barking.

"Amatilazo," Braggon said as he looked back. "It must be. Nothing else could earn such fury from my scrod."

Without a word, Maelich charged off behind the beast. The slippery footholds slowed him slightly but he made up for it by grabbing branches to help his balance as well as propel him through the murkiness more quickly. The screams gained volume as he charged forward following the fury of Mountain's bark. Mere moments passed before he could make out shapes through the mess of branches and brambles before him. There were at least ten large shapes chasing a smaller one. In the dim light, he was still too far away to determine what any of those shapes might be. The screaming definitely sounded like a small girl.

Ahead and to the left, there was a small clearing with a hut in the center of it. Hopefully that meant solid ground. Mountain made the clearing as soon as the first shape did, and it was a small girl. Maelich hit the clearing next and could only tell she was small—six to eight summers at best—and had light colored hair. Mountain made it across the clearing, leapt over the small girl's head, and pounded an amatilazo in the chest as soon as it exited the forest. He had the thing's bloody esophagus in his mouth before they hit the ground. The big scrod immediately lunged at the throat of another and earned more gore for his fangs. Three more that had been running with the newly deceased fled with Mountain biting at their heels.

By the time Maelich reached the other edge of the clearing, five more amatilazo had burst forth from the trees. Three of them leapt high at Maelich while the other two continued to chase the girl toward the hut. Maelich pulled his sword out and slashed one across the belly. Once the point of his blade had reached the bottom of the arc of that slash, he thrust it up into the soft spot under the jaw of another. As soon as the third hit the ground, crouching deep to leap again, Maelich brought his blade down on the back of its neck like an executioner and relieved the beast of its head.

A piercing scream sliced the murky air. Maelich glanced quickly into the woods to see Mountain furiously tossing body parts about in the trees. Confident the scrod had things well in hand; he turned and charged toward the hut. Ten long strides later he was kicking the door in. The screaming continued, but a quick scan of the room failed to locate the small girl making all of the noise. Both of the amatilazo were snapping and clawing at the fireplace.

"Hey," Maelich shouted at the two beasts.

The one on the left stood, turned, and screamed a hellish, screechy howl at Maelich. One step toward the warrior was all the beast could manage before the handle of Maelich's dagger was protruding from its forehead. Maelich stalked toward the fireplace as he watched the beast slip slowly to the ground. Saliva dripped off of its fangs onto black lips twisted up in an expression that made the yellow-eyed thing appear even more grotesque. The second beast barely had a chance to stand and turn before its head was flipping toward the wall.

"Everything is going to be alright," Maelich said toward the fireplace. "They are gone."

The screaming slowly subsided in place of a dull, exhausted whining.

"Are you stuck in there?" Maelich asked.

###

Ymitoth took a step to follow Maelich toward the screaming, but Braggon shot his foot out, kicking him the shins and depositing him in the swamp. The muddy slop slowed the old warrior down as he struggled to get free from the vines he had become tangled in. The struggle lasted several minutes until he finally managed to get his soaking self out of the sludge and onto a clump of roots. Braggon's betrayal didn't fully register with him until he turned back to see the traitor smiling and pointing his own blade at him. Instinctively, Ymitoth's right hand shot for the hilt of his sword. The effort served to prove the obvious. Braggon had stolen it as he fell into the murky waters of the swamp.

"Ye be a vile, traitorous bastard," Ymitoth spat.

"Not in the least," Braggon shook his head. "I serve my queen well. In fact, I have obediently served her for at least two hundred years now."

"I should have thrown me dagger at your heart," his teeth were clenched together so tightly it is amazing the words were able to make it out of his mouth.

"You probably should have," Braggon smiled. "You made my task quite easy. Maelich really is a hero." A hearty laugh momentarily paused his gloating. "I could almost hear trumpets blaring every time the man spoke. And the way he charged off after that scream," he lost himself in another fit of laughter, "well that was simply breathtaking. Oh, he just oozes heroism. I almost followed him into battle."

Ymitoth had no more words. His scowl was the only reply he had left for Braggon.

The gloating peacock continued, undaunted by the lack of response, "You though, I still have not figured you out. I mean, what are you? Those black, dead eyes are not the eyes of a man or anything else I have ever seen," he paused, "alive."

"And I ain't be like nothing you'll ever see again," Ymitoth finally spoke as he fired his dagger at Braggon's heart.

Braggon nonchalantly flicked the blade away with Ymitoth's sword. "Seriously?" he mocked. "You do realize I allowed you to capture me in the forest, do you not? I had to. The two of you had been wandering in circles so long Shellar was beginning to think you would never find her. I could have cut you down at any time. You will die here in this swamp with me while your precious hero is ground to dust by my queen."

Ymitoth shrugged, "The hard way then."

As the words left Ymitoth's lips, he crouched deep and leapt across the swamp toward Braggon. The blade of his own sword wielded by the traitor was flying toward his face before he made it halfway to the thick mass of roots the man stood upon. Ymitoth raised his left forearm up in front of his face blocking the strike as his right fist crashed into Braggon's nose and popped it in a flash of blood that appeared as gray as everything else in the dreary, swamp light. Braggon would have fallen into the muck had Ymitoth not followed up the heavy punch with a left that grabbed a hold of the treacherous bastard's collar instead of delivering another blow. Before Braggon could swing Ymitoth's sword again, the old warrior yanked on the traitor's collar and pounded his forehead into Braggon's nose. Then he did it once more for good measure.

Ymitoth pulled Braggon close and growled, "Me lad ought to be slaying your queen right at this very moment."

Blood and spittle flew out of Braggon's mouth as he laughed, "The queen of this swamp is eternal. No man will ever kill her."

Ymitoth wrestled his sword from Braggon's grasp and held it against his throat as he said, "If she still be living by the time I find her, I'll be killing her then." He pulled the blade slowly across the ancient man's throat as he spoke, and then watched the bastard's eyes cloud over. He didn't let the carcass fall into waters of the swamp until he was certain it had expired.

Ymitoth growled at his forearm as he assessed the damage. The mail of his sleeve had saved his arm from being completely hacked off. He could see a bit of bone through the severed meat though. It was a good cut. There was no time for worrying over a little blood and meat though. Maelich needed help.

As Maelich crouched in front of the hearth, the whining coming from behind the fieldstone of the chimney had morphed into a horrible growl. It sounded more like a chorus of massive beasts than an individual, small girl. There was something high pitched, almost squeaky sailing across the top of it while an inhuman shout danced about its middle. Layered at the bottom of those and other unspeakable sounds was this low, deep rumbling like the hooves of one thousand horses pounding solid stone while their riders clashed sword to shield without meter.

Maelich shouted at the hearth, "Is there something in there with you? Are you trapped?"

The chorus of horrifying sounds amplified in response. Then it spread like a net around him. He stood and spun slowly as the shrieking scream grew louder and louder, surrounding him. The walls of the hut began to quake, a slight tremble at first but in moments they rumbled and shook violently. Maelich gripped his sword.

Suddenly the hut exploded around him. Chunks of wood and stone as well as shards of glass flew away from him at an impossible rate for a split second and then paused. He circled again, marveling in confusion at the perfect dome of shattered debris surrounding him. It was completely still as if time had stopped. The fractured pieces of the hut slowly began melting together into a clear, jelly-like membrane rippling like water disturbed by a carelessly tossed pebble.

"What is this enchantment?" Maelich whispered.

The translucent membrane continued to solidify and then attain color. Brownish-green fluid, like swamp water, flowed inside the membrane. It was constantly moving, swirling, and gurgling. The screaming began again. Maelich had been so entranced by the rapid transformation of the hut he had failed to notice the complete silence that followed the explosion. A sound apart from the agonizing chorus pulled his attention back to the spot where the fireplace had been. The open hearth remained, yawning like a cavernous mouth waiting to swallow him whole. A few shuffled steps backward were all he managed before a thick, purple, vine—looking more like a muscle than any form of vegetation—shot out from it and wrapped around his leg.

Maelich fell to the ground and dropped his sword as the thick vine squeezed tighter on his ankle while slowly dragging him toward the yawning mouth, that black abyss, that doorway to emptiness. He stretched for his sword but it was already far out of reach. Struggling to grab a hold of the earth beneath him, his efforts earned nothing but handfuls of slippery muck. As the slow drag toward doom continued, the hearth surrounding the black abyss faded in favor of a thick, rounded beak lined with rows of menacingly sharp teeth. Maelich finally realized his folly. This was the trick. There was no illusion of a banquet and no feast. Shellar knew her victim and set the perfect trap to ensnare him. The frightened little girl, the amatilazo, the hut, none of it had been real. It was all a grand illusion to lure him close enough for an attack.

As Maelich struggled against the vine-like tongue gripping his ankle and slowly dragging him across the moist ground, he could barely hear Mountain barking above all of Shellar's horrible screaming. The scrod would be no help against the fangs dripping within that awful, black beak. A mere six inches separated Maelich's foot from the point of the horrible thing. It slowly, almost mechanically worked up and down as if it couldn't wait to grind him to dust. Despite all of his struggles and all of Mountain's furious barking and scratching at the ground, the heroic meal slowly slid closer and closer to a gruesome death.

Maelich quieted his mind, took a slow, deep breath in, and released it just as slowly. He pulled his dagger from under his cloak, leaned up at his waist and stabbed at Shellar's tongue several times. The ear shattering screams grew even louder as she lost her grip on him. He rolled backward, retrieved his sword, and slashed at the monster's shell as he stood. The swampy liquid filling the membrane serving as her body quickly oozed out of the cut Maelich's blade left in it. The screaming continued to gain volume as her massive, purple tongue whipped around the dome the witch of the swamp created with her body. Maelich ducked and rolled and flipped and dodged avoiding the wild attacks. Finally, he collected himself, crouched deep, and leapt toward the beak, slashing the tongue near its base. It writhed and whipped about on the ground as if it were motivated by its own thought.

Suddenly, Shellar collapsed on Maelich. The thick ooze covered him. The giant black beak was right next to him, still opening and closing in the same mechanical fashion. It grew ever closer as it continued to work open and shut. The weight of the beast crushed down on his chest. Breathing quickly became a labor. He could barely move and that damn beak was almost on top of him. He turned his wrist up. It was slow. All of the weight bearing down on him was impossible. A throaty groan forced its way past his clenched teeth as he pushed with all of his might. Finally, something popped. His entire arm felt free. Groping and pulling through the slop, he managed to slip his entire body through the hole his blade had punctured.

Once he had risen back to his feet, he was able to fully take in the globular blob surrounding him. The murky brown liquid that had filled the membrane oozed all over his feet. Brave Mountain remained at the edge of the thing, barking but unwilling to step onto it. The thing began rising around him. He slashed and slashed at it with his sword, leaving long gashes in it and hacking pieces off. Despite all of his efforts, Shellar once again surrounded him under a dome of dripping muck. The oily ooze splashed him and pooled around his feet as he continued to hack at it furiously. Meanwhile, the black beak was moving toward him again, still screaming and working up and down. He hammered at the shiny, black thing with his sword, cracking it with every strike. The screaming grew louder still. The membrane began to quiver and then slowly collapse around him again, suffocating him with the smell of death. Maelich's limbs kept working as he fell to his back, kicking, slashing, punching; all the while soaking in putrid, brownish-green, swamp water.

Finally through the murk, Maelich saw a dark mass floating among the rancid fluid. It was connected to the beak by two cords. Struggling to his feet, he charged toward that mass and slashed it in two. The chorus of screaming increased momentarily in one final crescendo and then stopped. In complete silence, Shellar fell to the ground around Maelich. He quickly glanced about. Mountain had stopped barking and sat just at the edge of the mass. Ymitoth was charging out of the trees from the other direction. Dizziness flooded into his head, swaying him and buckling his knees. The repugnant smell and lack of oxygen slowly blackened his vision until the trees seemed to fly up around his head. Then the canopy stared back as his eyes blinked slowly, once, twice, then darkness.

CHAPTER 33
GODS ON THE BEACH

Brerto hovered a few feet above the waves in the center of Biggon's Bay. Arms outstretched, his open eyes posed various contradictions. They appeared a void, the absence of color, shallow and empty. At the same time, however, they appeared deep and unending; all perceivable colors melting together like white light broken by a swirling and twisting prism. Those eyes stared up at the sky as outstretched arms wore palms facing the same direction. The god appeared like stone, unmoving, frozen in time. It was an illusion though. Brerto's will was hard at work filling the hearts of giants, trogmortem, and grongs with resolve and shouting at their minds to drive on, trample the men, and claim the prize. The greatest city of men lie waiting to be plucked from its pedestal so high above every other city, the favorite of Kallum brought low, seduced by the Dragon.

Standing on the beach with bare feet in the sand, two gods watched the spectacle. They had remained in that spot invisible to all but themselves and Brerto. Existing among the carnage, they let the violence fill them up and strengthen their opposition to the wily force they called brother. The scattering of Kallum had done nothing to stifle Brerto's ambition. He became even more brazen than he had ever been. The wet sand on their feet, saturated with the blood of the men who followed them, served to remind the two that the fight for peace had not ended over the Forgotten Forest with the scattering of the great Eagle.

"He is tireless," Moshat remarked.

"Indeed," Kaldumahn agreed.

"If only he would challenge me I would batter him from one end of this bay to the other and then across this world and back again," Moshat scowled.

"That is precisely why he will not."

"Brother," Moshat raised his voice out across the bay, "Brerto, defiler, enemy of peace, come test your mettle against me, coward. Pull back the monsters you would send to do your bidding in your stead."

A smile slipped onto Brerto's face as he lowered his hands to his sides. "I am here," he replied. "I have not left this bay since this war began. You call me coward. Yet there you sit idly watching me as I do my work."

"I wait for the moment when your monsters fail and fall before the resolve of the honorable men they fight. The moment when you realize you have lost and decide to enter the battle is the moment I wait for."

"Your men will falter and their great city will crumble to the ground beneath the feet of my giants. Havenstahl shall be no more. Bok will raise the flag of Maomnosett high above the ruins and leave it an empty shell. Then he will march on Alhouim and reclaim his brother's throne," Brerto goaded.

"All of this for a city of dwarves and an imagined slight against the name of a pompous family of giants?" Kaldumahn asked. "There must be more at stake than the shame of Maomnosett. Does Bok kneel before you Brerto?"

"Giants kneel before none," Brerto boomed.

"None to bow before the great and mighty Brerto," Moshat mocked. "You are no god. You are nothing more than a marginalized nightmare. A bad dream the people of this land once had, just like our scattered brother."

"Oh, Moshat," Brerto chuckled. "The two of you are both so simple. My goals soar far higher than the bent knees of men or giants could raise me. I will grind you beneath my feet in due time. Be patient my brothers. The days you remain to haunt this place are few."

"Enlighten us then, oh wise Brerto," Kaldumahn bowed dramatically. "What lofty goal have you set? What grand scheme do you hope to achieve on the backs of terrifying giants, horrible trogmortem, and savage grongs?"

"A wish from your lips to my ears that will remain unsatisfied," Brerto's expression became resolute. "A great power has been born into this world. Believe me when I tell you, mighty Kaldumahn, you will burn."

"Maelich's son," Moshat smiled. "Make a play for the son of the Lake and you will know what it is to burn."

Brerto's laugh was like thunder rolling up from his belly, "The lad has already been taken. While the forces of Havenstahl battled my nightmares and the two of you held vigil on the beach, the great Eagle came to claim his prize. This war is already lost. It does not matter how many giants die. It does not matter how valiantly the men fight. The greatest power on Ouloos is being trained to destroy all. This entire world will bow before me, and then you will know my goal."

"You lie," Moshat shouted. "Kallum has been scattered. We would have felt him had he returned."

"Whatever you say," Brerto shrugged. "Scurry off to that great city of men and test my words. This war is over." With that, he raised his arms back out to his sides and leaned his head back toward the sky.

Kaldumahn opened his mouth to speak, but Moshat touched his arm and said, "He is gone. Any further conversation will serve only to frustrate us and amuse him."

"He lies," Kaldumahn gritted his teeth.

"We should test the truth of his words," Moshat nodded. "He is not above spilling a falsehood to frustrate us when he has lost position in a debate, but what he said is possible. What if the assault on this bay was all a ruse? Bok may have raised an army to defend the name of his clan, but why now? Why would he wait so long when his nephews had tried and failed several years prior?"

"Why indeed?" Kaldumahn agreed as the two turned and walked toward the scarred field of stumps that used to be the forest. "Are we so narrow minded, so easily duped we could fall so fully into a simple trap?"

Moshat stopped and closed his eyes. Moments later they opened again and he answered the question, "It appears we are. Half the city of Havenstahl now flees for Druindahl and the catalyst for their flight was a visit from Kallum's priests. Those foul, dead-eyed creatures have stolen the heir to the throne of Havenstahl, heir to the throne of Ouloos."

A deep sigh poured from Kaldumahn's lips. It seemed to deflate him. "How could we be so blind?" he asked.

"How indeed?" Moshat shook his head. "The god will not be found until he comes to destroy us all."

Kaldumahn nodded, "We must force Brerto's hand. Havenstahl must not fall. The great White Tiger must take the battlefield so we might cut him down and even the odds."

Moshat shrugged, "We should and we will. But once Kallum unleashes the power of Maelich's son, none of us old gods will matter. That all-consuming fire will burn us to ash and scatter us on the wind."

"He will," Kaldumahn agreed. "Until that time comes, we shall fight with all of our might."

CHAPTER 34
THE OLD SOLDIER

Heels hammering the sides of his horse, Daritus charged down the trail. The men around him hollered war cries in celebration of their general charging into battle alongside them. All of the shouting mingled with the sound of thousands of horse hooves pounding the dirt of the trail and echoed off of the trees. Four sweaty horses across, the cavalry raced toward the monsters blocking their path. The old general raised his sword high above his head and let out a furious howl. The men behind him erupted in a cheer that peeled through the forest like an explosion.

"This is our land," Daritus's voice boomed above the chaos of ten thousand screaming voices. "Spill the blood of these monsters to feed our trees."

A mere five hundred yards down the trail a hideous parade of nightmares trudged on toward battle. Grongs marched alongside horrible trogmortem, those monstrous beasts that shook the ground when they walked. Those vibrations remained unfelt as the earth shook beneath the hooves of the riders bearing down on them. More than one nightmare thought of fleeing the terror of wild-eyed men perched atop wild-eyed horses. Two trogmortem led the army of horrors toward the coming storm, Beegam-Kur and Kyram-Nik. Their pace was slow and their march quiet.

Beegam-Kur turned toward the throng following him, "Crush these men. Grind them beneath your feet." Barely audible over the approaching stampede, his shout lacked sincerity.

Close enough to see the trepidation in Beegam-Kur's eyes, the wily general seized on it and shouted to the rampaging horde behind him, "These monsters have fear in their eyes. We men are the nightmares of the battlefield on this day. Today we bathe in the blood of beasts."

As impossible as it seemed, the furious cry of Havenstahl's cavalry grew even louder. The speeding cavalcade of riders cut through the column of trogmortem and grongs like a spear slicing into soft flesh. Blades flashed in the sunlight before hacking into skin, muscle, and bone splashing blood upon the trail and into the trees. Grong spears filled the air in response, but the quivering hand of one gripped with faith-shattering terror seldom finds its mark. Hooves of merciless horses urged on by riders consumed by their heroic objective trampled helpless grongs, battering the nightmares into the dirt of the trail, crushing bones and grinding muscles into goo.

Beegam-Kur hung onto the trunk of a stout tree. Blood pulsed from the gash Daritus had left in his neck. The trees blurred before his eyes as a cloud of dust poured into the trees kicked up by the hooves of those terrifying horses. A chill settled in between his shoulder blades as it grew increasingly more difficult to remain erect. Darkness seeped into the edges of his vision. He could barely see the bodies of grongs and even mighty trogmortem crashing into the trees around him. The sun faded as his fingers slipped away from the bark of the tree, and he fell to the forest floor. The last image dancing before his closed eyes as he left the physical were the eyes of that wild general who cut him down; the furious, relentless man who refused to be denied victory.

Men fell alongside the monsters they cut down, but their numbers were few. The real heat of the battle on the trail that day lasted only moments. Once the first one hundred rows of grongs and trogmortem had been trampled, slashed, or cast aside, fear wrapped itself around the hearts of stout grongs and mighty trogmortem. Quaking before the rage of the men bearing down on them, the balance of the force turned and fled. The horses of Havenstahl were far too fast to allow an easy escape, however, and many a fleeing nightmare was vanquished on the trail.

"To the beach," Daritus shouted. "Give them no rest and no peace. Cut them down like they would cut down your sister or your mother. Show them no mercy."

It wasn't long before the expansive column of horsemen reached the tree eating machines of the giants and a fresh force of fighting grongs. Spears—thrown with far more accuracy than those encountered on the trail—filled the air. The column of charging horses spread out into a loose mob of stamping hooves and slashing blades. Daritus took a moment to absorb the vast open space that only a week prior had been a dense bank of stout, old trees. Those mighty, ancient sentinels were gone. Trunks sheared a mere breath above the forest floor and thick piles of dust and woodchips were the only reminders the massive trees had ever lived. Sadness held sway in Daritus's heart and mind for the briefest of moments. An agonizing mixture of fear and pure, ferocious rage chased it away; rage for the gall of these monstrosities that would dare mar the perfection of the land he held so dear and fear at the sheer volume of nightmare creatures crowded into the wide clearing left behind. Column upon column and row after row of grongs and trogmortem had entered the fray.

Five men flew from their horses as a giant swung a wild backhand across them. A moment later, one of those horses that had just lost its rider sailed past Daritus's head, tossed by the same giant. The beast smashed men and stomped their mounts into the dirt. The riders of Havenstahl slashed and kicked and fought, but they failed to slow the giant at all. Daritus charged toward the beastly terror, recognizing him immediately. It was Bok. The missing left eye put out by Spang gave him away.

Within moments, Daritus was close enough to attack. By this time, Bok had noticed the brazen general's advance and stretched his arms out wide to invite the competition. Five feet from the giant, Daritus leapt up onto his horse's saddle and launched himself toward the giant's head. Meanwhile, Bok had already thrown both of his fists crashing down on the saddle that Daritus had occupied moments prior. The horse collapsed, crushed under the weight of the giant's fury. While his horse's bones were crushed and life fled from its body, Daritus sailed over the top of Bok, barely managing to tuck his head into his chest, hit the ground with his left shoulder, and roll back up to his feet. Sword drawn, he spun to face the giant just as his adversary did the same.

Bok smiled and said, "You're a spry little soldier, aren't you?"

"I am many things," Daritus spat. "Most importantly, I am the last thing you will see in this life." As the final word left his lips, he dove toward the giant's legs and rolled between them, spinning and slashing at the monster's calves as he regained his feet.

The cut on Bok's right calf was shallow, but Daritus's blade managed to sink a bit deeper when it tasted the left. The giant howled and spun toward him, swinging a wild, left backhand. Daritus easily ducked beneath the assault, but failed to avoid the massive right fist following it. Four granite knuckles pounded him from his left shoulder down to his waist and sent him crashing to the ground a solid ten feet from where he had stood. He rolled twice after pounding the hard earth and immediately scrambled back to his feet. Pain radiated out from his elbow, shoulder, and wrist as he made a futile effort at moving his arm. He stared down at the limp thing, probably willing it to move on some level. The more he tried to move it the more it hurt. He gave up the attempt just in time to dive out of the way of the leaping giant. A short breath later, Bok's right knee hammered into the stump Daritus had been standing on.

Daritus, the wily general, was a seasoned warrior. His limbs and fists and feet and teeth were all tools as useful and effective as his sword and daggers. He pushed the pain ravaging his left arm to a place deep in the back of his mind. That weapon was lost for this fight. He lunged toward the crouching giant with his left foot and pounded his blade into the right side of Bok's back, just above the waistline. The giant's hide was at least as thick as the stories suggested. It was definitely not impenetrable though. Daritus's sword sunk deep into that sturdy flesh, at least halfway up to the hilt. He lost his grip on it as Bok roared and spun toward him.

Daritus took several quick steps backward, fishing under his cloak for one of his daggers. Again Bok's speed contradicted his size, and the back of his hand connected with Daritus's torso and face. The blow sent him sailing through the air once again. Despite the tilting of the earth, the battered warrior struggled back up onto his unsteady legs in time to see his own sword flying toward his chest, flung like a small throwing knife by the giant. Even with fresh legs and a clear mind Daritus would have trouble avoiding the blade he had spent the prior evening sharpening for battle. A quick step to the right saved his heart but sacrificed his left shoulder. The impact of the blade slipping through his flesh and pounding into bone deposited him roughly back upon the ground. On his way back to the dirt and shredded bits of tree, he managed to retrieve one of his daggers from its scabbard. Though his left arm was completely useless, the aim of his right hand was true. A moment after he flicked his right wrist, Bok was blind in both eyes.

"Bastard," Bok roared as he stumbled and fell to the ground a few feet from where Daritus was again scrambling back to his feet.

Daritus had no words for the giant. His attention became completely focused on maintaining his balance and consciousness. He was not silent however. A roar at least as terrifying as anything a giant or trogmortem could muster rushed out of his mouth sounding more like a war cry than the bleak description of pain it really was. The blade of his sword had lodged itself deep between his collar bone and ribcage. It shredded the meat of his shoulder even more on the way out than it had on the way in. Daritus steadied himself and then stumbled over to Bok's massive, writhing form. Both of the giant's hands covered his eyes as he moaned. Daritus leapt onto his chest. Bok's roaring melting into loud, throaty gurgling as the sword sliced through his thick neck and ceased as the blade severed his spine. Daritus fell to the ground beside the giant's quivering corpse.

Men, grongs, trogmortem, and giants all paused to look over at the two when Daritus's voice had filled up the clearing with his supposed war cry. All of them saw the general of Havenstahl steal Bok's life with the might of his blade. The men cheered a chorus with such volume their revelry could be heard clearly at the palace like roaring thunder peeling across the sky. Giants, trogmortem, and grongs looked on in silent confusion. Bok the mighty, Bok the conqueror, Bok the irresistible power, was dead. The mightiest of all giants had been felled by the blade of a mere man.

As the riders of Havenstahl began to reengage their enemies, a small group of grongs led by Chark charged toward Daritus and the dead giant.

Chark was the fiercest warrior serving under Glung and considered by many to be the finest grong warrior to ever live. The razor sharp bicalchrin blades of the grongs he led yearned to taste Daritus's flesh and spill his blood while murderous intent danced across their reptilian eyes. Those hungry blades would remain unsatisfied as Kantiim charged up to the barely conscious warrior and dismounted. Chark and the ten grongs with him quickened their pace, but were met by other riders who circled their fallen general. By the time the legendary grong and the two left with him made it to Bok's body, Kantiim was already charging back up the trail toward Fort Maomnosett.

Daritus lay draped across the base of Glory's neck. Kantiim's right hand pressed against the small of his back to keep him from slipping off the charging horse. The ground raced by beneath him in brief bits he glimpsed in between long blinks. There were monsters in the trees. Bok had sent several small groups of grongs and trogmortem into the forest ahead of their tree eating machines to break up the camps of Havenstahl's forces. He would have to trust Kantiim's sword and expertise as a rider to protect him if they met any of them. All of his fight remained in the clearing hovering around the corpse of a giant.

"I killed a giant," he groaned.

"What?" Kantiim leaned closer his face.

Daritus mustered as much volume as he could and almost boomed, "I killed a giant."

Kantiim chuckled at his old, battered friend's enthusiasm and said, "You did. You killed the mightiest of giants. The great Bok is a terror no more. He has been felled by mighty Daritus, leader of men."

"Ott will seek retribution," Daritus croaked, his voice beginning to fail as weariness overcame him.

"He will," Kantiim agreed. "Do not trouble yourself with such things now. The day is won, and the battlefield is ours. You have delivered a devastating blow to our enemy and now need to heal. Sleep my friend. I will deliver you to Hagen. He will see you back to form."

The battered warrior finally drifted off to sleep as Kantiim urged Glory on to greater speed. His light-hearted demeanor had been an act for the sake of an old friend. Daritus had lost far too much blood and time was the enemy. Bok had taken nearly as much from Daritus as the old soldier had taken from the mighty giant. If Kantiim failed to get Daritus to Hagen in time, the two armies will have traded a leader for a leader and no gain would have been made.

CHAPTER 35
A NEW DAY IN DRUINDAHL

King Blancus rose from his throne after a long day of listening to the sorrowful lamentations of his people; how this one wronged that one and what so and so had stolen from so and so. The bulk of his time was spent passing judgment between neighbors. There seemed a never-ending supply of complaints, and they all found his ear. On this day, his mind was more detached from those complaints than normal. Cialia had returned to Druindahl in a literal blaze of glory. All but twenty riders burned to ash. Those twenty riders, along with one hundred swords that made up the royal guard, were the sum of what remained of Druindahl's defenses. Adding to the distraction was the fact that Cialia had made clear her intention of taking the throne from him. This would be the last day his rump would warm it. Whether that was more a frustration or a relief remained a point for debate.

The king had only managed three steps from the most important seat in Druindahl before Boringas stormed into the room and said, "Your Highness, may I present Cialia, former princess of the great city of Druindahl?"

King Blancus's form wilted slightly as he slowly closed his eyes and sighed, "Must you, Boringas? It has been a long, arduous day full of the complaints of the people who seem to find joy only in antagonizing each other."

Before Boringas could respond, Cialia stepped past him and took control of the conversation, "Thank you for the introduction, Boringas, but I am fully capable of stating my own business. Not to mention, the king knows full well who I am, and there is no need to remind him of my accolades." After a brief pause she turned her attention to the king and continued, "I wish I could say it is a pleasure to see you, Blancus, but I am a champion of truth. My disappointment with how far my fair city has fallen while in your care has removed any pleasure returning home could bring me. When my family ruled this place there were not a day full of complaints to be heard. The people were happy and led fulfilling lives. What has happened to my majestic city in the trees while she has been in your care?"

The king's smile was less than genuine as he replied, "Your family left few swords to defend this place when you departed, and the crown has found very few friends. This great city needs a great army. We are still charged with protecting the Lake and the Dragons residing there. I had to make some difficult choices."

"I heard of none of your challenges," Cialia retorted.

"Hubris," King Blancus shrugged. "Your mother trusted the rule of this great city I love to me. It was an honor I felt I deserved. How could I cry for help and admit I was not up to the task? I am not proud of how I ruled this place, and I am not happy about what it has become." He removed his crown and turned it over in his hands, examining it. Then he continued, "Look at this crown. The detail is amazing. Druindahl's entire history played out in images etched into fine prang. To me it is a beautiful and horrible thing, far too heavy for my head. You can have it, fair Cialia. I pray you wear it with more honor and better judgment than I did."

"You made some very poor choices," Cialia replied coolly. "However, I know you did what you believed to be right. I will relieve you your crown, but I would ask you to remain. Though your judgment has been questionable, I believe with guidance and the proper tools you could serve our city well as an advisor."

The former king dropped his left knee to the floor and bowed, "It would be my honor to serve the queen of Druindahl at her pleasure."

"Rise, Blancus," the new queen politely scolded. "The people I protect have no need to bow. My people stand tall. Go and rest now. Let the weight of the past five summers fall from your shoulders. I have tasks for you. Tomorrow will be a new day."

Blancus nodded slightly and replied, "Thank you, highness. I eagerly await your command." A relieved smile managed to work its way onto his face as he left the room.

Cialia walked up to the two thrones sitting against the wall opposite the entrance to the grand room. Both chairs were equal in elegance and craftsmanship and were a perfect match to all of the other chairs in the room. Leisha had explained the importance of this to her when she was a young child, "In kingdoms where men rule, the king's throne stands above the queen's in all aspects and hers above all the rest. In our city all are equal. I am the queen of Druindahl but I elevate myself above no one. I seek to lead not rule." Those words spoken so long ago were as clear as the day her mother spoke them. Despite her simple beginnings and the simple way she saw the world, Cialia admired her mother's brilliance in lifting the people up. She had an uncanny ability to help the people she led see things in themselves they never knew or believed were there. As Cialia sat down upon the simple throne on the left, that matched every other chair in the throne room perfectly, she hoped as queen she could be half of the leader her mother was. Leisha did not possess great physical strength, nor did she possess great military prowess. Yet she was a superb leader. People wanted to serve her, and she made them better at what they did by allowing them to do it.

"Was that your goal all along, Highness?" Boringas interrupted Cialia's reminiscing.

Cialia looked up at him and frowned, "If you believe that, old friend, then you never really knew me at all."

"I thought I knew you better than anyone," he shrugged. "However, with everything I've learned since you returned I can safely say I do not know you anymore. You are not the free spirit that loves the trail and refuses to shorten the tether on her anchor, if she even acquiesces to drop it in the first place. If I ever did know you, that time has long passed."

"I have not changed, Boringas. Duty places me firmly upon this seat, not desire. I yearn for the freedom of the trail, and I wish I could leave the rule of this place to someone else," Cialia countered. "Who would rule in my stead? Look at what it has become in only five short summers. I wish I could flee this place and hide away from everyone, especially after witnessing the horrors I wrought with my own hand. Alas, I shall have no time to process that. The few tears that wet your shoulder will serve as my only release. The rest will remain deep in my gut, eating at me while I attempt to return Druindahl to her former grandeur."

Boringas scratched his head, dropped his gaze, and began lightly scraping the front of his right boot against the edge of a tile sitting just a wee bit higher than the rest of the floor. An urge to be away from his old friend suddenly swept over him, "I have agreed to be your general, highness. What do you wish of me?"

"How many swords fall under your command?" Cialia asked as her left eye squinted and both moved to the left, back corner of the room.

"Twenty, my queen, only twenty men were spared the fury of your flame."

"One hundred and twenty," Cialia corrected him as her eyes lowered to meet his. "I have no need for guards. The elite force protecting this throne room is yours to command."

"Thank you, highness," Boringas bowed.

Cialia rolled her eyes at the gesture and responded with a shallow nod.

"One hundred and twenty swords are far better than twenty, my queen.

However, it is far fewer than necessary to protect our city. Unless you plan to burn everyone who dares approach our lovely forest home to ash," his lips thinned as he pressed them tightly together.

"Boringas, please," the new queen's eyes closed tightly as she spoke. "You have already helped me see the error of my ways. I feel that pain, and you can believe my flame will remain locked deep within me. However, the people in this place need protection, as do the Lake and the Dragons. I simply cannot shut down and grieve." Her eyes were moist when she opened them and looked into Boringas's eyes, "Now please, I have given you a task, old friend. Protect the city you love and the people sharing it with you. If you cannot accomplish that task with the tools available to you, you will need to find more tools. The swords remaining in your command are all swung by loyal riders of Druindahl, men who have lived and loved this city throughout their entire lives. Most of them were trained by my father. Let them share what they have learned with others. There are men in this city—and boys ready to become men—yearning for a chance to serve. Find them, recruit them, train them, and see our army return to its former glory."

"As you command," Boringas bowed, turned, and motioned to the guards lining each side of the throne room. "Men, on me," he instructed them.

"Stop bowing to me," she called behind him as she watched the royal guard file out of the room behind him. "I serve the same purpose you do," she added, mostly to herself.

After a few moments of the rumble of two hundred and two boots repeatedly clicking tile in unison, the room was empty and Cialia was alone. Alone normally didn't bother her much. In fact, solitude was typically something she welcomed, even sought. Somehow the echo of the heavy, wooden door as it finally finished its slow swing toward the jam and crashed shut behind the last of the guards amplified the emptiness of the place reminding her there were none left to distract her from her thoughts. Boringas's self-righteous banter was almost obnoxious, but it was far more pleasant than the dark thoughts swirling around in her head. Tens of thousands of voices melted together in a grotesque chorus of pain. She heard each of them individually as their shouts echoed from the back of her mind and filled her consciousness. All of them found their way home, but all of them felt the most pitiable fear and pain that—though brief— tormented every cell of their bodies until their souls were finally relieved of their flesh.

The room faded around Cialia as she listened to the accusations each of those unique voices called out against her. Walls vanished from her awareness as the ceiling evaporated and the floor disappeared until nothing remained but those voices. Her body floated among a black void as all of them roared loader and louder. Each presented their anguish to her. Her hands absently moved up to cover her ears, but she didn't need their aid to hear the horrible song. The sadness and suffering of those voices moved her eyes to tears again. Of course there was only one at first, one tear saturated in the suffering of tens of thousands of souls. That one tear proved insufficient to carry the weight of all of that pain away from Cialia as it slid down her cheek. More tears were necessary. They came like the rains of early spring; fat droplets of salty remorse soaking her cheeks.

"Stop it," she whispered.

The tears only came faster as if in defiance of her wishes.

"Stop it," her voice was far stronger this time, filling the vast chamber and echoing back at her from the walls. "The weak need a voice to speak to the strong in their stead. I am that voice."

As the tears slowly subsided, Cialia gathered the sad chorus of pained shouts sounding off in her mind together and released them from her mouth. Chairs tipped and the walls shook in response. The queen wiped the last of the sadness from her cheeks. The souls she sent to the Lake with her flame were vile and wicked. Those vermin had earned their fate and deserved the pain they endured before the Dragon guided them home to the Lake, hadn't they? Hadn't justice returned to Druindahl? It was becoming increasingly difficult to convince herself there was anything righteous about her actions against those wicked men. She could lie that justice had been her goal, but deep down she knew the truth. Anger, fury, and rage had driven her rather than a sense of justice. Though it was far too late to undo what had been done, she could promise herself never to release that horrible power at any man again. Sitting alone in the cold, quiet throne room, she decided just that. Never again would she release her flame to punish men, no matter what their crime.

CHAPTER 36
THE CRESTS OF OULOOS

The howling north wind ran its icy fingers through Maelich's hair, peeling it back from his face and freezing his forehead. The world was a dingy gray in every direction save directly below him. The ground beneath his feet was the clean, perfect white of fresh snow. No thoughts troubled his mind. Only two notable things entered his awareness and both of them had to do with the wind vigorously tossing his hair about and ruffling his clothes. First, there was the bone chilling cold it carried with it. The shiver shaking its way out to his limbs made it impossible to ignore. The other notable thing was the wild howl accompanying that deep chill. It didn't sound like wind. It sounded more like an animal in pain; a great mountain scarra with his leg caught in the jaws of a fur trader's trap letting the world share the agony dripping from his pitiable cry.

Then something tangible popped into Maelich's head. It was Mountain's face. He glanced around, but the scrod was nowhere to be found. Mountain was almost the size of a lowland scarra, probably not near the size of a mountain scarra. He had the same pointy snout and ears though, and the same icy, blue eyes. Maelich had never actually seen a scarra in real life. He had only viewed them in paintings and pictures built in his own imagination based on things he had read in books. It occurred to him—based on what he did know of the mysterious pack animals—it was quite possible Mountain had scarra in his bloodline. He was quite a bit larger than any scrod Maelich had ever encountered. Where was that animal anyway?

"Mountain," he called out, barely able to discern his own voice above the wind.

The dingy gray surrounding him slowly began to melt away. Melt wasn't quite right though. Evaporated was more like it. It dissipated like thick fog burning off of a field beneath the fierce glare of a rising sun. After a few moments Maelich realized he was standing atop a mountain. Based on the snow beneath his feet it was a rather tall one. Immediately after he made the discovery, he realized the gray hadn't completely left. It seemed as if he were inside a globe within a cloud. If not a globe, perhaps it was a dome on the mountaintop, forty feet tall and the same distance in any direction. The peak he stood upon was almost perfectly flat and ended just shy of the dome holding back the gray. Immediately to his left rested a perfectly round boulder that must have been at least ten feet tall and just as wide. Before he could question why it didn't roll one way or the other being almost perfectly rounded while at the same time being blasted by the fierce wind, a familiar, white horse walked out from behind it.

"Your journey yet awaits," the white horse's tone was so matter-of-fact it was almost unsettling.

Maelich shrugged, "I thought I had already begun." He scratched his head and added, "And I thought you weren't going to visit me again until I reached the Sea of Sadness."

The white horse replied in the same impossibly matter-of-fact tone, "You have meandered slightly off course and fallen a bit behind schedule. I told you I was your guide. I have come to guide you. Now you must make haste to the Sea of Sadness."

Maelich realized the wind was no longer blowing but couldn't figure when it had stopped. The thought held his mind briefly as he and the white horse stared at each other, both adding nothing but silence to the conversation. Finally, Maelich gave up the fruitless contemplation and said, "You told me you only knew the beginning and the end of my journey. The rest was to be my own. Have the rules changed, or did you lie to me?"

"The journey has not changed, and I have no cause to lie. As your guide, my only cause is to keep you on course."

Maelich squinted with his left eye and said, "Why the need for haste?"

"The journey has begun, and now it must be finished."

"The last time we met you told me it did not matter when I completed this journey just that it must be completed. I ask again, why the need for haste?"

"I said it did not matter when the journey was begun," the white horse corrected. "Now that it has begun, it must be finished."

Maelich turned and took a few steps away from the white horse and the big round boulder he was standing next to. As he turned back to continue speaking, he gasped instead. The mountaintop was gone along with the big, round boulder, the snow, the overbearing gray, and the invisible globe holding it at bay. Maelich now stood on top of perfectly-still water an equal distance from the white horse as he had been on the mountaintop. The stillness continued for roughly forty feet in any direction. Beyond that the waves were monstrous. They scraped the dull, red sky as they climbed ever higher before crashing down.

"You seem distressed, Maelich," the white horse continued in his damnably matter-of-fact tone. "What troubles you?"

"I am still not overly fond of your games, horse," Maelich's tone was far off and distracted as he continued to examine his new surroundings.

"I have no games for you to play," the white horse replied. "You remain in control here as you have always been. I am a bystander. If there is a game being played it is your game, and you play alone. As I have told you several times…"

Maelich finished his sentenced, "The journey is mine, and you are merely a guide to keep me on my path. Yes, you have told me that several times. It occurs to me though; you may not be the most trustworthy of guides."

"Now that is not fair, Maelich," it almost sounded as if there were something of a tone in his voice. "I have spoken only the truth to you."

"So you say," Maelich shrugged. "You say many things, but you provide little proof. In fact, you provide no proof just words. Words, words, words, you speak the same words over and over again."

"The truth does not change much from this moment to that. Why would my words change if the truth they describe remains the same?"

"How can I know what you say is true?" Maelich asked. "Like I said, words are not truth they are merely words."

The white horse paused briefly before replying, "You are correct. Words merely describe truth in the best way they can, and it is probably never perfect. Real truth is something you feel, and it is probably different for you than it would be for someone else. If you search yourself you will know I have only spoken truth to you."

Maelich drew in a slow, deep breath and let it out between slightly parted lips. "I do not feel any truth. I feel like you haven't told me anything."

"I have told you all you need to know up to this point. Apparently, you need to know more, so I will tell you more."

Silence filled the space between them for several moments until the white horse finally continued, "People will die if you spend too much time dawdling. The longer you take to complete your journey, the more innocent souls will make the journey home to the Lake far earlier than they should."

Before Maelich could respond, the great, invisible dome that had been keeping the titanic, crashing waves at bay evaporated. He raised his eyes in time to see one falling on him. At the same moment the smooth water beneath his feet supporting him during his conversation with the white horse stopped supporting his weight. Sinking quickly into the drink, the crashing wave forced him down even deeper, pushing him to the depths.

Darkness enveloped him as the crushing pressure swirled his body out of control. Once the pressure stopped, stillness surrounded him. He had no idea which direction he was heading in as he began to swim. Up or down didn't make any sense. Wet and dark were the only tangible things. His lungs burned as his body began to convulse. He couldn't hold his breath any longer. Water rushed into his lungs as an involuntary breath pulled the sea into his mouth and down his trachea.

Maelich jumped, tossing the water skin Ymitoth had been using to dribble water into his mouth. He flailed, rolling onto his belly as he slid off of Ymitoth's lap. Three deep coughs pulled moisture from the back of his throat. Another deep breath launched him into a violent fit of coughing that quickly melted into vomiting. The thick, brownish-green liquid rocketing from his mouth looked just like swamp water and smelled twice as bad. He heaved five times before rolling onto his back and looking up at a darkening sky. Mountain sauntered over and licked his face. The scrod's breath made him want to throw up again. Instead he reached up with his left hand, scratched the big animal behind the ear, and pushed his foul smelling mouth in a different direction in the process.

"Quite a dream ye been having," Ymitoth noted.

Maelich struggled to a seated position. Ymitoth tilted and swayed with the trees behind him as Maelich fought to bring his world back into focus. "It was the white horse again."

"What white horse be that, lad?" Ymitoth asked as he reached down to retrieve the water skin Maelich had forced from his hands.

Maelich scratched his head with his left hand as his right continued to scratch Mountain's head, "The white horse I dreamt about that sent us on this journey."

Ymitoth shook his head, "Ye never did tell me about no white horse."

Maelich squinted, "Didn't I?"

"No, I'd be remembering something like that," he took a long pull off the water skin and swallowed. Then he took a shallower hit, swished it around in his mouth, and spit it on the ground.

"I was sure I told you about it the first time," Maelich shrugged. "No matter, a white horse came to me in a dream the night before we left our hut to take this journey. He pushed me off of a mountaintop in that dream. That is what startled me so. This time he didn't push me or anything. I sunk into a great sea with horrible waves crashing on me. I could no longer hold my breath." He paused and thought for a moment before asking, "Why were you pouring water down my throat? That's probably why I thought I was drowning."

Ymitoth squinted and said, "Ye been asleep for two days. I thought ye might be parched."

"Two days?" Maelich shouted.

"Aye," Ymitoth nodded and scratched his chin. "Ye passed out after battling Shellar. Ye ain't woke since."

"Shellar," Maelich's eyes opened wide. "I killed that vile beast. What of Braggon?"

Ymitoth scoffed, "That vile, treacherous bastard be dead. He'd been nothing but a servant to that beast what ye killed."

Maelich scratched his head, "It was far too easy for him to trick us. Am I that eager to find adventure I dive in head first without a care for danger?"

"Aye," Ymitoth nodded and curled the edges of him mouth down, "ye be that."

After a few moments of silence, Maelich tested his feet. They were far less than sturdy, but he didn't fall. A dull ache behind his forehead refused to be ignored. He absently rubbed it with the first two fingers of his right hand. Mountain—apparently satisfied his new friend was beyond danger—glanced up at him and then lay down where he stood. Maelich walked a slow circle around the puddle of vomit that had just gushed out of him.

"I must have swallowed some of," he paused, looked at the disgusting brownish-green puddle, and added, "whatever filled her."

"Swamp water," Ymitoth shrugged. "That witch be nothing but a thin skin, swamp water, a big brain, and a hungry stomach. Well," he paused, "she be nothing but dead now."

"Where are her remains?" Maelich asked.

"I burned them up," Ymitoth replied.

"What about the crests for Goechal? We promised we would return any we found. Did you examine the remains?" Maelich's lips barely kept pace with his thoughts.

Ymitoth chuckled, "Look at ye there, prancing about like a scared child. Have ye no faith in me?" A sly grin found its way onto his face as he kicked over the open sack sitting next to his right foot. Hundreds of prang crests spilled out onto the ground in a pile. "Hopefully, the one she be wanting be lying among this pile I scavenged from that foul carcass before burning the lousy mess up."

Maelich clenched both fists and thrust them above his head as he let out a triumphant howl. "Yes," he added as if the howl needed any additional emphasis. "You are a true hero. Forgive me for doubting you."

Ymitoth smiled, clasped his hands together, raised them above the left side of his head, shook them twice, and then moved them to the right side to repeat the gesture.

As Maelich watched the old warrior cheer himself in mock fashion, he noticed the blood covered tear in the mail of his sleeve, "What of your arm? Are you hurt?

Ymitoth bent his left elbow, peered down at the same forearm, and replied, "Aye, that bastard took me by surprise and got a hold of me blade. I had nothing to block him with so I used me arm." After examining it for a few moments he added, "Hmm, would ye look at that. It be all healed on its own. She was a deep one too, clear to the bone."

"Interesting," Maelich scratched his chin and contemplated the idea for the briefest of moments. Then he added, "We should move. After all of the loss Goechal has suffered in her life, I don't want her worrying over us for any longer than necessary."

Ymitoth shook his head, "The sun already be low, and ye be needing a night of untroubled rest to be getting your strength back."

"Wise counsel as usual," Maelich nodded. "We can rest and start out at first light." He rubbed his belly and added, "How about some food then?"

CHAPTER 37
THE LONG, SLOW ROAD

Small circles of wagons dotted the landscape between the river and the road. They were packed as tightly as possible given the terrain and the sheer number of them. People milled about sticking close the wagons. Some washed along the river while others ate or chatted. Most just wished for something to keep their minds from contemplating their current situation or what dark terrors the future might bring. Leisha and Perrin sat beside a small fire burning in the middle of one of the circled groups of wagons. Both nursed bowls of some kind of stew far less compelling than the thoughts troubling their minds.

"How long?" Perrin asked as she examined her spoon.

Leisha looked up from her bowl, thrilled to have something to do other than stir its contents or think. "How long until what, dear?" she asked.

Perrin sighed, set her spoon in her bowl, and then set the bowl next to her on the log she sat upon, "How long before it stops hurting so much?"

"Which pain would that be, dear? I'm afraid you have suffered many different kinds of pain in a very short amount of time. I am unable to help with the burn or your husband's dishonorable behavior. I have never suffered a burn like that, nor has my husband ever acted in such a way. Sadly, my answer to the one question I can help you with will probably not fill you with joy." Leisha paused and tugged at the right side of her hair. "The pain never goes away. I ached for my boy until he returned to me. That is not to say you will never find joy while he is absent from you, but he will always be on your mind. Even if you manage to push it back to the farthest depths of your consciousness, it will always remain waiting for those moments when there is nothing to distract you from the sorrow. It is during those times when it will squeeze your heart and make you question whether or not you want to continue living."

Perrin managed a dry chuckle, "Ye be correct, Leisha. That answer don't be filling me with no joy. As for them other two things, this burn don't really be causing me no more grief, and I be just about done with your son. I love him. I do. But he put a hurt to me like none I ever felt, and it may be quite a time before I'll be forgiving him for that."

"I can find no fault with that," Leisha shrugged. "If I could lay hands upon my son right now, he would need Dragon's Fire to protect him from my wrath. Mind you, this is not merely for the pain he is putting us through, but all of these people need him. A whisper from his mouth would have ended this war before it began. There would have been no reason for us to flee like rodents in the face of a coming storm."

"Aye," Perrin agreed as her gaze peered deep into the dancing flames of the fire.

"Let us not forget the great Dragon's sister," Leisha picked her bowl back up and shoved a spoonful of stew in her mouth. She chewed twice before continuing around the mouthful, "She is as culpable in this as her brother. I birth two champions, two gods, and when my life and the lives of those they have sworn to protect are in the greatest peril many of them have ever seen, they are buried in their own sorrows and dramas."

She shook her head, swallowed the mouthful of stew, and continued the diatribe, "Look at Maelich. I can understand sorrow at the loss of his father, but I cannot imagine the dark place he occupies. I do not even want to think about it. That man has stood face to face with Coeptus. All of the secrets have been revealed to him. He should rejoice at Ymitoth's good fortune for being called home to peace. Yet he selfishly laments like any common simpleton who knows nothing of the good word or the real truths of this world. Cialia is no better. She is her brother's equal in all ways except believing in herself. She sits and waits for him to teach her. Did she not stand before Coeptus just as he did? Yes she did. She stood before Coeptus and was told the same truth from their mouths as her brother. Yet she still behaves as if he is greatness and she is his humble servant. That is why she is absent. She is afraid to lead. Someone always needs to tell her where to go or how to be." By the end of her rant, Leisha's voice was just shy of a shout.

Perrin had no more words. As she stared into the fire letting Leisha's comments sink in they at least took her mind from a place of lamenting the loss of Geillan to a place of deep anger with her absent husband. Anger was far more empowering than hopelessness, and she let it consume her. Maelich should be ruling by her side, and his mother was quite correct in her assessment of the situation. One word from Maelich's lips could have rained a storm of fire on those invading ships, and the people of Havenstahl would still be safe in their own beds. Instead they were strewn loosely about a dangerous trail with far too little to eat and far too little protection. Her hands clenched into tight fists as she watched the flames dance and thought about the words she would have for him if she ever saw him again. He would know all of the pain and hurt he had caused her, how it felt being cast aside for the company of a corpse, left unprotected with a son who had powers she couldn't possibly understand, and he would know in no uncertain terms she would never depend on him for anything again.

"The road be secure, highness," Glord's voice shattered the silence of the circle. "Ye both should be getting some rest."

"How safe are we, Glord?" Leisha looked up at him.

"I tell ye that we been at this trail for better than a week now, and we ain't lost more than twelve." He nodded before adding, "And those we lost to sickness, not any monsters this trail be offering up. Me men be watching the river to the South, the trees to the North, and the trail to the East and West. We be safe me lady."

Perrin looked up and asked, "What sickness be taking twelve of us home? Where be Meelah?"

"Meelah be doing all she can. She ain't got much to work with for medicines. I be doubting Hagen be having much better luck were he among us," Glord maintained an even tone.

"How long until we reach the Forgotten Forest and my old home?" Leisha asked.

"Better than a week, maybe less than two." The old general raised his eyebrows and added, "That be depending on how long we be taking to cross the Edge Mountains."

"Oh yes, the mountains," Leisha nodded. "I almost forgot."

Before Perrin could add a comment about sending soldiers out to find more medicines for Meelah to use in her healing practices, Fielstag charged in, gave a quick salute and addressed Glord, "I be having troubling news from the road, general."

Glord waited for the rest of the news. When it didn't come he asked, "And what be that news soldier? Come on ye, out with it now. Don't be keeping your queen waiting."

Fielstag remained silent, pleading Glord with his eyes instead.

Before Glord managed to understand the gesture, Perrin piped up, "Aye soldier, out with it now. What be this news from the road?"

"Forgive me, highness," Fielstag bowed. "This be news ladies need not be troubled with."

"These people that be in danger be me people. Be out with it now."

Fielstag bowed again, "As ye wish. About a mile or so from here, we be seeing the smoke of fires. Two gone off to be investigating and only one returned. That one be bringing a story of great, white, hairy beasts, that be looking like large men but with big claws and long fangs."

"Grizzly mongs," Glord sighed.

"Aye," Fielstag agreed. "I ain't never seen one meself, but I been hearing the stories since I been a wee lad. There be hundreds just north of the trail if ye be trusting the word of Borgan, and I ain't never found no reason not to be trusting him."

"Grizzly mongs?" Leisha's voice was far louder than she intended. She lowered it slightly as she continued. "What are grizzly mongs doing this far south and in those numbers?"

"That be the real question now don't it?" Glord replied quietly as his gaze travelled up toward the darkening sky.

"What be a grizzly mong?" Perrin asked.

"They are exactly what this fellow described them to be," Leisha pointed at Fielstag. "They are bigger than men. They are not the size of giants, mind you, but large enough. And they are ferocious. They are like humungous amatilazo with thick fur and slightly larger brains."

They all remained silent for a few moments. Perrin tried to picture what exactly a grizzly mong might look like while Leisha's mind fought against damning both of her children for the position she and her people were in. Meanwhile, Glord and Fielstag both puzzled over how they would combat this new foe with their limited numbers. A few hundred amatilazo would be far easier to deal with. Even a few hundred grongs would be no match for the couple of thousand swords the caravan boasted. Grizzly mongs were an entirely different story. They were nearly equal to grongs in intelligence, and they were far more savage than either grongs or amatilazo. One grizzly mong could take down twenty five well trained men in open battle. The horses would help but not significantly. If they encountered this troop of grizzly mongs on the trail, many soldiers would die and even more of the people they protected would follow them to the Lake.

Leisha finally broke the silence, "How long would it take two serious riders to make Druindahl if they hit the trail hard and rested infrequently?"

Glord scratched the back of his head as he peeled his gaze from the sky, "It might be the better part of two days, maybe three before they be seeing that forest."

"Do you have any willing to take that challenge?"

"Aye, any of me men be taking on any challenge at any time."

"Good," Leisha nodded. "Send your two swiftest riders. Tell them to let Druindahl know of our plight and ask them to send assistance."

Glord nodded.

Then Leisha added, "Be sure they inform King Blancus that Druindahl's former queen is among those in distress."

"I'll be seeing it done, me lady," Glord bowed just before he and Fielstag turned and left the small circle.

The suffocating silence returned. If not for the soft crackle of a dying fire, it would completely smother the small circle Leisha and Perrin occupied. Both of them stared at the slowly expiring flame. Neither felt a great desire to refuel it, both preoccupied with their own similar but very personal demons. Leisha closed her eyes tightly and shook her head. Perrin kicked a pebble back and forth between her feet. As the two sunk into their own little pools of self-pity, the moon rose high enough over the eastern horizon that it could be easily viewed above the wagons. Perrin glanced up at it, earning a brief distraction from her lamentations. The blessed diversion proved far too brief as her mind quickly traveled to the last time the moon was full.

"Look at that moon being all full and beautiful," Perrin sighed.

Leisha glanced up but had nothing to offer.

"The last time it be full like that, me life had been perfect. I'd been having everything me heart could be desiring." She sighed and added, "Now I ain't be having nothing of what I be wanting."

Leisha reached over and intertwined the fingers of her right hand with the fingers of Perrin's left. Neither of them said another word. Perrin leaned her head back on Leisha's shoulder and Leisha laid her head down upon Perrin's. Both women sat and watched that mystical, full moon slowly rise higher and higher into the sky as their minds searched faded memories for happier thoughts.

CHAPTER 38
THE BATTERED HERO

The difference between closed eyelids and opened eyelids was minimal enough that Daritus had to blink several times and squint to get a rough estimation of his surroundings. A dull ache permeated his entire body. Sharp points of pain in his chest and along his left side—mostly near the shoulder—stood out among the aching and grabbed most of his attention. The rough fabric of a tent wall against his right arm prompted him to roll to the left. The lesson that followed was quick. It felt like someone jabbed a spear into his shoulder as soon as his elbow hit the downy mattress beneath him. Shocks ran out to the rest of his arm causing him to cry out.

The briefest moment later, Hagen rushed into the small tent carrying a brightly burning lantern, "Daritus, consciousness has returned to you. Thank Coeptus." He set the lantern down on a small table in the middle of the tent as he rushed over to Daritus's side, reciting instructions the entire way. "Be still. Lie back. Do not try to move." Order after order poured from his lips in rapid succession.

The sigh saturated with equal parts defeat and frustration slipped from Daritus's mouth a quick second before he said, "I cannot lead a battle from my back, Hagen."

"No you cannot," Hagen agreed. Then he added, "We are lucky you have such able and faithful generals serving beneath you. They lead the battle in your stead."

Daritus blinked a few times at the bright light and rubbed his eyes with his right hand. "I ache, old friend," he mumbled at the ceiling. Then he turned his head toward Hagen and—with a far stronger command of his voice—asked, "How long until I am fit to return to the battlefield?"

"Your mind is your strongest weapon now, old friend," Hagen

shrugged.

Daritus shook his head, "Please search your mind for a more satisfying answer. How long?"

"Well then, why listen to old Hagen? He has merely been healing people since before you were born," Hagen's tone echoed his irritation. He scratched his head, shrugged again, and in the same irritated tone added, "You could probably swing a sword with your right arm in a week. Most of the ribs on your left side have at least slight fractures in them. That will make you vulnerable for an additional three weeks at best, longer if you refuse to give them proper rest. That left arm will need to remain set for at least six weeks. It, and that mutilated shoulder of yours, will never be the same. They will give you problems and pain for the rest of your days."

"That answer is not much more satisfying than your first," the old general lamented. Then he looked down at his left shoulder and added, "This damn thing will always give me pain?"

"Perhaps not, given enough time to heal," Hagen snapped. "I know you well enough to know you will not give it the time it needs. My elixirs can do much, but they cannot stop a stubborn, old bastard from breaking his worn body if he has a mind to do so."

"Fair enough," his expression lightened, slowly melting into a shallow smile. "I am a stubborn, old bastard. Thank you for standing up to me and keeping me humble." He grimaced slightly as he adjusted himself in the cot, "Do you have anything to take the edge off of this pain?"

Hagen smiled, "That is something I can help with."

The old healer moved to a small chest at the back of the tent, opened the lid, and shuffled around inside with both hands for a few moments. After a quick nod and some unintelligible mumbling, he rose from the chest with three jars. One was filled with a purple liquid, one with an iridescent-green liquid, and the last with a white powder. He set the three jars on the table and then turned back to the chest to retrieve a few more items.

"Here we are," Hagen said as he set a wooden bowl on the table next to the jars and a rounded, wooden stick next to that.

"That smells rather pleasant," Daritus remarked as he watched Hagen open the jar with the white powder in it.

"Indeed," Hagen agreed, "like wildflowers almost, with a bit of the sea mixed in. It comes from a plant that grows in shallow, mountain ponds. It is rare and very difficult to find. This jar may represent all of the chloricylt on Ouloos."

Daritus raised his eyebrows, "And you are wasting it on a battered, old scrod like me?"

Hagen looked up from his work as he poured a small dose of the chloricylt into the wooden bowl. "Ah, there is my humble friend," he smiled. "He managed to find his way through the pain. You may be a battered, old scrod, but you are the last hope of Havenstahl. Once I am able to return your strength to you, we will have words about a general's role in battle."

The old general smiled and shook his head, "Those words are already in my head, old friend, but when I saw the men's faces…" he trailed off.

Hagen nodded and produced a small, leather pouch from beneath his cloak, fished some dried leaves from it, and added them to the white powder in the bowl. Then he grabbed the stick and began grinding the leaves into the white powder.

After a few moments of silence, Daritus continued, "They all looked so full of hope. I saw a transformation. As I approached them, I called out. The faces that turned to me were twisted and downtrodden. Once they saw me, they lit up. You have known me long enough to know I am not an expert with words, so that is the best description I can give you. I can tell you though; my presence on that battlefield meant something to those men. It lifted them up. They cheered. They pumped their fists in the air." He paused again as his eyes moved up toward the ceiling of the tent. A wide smile spread across his face as he added, "I know this makes me sound like the greenest, young lad tasting only his first battle, but they made me feel invincible. Seeing how my mere presence affected them, how could I not lead them into battle?"

Hagen shrugged and replied, "Knowing you as well as I do, you could not." Then he pulled a cork out of the bottle containing the purple liquid.

Immediately after the cork had left the bottle, Daritus's face twisted into a grimace. "Oh, that is the foulest stench I have ever encountered. I hope you do not expect me to consume that," he groaned.

"It is foul, but you will grow accustomed to the smell," Hagen replied nonchalantly. "This liquid is my most powerful healing tool. It has stolen many battered soldiers from the Lake, and it is the only reason you still grace the sweet face of Ouloos. The powder and the herbs will dull the pain, my special elixir here will heal your wounds, and this green liquid is nothing but a super-concentrated mixture of natural juices that will improve the flavor of this concoction and help return your strength. Your body needs all of these and rest if you hope to return to something that resembles Havenstahl's greatest general."

As Hagen poured, Daritus's face twisted further, "How can you just stand there like that? I could vomit all over the floor right now. That is horrible."

"Now you sound like a lad," he replaced the cork on the bottle, but the rancid odor remained. Then he uncorked the jar with the green liquid and a fresh, fruity smell drifted through the tent, mingling with the foul scent that seemed to permeate everything. Somehow the contrast made it worse.

"It is in my throat," Daritus complained. "I will be dead before you are able to attempt making me drink that foul spirit."

Hagen sighed and rolled his eyes as he grabbed the stick and began stirring, "The great Daritus, leader of men, has been reduced to a whiny, whimpering lad by a bad smell."

Before Daritus could complain any more, the door to the tent flung open and an excited Doentaat stormed in, "There be the greatest warrior of men. Aye, let giants and trogmortem and grongs and all form of monster quake in fear and flee at the sight of him. Be there any that can stand and face this man, this giant slayer who be mightier than Bok?" Immediately after his rant, the dwarf king drew a deep breath in. His eyes squinted as a confused look spread across his face and he choked, "What in the sweet name of Coeptus be that foul smell?"

Hagen rolled his eyes again, "Two of the greatest warriors on Ouloos defeated by an unpleasant odor. If only your men and dwarves could see you now."

"Aye, if only they could smell this they'd be understanding," Doentaat grunted.

The old healer ignored the last jab. Grabbing the bowl, he walked over to Daritus and handed it to him, "Drink this now. Drink it all and lie back."

Doentaat's eyes grew wide, "Ye'll be killing him if ye be making him drink that."

"The source of that foul smell is the reason this hero yet lives," Hagen snapped.

Doentaat didn't respond. He merely shook his head and tied the door of the tent back to allow some fresh air into the room.

Daritus closed his eyes and grimaced as he raised the bowl to his lips and began drinking. His eyes snapped open. The flavor didn't match the foul smell. It certainly wasn't something he would seek, but it really wasn't that bad. The faint, fruity taste was slightly muted by a dim metallic flavor and the whole thing carried the essence of sea water. Even still, though it wasn't delicious, he could at least stomach it.

Hagen watched as the old general poured the mixture down his throat. "Chew those herbs," he commanded.

Doentaat gagged and stuck his head outside of the tent.

After finishing the concoction, Daritus shook his head, and said, "That was not quite as awful as I expected it to be," around a mouthful of herbs.

"Chew those well and then have a drink of water," Hagen handed him a water skin. "Then I want you to lie back and rest. The more you rest the quicker you will heal."

"Bah, he been laid up in this tent for two whole days. He be needing to come out of this tent and walk among the troops," Doentaat stuck his head in, braving the awful stench. "Them soldiers be needing to see that the slayer of giants still be walking among the living."

"He needs his rest," Hagen disagreed.

Daritus swallowed the herbs, took a good, strong pull off of the water skin Hagen had given him, touched the old healer's arm, and said, "You know more about healing than any man on Ouloos, probably more than the gods even, but you know nothing about leading men, old friend. Doentaat is quite right. The men need to see me alive. Even as broken as my body is, it will lift their spirits to see me walking about. I killed a giant in one on one combat, and though I am not certain I deserve it, the fact will raise me to legendary status in the eyes of the men who follow me."

"And the dwarves," Doentaat piped in.

"They need this, and I need this. Their expected enthusiasm will fill my sails as much as theirs," Daritus's expression pleaded as he maintained eye contact with Hagen.

The healer frowned and stroked his chin. Then after some internal debate, he conceded, "Well, it is not as if I could stop you if I tried. You are a stubborn, old scrod. Your arguments do have merit. Go then, frolic with the other barbarians. Please keep that left arm as still as possible, and please be as brief as you are able."

Daritus flashed a wide smile as he rose and patted Hagen on his left shoulder, "Thank you, old friend. I am stubborn, and I appreciate your blessing." Then he turned to Doentaat and asked, "Shall we rally the troops?"

Doentaat failed at suppressing a yell, "Aye, let's show them there ain't no giant what can stop the greatest of all generals."

As the two stepped into the orange, flickering glow of a blazing fire, they caught the attention of the twenty or so soldiers lounging around it. A voice among the crowd shouted, "The giant slayer lives!" The rest of the small group erupted in a cheer that brought more soldiers from other fires burning around the camp. In a few moments, hundreds of men were crowding as closely as they could to the hero that led them into battle and killed a giant.

"Don't be crowding too close," Doentaat hollered above the murmuring throng. "The giant slayer still be needing to heal." Then the king of dwarves paused, collected himself, and shouted with every ounce of force his lungs could muster, "But Daritus, the killer of giants, lives!"

This sent the crowd into a wild frenzy. A cheer louder than a crack of thunder erupted from the throng of wily soldiers.

"Let them giants take note," a voice rose above the rest.

"General Daritus fears no man, no beast, and certainly no giants," another answered.

Still another shouted, "Long live the king."

And yet another answered, "Yes, King Daritus."

The buzzing and shouting continued. Congratulatory remarks filling the air as the soldiers reveled in their general's glory.

Finally, Daritus raised his right arm and shouted, "I am no king."

"Quiet," Doentaat yelled. "Let the general speak."

The murmuring slowly subsided as Daritus continued, "My friends, soldiers, comrades, I am no king. I am a man, a soldier just as all of you are. I am a man who stands tall against fear, as all of you do. I am a man who is willing to give my life for the good of Havenstahl and Alhouim and all of Ouloos." He paused as the crowd finally grew completely silent, finally adding, "But I am only a man."

Daritus began to pace back and forth in front of his tent as he continued, looking around the crowd into as many eyes as he could, "I am not a god. I am not special. I believe the people I represent deserve to live in a world free from the fear of being trampled, ripped apart, or even eaten by the likes of the monsters challenging our shores. But...I am just a man."

"Just a man who kills giants," a voice answered from the crowd that erupted again in response.

Once the crowd calmed back down, Daritus stopped pacing and continued, "Yes, I killed a giant. And not just any giant, I killed their leader. It was a general against a general, and a leader of men prevailed. I have been battered, teetered on the brink of death, and yet here I stand very much alive. What does that tell us?" He paused, glanced around the crowd, and then answered his own question, "It tells us giants are not invincible. They bleed and die just as we do. Their hides are tough, but our swords are sharp and strong." He paused again as a murmur swept through the crowd. Finally, he added, "When the sun rises on a new day, I cannot lead you into battle, but I will be with you in spirit. Every grong you cut down, every trogmortem you slay, and every giant that falls before the might of men and dwarves will strengthen my spirit."

A brief cheer blasted from the crowd.

"All of you, men and dwarves, you all share my desire. All of you have the strength to see your will done on the battlefield. What stands in the way of your glory? Giants, trogmortem, and grongs are horrible, nightmare creatures that trample everything and leave a path of destruction in their wake. Yes, they are terrifying. They growl and snarl and snap. They fight for no cause though. All of you standing before me, all of you fight for a cause. Do not be swayed from it or intimidated by their posturing. Think about the innocent folk who sit huddled in their homes, terrified by the monsters threatening their peace. Think about those who have fled the coming storm and challenged the dangerous trail to Druindahl, ripped from their land by fear. Think about your fallen friends who have died by your side. They are your cause. They are whom you fight for. Let those images burn into your brain, and unleash that fury on the beasts that dare challenge your might. I am just a man, and I killed a giant. Who among you will be the next to make that boast?" The volume of Daritus's voice had slowly been rising as the words poured from his mouth. By the time the last words fired from his lips, they were carried along by the strength of an all-out shout.

The crowd erupted again, cheering and pumping their fists in the air. Daritus walked among them. As he did, hands reached out to touch him, patting him here and there on his back and shoulders. Some patted a bit too close to his wounds. He hid the pain well as he patted backs and shook hands in return. Such strong energy coursed through the crowd, he nearly forgot his injuries. If not for the cast and the brief moments of excruciating pain when an eager soldier pounded his back too briskly or bumped into his injured, left arm, they would have been completely removed from his awareness. He remained among the crowd possibly a bit longer than he should have. The reminders of his injuries became stronger and more frequent as the elation of his men continued to grow. Finally, a familiar voice piped up over all of the celebratory bantering.

"That is enough for now," Kantiim shouted over the crowd. "The giant slayer needs rest. If you wish to honor his great deeds, rest well and stand tall on the battlefield tomorrow. Let his unwavering bravery be an example to you, and show our enemies all the fury Havenstahl and Alhouim have to offer."

Kantiim and Doentaat pushed their way through the crowd, eventually carving a path to Daritus. After far less convincing than an uninjured Daritus would have required, they managed to pull him from the throng of admirers. The grimace that jumped onto the battered hero's face was unmistakable as the energy of the moment began to wear off. He would pay for the brief rally with pain. The energy of the crowd and the looks on the soldier's faces made the discomfort worthwhile.

"Ye got a silver tongue there, old friend," Doentaat shouted up toward Daritus's ear as he pushed a path through the crowd, back toward the tent.

"That is certain," Kantiim agreed. "They are flying high. I should lead them to battle at this very moment."

Daritus sighed as they finally made it back to the door of his tent. The pained grimace remained on his face as he replied, "I wish I had more than words to offer them. I should like my sword to be on the battlefield with them rather than just fond thoughts of my deeds."

Just as the words finished leaving Daritus's lips, Hagen poked his head out of the tent and scolded, "You have done more than you should have." After examining the battered hero's face he added, "Much more based on the twisted grimace you are wearing. Your sword will remain safe in your scabbard, and you will remain safe on your cot."

Daritus forced a smile to his face, "It will not be easy to remain behind. I had forgotten the taste of the battlefield. Now that I have been reminded, I yearn to be back upon it fighting beside my men." He paused, looked over at Doentaat, and added, "And the stout dwarves we have always depended on in times of need."

A stern look crept onto Hagen's face as he replied, "Take satisfaction in the fact I allow you to remain in this crude tent rather than the safety and comfort of the castle. I would prefer to see you resting and healing in your own quarters. Consider this a compromise, and set your mind away from the battlefield."

"That be sound advice," Doentaat agreed. "We be leading this battle in your stead."

"Rest now, old friend," Kantiim added.

With that, Daritus entered the tent and finally let the pain take him. His form crumpled onto the bed as darts of fire shot through his body, radiating from his mangled shoulder. He had done too much. Hagen's advice had been good and sound. Sadly, once Daritus set his mind to something, he had a difficult time following even the best advice. Especially when it ran contrary to his desires and the only penalty was his own suffering. Luckily, sleep ambushed him so abruptly once his head landed on his downy pillow he didn't have to suffer his mistake for very long.

CHAPTER 39
LOSS AND FURY

Maomnosett Ott's massive form slumped before a raging fire. The night had already grown rather old and did not have long before dying to make way for the sun of a new day. Ott had been sitting in front of that fire since two nights prior after washing his dead son's body and placing it on the pyre. He had lit the blaze himself and watched the body blacken and eventually disintegrate. Even after Bok's body had long turned to ash, Ott remained. After his youngest son—the only son he had left—and his grandson's had all finished paying their respects and moved on, the mourning, old father remained staring into the dancing flames. Two days of battles had raged a mere few hundred yards from him, but he paid them no mind. His eyes remained completely absorbed by the consuming flames. His second son was dead, killed by a man. Bok was not only his second son, but he was the second son Ott had lost to the city of Havenstahl. Ahm had been his eldest, a glorious king. Bok was even mightier than his elder brother had been, and he was cut down before he could claim the throne left vacant upon his brother's death and due to him by right.

Ott never really cared about Havenstahl. When Maelich killed Ahm, the elder giant was angrier at what it meant to the Maomnosett name that a mighty giant was killed by a mere man than the throne of a city of dwarves. When word of Maelich's true nature spread, his anger and disappointment lessened. When Ahm's sons, Aht and Ahn, failed to regain their father's throne and perished in the process, he was far angrier with them for being unprepared. The men of Havenstahl helped thwart the efforts of his grandsons' though. That was the second time Havenstahl interfered with his family and his name. Even all of that was not enough to raise his hackles to a point worthy of crossing a sea to wage war against a foreign land.

Though he was not blind enough with rage to be pushed into an assault on Havenstahl, his ire had been ignited. Most of the rage he felt was still aimed at the empty throne one of his sons should occupy. When Brerto came to Bok, the time was right. He would join the assault on Havenstahl but his focus would be on the throne of Alhouim, the former Maomnosett. Bok would occupy that throne. That had been his plan. Havenstahl would serve as the catalyst, but Alhouim would be the goal.

A wee man changed Ott's plan for him. With Bok dead, Ohm would take the throne of Alhouim and return the city to the former glory of Maomnosett. That throne seemed far less important than it ever had though. His second son was dead, killed by a man. Havenstahl had interfered in his life for the last time. He would burn that city down with his own hands and trample or eat any man that dared stand in his way.

The sound of cheering filtered through the trees that had yet to be cut down and reached the old giant's ears as he mourned. 'My son's slayer must live,' he thought, as his jaw set tight. The cheering continued to grow louder as Ott stewed. Sadness for the loss of his son quickly gave way to blinding rage. It began like fire in his belly, raced out to his limbs, and flushed his cheeks. His jaw clamped tighter. The skin of his face shook from the force. He stood, stretched his arms out wide, and roared back at the wild cheering. Pain and frustration laced itself around the furious sound that poured from the giant's lips for a solid minute. Then he drew in a deep breath and released an even louder howl.

Grongs, trogmortem, and other giants stopped what they were doing and began to wander over to the old giant as he roared. As they approached, one roar finished and another began. It was equal in volume and angst to the prior. Five times the giant sang that pitiable song, a chorus of pain, sadness, anger, and foul intent.

Finally, after the last roar had spent all of the air in Ott's lungs, he sucked in another deep breath and shouted, "My son is dead!" He looked around at the crowd gathering around him and continued in a more reasonable tone, "The mighty Bok was killed by a wee man. His pathetic body has burned to nothing, and he is a memory. I loved my son. I still carry a strong love in my heart for him. I always will. That love is marred by disappointment though. He was the mightiest of giants, a specimen to behold. His form embodied the perfection that is the giant, and he was killed by a mere man. I cannot forgive that weakness."

Bok's eldest son, Oyg, took exception to his grandfather's harsh words, "My father was many things: a brilliant leader, an unyielding warrior, a furious defender of his kin, and your son. However, weak is not among the words you could use to describe him."

The old giant laughed, "He was killed by a man. I might find less fault if he were killed by an army of men. Sadly, he met that man in one on one combat in an open battle field and fell on the worm's blade."

"That man was named Daritus, and he is the mightiest warrior serving under the banner of Havenstahl," the young giant challenged his grandfather.

Ott fell into a mad fit of laughter at his grandson's statement. It took him a few minutes to compose himself. Once he did, a menacing expression replaced his smile and he said, "The mightiest man on Ouloos is no match for even the weakest of giants. The man's name means nothing to me, and your exultation of that name means even less. Your father was felled by a man. You should be embarrassed not defensive."

A growl louder than the cheering of the men and louder than Ott's roaring had been filled the clearing and ended the conversation. All eyes—including Ott's—turned to give form to the creature that could conjure such a terrifying sound. The great, white tiger sauntered toward the gathering of giants, trogmortem, and grongs. He was easily the size of six large men. The ground shook under his massive paws after each step he took. Even in the orange glow of the fire light, his white fur blazed like the sun interrupted by stripes of the deepest black. The great, white tiger continued until he was looking eye to eye with Ott, whose head sat fifteen feet above the ground.

Every soul in that clearing fell to one knee with Ott. Then the old, giant said, "Brerto, great, white tiger that rules the skies, we are unworthy of your presence. Please grace us with the sweet boom of your voice. God among gods, what is your bidding?"

Brerto's voice was deep and powerful, primal, "Bok has failed me. Your son has failed me. I blessed him with the gift of service to my name and filled him with my glory. Yet he faltered and wasted his good fortune. He has left a black mark upon your name."

Ott remained bent on one knee with his head down as he replied, "None feels the sting of those words stronger than I. My son has marred my name and failed all of these faithful souls that followed him. Worst of all, he has failed his lord. He has failed you, my lord, god, and king. In his failure to faithfully honor you with the blood of men and dwarves, I have failed you. I raised him to be a great warrior and he proved deficient. Oh great Brerto, I know I do not deserve your mercy or your pity, but please, my lord, forgive my transgression. I seek only to serve you."

"Rise," Brerto boomed.

Though Brerto remained on all fours, Ott's face was level with his when the giant rose. Rather than disrespect his god by returning his gaze, he averted his eyes toward the ground. "Your word is my command, lord," Ott's tone carried a note of awe.

"Look me in the eye, faithful servant."

Ott raised his gaze to meet his lord's. The great tiger's eyes were without color. They weren't black. They were at once nothing and everything, empty and full all at the same time. Those eyes grabbed Ott's stare and held it. "Your gaze is both terrible and mesmerizing my lord," he stammered.

"You have not failed me," Brerto boomed. "Your son has proven to be a disappointment, but you remain a faithful servant. You have the strength to repair the damage your son has brought to your name. Lead my army and destroy the men of Havenstahl. Trample them beneath your feet, and crush them into the dirt they fight so hard to protect. This is my will."

"You honor me, lord," Ott replied graciously. "Your will be done."

Immediately after the last word had left Ott's mouth, the great, white tiger vanished, but his voice remained, "Remember your promise, Ott. Kill them all."

The rest of the crowd behind Ott began to rise back to their feet as Ott fell back to his knees. His god had spoken to him. He had levied a direct command. An odd mixture of awe, fear, joy, and honor swelled in his chest. The queer combination sent his thoughts flittering this way and that. Closing his eyes, he drew a deep breath in and rose back to his feet. Where his son had failed, he would succeed and return honor and glory to his family's name.

Ott turned to face the crowd gathered around him. "Our god has come down to bless our mission. Bok failed us. Men do not kill giants. They are crushed beneath our feet, ripped apart by our hands, or ground up in our teeth. And dwarves," he paused and looked around the crowd, "dwarves should not even exist. They are abominations, even lower than men. They exist merely to worship us."

The awed crowd before him was unable to do much more than mumble. God had spoken to them. Brerto, the great, white tiger, had shown himself to them and given them a mission. Drunk with excitement, they milled about absently congratulating each other. Ott was their leader now, their general, and their king. His reign commanded by Brerto himself. They would follow him into battle. They would stab and bite and tear and crush. They would rip men apart and trample them under foot. They would not be swayed from their righteous purpose.

CHAPTER 40
PEACE

Two days had passed since Maelich awoke after slaying Shellar, and the sun was setting on a third by the time he caught the first glimpse of Goechal's hut through the trees. The road back from the swamp had been far less clumsy than the road in. Maelich shook his head as he glanced over at Ymitoth with a smirk. No words were necessary. The old warrior perfectly understood the sentiment behind Maelich's grin. Two great trackers, hunters, and warriors had doubled their journey by wandering around lost in the woods. Had it not been for that treacherous bastard Braggon, they would probably still be wandering lost in the woods, just skirting the edge of the swamp.

As the two hurried up toward the old hut, Maelich noticed there wasn't any smoke coming from the chimney. Night was quickly approaching. Even if she wasn't cooking anything for an evening meal, she should at least have a fire going for warmth. He gave Ymitoth a nudge and said, "No fire. Why do you suppose that is?"

Ymitoth shrugged, "We been at the trail better than a week. Perhaps she ain't about. Maybe she'd errands that needed running."

Shaking his head, Maelich replied, "That old woman was far too frail for any journey, and there is nothing close enough for an errand."

"Well there be the door," Ymitoth pointed. "Knock and be having your answers."

Maelich gave the weathered, wooden door three solid knocks. After a few moments passed without a reply, he gave it three more that were just a wee bit harder. Still the hut remained silent. He pressed his ear against the door. No sounds were about on the other side of it. Ymitoth sauntering around the corner of the old place grabbed his attention. As he watched him disappear around the corner, he knocked again. The hut replied with nothing but more silence.

"There be a shape on the bed," Ymitoth hollered from around the corner. "She looks to be sleeping."

"With no fire?" Maelich replied. "She will freeze once the night takes hold."

He slowly pushed the door open, poked his head inside and in a soft voice asked, "Goechal, are you well?"

Goechal didn't reply.

Maelich tried again, his voice a bit stronger this time, "Goechal?"

The shape on the bed stirred, but remained silent.

Ymitoth pushed past Maelich into the hut and said in a rather loud tone, "Goechal, the lad here ain't about to let ye be resting your weary eyes. Tell him that ye be resting and he ought be leaving ye to be."

Goechal finally rolled toward them and opened her eyes, mumbling something inaudible.

"What was that?" Maelich asked, far more relieved than he needed to be.

"I be weary, lad," she replied weakly.

Maelich practically skipped over to the bed, reached into the sack containing all of the medallions Ymitoth had salvaged from Shellar's remains, and produced a stack of five he had tied together. All of them were etched with the image of a great fish breaking the surf, the symbol of Belscythia. Hopefully one of them had belonged to Brakken. Maelich untied the bundle and spread them out on the bed next to Goechal.

"Oh sweet lad," she said, her voice faint, weak, and slightly crackling. "Ye killed that witch and brought home me sweet Brakken's crest."

"I did kill Shellar," Maelich smiled. Then he picked up one of the medallions and examined it, "I have five medallions bearing the crest of Belscythia. Are you able to determine if one of these belonged to Brakken?"

"Aye," Goechal's voice remained weak, but her eyes sparkled. "Be there anything carved in the back of any of them?"

Maelich began flipping them over and examining their backsides. "Yes," he replied. "Two of them have some form of inscription on them."

"Put them two in me hands," her voice gained a bit of strength and she sat up in the bed. A smile using every inch of her face spread across it.

A matching smile spread across Maelich's face. Goechal's enthusiasm made her appear at least 20 summers younger than she seemed when he first met her. He handed her the two potential emblems, nearly as excited as she was.

The gleam of her eyes was so bright it remained remarkable even through her deeply squinting expression. Those eyes examined the first one closely for a few moments before Goechal tossed it to the side and said,

"That ain't be the one." Then she pulled the other closer to her face and applied the same scrutiny. After an equal amount of time, her form deflated, those twenty years she seemed to drop only moments prior rushed back like a herd of stampeding tubber. She threw the medallion across the room. "That ain't be the one neither." A tear perched itself on her left eyelid, threatening to fall. Before it could, her eyes widened and her smile returned, "Them ain't be the only two. Give me the rest."

Maelich quickly collected them all and handed them over. He thought about reminding her he hadn't found any inscriptions on any of them but decided against it. She would learn on her own soon enough without his help. Commenting on it would probably only make it worse. As he prepared to console the poor, old woman, who was most certainly about to be crushed by the lack of evidence of her husband's honesty, his mind drifted.

"Aha," she cried. The volume her small, frail form achieved was shocking enough to make Maelich jump. "Aye lad, with your eyes so young and fresh, ye ain't seen nothing years of loving someone be helping old, failing eyes to see."

Goechal used her sleeve to polish up the one prang medallion remaining in her hands. The tears finally came, but they poured onto a wide smile. As Maelich watched her admire the crest, she appeared more like a young maiden gazing at the object of her affection than an old woman just waiting to die alone in the woods. "Oh Brakken," she gushed, "I knew ye'd been faithful to me. I ain't never doubted ye for a moment."

Goechal remained like that, glowing and doting over the symbol of her love. Ymitoth sat at the table while Maelich leaned on the edge of the bed. Both stared dopey-eyed and smiling at the result of the good work they had done. Maelich looked back at Ymitoth and winked. The scene playing out before them on the bed was the hero's payment. It is a hard life. The trail is unforgiving. But the payment is oh so sweet. No amount of prang or precious jewels could ever match the value of true appreciation. Goechal had been holding onto a belief. To see that faith justified was everything she had been living for.

Finally Goechal looked over at Maelich and held the back of the medallion up close to his face. "Look here lad," she said, continuing to smile through the tears. "Be looking close now too. It be faint, but it be there."

Maelich squinted at the spot that Goechal's wrinkled finger pointed to. There was something there. It was so faint the quick examination he had performed earlier missed it. It was definitely there though. He read it out loud, "Root."

Goechal pulled the medallion back to her bosom, leaned her head back, and in a joyous tone shouted, "Aye, Root. That be what me Brakken had been calling me since the day I said I'd be his wife and spend all the rest of me days with him."

Maelich leaned his head to the side and asked, "Root?"

Goechal laughed in his face, her excitement getting the best of her and stealing her control. "Aye, Root," she shouted again.

"That be an odd name to be calling somebody," Ymitoth interjected.

As impossible as it seemed, Goechal's smile widened even further, "Not if ye be knowing me Brakken it ain't. That day he married me he looked dead in me eyes and said, 'I be calling ye Root from this day on. Ye be the root that be keeping me grounded, the root that be keeping me centered, and the root our family be growing from." The tears kept pouring from Goechal's eyes as she continued, "It may be sounding funny to ye or any other that be hearing it. Me Brakken he ain't been no poet or nothing, but them words he spoke right out of his heart. And I knew what meaning they carried to him. I been his Root since that day and that name be meaning the world to me. I be hearing his voice in it."

"It does not sound funny to me at all," Maelich replied. "Your Brakken sounds like a fine man who loved you above all else."

"Aye," Ymitoth agreed. "He be sounding like a fine man indeed."

Goechal didn't say another word. She kissed the medallion and pulled it back into her bosom. Then she laid her head back on the pillow, stared at the ceiling, and continued to mumble words of affection to her husband who had died so many years ago. After a few moments, her mumbling stopped. After a few more moments, her chest stopped shallowly rising and falling. A few more moments after that, her eyes grayed over and one final breath left her body. The smile never left her face, and Brakken's medallion with the term of endearment scratched onto the back of it remained tightly in her grip, firmly pressed against her heart.

Warmth began in Maelich's chest and swelled up into his cheeks. A moment later, tears quickly spilled over his eyelids. He was swift to wipe them away and close his eyes up tight in an attempt to stop more from coming. It proved a fruitless effort. When he opened them back up a fresh batch poured forth freely and ran down his cheeks. Ymitoth glanced over at him when a sniffle took him by surprise and filled the small hut with its sound.

"Ye be crying?" Ymitoth asked with earnest concern. The sarcastic tone that would normally accompany a question about tears amongst warriors was thankfully absent.

"I cannot help it," Maelich gave in and lost himself in sobs as he fell to his knees beside Goechal's bed and rested his hand on her cool forehead.

Ymitoth walked over, placed his hand on Maelich's shoulder, gave it a squeeze, and said, "There ain't be nothing to be crying about lad. Ye brung peace to this poor soul. She'd been hanging on hoping for someone to make an end to her story. Ye gave her that gift lad."

"I know that, but this does not feel like a happy ending," Maelich's cadence was slow and choppy as his words fell inelegantly from his mouth, randomly interrupted by sobs.

"Sure it be happy," Ymitoth gave Maelich's shoulder another squeeze. "Just look at that smile what ye put on that face of her's. That be real joy right there, lad, and ye brung her that joy. This be a happy ending."

"I know but…" Maelich's voice trailed off as he laid his head down upon the bed next to Goechal's body and wept. Ymitoth gave his shoulder one more squeeze and then he stepped out of the hut to give Maelich a chance to get all of his emotion out.

As Maelich knelt, weeping next to the corpse of a woman he didn't really know, life seemed completely absurd. Why do it? Why do anything? If all anyone had to look forward to was dying, what was the point? What did it all mean? Goechal probably lived fifteen summers more than she should have clinging to a hope that someone would bring her peace. In the end, what difference did it make? She died with a smile. So what? She was still dead. What purpose did it serve?

Questions continued to swirl around Maelich's head. Sadly, there were no answers to accompany them. They were all the questions great minds ponder but never really answer. Sure they theorize, but none of them really know anything. They merely weave something that makes them feel like there might be some point to everything, but really there isn't. People live, they fill their lives with distractions, and then they die and return to the Lake. At the end of it all, there is no difference between the man who spends his life sitting on a rock and the man who spends his life saving the world. In the end they are both the same, food for the Lake.

Ymitoth was sitting on a log, splitting a long blade of grass into several thin strips, challenging himself to see just how thin he could get them when Maelich finally emerged from the hut. "Did ye say all of your good-byes to the old soul?" he asked.

Maelich nodded as he rubbed his puffy, red eyes and replied, "I did. I have nothing left to say or think about it. I left it all in that hut."

The two men gathered wood and built a pyre. They were able to find plenty of solid, dry stuff around the hut. When the platform was finished, it was about six feet long, four feet wide, and four feet tall. After all the heavy lifting was finished, the two men washed Goechal's body and prepared her for the pyre. Ymitoth laid her out on the platform of sticks while Maelich gathered as many trinkets from the hut—that appeared to have some meaning—as he could find. After all of those trinkets had been placed around the body, Ymitoth used his flint to fire up a brand.

Ymitoth paused with the burning stick in his hand, looked at Maelich, and asked, "Have ye got any words ye would be sending her off with?"

Maelich stared at the body in silence for a few moments and decided, "No. I am all out of words. There is nothing I could say at this moment that would carry any meaning."

"Aye," Ymitoth nodded and offered some of his own. "Oh great Lake, father of all life, take this woman into your peaceful waters. She been a good, faithful soul for all her days. Please be showing her the peace she be deserving."

Ymitoth bowed after delivering his brief prayer. Then he tossed the brand onto the pyre. The dry wood caught immediately. In a matter of a few moments, a healthy fire was quickly consuming it. Ymitoth stood with his head bowed as the fire burned. Maelich watched though. He kept his eyes on Goechal's body as the fire first licked it, then caught hold of her gown, and finally covered it completely. The flames danced and zigged, racing up her form and back. Maelich lost himself in their movement. The soul finds water and the body finds flame. In the end, the only evidence is ash blowing in the wind. What was the point of it all?

CHAPTER 41
THREE QUEENS IN DRUINDAHL

Three days had passed on the trail by the time Fielstag and Borgan reached the edge of the Forgotten Forest. They would have made the trip far more quickly if not for a run in with a small pack of exceptionally brazen Amatilazo. There were only five of them and they appeared sickly. Not to mention the sun had barely dipped below the horizon, and the sky was still splashed with color. Amatilazo typically waited for the safety of the darkest hours of night. They were fierce, but no match for two battle-hardened veterans of Havenstahl's army.

"Be minding the treetops," Fielstag said quietly as both men slowed their horses to a trot. "I only been in this forest once after fighting a battle right on this very spot. Druindahl be having scouts all up and around them treetops. They probably been watching us all the way down the mountain."

"Aye," Borgan agreed. "I fought in that battle too. I had been pretty green at the time, but I saw them arrows flying out of them trees."

Fielstag nodded and looked up toward the canopy. A memory of what might be lurking within the cover of the dense leaves slipped through his mind before slithering down his spine in the form of a subtle chill. After trembling its way through him, that chill settled into an odd coolness between his shoulder blades; something closer to fear than a warrior would like to admit. Aside from being masters of the horse, the warriors of Druindahl were also masters of the trees. They could move about the canopy in near complete silence, like ghosts slipping through the foliage. He had witnessed the prowess of those ghosts first hand. Hopefully, he would have a chance to identify himself as friend before earning an arrow in the heart.

"We'll be losing the light soon," Borgan interrupted Fielstag's thoughts.

"Maybe we ought camp for the night and be attacking this dark forest when it be at least dimly lit. It be pretty dark in there already."

Fielstag shook his head, "We already been taking too much time. For all we know, them grizzly mongs what you seen may already be cutting our people down. We'll be taking it slow and walking our horses."

With that, Fielstag leapt down from his horse and looked around the ground at the very edge of the trees. His long, blonde hair hung down into his face. He brushed it back as he stooped to snag a fallen branch. It was about six feet long and a good three inches in diameter. With a few slight modifications, it would suit his purpose perfectly. He grabbed the thicker end with his right hand and about halfway down the shaft with his left hand. Then he broke the thing over his knee. The result was a piece just over two feet long and another piece just under four feet long. The latter he snapped over his knee in the same fashion, not quite in half. After the effort, he rose with his prize of two sticks just over two feet long. Sticks in hand, he walked over to his horse and fumbled around in one of his sacks until he found what he was looking for. After a few moments, a strip of cloth had been ripped in half and each half had been wrapped around one of the sticks. He set one down on his saddle, picked up a jar of liquid and soaked the fabric on the stick remaining in his hand. After setting the jar down on the ground, he picked up his flint, struck it near the fabric, and the torch sparked to life. He walked over and handed the blazing thing to Borgan. Then he repeated the steps with the other stick.

"These will definitely be helping," Borgan nodded as he hopped off of his horse.

Fielstag smiled, "They won't be helping us see them scouts up in them trees, but they'll certainly be helping us find our way."

"Aye, but what be our way?" Borgan asked. "We ain't got no idea where we ought be going once we get inside them woods."

"Now that ain't all true," Fielstag shook his head. "We ain't spent a long time here, but we spent some after that great battle. The going will be slow, but we be finding our way. Besides, it won't be long before their guards be coming to challenge us."

Hours slipped by as the two men led their horses slowly through the dark forest. They had to stop twice to rework their brands after exhausting all of the fuel and fabric. The torches cast an orange glow surrounding them in a dome of light with about a ten foot radius. Beyond the dim glow sat blackness upon blackness. No starlight or moonlight proved hearty enough to penetrate the thick canopy of the forest. On a few occasions they heard rustling sounds from beyond their small dome of protection. Some of those sounds seemed loud enough to be made by men. No one came to accost them or question them though. Two battle hardened soldiers slowly shrunk into a couple of frightened lads; eyes darting around at every out of place sound, quietly begging for the light of day. A screech tore through the darkness. It was loud enough to make both men jump and send their horses into a fit of stamping and whinnying. Borgan even dropped his torch.

"What on Ouloos be that?" Borgan whispered as quietly as he could amid heavy breaths and a racing heart. The only sound he had ever heard that remotely reminded him of the horrifying screech was a squeal his sister Pinella had made when they were both very young. Dingum, their scrod, had begun behaving strangely, displaying unusually high amounts of aggression. One day during a game of chase, the scrod caught up to her and bit into her hand. His fangs pushed all the way through from one side to the other. The sound she made as Dingum chomped into her flesh was almost as horrible as that screech. Dingum was killed for the assault and Pinella's hand was never the same. The sad memory somehow made the awful sound from somewhere among the trees even more terrifying.

Fielstag quickly regained his composure. Unlike his shivering comrade, he had heard the sound before. "That be a horny witch," he replied. The oppressive dark still had him feeling rather timid and small, but knowledge of the source of that awful sound somehow placed his mind just a bit more at ease. Knowing what creepy things were eyeing them from beyond the safety of the dim glow of their torches gave him the slightest feeling of power.

"What be that?" Borgan whispered. "I ain't never been hearing of no such thing as a horny witch."

"It be nothing more than a big bird that be hunting the small things scurrying about the forest floor in the darkness. There be myths about them turning into powerful, horrifying witches what can turn men into beasts like fallon or tubber. There ain't no truth to them tales though. They just be big birds that make an awful shriek. That shriek be what earned them that name of witch. And the feathers that be above their eyes be standing up tall like horns. Ye be putting them two ideas together and there ye be having horny witches. They ain't no cause for fear." As Fielstag assured his companion, his own fear continued to diminish.

The two men continued on into darkness for roughly an hour more before another notable sound stood out among the eerie song of a night in the forest. The rumble of hoof beats on the trail increased as a horse obviously approached. It would be quite odd for a rider of Druindahl to make that much noise while moving through the forest. They were normally far too stealthy to be heard until they were right on top of their target, if they were heard at all. On the other hand, unless a horse was spooked, it more than likely would not be moving that quickly through the forest without a rider. Both men stopped and stood their ground. Neither drew their sword. Within moments, an orange glow matching the dome surrounding them came into view up the trail a stretch. The speed at which it approached was impressive considering the darkness surrounding it.

Borgan and Fielstag kept their eyes trained on the approaching orange glow. The hoof beats of the horse were downright loud by this point. The rider's mission definitely had nothing to do with stealth. As the stranger approached, the two warriors of Havenstahl were increasingly able to make out his form in the orange glow from his torch. His helmet and chest plate were prang, brilliantly shining even in the dim, orange glow. His sleeves were red, the color of Druindahl. Their particular hue matched the ribbons streaming behind his massive, brown horse perfectly. Once he was roughly ten feet from Fielstag and Borgan, the rider abruptly stopped.

"You have entered into protected lands," Boringas's voice was strong and dripped authority. "State your names and what business you have in this wood."

Fielstag's voice failed to match the authority accompanying Boringas's words. On the contrary, his were quick and fell from his mouth amid heavy breaths, "We be riding under the banner of Havenstahl. Monsters and giants from across the Great Sea have lain her under siege and her people be fleeing to the safety of your forest. Them people be riding a slow caravan down the road from Havenstahl, and ye be knowing what a treacherous road that be."

Boringas gripped the reins of his horse as he continued his line of questions, "I can tell you are soldiers. Why have the two of you fled your posts and journeyed ahead of the people you protect?"

"We be riding by command of our queen, sir," Fielstag replied. "She be requesting assistance from the great city of Druindahl. We be on an errand to take her message to your king. There be grizzly mongs just a mile or so off of the trail when we left. I be praying the queen ain't dead."

"Grizzly mongs?" the authority in Boringas's voice briefly fled in place of shock. "What are grizzly mongs doing this far south? They have never ventured this far south." He paused as the idea turned over in his head a few times. It would have to wait. "Things have changed dramatically here in Druindahl. We have no riders to spare, and our king has been dethroned in favor of a former princess. Cialia now rules this land as her queen."

"Cialia," Fielstag gasped. "Her mother be in trouble as well. She be on the trail too."

"I will take you to my queen," the authority had returned to his tone. "I believe she now slumbers, but this is news she will wish to hear." He turned his horse around, looked back, and said, "Mount your horses and stay close to my backside. The trail is ample if you know her twists and turns."

Fielstag and Borgan did as Boringas had commanded. Neither had experienced a night ride through the forest at the speeds they were achieving. Boringas knew the wood well. They traveled roughly five miles in just around fifteen minutes. That was good time for a ride through the forest during the light of day. Fielstag had forgotten much of what he had seen when last he was in the city. He remembered enough to not be surprised when Boringas halted them in what seemed to be just a random spot on the trail. Immediately above their heads, torches blazed and well-lit wooden walkways spanned from tree to tree where large platforms and buildings wrapped around them, even among their highest branches. They couldn't see any of it from where they stood. That was the secret, the mystery of Druindahl. Lights shined up in the canopy, but from the forest floor no one would ever know. The city in the trees was completely hidden.

Boringas let out a sharp, brief whistle. Shortly after, an elegant cart smoothly lowered to the forest floor from far up in the canopy. Immediately after it touched down, three men rushed up out of the darkness. Once the riders had dismounted, each of those three men ushered one of the horses away into the blackness surrounding them. Borgan looked over at Fielstag and raised his eyebrows over a frown.

As if Boringas had noticed the gesture, he said, "Do not fret over your horses. They will be taken to the stables, fed, cared for, and given proper rest." Then he raised his right arm toward the cart that had lowered from the trees, bowed, and said, "Welcome to Druindahl."

Both Borgan and Fielstag bowed in response. Then the three men entered the cart together. The movement of the thing was far smoother than either of the visitors imagined a cart being hauled up into the trees would be. Some serious engineering had obviously gone into its design. The entire journey lasted roughly half a minute, and by the time they reached a wide, wooden platform, the forest floor was lost in darkness.

Once off the cart and on the platform, Fielstag took a moment to look around at the construction. Wooden paths sprawled out in every direction, connecting large, circular buildings that incorporated the shapes and angles of trees into their construction. This was no rude structure slapped together haphazardly by hurried men with crude tools. The paths were smooth, and detailed reliefs had been carved into the wide posts supporting the railings. Those reliefs told the history of Ouloos through the images they portrayed. As Fielstag appreciated the design and construction of the place, the idea that all of the grandeur of it could exist completely invisible to the ground below made it appear even more amazing to him.

The two soldiers from Havenstahl fell in step behind Boringas, neither able to hold back their awe. The leader of Druindahl's army led them across a great bridge, then left and then right, through numerous curves the path made around trees, up several steps, and then across another great bridge. The three kept a swift pace, any faster and they would have been jogging. Even with the speed with which they walked, Fielstag and Borgan found time to admire their surroundings. The lights were perhaps the most amazing feature. It wasn't really the lights themselves that were notable though. The shades they bore, those were truly amazing. Cast of fine prang and resembling two bells—one above and one below—they were connected to each other by a wide strip. The lower bell was upside down with its mouth opening to the bell above it. The space between them was impossibly thin. Still, each lamp cast an ample beam of light on the path, bright enough that it appeared to be bathed in the sun's full glory. Fielstag thought on what the inner workings of those lamps might be, probably something with mirrors.

Boringas finally halted at a wide stairway leading up two stories to an ornate archway, "It is amazing. The name of the man who crafted it escapes me, but he carved much of what makes Druindahl so beautiful to behold with his own hands." He paused for a moment and added, "And his work has stood the test of time."

"The detail in all of these carvings be like nothing I ever seen," Borgan commented, his voice drenched in awe, "but that arch be a gem that be standing out among the treasures."

"It is," Borgan agreed. "Look at the detail on those dragons. That deep red color they all share has never been touched up or reworked. That work stands as it has always stood. It is truly amazing. I have walked beneath that arch more than one thousand times, and each time I am overcome with reverence for the great work Coeptus can do through the hands of men. It is hard to believe the piece was carved from one big chunk of wood."

The three men stared up at the thing for several moments, admiring the beauty of it. The top of the arch consisted mostly of a perched dragon spreading her wings—an image of Helias no doubt—with her head turned up and fire ushering forth from her mouth. Along either side of it were other, smaller images of dragons; some flew, others walked, and still others perched. Each of them appeared so life-like they might fly up into the darkness at any moment. Each man—even the one who had spent his life admiring the work—let out a slight gasp at one moment or another when sheer amazement finally filled them to the point they could no longer hold it all in. Such was the quality and detail of the work. If the eyes of a man stared long enough, those dragons seemed to come to life, moving as if sweet Coeptus had blessed them with souls and beating hearts. It was always the trick of an overly impressed mind, of course, but none could spend very long admiring it without being fooled.

It was Boringas who broke the spell when he said, "Unless she slumbers, the queen sits beyond that arch. We should make our way to her."

Fielstag and Borgan both nodded their agreement, and the three men began up the stairs. Unable to completely break free of the spell those expertly crafted dragons held on them, the journey up the tall flight of stairs lasted far longer than it needed to. Eventually, they made the peak and passed beneath the object of their fascination only to be faced with a doorway matching it perfectly ten feet beyond it. This one was not carved from wood and painted to perfection. This one was cast of fine prang and glimmered in the light shining on it from those amazing lamps. Two guards stood at attention, one on either side of the doorway. Both bowed slightly as the three men approached.

Boringas faced the guard on the right and said, "Is the queen inside?"

"She is, sir," the guard replied. "Shall I announce your presence?"

"That will not be necessary," Boringas shook his head. "There have been developments demanding far more haste than ceremony. I will announce myself."

Boringas pushed the two, heavy doors open. Crafted in the same shimmering prang as the doors, the walls inside the room they opened into seemed to glow. Reliefs—obviously carved with the same meticulous care and attention to detail as those decorating the wood along the paths of the city—adorned all four of them; stories played out in pictures evenly spaced around the room, midway between floor and ceiling. The artfully-crafted memories seemed to float in the warm glow like silhouettes of gulls soaring in the blazing, orange brilliance of the setting sun. Both Fielstag and Borgan lost another gasp as they entered the throne room and stepped onto a carpet running the length of it from the doors to two thrones; one empty and one occupied by a person who bore a face both men recognized. Somehow that face seemed older and more terrible than either man remembered.

"Where are the guards?" Boringas asked with the slightest hint of irritation in his voice. "I realize you said you had no need of them, but I sent them back to you for a purpose."

Cialia raised her vine-crowned head and replied in a matter-of-fact tone, "I told you I have no need of guards. That has not changed, and it will not change. My mind is connected to everything, sweet Boringas. You need those men for your army far more than I need them standing around my throne room."

"If your mind truly be connected to everything, then ye be knowing of the plight of our people," the words tumbled out of Fielstag's mouth before he could stop them.

"What plight?" Cialia's eyes narrowed.

"Apparently your focus has been elsewhere," the irritation in Boringas's voice grew to something just shy of disrespect. "These two soldiers have come to us ahead of a great caravan from Havenstahl. It appears the greatest city of men has been set upon by an enemy who has no fear of her might."

"The army of Havenstahl has fallen?" Cialia's tone echoed her shock.

"Not at all," Fielstag held his head high. "The great fallon be waging war against giants, trogmortem, and grongs. Borgan and me seen many battles, right at the front. That enemy came with great numbers though, and they be fighting with a fury we ain't before seen. Your mother, she be guiding the people that ain't built for the fighting here; all that be going anyhow. The road from there to here be treacherous, and we be boasting but a small number to defend the lot of them…"

"Grizzly mongs," Boringas interrupted, "hundreds of them threaten the trail. These two come in search of assistance from the great riders of Druindahl. Sadly—due to recent developments—we haven't the numbers to be of much assistance."

Cialia's head dropped into her right hand and she remained that way for several moments. When she finally raised her eyes back up to the three men addressing her, fear danced all about them. "How long ago?" she asked.

"We been to the trail three days," Fielstag replied.

"They could be dead," the volume of Cialia's voice had fallen to barely a whisper. "My mother could be dead."

"Aye," Fielstag agreed. "I be hoping it ain't so, but them monsters from the north been well too near to that road than to think it could be otherwise. Thousands upon thousands be travelling in that caravan. There ain't no place for numbers like that to be hiding and they ain't moving nowhere with any kind of speed. That confrontation be inevitable. I just be hoping it ain't happened yet."

Cialia raised her arms up to them, bringing the room to silence. Then her hands moved to either side of her face as her index fingers began to rub slow, deliberate circles on her temples. She closed her eyes and inhaled deeply through her nose. That breath remained in her lungs for several moments. When she finally released it slowly through her mouth and opened her eyes back up, they were as red as the dragons carved into the archway outside the throne room. Her body trembled slightly as her breathing became even and steady. Fielstag looked over to Boringas as if to speak, but the general raised his index finger to his lips and then pointed to Cialia.

Several quiet moments passed as the queen continued to rub slow circles on her temples. All the while those red eyes gazed through the three men standing before her. Physically she sat before them, but her mind had left the room. It travelled through the paths of Druindahl and down to the forest floor. It raced over the mountains and along the road Fielstag and Borgan had followed to find the hidden city in the trees. Finally, she found men fighting massive beasts with long, matted, white fur, horrible claws, and fangs that looked useful for tearing flesh. She drew the men in and away from the fight.

Pulling the men close, Cialia continued just a little farther down the trail where hundreds upon hundreds of wagons sat parked in random circles on either side of it. In and around those were the thousands of scared, hungry people huddled together, terrified by the impending doom. Cialia drew them all to her. She reached out with her mind and connected them all as if she were physically tying them to a long rope. Once she was connected to each and every one, she pulled them back with her; back along the trail toward Druindahl, back over the mountains, and back into the trees. Once there, she left the wagons and the people on the forest floor with peaceful thoughts in their heads. After all that had been alive on the trail from Havenstahl were safe within the trees below the great city of Druindahl, she pulled back to throne room and closed her eyes again.

The three men cowered before the horrible queen, dreading the moment those fiery eyes would open again and what that might mean to their hides. All of them gasped when two more queens appeared next to them, seemingly out of thin air. Leisha, the former Queen of Druindahl and Perrin, Queen of Havenstahl materialized before their eyes, holding each other tightly and burying their faces in one another's shoulders. Thankfully, when Cialia's eyes opened again, the red color had fled in favor of the soft blue Boringas had fallen in love with so many years ago. She leapt from her throne and ran to the two bewildered women whom she had just pulled through space.

"Mother, you are safe," she cried as she wrapped her arms around both women.

Leisha raised her head up and looked around. "Where are we?" she asked. Before anyone could respond she asked another question, "How did we get here?"

"You are safe in Druindahl, mother," Cialia replied quite breathless. "I brought you here."

Then Perrin lifted her head and looked at Cialia, "Where be all me people?" She pulled away from the new queen's embrace as she asked the question. "If ye have left them to be fending for themselves, send me back there so I can be dying with them."

"Your people are quite safe," Cialia comforted the bewildered queen. "I brought you all back here to the safety of Druindahl. They are under the city on the forest floor. All of their wagons and supplies have made their way as well. You are all safe and under my protection."

Leisha looked her daughter in the eye and asked, "Where is the king?"

"Druindahl has no king and probably never will," Cialia's reply was curt.

"What did you do Cialia?" Leisha's eyes narrowed. "Where are all the guards?"

"I have no need of guards, mother. I am perfectly capable of caring for myself," she paused, "and anyone else who comes along."

"It would appear you are getting quite comfortable with your power," Leisha continued to eye her daughter suspiciously. "What have you done with the king?"

"Honestly, mother," Cialia sighed and withdrew from the embrace, "you look at me as if I am some kind of monster. The king was unfit for the throne, so I relieved him of it. He now serves as my advisor."

"What did he do to make him unworthy of the throne I gave him?"

"He let our fair city fall to vicious men who cared more for coin than the people they were sworn to protect and he…" Cialia stopped as she noticed the burn on Perrin's face. "Sweet girl, what has happened to you?" she asked. "Where is my brother?"

Perrin shook her head, "Your brother still be absent. He might be too much for the trail, but he wouldn't never be causing me no harm like what me face shows. What's been done to me face been done by me son."

"Your son did this to you," Cialia gasped, "but how, he is only just born?"

"That is a story for later, Cialia," Leisha interrupted. "First you need to tell me what has been happening in my city."

Cialia's head drooped as she turned her gaze back toward Leisha. An attempt at a stern expression failed as she replied, "The man you left to occupy your throne peopled his army with mercenaries, thieves, and murderers." She paused briefly and added, "Perhaps even rapists. Luckily, I arrived in time to stop at least four from earning the last title. Those four had set upon a young girl, Keiryn…"

"Tesha's sweet daughter?" Leisha interrupted.

"Is dead," Cialia answered. "She earned the interest of one of those men and when she rebuked his advances, all four attacked her. She managed to escape by clawing and kicking, but they ran her down in the forest. I gave them every opportunity to handle the matter with civility. They refused and fought with me until two of them had returned to the Lake. Then the glorious riders of Druindahl assaulted us on our way into the city. Only one of them fired the arrow, but almost all of them were culpable in her death."

"You killed them all," Leisha's tone echoed the numbness she felt, as her eyes reflected the horror of her realization. "You have found your fire."

"Yes I have, mother. I have done terrible things in the name of justice," Cialia's tone swayed between defensive and regretful. "I searched their hearts. All but twenty-one wished it had been their hand that drew back the string launching the arrow through Keiryn's throat. She was innocent. Those men were like a disease, settled into the city I love. Sadly, I am torn about what I have done. On one hand I feel those vile creatures deserved the punishment I gave to them, but on the other hand…" her voice trailed off as her gaze dropped to the floor.

Leisha closed her eyes as her head slowly shook back and forth. There were so many things she wished to express at that moment, but she had no words to give meaning to them. They were feelings mostly, pain and emptiness, a hollow in her soul. She had given birth to a god and that god was truly great and terrible, filled with an unwavering sense of justice allowing no room for error. Simply harboring ill intent was crime enough to earn death.

Cialia raised her head back up and watched her mother wilt under the weight of what she had just learned. Is it weakness to temper justice with compassion? The innocent require a champion who can protect them. Is it wrong to remove a threat before it injures or kills them? Once the threat becomes an act, doesn't punishment become vengeance? Is justice nothing more than vengeance then? Justice and vengeance; the two seem closely related kin. Why take the life of one who has killed another if not for vengeance? It is a lesson, of course, a lesson to all others that murder will not be tolerated. Is waiting until the innocent victim has been cut down, tortured, or battered to deliver justice any nobler than stopping the author of that threat before they can write the horrible story growing in their head? If the intention is known, why wait until the crime has been committed?

Cialia sighed as she turned her attention away from the doubt stomping around her conscience. Forcing a smile back to her lips, she returned her gaze to Perrin, "Sweet Perrin, so beautiful, just look what they have done to your face. Come here sweet sister."

As Perrin fell into Cialia's embrace, she rested the burnt side of her face on the queen's shoulder. She had grown accustomed to the pain any touch caused the wound. It fueled her desire for vengeance against those who stole her child and brought about the tantrum that released his flame. The pain didn't come though. Streams of fire should have been rushing away from the burn that engulfed the entire right side of her face, sending fire down her neck. There was no burn, no fire, and no pain. Instead, her cheek felt cool against Cialia's shoulder, like a light, evening breeze gently kissed it with relief. The spot began to tingle, from her jawline up to the very top of her head and from her right ear to that side of her nose. It was not quite a tickle, almost an itch; something that balanced a narrow path between those two and mingled with the cooling sensation slowly washing away the memory of any pain. A faint glow danced in the periphery of her vision. It emanated from the spot where her face touched Cialia's shoulder, the source of that not quite a tickle and not quite an itch as well as the glorious cool. The idea to be afraid of what was happening to her almost popped into her head. However, the sensation was too calming to allow it.

Cialia pulled away from Perrin and held onto her shoulders as she pushed her back to arm's length to admire her work. "There you are," she said as she caressed Perrin's right cheek with the back of the fingers on her left hand, "just as beautiful as ever. You have such soft and perfect skin. My brother is a lucky man."

Perrin's right hand shot up to her cheek and examined the spot that had been so charred just moments prior. Her heart was immediately torn between sadness and elation. The burn was gone. The pain was gone. Both of those were good things. However, the only tangible piece of her son she had left was gone with them. There was enough of him in her heart. That would have to do. She finally answered, "If only he be knowing it."

Leisha finally managed to get past the mess of mangled emotions stomping through her heart and gave voice to more pressing matters, "Your father leads the armies of Havenstahl and Alhouim in a battle they cannot win."

Cialia turned her gaze back to her mother and did her best to appear confident, "Father is the greatest general to ever grace the face of Ouloos, mother. And Havenstahl still boasts the mightiest army ever to march into battle."

"They fight monsters and giants, Cialia," Leisha sighed, "things that cannot be killed by men."

"Maelich killed a giant," the new queen countered.

"Your brother is hardly a man though, is he?"

Cialia shrugged, "That is true. However, at the time of his trial, he was but a lad. I think father can do at least as much. You have never traded blades with him. He trained me. I have witnessed his mastery with a blade first hand. Believe me, my father is one man who can kill a giant."

"I wish I shared your confidence," Leisha sighed. After a few moments, she added, "It troubles me you were unable to sense the danger. You have always been so connected to everything."

Cialia considered this for a moment, "That is troubling. My mind was so full of everything; I suppose I had to release it for a while. I have found my center again. This is where I belong. These people are without a champion. I am their champion."

"And the people in Havenstahl who still view you as the same?"

The forced smile remained on Cialia's face as she answered, "I have faith in my father. He is the greatest general this world has ever known. I will check on him tomorrow. I will send my thoughts to the battlefield and see how he fares."

"I have faith in your father too, but I also had the benefit of looking into his eyes before he marched to war. They were not the eyes of a great general confidently stalking off to victory. He looked like a man walking to the gallows," Leisha's gaze traveled to the floor, but her mind wasn't registering anything it showed her. Instead it was full of visions of blood and death.

"Come," Cialia draped her arm over her mother's shoulder. "You have faced a difficult journey. Let us rest and solve all of these problems when the sun is on hand to free us from dark and terrible thoughts."

"Wait," Leisha said as she pushed Cialia's arm away and turned to face her daughter. "Perrin's and your father's stories have distracted us from your actions. You defend and you justify, but I don't think you believe your own words. You need to work through those feelings. How can you present yourself as a champion of these people if you doubt the actions you use to defend them?"

Cialia's eyes narrowed for a moment while a stern expression crept onto her face. The moment was brief as her eyes widened and the sternness fled, chased away by something more akin to hopelessness. "I have done terrible things, mother," her voice cracked as her form slumped into Leisha's embrace.

CHAPTER 42
THE BATTLE OF MAOMNOSETT

First light, the moment before the sun has peeked over the horizon, when the dark of night first begins to recede in fear of the sun's fury. That first glow from the east caught Daritus's eyes. Unable to sleep, the battered, old general leaned—with his good arm—on an old staff and gazed back at the great city atop the mountain he had nearly given his life to protect. The faint first bits of orange and red on the horizon gave the place a magical glow. How many had Leisha saved, and how many remained? Those remaining were far more confident than he was in his ability to defend them against the monsters at their gate. What if he failed? How many would die along with him?

The plan was solid. It was good. Ymanchol's progress had slowed on the northern pass to Biggon's Bay and eventually stopped. That merely meant their enemy would have a clear path to flee back to their ships when faced with a mighty force at their front and equal forces at their flanks. It was a good plan. Why couldn't he bring himself to feel as confident about it as Doentaat and Kantiim? It was his plan after all, and things were going mostly as he expected them to, even better in some regards. Still, something in his gut—emptiness maybe or this crippling sense of foreboding—kept him from sharing the bright outlook of his generals. They all cheered his name hollering, "Giant slayer," whenever they caught sight of him. The entire force was flying high on wings he earned for them with a shattered arm, broken ribs, and the blood of the fiercest of giants. Why couldn't he soar to those same heights with them? His gaze drifted down to his useless arm. If only he could blame his trepidation on his wounds. Sadly, they weren't the cause at all. Despite an inability name to it, he was sure it wasn't that. He would march into battle with no arms and only his forehead as a weapon if the need arose. It wasn't a fear of dying holding him down. It was definitely something though, perhaps a fear of failing.

Then something changed. It was subtle, barely reaching the periphery of Daritus's thoughts. It was definitely there though, out of place with the grumbling of soldiers rising from slumber and the snores of those who had yet to join the new day. The battered, old general focused on that out of place…something. A slight change in the direction of the wind, faint, odd whistling, or something else entirely? His mind continued to chase after that intangible thing that was there, however impalpable. That something slowly grew stronger than just the raw beginnings of a hunch. The air had changed. It was the slightest current, but it was out of place with the light breeze gently tossing his hair around while he stood gazing to the east. Accompanying that minute change in the air was the faintest of whistles. It was barely a sound at all, but more than ample for the trained ears of a skilled hunter. Daritus had been that in his day. He had learned to pick the most imperceptible of sounds out of the white noise that was the wind and the leaves in the trees. This light whistling stood out amongst those other sounds to his keen ear, if to no one else's.

After a few moments of intense focus, Daritus turned his gaze to the western sky just above the open field that spread out before Fort Maomnosett. The big, dark shape was almost perfectly camouflaged against the still-dark, western sky…almost. Despite the near blackness of the sky, the battered, old general made out the shape of a large boulder. No siege weapons had been reported by any of the scouting missions. Giants probably didn't need any though. The boulder looked to be just a hair shorter than an average-sized man, and it was not quite perfectly round. Before Daritus could fully process what his eyes were seeing, his mouth opened and the words came out. "Run!" he shouted. "Run away from the fort."

The words had precious, little time to reach any ears before the massive boulder crashed into the front of Fort Maomnosett. Only a few men camped within those walls. If those few men were slumbering, they were definitely dead. As Daritus continued to shout with all his might, two more boulders followed closely behind the first. By the time the last crashed into it, the structure was all but demolished, an empty shell of falling sticks. After each of those boulders struck, they continued to roll, bounding over the trench at the back of the broken fort, and over tents and men that were too slow or unaware of the need to get out of their way. The entire camp awoke, at least all of those who weren't dead.

Daritus yelled, "The enemy is upon us, to the front, men!" The order was unnecessary. In fact, his ears were more than likely the only ones to hear his command. The soldiers of Havenstahl were difficult to surprise, and he who managed it gained precious little advantage by doing so. In moments, horses were saddled and forming into their columns while foot soldiers did the same. Kantiim was up and down the ranks of his men, prepping them for the day's battle. The field Daritus had marked for Havenstahl's last stand would finally taste blood.

Meanwhile, the catapults that had been sitting idle a short distance behind the fort waiting for a target finally let loose. Six fire balls raced over columns of foot soldiers standing ready for battle and over columns of horseman already racing toward what remained of the trees. Those fireballs had been fired in the general direction of the enemy. If the giants were close enough to fling boulders, they were close enough to be reached by catapult. Hopefully, if they didn't cause any damage, they would at least instill a bit of fear. Once the scouts that had been dispatched to survey the strike returned, the weapons would be adjusted accordingly and fired again with ill intent.

The horses had barely made the tree line when the monsters came. Before a hoof touched the trail, three trogmortem crashed into the charging cavalry, swatting, clawing, and biting. The collision caused more than a few men to fall from their mounts while those close enough to see it, yet still far enough back to take evasive action, circled left to come around for another pass. Meanwhile, more trogmortem came with grongs close on their heels. Accompanying them was the terror that no man wants to see on the battlefield, giants.

"Hold!" Kantiim shouted down the first row of foot soldiers formed up in front of the ruins of Fort Maomnosett.

The eyes of those men glaring out from beneath their helmets should have been glazed over with fear. Near twenty giants roamed the battlefield, tossing horses and men far into the trees with every swipe of their mighty arms. Some of them stomped, the bones of men and their mounts cracking and crumbling beneath their feet. Others grabbed and tore and bit and chewed. None of that had any effect on the resolve of the men standing tall in front of their crumbing fort and thirsting to taste the blood of battle on their lips. Their general had killed a giant in single combat. One on one, their leader stood tall and bested the fiercest of all giants. A man could kill a giant. Sword against sword, flesh against flesh, man could prevail. Many men swelled the ranks of Havenstahl's army. The rampaging giants had taken the horsemen of Havenstahl by surprise. Those fallen would be avenged.

"Hold!" Kantiim shouted again, as Daritus stalked over to stand by his side.

"This is your time!" the battered, old general shouted with a voice like thunder against a sky still dark with the last breaths of a dying night. "I cannot march into that battle, but I am with you. We are all men. Our hearts beat as one, fueled by the fire of the Great Mother. Feel that fire. It burns in me, and it burns in all of you. I have shown you the way. Who will join me as a slayer of giants?"

With one voice, each soldier in those columns of men together shouted, "Hoy!"

"Hold!" Kantiim shouted again, noting the eagerness in each eye looking back at him from the crowd. They would descend on the field like disease on broken skin. He shot a grin in Daritus's direction. Despite being beaten and crushed, the battered, old general carried himself with a swagger only the finest warriors can flaunt without appearing silly. There was nothing silly about Daritus. Kantiim walked over to him and said, "I see that light in your eyes, old friend. This battlefield is not for you on this day. Stand here and watch if you wish, but do not pick up a sword."

Daritus smiled wide, "That depends on how well you have trained your men."

The battle in the field raged on before those eager soldiers. The horsemen of Havenstahl made a fight out of it once they overcame the surprise. They lost ground every time they circled back around though. By the time the sun showed its full form in the sky, half of the battlefield belonged to the invaders. Grongs fell, trogmortem fell, but no giant earned even a scar. Not one man in the thick of it proved equal to Havenstahl's general. None could share the claim of the giant slayer.

Kantiim shouted, "Hold!" once again. Then he glanced over at Daritus who gave him a nod. When he turned back to his men, he spoke the one word they had all been aching to hear, "Charge!"

Daritus stood back as Kantiim's force erupted toward the center of the battle. At that same moment, moved by the same command, the horsemen of Havenstahl disengaged and raced toward the trees, leaving the enemy to face a fresh batch of furious hell. Immediately after the horses disengaged, a volley of arrows filled the sky from behind the ruins of Fort Maomnosett. They blotted out nearly all the light the sky had earned with the rising of the sun. Grongs fell, trogmortem stumbled, and giants raged on. Kantiim's men stopped abruptly roughly one hundred feet in front of the invading force and set their shields. Another volley of arrows filled the sky.

Then a voice louder than ten men shouted from the mass of attacking monsters that had paused ever so briefly to collect themselves after being pummeled by arrows, "Attack!"

The moment the words had left his mouth, Ott raced toward the line of men. Spears flew at him. Some glanced off, fewer stuck, but none slowed him down. When he crashed into the front line of Havenstahl's force, five men fell back into the row behind them. Blades flew at the furious giant. Blood splattered from his arms and his legs. It didn't stop him from swinging those mighty arms and kicking those stout legs. Men flew through the air. Men were crushed. Men were trampled under his feet. Finally, the rest of his force caught up with him and the battle began in earnest.

The moment the two lines collided, a horn blew from somewhere in the trees on the northern edge of the clearing. Immediately after that horn blast, an answer blared from the trees at the southern edge of the clearing. Moments later, bodies poured out of both tree lines. Men and dwarves charged at the flanks of the invading force and smashed into both sides of it. Dwarf axes chopped down grongs and hacked through the legs of trogmortem, while the spears of men dropped beasts where they stood. Hountmytall Dik, of the first generation of giants, second in age only to Ott in the campaign, turned his attention to the force attacking from the north. Thousands of dwarves and men all mingled into one group pushed against the flank of his column. Dik forced his way past grongs and trogmortem, working toward the northern flank.

Bindaar roared, "Thar blow the beast we be wanting for our wall lads! Follow me now, and cut the bastard down!"

One hundred dwarves hacked their way through columns of monsters, fighting to reach the giant. In moments, mighty dwarf axes were chopping at Dik's legs as if they were the trunks of great trees. Every time his mighty swat sent one sailing back into the trees or east toward the crumbled fort, another stepped in to take his place. Meanwhile, a group of dwarves had managed to work their way behind the mighty giant. Eight of them climbed up his back as if their prize were the peak of a mighty mountain, Mount Hountmytall. The glory didn't lie in placing their flag on a great summit, however. Their glory lay in hacking away at the stone-fleshed monster, finding the soft spots to bury their daggers, searching for the veins and arteries that would spill the life's blood out of the beast.

Dik's sons, Mon and Mob, his eldest and youngest, each witnessed their father fall. The battlefield filled with the sound of their rage. Each face of each dwarf—hammering with their axes and stabbing with their daggers, climbing all over their mighty father, picking away at him until blood loss rendered him too weak to stand and far too weak to fight—was etched into their minds. Half of the dwarves responded to the cries with smiles for the wailing giants and more vigorous hacking and slashing for the falling mountain, Hountmytall Dik. The other half leapt off the dying giant to follow Bindaar as he charged toward the two sons with a mind to hack two more limbs off of the Hountmytall family tree.

Grongs got in the way of the dwarf general's rage. He hacked at them with the fury of a dwarf who well knew the weight of the shackles accompanying the rule of giants. Maomnosett Ahm had ordered him strung up on the Sacred Pine when that giant's fat ass sat on the throne of Alhouim—Maomnosett at the time. Never again would Bindaar submit to a rule as cruel as that. He would swing his axe and his fists. He would smash with his forehead and kick with his legs. He would fight them until they were all dead or fled or until all the life had left his body. Bindaar was a dwarf who had tasted sweet freedom and would never relinquish the delicious morsel from his mouth again. The waste he was when Doentaat hounded him daily to get off to the mines and do his work—when he would instead skip off to the mountainside to smoke fairy weed and admire magnificent, fluffy clouds playing out a drama at this moment and a comedy the next—had long fled in favor of a furious general. When Doentaat had taken the throne and named his old friend and housemate a leader in the newly freed army of Alhouim, the shifty rascal in Bindaar was snuffed out by a noble dwarf with a mind for protecting the dwarves he served. That was the dwarf hacking at the legs of Mon, eldest son of the fallen Hountmytall Dik. The blood of the giant saturated his beard and stained the grass of the field while Bindaar hacked and slashed and dodged and rolled, chopping the beast down as if he were felling a mighty oak.

Another giant fell and then another. The first and second generations of the house Hountmytall had all perished. The axes of dwarves and the swords of men proved mighty enough to cut them from the sweet face of Ouloos. Men fell. Dwarves fell. Many souls of both Havenstahl and Alhouim were called home to the Lake. But giants fell too, and their numbers were few. Within an hour of the first drop of blood staining a blade of grass, the terrible monsters from across the Great Sea gave ground, forced back by the shields and swords of men and the mighty axes of dwarves. Small groups of grongs even broke rank and fled back toward the sea, back toward the trail leading to Biggon's Bay. Those cowards found their retreat to be painfully short, as the horsemen of Havenstahl circled them round and cut them down. The battle raged on.

A battered, old general watched in awe as his men and the dwarves of Alhouim stood tall against monsters, nightmares from across the Great Sea. The essence of a smile graced the lips of the old warrior, almost ready to feel the slightest hint of confidence. As Daritus watched his armies and those of Alhouim push the terrible beasts back toward the sea from which they came, pride filled his chest. 'I am a man,' he thought, 'and I killed a giant.' All of the warriors battling those beasts back on the blood-soaked battlefield knew of the deed, and every soul with a sword or an axe wanted to match it. For the first time during the campaign, he actually felt Havenstahl might prevail.

As the sun reached the apex of the arc it burned across the sky, the battered, old general's confidence faltered. A great scream, one thousand times more terrible than the cry of a horny witch, ripped across the sky. Daritus held his ears as a grimace found its way onto his face. Even with his hands pressed firmly over them, the horrifying sound caused pain. That high pitched scream was only one aspect of the sound, merely a piece of it. Beneath that lay a growl as deep as the Great Sea and as terrible as the eyes of a god. The sound was like death and pain and sorrow and sadness and hopelessness all rolled into one petrifying emotion. Daritus turned to see what manner of creature boasted vocal chords so mighty as to produce a sound like the noise punishing his ear drums.

A gasp forced its way past his lips a moment before he shouted, "To the castle!" without turning his head.

Time slowed around him as he witnessed the horror. The eagle had returned. The dead god Maelich and Cialia scattered to the wind had somehow found a way to pull himself together. Giants were terrifying, but a god was something worse. The gods had power no man nor dwarf nor giant nor any other creature gracing the sweet face of Ouloos could hope to understand. Beholding a god was like stepping into a pit of murk that pins your limbs and fills all of your orifices, choking away your breath. Daritus could not bring himself to move as the mighty eagle cried again. His hair blew back behind him as the mighty flap of the eagle's wings beat the air toward him.

Kallum, the great eagle, hovered above the castle at Havenstahl, waiting. Once the rest of the eyes on the battlefield had turned to behold him in all of his brilliance, he swooped down on the castle, tore into the great stone of the tallest tower, and ripped it from its foundation. Tons of rock broke upon the village and small settlements that dotted the hill leading down into the valley. The screams of those not crushed under the weight of ancient stone filled the sky, reaching all the way back to a battlefield that had paused in its bloodshed to witness the return of a god.

The great eagle swooped again and again at the mighty symbol of the strength and resolve of men, the castle crowning Mount Elzkahon, the castle of Havenstahl. The walls crumbled and the rocks flew. The terrible eagle tore rock from rock, flinging heaps of it at the surrounding countryside. In moments, all of the towers of that mighty castle, that testament to the ingenuity of men, were toppled and tossed about the grass and trees. All along the sloping hill leading south away from the castle gates, mighty, carved boulders once serving as the walls of a great castle littered the ground. Havenstahl was falling, a victim of the wrath of the vanquished god.

Every man, dwarf, giant, grong, and trogmortem on the bloody battlefield in front of Fort Maomnosett halted. Dumbstruck, as they watched the greatest city of men expire, ripped apart by the fierce talons of that vengeful horror. Kallum was not dead. He was not scattered. Wherever he had been was a prison too feeble to hold him. His rage poured onto the city that spawned the man who challenged his rule. Let there be no question. Kallum is the king of gods.

"To the castle!" Daritus shouted again, his voice finally returning. "Our people will be crushed under the weight of that stone."

Men and dwarves began walking at first. Then slowly—as the awe that watching a god in all his fury inspired gave way to something more akin to rage than reverence—they all began to run. Few steps had been taken by any counting themselves as defenders of Havenstahl when another primal and horrible sound filled the clearing. This was not the screech of mighty bird, but the roar of a monstrous beast. Brerto, the mighty tiger leapt from behind the trees at the western edge of the clearing, sailing over the giants, trogmortem, and grongs that marched in his name. By the time his mighty paw felt ground beneath it, he was standing atop the ruins of Fort Maomnosett and the bodies of men and dwarves crushed beneath his might. Claws and fangs flashed in the sun as he swiped and chomped, slashing and biting. Neither man nor dwarf stopped to challenge the great beast, save one.

Men and dwarves scattered, all fleeing in the direction of Havenstahl. It would be hard for any on the battlefield that day to say for certain whether it were fear or duty leading them in the direction of Havenstahl. Perhaps it was a mixture of both. The monsters from across the Great Sea wasted no time in giving chase. Their god fought beside them, cutting down their foes. The claws of rampaging trogmortem tore into the flesh of fleeing men as the spears of grongs ripped through meat, organs, and bone. The handful of giants still living trampled, crushed, and tossed as they leapt through the mass of fleeing heroes. Havenstahl's soldiers bled and died as her walls crumbled. The greatest city of men was dying.

One man stood alone. He was half lame and dazed as if drunk from ale, but he stood tall. Daritus ignored the pain ripping through his body from his neck down to his waist and drew his sword. It was like moving through a dream. The world slowed around him as he skirted the thick legs of giants and navigated a mob of grongs with his eyes remaining fixed on his prize. The blood of a god—the great tiger, the mighty Brerto—would stain his blade. It wasn't pride driving him toward that destiny and filling him with the idea he could kill a god. He didn't know what it was. Honor? Duty? Neither of those words quite described it. Whatever it was, it filled his heart and pushed him ever closer to that massive beast, that god in giant animal form.

Finally, Daritus stood before the great Brerto, the fierce, white tiger who rules the land with claws and fangs. The mighty god didn't notice him at first, occupied with slashing, tossing, and biting dwarves and men. The great general wasn't swayed. He raised his sword, the tip of the blade aimed at the god's heart—if the monster had one. He remained there, frozen for several moments as the melee continued around him, until at last the mighty, white tiger looked down at him.

Laughter, like oily metal on stone, poured from the god's mouth, "Well, well, and what do we have here? A hero stands before me, brave among the cowards who flee around him." Brerto's eyes narrowed, "I know you. You are the one they call Daritus. You have served the lion and the Dragon for your entire life. More importantly, you are the slayer of giants. One man, all alone, cut Bok down and sent him to the Lake. Mighty you must be."

Daritus raised his head defiantly to the god, "I am no mightier than any other man. I have a duty to those who follow me, a duty to stand tall no matter what horror stands before me. You threaten those men and dwarves who look to me as their leader, and I will not fail them."

"Of course," Brerto laughed again, "the hero always points to duty as if there were nothing else of import. You will play the martyr, wagering a life spent in the service of others. Yes indeed, you are the picture of what a hero should be."

Daritus managed only one step before the great tiger was gone, rolling into trees and crashing them down with Moshat, the mighty bear, snapping and swatting at him. The battered, old general had only a few moments to digest what had just happened before a dark shape raced out of the brawling mob, and carried him away. By the time the old general's wits returned, he was deep in the trees to the north of the ruins of Fort Maomnosett being set back down upon his feet.

Again he raised his sword and leveled it at the man who had carried him from the battle, "What on Ouloos are you doing?"

Spang looked up at his general, pushed the hood back from his face, and said, "All of the men and dwarves who fight today see you as something more than merely a man, even more than a mighty slayer of giants. You are practically a myth among them already, and your name will endure long after your life has expired. We cannot have you dying today, however. The spirit of our forces has been flying so high. Watching the walls of Havenstahl fall brought them low enough. Your death would go far in sucking the rest of the wind from their sails. I refuse to allow that. Please forgive me, but I mean to keep you alive."

Daritus scowled at the Red Dragon—leader of the Dragon's Flame—for several moments until the adrenaline finally began to fade from his blood. Once he had reached a more reasonable state of mind, he said, "Today you prove far wiser than I, old friend. Where are the rest your flames?"

"Dead," Spang replied somberly. "They are all dead. They fought bravely and all of them died well. They all died though. We count masses of grongs, hundreds of trogmortem, and two giants among our victims. Oyn, of the house Maomnosett, and Moh of the house Hountmytall, both fell to the Dragon's Flame."

"All of the flames have been extinguished?"

"All except me," Spang affirmed.

Daritus's eyes narrowed as he pushed further, "How did you manage to survive if all of your brethren proved less lucky?"

Spang shrugged, "Call me a coward if you will, but once all of my flame's had been extinguished and there was nothing more I could do for them, I fled. I have executed many missions, and I have fought many battles. Each of them has taught me a lesson whose sum is, I cannot win a war on my own. I believe you realize this, and I am uncertain why you would risk so much. I refuse to let you forget it though. You cannot win a war on your own, and you cannot kill a god."

"I know this," Daritus shook his head. The brief chuckle that fell from lips immediately following those words belied the tension wound around his spine. "I am uncertain what possessed me to challenge the tiger, but my plan definitely was to kill him. I am certain I would have failed."

"You would have," Spang reassured him. "The great bear battles with him as we speak, and I promise that even if he defeats the god, he will fail to kill him."

"Thank Coeptus Moshat has joined us on the battlefield," Daritus sighed. "Perhaps we can still win the day, or at least survive. What of Kaldumahn, I wonder?"

"Can you climb?"

"Perhaps, but only if the climb you suggest is an easy one."

"Come," Spang leapt up onto a tree with low branches in ample numbers. "You should be able to manage this one."

The going was slow for the old soldier, but eventually he earned a view of what was left of Havenstahl. Directly above those ruins, two gods battled each other in the sky. Kaldumahn, the great, silver lion, swatted at the mighty eagle, Kallum. That mighty paw missed its mark as Kallum flapped his broad wings, propelling himself even higher into the sky. The lion leapt up toward him, all jaws and fangs. Again his aim was off the mark. This time he earned the eagle's talons. Kallum shoved them deep into Kaldumahn's back, attaining a roar so robust only a god could muster it. The mighty eagle tossed the great, silver lion to heights no hawk could boast. The great lion's trajectory, as he careened through the air like a meteor plummeting toward the sweet face of Ouloos, sent him crashing deep into the trees of the Sobbing Forest. The great and fierce eagle soared high, spreading his majestic wings at the apex of his flight so all might revel in his glory.

"Mighty Kaldumahn has been tossed aside like a bag of dead bones," Daritus gasped. "Who can stand up against the might of a resurrected god?"

"Moshat fairs far better," Spang replied as he tapped Daritus's shoulder and motioned his head toward that morning's battlefield.

In the blood-soaked clearing, mighty Moshat, the fierce bear who lumbers the tree-lined hills of the north, blasted the white tiger, the great and terrible Brerto, across his jaw with a paw so mighty it could crumble mountains and crack Ouloos to its very core. The tiger fell to His side, rolling back to his feet only to be swatted again with equal force. The relentless bear stalked the failing god, offering no reprieve. Unrelenting, Moshat stood tall on his hind legs, measuring his opponent, and attacking with a speed that seemed impossible from his bulky form.

A brief and minute speck of hope glimmered dimly behind Daritus's eye. Mighty Moshat, the great bear, battered the author of this war—the great force filling giants, trogmortem, and grongs with fury and horrible purpose—pushing him back to the sands of the beach at Biggon's Bay. Perhaps there was cause for hope. But then, there was still a resurrected god, a god who appeared far mightier than any force existing in all of Ouloos. Even if Maelich were on the battlefield, would he prove strong enough to fell that primal power, and scatter the god into the atmosphere like dust again? Speculating on the outcome of a fantasy was fool's work when men and dwarves were dying all around the tree Daritus occupied with Spang, hiding from the fight. Maelich was not on the battlefield. The lad of the Lake was nowhere to be found. Who else could match that might?

"I should be with my men, fighting by their sides," Daritus groaned. "Instead I hide in the trees like a coward. Damn you, Spang. Damn you and your logic and sensibility."

"I accept your damnation. It pains me just as much as it does you to sit idle and watch while the men I have served with for years fight and die. However, this battle will end. This war will end. Men will still live. They will need a leader to gather them up and prepare them for the next war; the war that sees the fighting men of Havenstahl march on the ruins of their lost city and take it back from the vile monsters who have stolen it away," Spang's tone carried none of the bravado his words might have inspired. Instead, it remained rather even and flat.

"Havenstahl is lost, is it not?" the words caused the battered, old general more pain than any of his physical wounds ever could. His plan had failed. The walls of his great, adopted city came crumbling down while the men and dwarves who had placed their hope in the might of his sword and the cunning of his mind died beneath the feet of giants, the claws and fangs of trogmortem, and the dirty spears of lowly grongs. He had failed, allowing the hope that had flashed behind the eyes of those faithful to fade with the grandeur of their fair city.

"All is not lost," Spang replied, his tone remaining even and flat. "They haven't moved our fair city and hidden it from our eyes. It is where it has always been. They have crushed our castle and knocked down our walls, but the city remains atop the mountain. More importantly, it remains in the hearts of the men who believe. Those men will fight to regain it, and you will lead them. There will be nowhere for our enemy to hide. This battle is lost. This war is lost. But our fight has only just begun."

Daritus remained silent, mulling over Spang's counsel. Could he ever lead these men again after failing them so miserably? Kallum was a surprise, but hadn't the dead-eyed men returned to announce the fallen god's rebirth? Surprises cannot happen. A great general accounts for every possibility and weaves it into his plan as if he were creating a great tapestry. If the correct threads are not used, the glory of the piece will be lost. Too many colors were missing from the threads he had used to weave the work that would be the war of Havenstahl. Perhaps the slayer of giants was more warrior than general after all. Perhaps the men who looked to him to guide their steps on the battlefield should avert their eyes and find someone worthy of their faith and admiration. As the beaten general swam through the muck of self-doubt, he glanced back up at the mighty eagle, soaring above the broken shell of the greatest city of men and her crumbling ramparts.

CHAPTER 43
THE DRAGON QUEEN

The sun had reached its highest point before Cialia appeared in the doorway of her mother's room. She found Leisha talking with Perrin in a small sitting area just off the main bed chamber. The two women seemed far less than content talking and fretting over cups of tea.

"I have slept far longer than I intended," Cialia said as she slowly entered the room.

"Many dark thoughts and doubts weigh heavy on your mind," Leisha shrugged. "Rest is always helpful in sorting out opposing ideas. You remain full of doubt."

"I am," Cialia frowned. "On one hand, I feel the vile men I sent to the Lake earned my wrath with the darkness in their hearts and their failure to righteously serve the people they swore to protect," she paused as she pulled the vine crown from her head and turned it around in her hands, examining it.

Leisha's eyes narrowed, as she looked over her tea at Cialia, and said, "Go on. What other ideas battle with your feelings of justification?"

The fretting queen scratched her head with her right hand as she continued to examine the crown she had made with the power of her will. Finally, she held the crown up toward Leisha and said, "I made this," the words tumbling out of her lips amid awkward laughs. "I called these vines to me and ordered them to wrap themselves around my head."

"And?" Leisha asked as she sipped her tea.

Cialia's eyes closed tight as the crown in her left hand began to crumble under the weight of her grip. When her eyes opened and looked back into Leisha's, she said, "I created fire. I pulled it out of the sky and burned men with it. My mind invaded their thoughts. Then I judged, sentenced, and executed them. None were safe from my scrutiny or my power."

The former queen stared at her daughter silently for a few moments. Her expression softened slightly as she finally said, "So you do feel remorse, if only slightly. You should feel that. You sentenced thousands of men, who had committed no crime, to die by fire because they harbored wicked thoughts. If not downright evil, it is at least a gross misuse of your great power."

Cialia's expression hardened as she reflected on her mother's words, "I am this monster you describe, and I am finding it terribly difficult to justify my actions even to myself. When Coeptus gave me this great power, it changed me in many ways. They showed me things you could not possibly understand. No one who hasn't seen them could. That changed me. However, one thing about me that has remained consistent is my idea of justice and how it is administered. This is not something new. Nor is it something I came up with on my own. I have been given a gift of great power by the authors of our world, but my sense of justice was planted and cultivated by you. It grew under your guidance. You are no warrior, but that does not mean you do not wield great power. Your lips whisper into the ears of the greatest general this world has ever known, greater than Ymitoth or any of the mighty leaders of Havenstahl who have come before him, and you have never hesitated to unleash the great power you wield. Just because you do not thrust the blade into the breast or fire the arrow that pierces the flesh, do not think you are not the killer. You have trained me to be this monster you see. If you look at yourself, and I mean really look at yourself, I believe you will see the resemblance. Think of that as you sit there in judgment of me."

Leisha's eyes widened as she stammered, "How dare you attempt to lay the souls of the men you slaughtered at my feet? I spent the better part of my life defending this world from evil, defending the last Dragon from the monsters who would cut her down and end our world. How can you compare that with the torture you committed? Their only crimes were impure thoughts. Thinking about evil acts is not the same as committing them. Where does this twisted logic come from?" She paused and added, "Wait. Don't tell me. I am also to blame for that."

Perrin shifted, thought of interjecting her opinion into the debate, and opted to remain silent. Though she felt a kinship with both women, being married to the son of one and the brother of the other, this family debate seemed something she should sit out. On top of that, her own demons had dragged her mind to a place that left her nearly bereft of emotion. Questions of the meaning of life seemed infinitely bigger than questions of justice, duty, and loyalty. What did any of it matter in the grand scheme of things?

Cialia stared at her mother for several moments in silence. Her blue eyes that had always appeared so innocent and full of wonder carried coldness, like something had ripped open the shades and allowed the heartless reality of life to flow into them. She finally broke the silence and said quietly, "This is not blame, mother. It may be an attempt to justify my actions, not only to you but also to myself, but my words are true. How many men were slain at the hands of the riders of Druindahl while they rode under your command?" She paused for a few moments, eyeing her mother intently, and then continued, "I don't expect you to know the number. The number you should have no trouble recollecting is the number of Dragons who have been slaughtered during your lifetime. That number is zero. All of the dragons hunted down and killed by men were murdered generations before you were even born."

"And the point of all of your words, dear daughter?" Leisha's head shook slowly as the tension left her face.

"The point is none of the men you sentenced to death at the hands of my father, his men, or I ever committed the crime which earned them their deaths. None of those men ever killed a Dragon. They were killed in defense of the last Dragon and therefore, killed because of their desire to destroy her. They were killed because they wished to commit evil against Ouloos just as the men I ended in the forest were, and they were all killed at your command."

Leisha remained silent as her gaze drifted toward the floor.

Finally, Perrin decided she had remained silent for long enough. She looked to Cialia and said, "It ain't no easy answer what ye two be trying to get to. Meanwhile, them warriors of Havenstahl be fighting for the lives of me people, and though I be having just as much faith in your father as ye do, I be having terrible fears of what may happen if they falter. Only half of them people they be defending followed us here to Druindahl. I be carrying a mighty fear for what them monsters might be doing to them people what didn't."

Leisha rubbed her eyes, sighed, looked back up at Cialia, and said, "The young queen has a point, and her fears are very valid. You and I have many things to discuss, but they are far less important at this moment than the lives of the innocent people of Havenstahl whose only crimes are trusting in the strength of the army that protects them. You have the power to end the battle with a whisper of your voice."

"My flame," Cialia nodded as she sat in a chair opposite Leisha and Perrin. "Though I do not share either of your fears—I have complete faith in my father to turn back any assault on the city of Havenstahl—I will grant you the peace you seek. Once my assumptions have been validated, we can discuss the irony of asking me to use my power after damning me for the same."

Cialia—new queen of Druindahl, child of the Lake of Dragons, master of Dragon's Fire, time, space, and all of the elements, and protector of Ouloos—closed her eyes. Leisha and Perrin watched, seeing only what appeared to be a sleeping queen. Cialia saw much more. In an instant she was on the battlefield that poured into the valley at the base of Mount Elzkahon and up the hill toward the castle. Huts burned as villagers screamed and fled. Many fell as vicious grongs leapt upon their backs, scratching and biting, or felled them with spears. Soldiers and solidas gave ground up the hill. Their ranks were discombobulated as some faced the attack while others charged toward the castle. As her gaze followed the men and dwarves charging up the hill toward the gates of Havenstahl, it finally came to rest on the fallen castle and the busted ramparts of the city. The horror of the image paled when she beheld the terror soaring above it. The eagle, Kallum, the scattered god yet lived.

Back in the throne room at Druindahl, Cialia's eyes snapped open. "I am sorry I doubted you, mother," was the only explanation she gave before her body vanished from her chair.

Cialia materialized in the valley at the base of the hill. Laenkishot Kik of the third generation of giants, son of Kil, and grandson of Kon stood immediately before her. A broad smile spread across his terrible face as he raised his right fist high above his head. Though she fought against the fire, images of innocents impaled on spears and gnawed on by scaly beasts filled her head and beat down her resolve. Flames immediately danced up her arms and then around her entire body. Kik's fist barely made three inches toward the queen of Druindahl's head before he burst into ash and his conceited smile was vaporized.

Cialia's focus moved to the Eagle. Her eyes blazed fiery red as the flames swirled a great circle around her. A mighty roar from far behind her slightly tugged her attention. It wasn't enough to turn her gaze from the eagle, but it was enough to stay her flame momentarily. In that moment of hesitation, the great, silver lion soared above her head, paws digging into air as if the god were galloping across the sky. In a moment, Kaldumahn and Kallum were locked in battle above the ruins of Havenstahl. Kaldumahn, the great, silver lion who stalks the skies fought with the ferocity of a mother scarra defending her cubs. However, Kallum, the great eagle proved to be master of the air. He beat Kaldumahn with his wings, sliced him with his talons, and ripped off hunks of his perfect flesh with his mighty beak. The two gods appeared a blur to all but Cialia who witnessed the full ferocity of the assault. Eventually, the battered lion was tossed back to the Sobbing Forest.

Cialia's eyes narrowed to slits as her gaze fell back to a battlefield littered with the bodies of far too many innocent victims. When a man picks up a sword and swears an oath to defend a city or sets his intention toward adventure, he accepts the risk of death accompanying either occupation.

When a god takes physical form and openly wages war against another god, he accepts the risk of being scattered on the wind. When a dwarf picks up the mighty dwarf axe and proves himself worthy of the title solida, he too accepts the risks of that post. The corpses of unarmed victims scattered among those of fighting men, dwarves, grongs, trogmortem, and even giants were more than Cialia could stand. They had chosen a life of peace; farmers, herders, smiths of all kind chose to serve in ways that left them unable defend themselves. Their choices set them at the mercy of the honor of warriors. The monsters attacking Havenstahl showed no honor, cutting down all before them. Whether those innocent souls were hiding, fleeing, or making a stand to defend those they loved, their enemy made no distinction between trained soldiers and innocent victims.

The blood-soaked hill covered in corpses and pieces of corpses, faces frozen in expressions of pain, fear, and hopelessness, pushed Cialia beyond the fragile edge of control. The fire swirling around her form paled in heat to the fire burning in her belly. That rage filling her, consuming her, aching to lash out and destroy, pushed against her will, beating it back and crushing it down. Tears that would have flowed freely over the softness of her cheeks evaporated before they had a chance to drip from her eyes. She fought to hold back the rage, almost succeeding completely. However, the fury burning through her was strong and relentless. She managed to hold it back from burning through every evil her mind touched, but it succeeded in slipping through at each monster that fell under her gaze. The tough skin of giants sizzled before erupting and casting chunks of burning flesh all about them. Trogmortem hides did the same. Grongs exploded where they stood.

It didn't take long for the ferocious nightmares from across the Great Sea to realize what great power had joined them on the battlefield. It took even less time for them to learn to fear it. In moments, giants, trogmortem, and grongs—the fury and ill intent stolen from their eyes by mind-numbing fear—raced away from the castle at Havenstahl. Furious monsters fled in every direction desperately seeking a safe place to hide from the fury of Cialia's fire.

Once the monsters had been burned or fled the battlefield, Cialia cast her gaze back toward Kallum, the mighty eagle, lord of the sky. Her rage swelled again, lashing out in a ball of flame the size of a hut. Kallum showed his true nature to all remaining in the field by retreating back to the east. Racing on mighty wings, he made his escape, fleeing the heat of Cialia's rage.

After a long, quiet moment of confusion, a voice rang out from the hillside, "The great Cialia has returned! She has found her flame!"

A cheer erupted from all of the souls still drawing breath on the battlefield. Soldiers, solidas, and the innocent villagers they fought for all sung boisterous praises to the glory of her name. They damned the names of the monsters that had brought them war from across the Great Sea. They stomped and crushed the charred remains of their enemies. With one voice, they shouted to the sky. None could challenge the might of Havenstahl; the greatest power on Ouloos defended her.

A breathless Cialia collapsed where she stood. As her skin cooled, tears finally began to fall down her face. What had she done? Her clammy skin had only moments to feel the grass before she slipped back to her throne in Druindahl. The gratitude and songs of praise flowing from those surrounding her and those scattered all the way to the gates of the city almost stung. Relief danced among those praises, but it wasn't alone. A vengeful joy fraternized with it. It felt dark and bold and—worst of all—unfinished. Thoughts of retaliation and eradication filled too many of the minds on the battlefield. What had she done? What did they expect from her now?

When Cialia opened her teary eyes back up, she was back in the chair in Leisha's sitting room, looking to her mother and sister-in-law. The benevolent expression that had taken up residence on her face since she had first found her flame in the Forgotten Forest had fled. In its place was a conglomeration of fear, confusion, and sadness. "I have done terrible things, mother," she wept. As the words left her mouth, she counted each of the lives her rage had ended. One by one, each face, each story, and each history sailed through her awareness. They were living, breathing, cognizant beings, and she utterly destroyed them on a whim. The justification she had been clinging to so tightly scurried away as the realization her vengeance reduced her to something equivalent to those she found so vile settled into her consciousness.

"Yes," Leisha agreed quietly, "you have done terrible things. We all have for our own reasons." As the words softly left her lips, she went to her daughter—the great and mighty power—and held her to her breast like a weeping babe. They remained like that, weeping together in silence for several moments. They may have remained for eternity if Perrin had not interrupted the sadness.

"What did ye see? What of me kingdom and me people?" Perrin implored.

Cialia pulled away from Leisha's embrace and turned her eyes toward the young queen who seemed so much older than she remembered, "Your men fought bravely, but their enemy was unrelenting and furious. And there were gods on the battlefield with them." She trailed off as her gaze moved to the floor.

"And?" Perrin shook her hands as she crouched toward the floor. "What happened?"

"Many of your men died trying to protect your castle and the villagers who remained. Many of those people died too," Cialia brought her gaze back up to meet Perrin's. "Your castle has been destroyed, and Kallum yet lives."

Tears filled Perrin's eyes before cascading down her cheeks. How much loss could one soul endure? First her husband had left her, chasing death rather than focusing on the new life he had created. The sting of that was still strong. His relationship with Ymitoth had been so important to him deep, emotional scars wouldn't be a surprise. In fact, they would be expected. However, why seek solace in a corpse when the celebration of new life was so close at hand? Then, as if losing her love to a carcass wasn't enough, her parents died trying to protect her and her new son. Though she shared no blood with them, they raised her with love as their own. Were it not for them, she would be swimming in the Lake in their stead. Before she even had a chance to digest—much less grieve—their loss, Geillan was taken from her. She had such precious little time with him before those monsters came to claim him for the god, that bastard. Finally, many of her people were dead, and Cialia's grim mood suggested their numbers were great. Taken together, it was more than the young queen could bear.

Perrin slipped from her chair and fell to her knees. All of the events since the return of the dead-eyed men, since Ymitoth's death, happened so fast she hadn't proper time to process them. As the tears rained down her cheeks, all of it flooded into her mind at once. "Where be all the peace promised by the death of that wicked god?" she wept. "If only me eyes would have never fell on that perfect face and me heart didn't be fluttering so whenever me Maelich been around. If only he ain't never found me in that hut, I might have died there and never been feeling any of this."

Both Leisha and Cialia rushed over to her, knelt beside her on the floor, and began rubbing her back. "We have all suffered great loss, Perrin," Leisha whispered.

Perrin pushed them away and stood wrangling the sadness and stuffing it deep down into her belly where it could boil into rage. The tears ceased as fury washed over her face. "No!" she shouted. "Ye with your causes and your missions and your terrible purpose, I don't be caring about none of it. Both of ye pushed me husband to fight that god. All I ever be wanting was to hold him and love him and give him children for us to be raising and teaching and loving. Ye two witches pushed him into fighting Kallum. If he didn't always be feeling like he had to be saving everybody, maybe we'd have been having a peaceful life."

"Perrin, please," Cialia implored, reaching her hand out toward the frantic woman.

Perrin batted the hand away. "No!" she shouted again. "I be going back to me castle. I'll be leading me people to rebuild their homes. Ye two witches can be staying here and plotting and scheming. I'll be finding me husband and me son on me own. And when I be bringing them both back home, I'll be keeping them for me self."

Leisha looked toward the ground, took a deep breath, and said, "Love, I understand your pain, and I feel your loss. Your husband is still my son, and your son my grandson. I love them just as much as you do. We are all feeling loss right now. I think if you search your heart though, you will realize the things you love about Maelich are the very things that make him do what he does. He is a hero. He stands up for those who cannot stand up for themselves. He is larger than life."

Perrin absently wiped at her cheek and continued to stare into Leisha's eyes.

"I do not know why he left us," Leisha continued. "I have my suspicions, but all of them are loose conjecture based on what I know of my son. Fleeing with a corpse is definitely something I would not have expected from him."

"I do be loving him," Perrin's tone had lost all of its fury and shrunk into something that sounded like complete defeat. "It hurts me that he be leaving me on me own. I be aching for his pain too, but I ain't got much more heart to be giving. What of me son, me beautiful babe so new to this world? What could be happening to him right now, me perfect Geillan? Me husband be having to battle his own demons, and I be hoping someday he be coming back to me. I can't be waiting for that though. Life be trudging on with or without him in it."

Leisha put an arm on each of their shoulders and pulled both women toward her, "I think we have had enough for one day. Let us rest now. Tomorrow, we can look at this with clear eyes. Kallum yet lives. He has shown himself. I have no doubt it is he who holds your precious Geillan hostage. There can also be no doubt the Dragons will soon need the warriors of Druindahl to defend them. Perrin, I feel it would be wise to call our people and our warriors here, especially in Maelich's absence. The forest will provide us security to regroup and prepare for the coming storm."

Perrin simply nodded. She had more words, more arguments aching for a voice, but the voice that would carry them into the world had neither the energy nor the desire to propel them into reality. In fact, not one of the queens huddled together in that circle found any desire to share any further words. All three of them bore heavy thoughts requiring processing. Too many emotions flooded their minds for any of them to view anything logically until there was time to sort through it all. Each of them retired to her respective room to rest and reflect on everything that had happened and everything that was to come.

CHAPTER 44
THE TIGER AND THE BEAR

No life remained in the vast, scarred clearing that used to be a forest filling the space between the great field west of Fort Maomnosett and the beach at Biggon's Bay. Many corpses of men, grongs, and trogmortem littered the ground, but no souls haunted the place. The beasts from across the Great Sea would never allow the men of Havenstahl to collect their dead and—aside from the giants—most of those monsters didn't care enough for ceremony to bury or burn their dead during times of war. A handful of trogmortem clans would mimic the ceremonies of the giants. However, more of them left the carcasses to feed the circle of life. Traditional trogmortem beliefs were far deeper and more complicated than their monstrous appearance would suggest.

In that field—a wasteland of broken carcasses—two gods battled with all the fury of Ouloos. Moshat, the mighty bear, pushed the great, white tiger back almost as far as the short cliffs bordering the beach at Biggon's Bay. Swatting with his powerful arms and snapping with his massive jaws, the god of the mountains slowly gained ground. Brerto was not one to submit easily though. He fought back against the mighty bear, slashing and tearing with his claws while snapping and biting with his equally massive jaws. The two smashed and hammered each other, ripping flesh and spilling the blood of gods all across the scarred field. They remained locked in combat, viciously attacking one another until the last lights of day threatened to expire.

Finally, with the waves of Biggon's Bay crashing against his back paws, Brerto hollered in a voice both beautiful and terrifying, "Enough!"

Moshat, the great and mighty bear, paused in his assault. "What is this?" he asked. "Is the mighty and terrible Brerto submitting beneath my

259

strength?"

"See it as you will. Your views mean very little to me, brother," Brerto scoffed as he gave up the form of the mighty tiger in favor of the old wizard of Alharin. "Our reason to claw and tear at each other has been eliminated. Cialia has scattered my army and Kallum has fled before her might…coward."

"The princess of the Lake has found her flame," Moshat smiled as he followed his brother's lead and abandoned his animal form. "It appears you have failed."

"Cialia finding her flame was definitely not part of my plan, but do not fool yourself into believing you have won anything. That flaming wench has burned some of my armies and scattered the rest, but those remaining will regroup. Havenstahl has fallen. Alhouim will follow. Both will be mine."

"After all your boasts about how cunning you were to dupe us into this battle, your true colors show," Moshat's eyes narrowed. "Kallum gets the fiery heir, and you get the greatest city of men."

"Havenstahl?" Brerto chuckled, "It is a wasted ruin. More importantly, it is only the beginning. All of Ouloos will burn. Men, dwarves, Dragons, even you and our pathetic brother, you all will burn. Maelich's son will unleash a fury like nothing this world has ever seen. Once it has been completely destroyed, I will rebuild it and rule it all."

Moshat leaned his head back and laughed, "You will not even have Havenstahl. I will fill your eyes with my glory at every turn; the armies of men and dwarves will fight with every scrap of determination in their hearts; and do not forget about our mighty brother, Kaldumahn." He shook his head as his lips twisted from a wide smile to a contempt-filled sneer, "Besides, even if you proved mighty enough to make good on your boasts, this world would belong to Kallum. You have only ever been his faithful pet; a scrod sniffing about his feet sustaining yourself on the scraps that fall from his table."

"Your bravado amuses," Brerto beamed. "Say what you will. We both know you and our brother Kaldumahn will burn as you fruitlessly defend a lost cause." His smile faltered the slightest bit as he added, "And I am equal with Kallum. I will rule beside my brother, not beneath him.

Moshat remained silent while a scowl cut deep lines into his face. The debate had become useless. On top of that, it was becoming more and more difficult to believe the bold words trumpeting from his mouth with all the bravado Brerto had suggested. As much as he hated admitting it to himself, Brerto was probably correct. Geillan was a power like nothing Ouloos had ever seen. In Kallum's hands the boy would become a destroyer. Of course, he and Kaldumahn would search and attempt to find the fiery heir; try to stop Kallum's scheme before it had a chance to mature. The odds of finding the child were so slim it was challenging to harbor any real belief in the idea.

In an instant, Kaldumahn stood before them both, "I have failed. Havenstahl has fallen, and many of her souls have returned to the Lake."

Before Kaldumahn could address him, Brerto said flatly, "The odds no longer favor me. Farewell, my brothers. Feel free to contemplate your demise until I return in glory to destroy you both." He vanished as quickly as Kaldumahn had arrived.

"Coward," Moshat spat. Then he turned his attention to Kaldumahn. "What of Kallum? How did you fair?" he asked.

"That was not Kallum," Kaldumahn replied somberly. "During the battle, I believed it to be. However, as I tended my wounds in the Sobbing Forest, I realized the being I fought in the skies over Havenstahl was not quite him."

"Perhaps he has changed," Moshat shrugged. "The twins did scatter him to the wind."

Kaldumahn shook his head, "No, this being was something else."

Moshat's eyes widened again, "Has Ijilv found a way to mimic our fallen brother and show his true nature?"

"Perhaps," Kaldumahn stroked his beard. "Ijilv has been such a mystery—remaining withdrawn as he is wont to do—it is difficult to say if it was truly him. I remain uncertain."

"If not Kallum and not Ijilv, then whom did you face?"

"I do not know. He was more powerful than any of us though, even more powerful than Kallum had been."

Moshat pondered the idea for a moment, "Brerto spoke of Kallum and his priests. Surely if they are in league together, Brerto must know with whom he is dealing. He is damnable and evil, but he is perhaps the wisest among us."

"Perhaps," Kaldumahn agreed, "he may be the wisest among us. That does not make him infallible though. His ego gets in his way often enough. He may believe the eagle I faced over Havenstahl is, in fact, Kallum. However, I do not."

"Whoever it was who took the form of the eagle and bested you over Havenstahl, one thing is certain."

"What is that, Moshat?"

"Though it seems impossible, we must find and destroy him," he paused and gazed out over the bay. "And retrieve Maelich's stolen son."

CHAPTER 45
ACROSS THE SEA OF SADNESS

Maelich leaned up against a barrel, rocking back and forth as high waves tossed Melancholy Mistress—the ship he and Ymitoth had procured to ferry them across the Sea of Sadness—enough to earn a bit of grumbling from his belly. The crew buzzed; sailors ran back and forth doing this and that, making the final preparations to drop anchor in the Bay of Danggytrint. Maelich paid them little attention. It took all of his focus to keep the meager contents of his belly from spilling out onto the deck. The three-day sail represented his first time at sea—or even on a boat at all for that matter.

"Ye be looking a bit green, lad," Ymitoth strolled up sporting a devious grin. "The sea she don't be counting ye as friend."

The simple act of shaking his head made the world dip this way and then that. "No, no she doesn't indeed," he replied softly.

Ymitoth chuckled, "Just try to be keeping it together a wee bit longer. The captain be giving us a small boat what will carry us to the shore. I'll be doing the rowing so ye can be focusing on the pier and keeping all what's in your belly down. We'll be looking for a fellow with the name, Kinner. He'll be taking that boat from us and supplying us with some horses for the rest of our journey."

Maelich drew in slow, deep breaths, filling up his cheeks as he released the air through a thin slit in his lips, "Horses will be good, far better than these waves at least."

"Aye," Ymitoth agreed as he strolled away chuckling.

The rest of the journey into shore took the better part of two hours, all of it a blur for Maelich. Luckily, Ymitoth handled everything. He dealt with the ship captain, rowed the boat, and finagled with Kinner over the horses.

By the time Maelich slipped free from the grasp of the Sea of Sadness, Ymitoth had managed all remaining necessities for the final leg of their trek. He had two solid-looking horses in tow as he strolled up to the bench where Maelich slumped.

"Ye be looking a bit fresher than the green muck I spoke with on that ship," Ymitoth said as he tied the horses off. "Are ye looking to take some food before we get back to that trail, or would ye rather be hitting it hard straight away?"

Maelich shook his head, "I am feeling much better, but I couldn't eat a thing right now. If you can manage without food, I would just as soon get a head start on tomorrow's journey."

"Aye," Ymitoth nodded. "The trail she be a calling me too. That sun will be giving us half a day more. Let's be taking what he be giving." An odd smirk slipped onto his face as he scratched his head and added, "There be just one more thing what's been bugging me since the second night out on the Sea of Sadness."

"What is that?" Maelich asked as he slowly rose to his feet.

"Ye'd been tossing and turning. Of course I figured that been on account of how the waves affected ye so. But ye were mumbling all sorts of oddness, like blue men and caves," he paused a few moments before adding, "and that white horse again."

"Oh yes," Maelich nodded and looked toward the ground. "I forgot to mention my latest visit from the white horse. That sea sickness kept all of my focus. Indeed, the white horse came to see me again. He spoke a little more plainly to me this time, and I didn't have the sensation of falling off of a cliff or drowning. I did wind up alone in pitch black just before waking. It wasn't nearly as bad as the other two meetings. In any event, he told me we should follow the southern road out of Danggytrint. It will veer slightly east after a day or so when we'll reach a river. We should follow it another two days into a low mountain range where the blue people will find us."

"The blue people?"

"That is what the white horse said. The blue people are our destination."

Ymitoth shrugged.

The trail was easy, dry, but easy. Mostly cracked earth and sand surrounded them. Occasional patches of hearty, green plants dotting the landscape were almost too infrequent to mention. Luckily, Kinner had schooled Ymitoth on the dangers of running out of water in the "cracked land" as he called it. Between them and their horses, they drained all of their water skins on the first day of scorching heat with the sun beating down on them and no shade for protection. Once they made the river, it provided everything they needed aside from bits of food the occupants of four small villages gave them along the way. The common tongue wasn't common in any of those settlements, but the inhabitants were friendly enough, not to mention eager to share with sun-weary travelers.

They lingered a bit long in one village where the people were particularly generous. That set them back a bit, as did their full bellies and full horse sacks. Additionally, the sun proved exceptionally rough on Mountain. Since the big scrod was setting the pace, it was a slow one. By the end of the third day, they could see the mountains the white horse had described to Maelich during their last meeting. However, those rocky peaks scratched at the sky a great enough distance before the travelers it was obvious they would never have made them by nightfall. The fourth day, just before the sun had reached its highest point, the trail began to wind up into the low foothills marking the northern edge of those mountains.

"Well, here be them mountains ye spoke of," Ymitoth leaned over toward Maelich. "So what we be looking for now?"

"The white horse said the blue men would find us here," he replied as he scanned the horizon. Large boulders dotted the landscape before them and the random greenery grew a bit thicker.

A flash of blue caught Maelich's eye from the periphery of his right side. As he turned his head toward it, he caught sight of a spear flying toward them a moment after he heard the whistling sound it made as it sliced through the air. Mountain's hackles shot up from the base of his neck to his tail a moment before the spear pounded the trail immediately in front of the horses. The scrod lost all of his sluggishness as he bounded toward the source of the spear, a giant boulder roughly fifty feet up the trail.

"Mountain, no," Maelich's tone was sharp and loud as he threw off his cloak and leapt down from his horse.

Mountain paused. Then he growled, whined, looked back at Maelich, and took a few more steps.

"Mountain," Maelich hollered again as he drew his sword.

Ymitoth appeared next to him, sword drawn, and ready, "I be thinking them blue people ain't eager to be seeing us."

"It would appear not," Maelich replied quietly to Ymitoth. Then he raised his voice and shouted toward the boulder, "I am Maelich of Havenstahl. This is Ymitoth, my father and mentor. We mean you no harm. We were sent on a quest by a white horse to find the blue people. I must assume you are the people we seek."

A head peaked out from behind the boulder. It was a man and he was indeed quite blue. His skin wasn't blue, or maybe it was. The actual color of his skin was impossible to ascertain as a deep, blue substance was smeared thickly over it. It was the color of the sky at twilight, just before the last light of day has given way to the black night sky. The man's dirt-streaked hair was black, long, and straight. Random braids with some form of decoration woven into them settled in between the snarls. His gnarly beard was the same dirt-streaked black and bore the same random braids and decorations. A string of brightly-colored beads hung around his neck, each bead catching the sun and shining. The only clothing the man wore was a rectangular strip tied around his waist and ratty foot coverings loosely resembling boots. Both appeared to be made from some kind of hide.

"That man definitely be blue. These must be them people we be seeking," Ymitoth commented.

"It would appear so," Maelich replied. Then he looked down at Mountain who was stomping his feet, shifting between whining at Maelich and growling at the blue man. "Mountain, sit," he commanded the eager scrod.

An idea popped into Maelich's head. He sheathed his sword and turned toward the spear jutting out of the trail in front of the horses. As he turned, the prang crest of Havenstahl fell out from within his shirt. It reflected the brilliance of the sun, blazing bright enough to cause the blue man to shade his eyes. As the flash of light moved away, those eyes grew wide with recognition. The blue man jumped and shouted something like a cheer, "Aiyeeee." Then he rushed toward Maelich, leaping and howling. Nine additional, blue-painted bodies poured out from behind the boulder and fell into the same excited behavior.

The wild leaping and screaming was all Mountain needed to forget his master's command. The growls that had steadily been pouring out of the scrod quickly escalated to furious barks. The beast leapt toward the people, almost gaining enough distance to escape his master's reach. Maelich was quick enough to stifle the scrod's effort though. He leapt upon his back and dragged him to the ground.

"Mountain, no," he yelled again in the scrod's ear. Then he held him tight with his right arm while he petted his belly with his left hand, and whispered, "Shh, it's alright," in his ear.

Mountain's continued growling slowed the excited group of blue people and eventually stopped their approach altogether by the time they made it within fifteen feet of him and Maelich. As soon as they stopped moving, all of them fell to their knees, folded their hands, and bowed in unison. The scrod's growling eventually ceased completely while Maelich continued to whisper soothing words to him. After a few moments, his struggling stopped as well. When Maelich finally released him, he charged over to the prostrate blue people and began sniffing all about them. All of them remained completely still. Apparently satisfied they no longer posed a threat, he trotted back over to Maelich, gave him a far less aggressive bark, and then lay down by his side.

"Good boy," Maelich leaned down at patted him on the head. Then he stood, looked over at Ymitoth, shrugged, looked back at the crowd of bowing, blue people, and said, "Please rise. Do you understand my words?"

The first man they had encountered, Ding, looked up at Maelich with wide eyes and a gaping jaw. He stuttered over some garbled gibberish before saying, "Yes, words. You Maelich, king, Maelich, savior."

Ymitoth shrugged when Maelich looked back at him again.

"My name is Maelich, but I am a warrior not a king. What is your name and who are your people."

"Me Ding," the blue man replied. Then he waved his arm behind him and said, "Them Shaiwah." He pointed at Maelich and added, "You Maelich. You king."

"The Shaiwah," Ymitoth interjected. "Me uncle had stories of them when I been still a lad. Them stories had all but fled me old mind."

Maelich glanced back at him once more, "Well, why do they think I am their king?"

"Please, come," Ding's voice had a pleading quality. "Meet Maulom. He wise. He tell you, you king."

By this time, Mountain had completely overcome his distrust of the blue people, the Shaiwah. He probed and sniffed at them, earning a scratch behind the ear here and a pat on the head there. The attention was tentative at first. Once the Shaiwah determined the beast would not maim or devour them, the affection became more open and friendly.

Finally Ymitoth said, "We should be heeding their word and meeting this Maulom they be speaking of. Maybe he'll be filling us in on how ye became a king."

With that, the two men grabbed the horses and led them on foot behind the Shaiwah who were buzzing with excitement. Each in turn touched Maelich. When he smiled in response, they grew bolder and hugged him. An odd sense of serenity, even belonging, filled him. The fact he had a purpose with them was apparent. What it could be would have to wait until he finally met the one they called, Maulom. Until then, their reverence of him would have to serve as proof enough.

Ding led the group past the boulder the ten Shaiwah had been hiding behind when first Maelich, Ymitoth, and Mountain arrived and up into the foothills in a westerly direction. The path they followed was the basest approximation of a trail. Narrow and covered in loose rocks and dust, it wound its way around monstrous rock formations that grew larger the higher the trail took them. The going was slow with the horses trailing behind, but the tall mountains grew ever closer. Finally, Ding called a halt to the group as they reached the point where the foothills gave way to the mountains proper. The first peak of the range loomed above them like a stalking monster puffing out its chest and stretching up toward the sky.

Ding turned toward Maelich. "There, home," he said as he pointed toward the base of the massive giant.

"The mountain is home?" Maelich asked as he looked closer.

As Maelich continued to gaze in the direction Ding was pointing, he finally made out a black spot partially obscured by a mammoth boulder. The sun had long fell behind the mountain and the shadow of the giant gave the surrounding land the appearance of dusk. There was movement around the boulder, more blue people, more Shaiwah.

"They're cave dwellers," Maelich said as he leaned closer to Ymitoth.

"Aye," Ymitoth agreed. "There ain't be no place else to dwell in this land."

More blue people appeared from behind the large boulder. All of them buzzing and skipping along; surrounding a man dressed in clean, white, loose-fitting trousers and a shirt that matched them in every way. The man's hair was equally white and cropped close to his head. A white beard and mustache wrapped around his mouth cropped in the same close fashion. Everything about him seemed completely out of place in the dirty hills at the base of the mountain.

Ding motioned his hand toward the approaching group and said, "Come, come, meet Maulom."

As the two groups approached each other, a deep sense of recognition filled Maelich. Though he couldn't quite figure why, something about the man in white—the one Ding referred to as Maulom—was terribly familiar. Like seeing a face you haven't seen in twenty summers; the essence remains, but the features aren't quite where you remember them.

Maulom looked toward the sky, raised his hand up on either side of his head, and said, "Maelich, thank Coeptus you have arrived."

"You obviously know me, but I am afraid that, though you stir feelings of recognition in me, I am quite unaware of who you might be." Maelich chased memories around his head, desperately trying to give meaning to the sense of knowing this Maulom awakened in him. It finally struck him. It was something about his eyes. He didn't know why, but Maulom's eyes were familiar. After a few moments he added, "And who is Coeptus?"

Maulom smiled, "Forgive me. Thank the gods you are here. We will speak of Coeptus in due time. For now, of course you know me. You have never seen me like this, but we have had a few recent conversations."

Maelich's eyes narrowed as Maulom's clue solved the riddle for him, "You are the white horse in my dreams. You lied. You told me you had no name other than the white horse."

"That was not a lie," Maulom shook his head. "In your head I was the white horse. You see, I projected myself to your subconscious mind. Picture me as a writer and you as the reader of my work, or your subconscious rather. I projected myself to you or wrote the story, so to speak. You—or your subconscious rather—read a white horse from that story. As the reader, or the receiver of the message, your interpretation is just as important as my intended meaning as the writer, or the deliverer of the message. In fact, being that we were meeting in your head, your interpretation was far more important—and even more valid—than my intended message. Therefore, I was the white horse."

Maelich shook his head, "Well you are consistent in one thing. You continue speaking in riddles."

"Aye," Ymitoth interjected. "Ye be saying a lot of nothing from where me fool ears be sitting."

Maulom flashed a patronizing smile to both men, "In any event, the important thing is you are here now. The Shaiwah have been waiting for you for hundreds of years."

"Hundreds of years, how is that possible?" Maelich asked. "I have only been alive for…" he trailed off as he glanced back at Ymitoth.

"Thirty, lad, ye been gracing the sweet face of Ouloos for thirty summers now," Ymitoth helped.

"There you go," Maelich looked back at Maulom, "thirty summers, not hundreds."

Maulom's smile lost its patronizing quality, "Thirty summers or hundreds, what is the difference to a people who could have no idea of your existence based on the vast distance existing between them and the land you call home? The simple answer is it makes absolutely no difference. They did not know when you were born, nor did they know when you would come. They did know, however, that someday you would. The obvious question vexing your brain right at this moment must be, 'How did they know?' The simple answer to that question is Coeptus.

"A few moments ago, you asked me who Coeptus *is*. The question is incorrect. Who *are* Coeptus would be the correct phrasing of your query. Coeptus are everything. The air above your head, the ground beneath your feet, you, me, everything you see and everything you do not see, all are Coeptus. Even the gods, those you worship and those you fear, all of them are Coeptus. Being we are all connected to and by this same energy, all have access to all. Some things can be learned through careful and thorough examination of one's self. Others are readily available to our subconscious mind. That is where real, powerful connections can be made. See, for most us, our conscious minds are guarded by barriers, walls built of the things we are told and taught throughout our lives. The possible and the impossible are dictated through our interpretations of the world we occupy; while those interpretations are guided by the principles and laws we have been taught. Most accept these definitions of possible and impossible as facts, givens that need not be tested because they are known and accepted laws. This is not the case for the few who ignore the limitations placed upon them by the beliefs and superstitions of those who came before. For those initiates into the mysteries of Coeptus, words like impossible do not exist. For them, there is only possibility.

"But, Coeptus are something that cannot be learned or understood in a short lecture given in the shade of a mountain to a traveler weary from the trail. The question is, 'How did they know you would come?' Though Coeptus are the easy answer to that question, Coeptus will remain beyond your comprehension for a time. For now it is enough to know that through Coeptus, all things are possible. Hundreds of summers past, Coeptus told the Shaiwah of their coming king. They painted the story in the same blue they use to protect their fair skin from the blistering sun. My search for truth through Coeptus led me to them when I was a young man of only twenty summers. After forty summers among them as their teacher and guide, I found you for them through the grace of Coeptus. Once I found you, I found your mind was bound tight by the bonds of things you had been told; lessons learned through the teaching of men shackled by the concept of impossibility. Therefore, I was unable to communicate with your conscious mind. However, the unconscious mind is a miracle that refuses to succumb to those chains. That is why we met in your dreams."

By the time Maulom finished, Maelich's eyes were wide and his head shook slightly. "I am a simple warrior. I live in a hut with my mentor, this man," he pointed at Ymitoth, "whom I call father. I am not a stupid man though. I know Kallum created all and it is through him that all things possible are possible. These ideas you speak of are blasphemies against my god."

"These ideas are things you have known, Maelich," Maulom contended. "Your mind has been scarred deeply by great tragedy. It is something you would not believe right now if I told you, but it has erased much of your memory. That can wait. First, give me a few moments to show you the story of the Shaiwah. They are a people who have suffered for centuries at the hands of Tiakwah and her savage armies. The Shaiwah are peaceful and ill-equipped to defend themselves. You are the savior they have been waiting for, Maelich. You are the great power sent by Coeptus to protect and defend them."

"I am weary," Maelich decided. "I will give you the moment you desire. Show me the story of the Shaiwah. Later we can discuss these ideas about this Coeptus you speak of."

Maulom's smile widened, "Come, the prophesy is painted all about the walls of the cave. You will be a great king, and you will deliver these people to the peace Coeptus have promised them."

CHAPTER 46
THE SEARCH BEGINS

Perrin sat upon the floor in the throne room of Druindahl. Her heavy head rested in her hands, as her eyes looked up at two empty thrones. Kallum's fury had destroyed her throne and the city surrounding it. The more time she had to think about what her life had become, the less important it seemed to restore each stone, each plank of wood, every pane of glass, and every sheet of fine, crafted prang to its former home. Initially, seeing that her castle and her city were reborn seemed more important than anything else. However, the longer she processed everything, where her rump sat quickly became the least of her worries. Maelich and Geillan beat all of her other thoughts back. Death was the least plausible idea for either of them. The lad of the Lake seemed expert at avoiding his return to that place no matter what peril he might find himself in, and sweet Geillan had undoubtedly been stolen for a far greater purpose than merely to be killed. Her sweet baby, her newborn son, had no control of his journey. Her absent husband was a different story entirely. Wherever he was, it had to be a place he wanted to be. There wasn't a power on Ouloos that could keep him shackled. If only he wanted be at his wife's side.

Geillan was foremost. The future king of Havenstahl needed to be found. The child obviously had great power. Perrin had witnessed it first-hand. Even absent the scars Cialia had stolen from her, the memory of them would linger for all of her days. Sweet Geillan had been blessed with the power of Dragon's Fire. Based on history, it was easy enough to determine why a creature as wicked as Kallum would want him. Yes, the *why* was easy, controlling a power as great as Geillan would make him unstoppable. *Where?* That was the challenge. Where on Ouloos could her sweet babe be? When the gods abandoned their physical forms, they existed outside the rules binding the physical. Maelich had taught her much before leaving her alone to bring their son into the world. How do you find something that may not exist, at least in the same sphere of existence?

"My dear, sweet girl," Leisha said as she entered the throne room and walked up to Perrin's slumped form, "you will not find him. When it is time for him to return, he will. Until then, you must continue to live."

Perrin glanced up at her, "Do ye be speaking of Geillan or Maelich?"

"Geillan, of course," Leisha's smile was forced. "Maelich has chosen his path. Hopefully it leads him home. Whether or not you welcome him is something you have to decide. I hope it is not him you dwell on. If you were to ask me, I would tell you he does not deserve your attention."

"Geillan be ruling me thoughts," Perrin conceded. "Maelich broke me heart. I ain't the time to be wasting on hurting over him."

"That is a truth," Leisha agreed. "According to Cialia, the war claimed many lives. Most of them were warriors, well aware of the peril of their rank. But it appears far too many innocent souls were sent to the Lake with them. Our people have been scarred. There is much healing to do, and you will have to be the one to lead them in their healing. Your castle has been destroyed, but the throne is still yours. You still lead those people."

"No, that seat be far too big for me to fill. The road, the search, it be beckoning. I be leaving with the sun." The queen shrugged as she finished, "There be nothing here for me now."

"You are the queen," Leisha's tone was a bit louder than she intended. "The people of your city need you to lead them."

"They don't be needing the likes of me. I ain't any kind of leader. Me husband, he be a leader," she paused before adding, "like his mother. Ye be the mother of the king. The throne of Havenstahl be far more fitting for your rump than mine. Ye can be guiding these people through their healing."

"Sweet Perrin, the trail is no place for the queen of the greatest city of men," Leisha countered, "and like it or not, you are that. Besides, you will not find Geillan. Kallum represents a power far too great for you to overcome. The trail will bring you nothing but more heartache."

"Aye, the road be a dangerous place. That be why Glord and five stout men of his choosing will be acting as me escort and guard. He be teaching me the ways of the warrior and how to be swinging this sharp hunk of metal with deadly purpose too," Perrin's tone turned grim as she rose. Her meekness had been melting away quickly since facing Kallum's dead-eyed men in the halls of Havenstahl. When she stood and hauled the glinting hunk of metal out from beneath her gown, it fled completely.

Leisha's eyes widened. "That is fine craftsmanship," she decided after a few moments of inspection. "Equal, at least, to my husband's. Where did you get it?"

"Me husband had it made for me before he fled his duties," Perrin replied, holding the glimmering blade high above her head. "The smiths of me city be having no equal."

Leisha shook her head, "Glord is a good man, and he is handy with a blade. But you are a queen and a mother, not a warrior. The road is dangerous, my dear. You must abandon this plan."

Perrin shrugged, "I be leaving with the sun of a new day. I ain't for words, so I be asking ye to speak me message to me people in me stead. They be your people now."

"Of course," Leisha took the queen's hand. "I fear for you, but I see you will not be swayed. A fire like that once burned in my belly. I will do as you wish. The people will know you have been called to the trail with great purpose, and I will mind their safety in your absence."

"Ye would be minding it in me presence," Perrin quickly replied, "ye and the queen of Druindahl."

Leisha nodded, bit her lower lip, and asked, "Where will your search take you?"

"First, I be speaking with Cialia and learning everything she might be knowing about me enemies. She be wise and knowing much of what the rest of us don't. She can also be learning me on how I might be finding that Lake and them Dragons what might be telling me more. Me journey beyond that will be depending on what I be learning from them."

"You should rest, my dear," Leisha took Perrin by the shoulders and then added, "And I will prepare words for our people."

EPILOGUE
THE SLEEPING DRAGON

In a small room at the top of a tower stretching farther up into the sky than any other structure made by men on Ouloos, the baby, Geillan, prince of Havenstahl, slept; his small form hovering between four obelisks. The obelisks—clear crystal glowing with perfect, white light from within—formed a perfect square. Like a creeping voyeur examining the object of his devotion, a clean, bold-looking, old man observed him intently. The old man, of course, was no man at all. A contemporary of Brerto, Kaldumahn, Moshat, and even the scattered Kallum, Ijilv was one of five gods tasked with maintaining balance on Ouloos.

"What a precious gem you are, little Geillan," Ijilv spoke soothingly to the sleeping child. "Such a little thing and look at all of the drama you have caused. They all search for you in vain."

Ijilv's eyes closed as his staff pulsated with blazing, white light. The obelisks surrounding Geillan's sleeping form mimicked the perfect, white emanations of the staff while the circular, stone room began to flash; at one moment the blackest dark and the next brighter than any natural light. The transitions were slow at first, like a beacon to sailors cresting great waves in the darkest hours of night. Gradually the pulsations increased until the time between dark and dark, and light and light was so minute it was barely perceptible. At once, the room appeared in total darkness and in total light, both conditions seeming to exist side by side at the same time rather than at alternating intervals; dark and light in equal parts running down the same path.

The god's eyes remained closed as he walked to the northernmost point of the circular room. A prang basin filled with water hovered there, exactly four feet from the stone floor. Ijilv plunged both of his hands into the

273

water and rubbed them vigorously against each other. Then he cupped them together, gathering water in between them, and said, "From the cleansing water's life comes the soul, ever yearning to return and wash off the filth of the physical." After the last word left his lips, he lifted both hands above his head. The water rained back down onto him.

After three deep breaths, he moved along the wall to the east. There he found fire burning in a basin matching the one housing the water exactly, save its contents. No fuel existed in this basin, only flame burning of its own volition. Ijilv performed the same exercise he had with the basin of water; plunging his hands—this time into flame—and rubbing them vigorously against one another. Finally, he cupped them together and said, "The fire is light. At once nurturer and destroyer, conquering darkness while consuming life." Again he lifted both hands quickly into the air, showering dancing flames over his hair and face.

Ijilv drew three more deep breaths and then skirted the wall to the southernmost point of the room. A basin matching the other two hovered there. It was filled with dirt, simple, fine granules of dirt. The god plunged his hands in and rubbed them together. Finally cupping them, he said, "Ouloos, the fertile soil from whence all growing things come. The power to sustain the physical while the soul matures and feeds lives within you." Dirt flew up and around him as he raised his hands, showering him in the fresh soil.

Finally, he continued to the west. The basin hovering there appeared empty. Still, Ijilv performed the same exercise he had completed with the other three basins. Once his hands were cupped, he said, "Nothing is ever empty as air fills in the voids, breathing over the land, fueling fires, and rippling waves into the waters." Again, he raised his hands above his head.

Once Ijilv's hands stretched toward the ceiling of the circular room, a brisk wind began swirling around the walls. The god moved toward the center next to the square of flashing obelisks surrounding Geillan. The four basins remained motionless as the wind slowly gained intensity. The elements those basins contained did not, however. As the air spun faster and faster around the room, the other three elements mingled together with it until they were not discernable from each other; each of them giving up their individuality to merge into one force. Finally, when none of the four could be recognized among them, Ijilv's eyes snapped open and saw everything.

The ceiling of the room shifted from the cold stone that formed it into something fluid and flickering. The scenes playing out upon it flashed as quickly as the dark gave way to light and the light gave way to dark. Nothing was invisible to Ijilv as he watched everything on Ouloos happen all at once. For him, things didn't move quite so quickly. Each scene played to him as if he were part of it. As he moved through these scenes, little bits of Kallum sparkled to him; sometimes in the air, sometimes in the dirt, sometimes in the fire, and sometimes in the water. Each time he happened upon a piece of the scattered god, he snatched it out of the scene and consumed it—little pieces of Kallum feeding him, strengthening him, and preparing him for what was to come.

The End

ABOUT THE AUTHOR

E. Michael Mettille is the pen name of Mike Reynolds. Mike Reynolds is the author of Lake of Dragons and Hell and the Hunger. Mike has also written numerous short stories and poems. He has spent the last twenty years in direct marketing, print, and communication. Mike is fascinated by history, belief systems, the human condition and how all of those things work together to define who we are as a people. The world is a wonder and, based on the history of us, it is a wonder we have a world left to wonder about. Born and raised in Milwaukee, WI, he now lives in Los Angeles with his wife, Shelia.